The Tournament of Heirs

Amilea Perez

Content Warnings

This story contains content that may be troubling to some readers, including but not limited to, **brief mentions of miscarriage and stillbirth, depictions and references to violence and death and sexually explicit scenes**. Please be mindful of these and other triggers before continuing.

PLAYLIST

This playlist can be listened to in order or on shuffle mode! However, for a more theatrical experience, listening in order is recommended.

GLOSSARY/PRONUNCIATION GUIDE

PEOPLE

Metztli Amos (Mets-Tle): Second Born Heiress of The House of life

Acalan Amos (Aca-Lan): First Born Heir of The House of Life

Tenoch Amos (Ten-O-Ch): Emperor of The House of Life

Xara Amos (Sa-Ra): Empress of The House of Life

Atzi (At-zee): Head Priestess of The House of Life.

Shaman (Sha-Man): Witch/Spiritual Healer

Nemiliztli (Nemi-Lis-Tle): The God of Life

Nenetl (Ne-Ne-Tl): Seamstress/Xara's best friend

Ohtli Flores (Aw-T-Lee): Emperor of The House of Flor

Ahuic Flores (Ah-We-Ic): Empress of The House of Flor

Xochitl Flores (So-Chi-Tl): First born Heiress from The House of Flor

Atlatonan Flores (Al-Ta-Toe-Nan): Second born Heiress from The House of Flor

Xochipilli (So-Che-Pe-Lee): Third male Heir from The House of Flor

Eztli (Ez-Tle): The Goddess of Blood

Yaotl Cruz (Yah-O-Tl): Emperor of The House of Blood

Chimalli Amos (Chim-al-lee): Deceased uncle from The House of Life

Necalli Cruz (Ne-Call-E): First Born Heir of The House of Blood

Coatl Cruz (Co-Alt): Second Male Heir of The House of Blood

Citlalic Cruz (See-Tla-Ic): Second Born Heiress of The House of Blood

Cuauhtémoc (Kwa-Te-Mok): Male Heir from the House of Wind

PLACES

Tu'nethe (Two-Neth): City where the House of Life resides

Texcoco (Tex-Coco): City where the House of Blood resides.

Chalco (Ch-al-Co): City where the House of Flor resides.

THINGS

Tlaxcalli (Tlaj-Ka-Le): Corn Tortilla

Netl (Ne-Tl): Beans

Mantecah (Man-Te-Kah): Lard

Tepoztopilli (Te-Pos-Toe-Pille): Spear

Pulque (Pull-Kay): Traditional fermented Alcoholic beverage made from the Maguey (agave) plant.

Macuahuitl (Ma-Ca-Hui-Tl): Wooden club with several embedded obsidian blades around its silhouette.

Ōllamalitzli (Olla-Mal-Etzi): Meso-American ball game similar to basketball but with significant ritual and ceremonial importance, often associated with themes of life, death, and the cosmos.

Taquito (Ta-Key-To): A taco, but rolled up.

Xocoatl (Sho-Co-Alt): Traditional Meso-American beverage often compared to modern hot chocolate.

Tamales (Ta-Mal-Es): Corn dough filled with various ingredients such as meats, cheeses, or chilies, wrapped in corn husks or banana leaves and steamed.

Pozole (Po-Zol-E): A soup made from hominy (dried maize kernels), pork or chicken, and seasoned with herbs and spices, often garnished with radishes, cabbage and lime.

Tlacoyos (T-La-Coy-Os): Oval-shaped corn masa cakes stuffed with beans, cheese, or other fillings, often topped with nopales (cactus), salsa, and cheese.

Mole (Mol-Eh): Traditional Mexican sauce made from a blend of chiles, nuts, spices, fruits, and chocolate.

Tlatlauh (Tla-Tauh): Root known to be used as a toothbrush in Mesoamerican times.

Copalli (Ko-Pal-E): Species of trees found in Mexico and Central America.

Xoloitzcuintle (Sho-Los-Queent-Tle): Aztec/Mexican breed of hairless dog.

Chachalaca (Cha-Cha-La-Ka): Birds native to Mexico/Mesoamerica

Messi (Mess-E): Messiah

To be loved is to be seen;
And I see you.

METZTLI

etztli Amos frowned as pain pulsed through her body.

The pitch black sky offered her little comfort in her despair. It had been even darker when they had begun their journey through the city and into the forest.

The soles of her feet felt wet despite the fact that they had been walking through sand and dirt. Metztli wondered if she'd find blood pooled beneath her when the sun finally rose to greet them, or when they arrived at the temple. Whichever came first.

With every footstep, she tried to remind herself that she wasn't the first to walk this path, nor was she alone. Her brother, Acalan, walked beside her with his chest held high, his gait peaceful and unhurried. He'd always been better at these sorts of things than she was.

In front of them were their parents, Tenoch and Xara, the emperor and empress of the House of Life, their house, their legacy. Behind them, they were joined by all of their people who were fit to make the journey. Some old, some young, all willing to sacrifice their own comfort, to join them as they took the treacherous path to the temple of Nemiliztli, The God of Life.

The hike was brutal, hours of walking barefoot through difficult terrain wasn't easy even for Metztli, and yet their people seemed joyous at the opportunity to join them.

She had to stop herself from scoffing outwardly at the sight of their followers. Metztli would much rather be enjoying the comfort of her silk sheets, woken up by the sun warming her golden skin. But that morning had begun with her older brother shaking her with such enthusiasm that she couldn't quite understand or have herself.

"Duties," she whispered to herself, earning a sidelong glance from her brother. She had to remind herself that they all had duties to fulfill and this was just one of hers.

Metztli faked a grin when she caught her brother's eye, knowing Acalan would likely scold her later for being anything less than serious on this sacred day of worship. The gods knew it wouldn't be the last time she'd need one before they entered the Pyramid of Tributes in just a few days. Whether she would receive any additional scoldings after the Tournament of Heirs depended on whether they survived or not.

"Is it really wise to put our bodies through this just a few days before the tournament begins?" Metztli turned to ask her brother in a half playful, half serious tone.

Acalan shook his head and gave her the same look he always had since they were children. It was the look that said, *Can't you ever be serious?*, without ever having to mutter a word.

"Don't look at me like that, I'm just saying, the tournament will be difficult enough without our feet aching from this," Metztli quipped.

Xara, their mother looked over her shoulder to reprimand the both of them. Metztli had to hold in her laugh. Despite her mother's repeated efforts throughout their lives, she had never quite mastered the ability to scare them with a simple glance. Her eyes were far too soft and gentle for either of them to be able to sense anything but the love she had for them. Acalan was quite the same, he'd always resembled their mother in that.

"If you stop complaining and keep walking, perhaps Nemiliztli will reward us with an easy victory," Acalan whispered in return.

Metztli rolled her eyes at his response. If the gods had any appreciation or love in their hearts for their children, they would have ended this vile tradition centuries ago. Despite wanting to argue further, Metztli opted to surrender. She was only wasting her breath, and it was far wiser to conserve her energy for the rest of their journey.

They were still surrounded by the thin tall trees that covered the wide breadth of the forest that stood between their home in Tu'nethe and the temple of Nemiliztli. She'd only visited the temple once before when she'd been a child, so small that she didn't actually remember the temple itself.

She had, however, heard stories of its beauty. Her father Tenoch loved to rave about how the structure was lined with gold and shimmered from every angle that one could look upon it. From Metztli's understanding it was vast enough to fit the entirety of Tu'nethe within it as well.

But the temple couldn't be that beautiful if she couldn't recall it now.

When she and Acalan had only been a few years old each, her father had made the journey from their home in Tu'nethe to the temple, carrying both Acalan and herself in his arms. He came to the temple in hopes that in return for his suffering and pain, Nemiliztli would spare his wife Xara, who'd grown terribly ill after a difficult childbirth that resulted in a lost heir. Tenoch had already pleaded with every Shaman to aid his wife, to cure her from whatever sickness was plaguing her body, but despite being spoon fed every remedy that they knew of, she only grew sicker, and it wasn't long before Atzi, the head priestess of the House of Life, warned Tenoch that their mother was balancing on a thin line between life and death.

Metztli had been too young to really understand what was going on. But being that her mother was still with them, and that at this very moment she was walking far too enthusiastically in front of them, Metztli couldn't help but wonder if Nemiliztli had indeed taken pity on her father and kissed their mother with the spirit of life, giving her the opportunity to raise her children and live by her husband's side for a little longer.

Though her feet ached, Metztli quickened her steps as she recalled that memory. Perhaps it had been a coincidence that their mother had begun recovering so quickly after their father had made the journey to the temple. But if that wasn't the case, Metztli herself wasn't jumping at the idea of disrespecting Nemiliztli in his own temple either.

She would be lying if she said she had any amount of faith in the gods, but there was no doubt she and Acalan were going to need every bit of help they could get once they were inside the Pyramid of Tributes. For the entirety of her life, everyone around her seemed to have an abundance of faith in Nemiliztli and his ability to aid the both of them, guiding them to victory.

Metztli didn't want to begin entertaining the idea that due to her lack of faith he wouldn't, but she couldn't force herself to believe. She'd never been able to despite years and years of trying to do so. She did however, believe in a lot of other things that didn't depend on Nemiliztli showing her or Acalan an ounce of pity.

Metztli believed she had the ability to be lethal during the Tournament of Heirs. She had trained and hunted enough throughout her life to prove that to herself. She believed that surviving would be an easy feat if she kept her mind balanced and at ease, she was aware that the latter would likely be harder to do than she assumed. Most of all, though, Metztli believed she could protect her brother when the time came and bring victory to their home.

The princess tried to justify this in her mind by telling herself it was simple.

Kill. Survive. Protect. Win.

Those were all tangible things that she'd proven herself capable of over the years. She'd heard far too many stories of heirs who had assumed faith was all they needed to win. The idea was a lovely one until someone was coming at your throat with a blade. Faith wouldn't do much to save anyone then .And besides, her own father had taught her that faith could only take you so far in the tournament itself.

Acalan could spend all the time in the world praying to Nemiliztli, but it was Metztli who'd be by his side when an heir from a neighboring house came for his life.

"What are you thinking about?" Acalan asked, interrupting her reflection.

"Nothing really, just trying to figure out the best way to

disembowel someone without a blade," Metztli responded in a tone far too plain for her sentiment.

Acalan raised his brow, scrunching his face in disgust.

"Okay well, stop thinking about that," he replied, half arguing, half commanding. "We'll be there soon and I don't think the god of life would appreciate a thought like that."

Metztli barely bit back a burst of laughter, and settled for a cheeky grin instead.

"How do you know we're clo-" Meztli started questioning.

"Look up."

As Metztli's gaze moved away from her brother and towards the sky, she found a stone pyramid larger than any of the others that resided in Tu'nethe, rising up above the treetops. It sat on the top of the mountain they were about to scale, and from where she stood, it looked like the stone pillars adorning the pyramid were made of gold. But she wasn't yet convinced that the rising sun wasn't simply playing tricks with her eyes.

"It looks like…like it belongs in a different world," she said, finding it difficult to choose the correct words to describe what she was looking at.

"Heavenly, right?" said Acalan. "Almost too beautiful to disturb. It's a marvel to me. I mean can you actually believe this was built centuries upon centuries ago, and it still remains so presetine? It's…Glorious."

Metztli shook her head in response. There was no doubt that the temple was beautiful, but that wasn't the reason she'd been unable to find the words to describe the sight of it.

"No, it just seems a bit narcissistic to have a temple built in your honor. Even if you are a god," Metztli responded, sarcasm coloring her words.

"I'm sure your first request will be to have a temple built in your honor if we return home victorious," Acalan retorted.

"No. Actually, *if* we return home, I think my first request will be to be left alone for the first time in what…seventeen years?" she said, turning to meet her brother's cool brown eyes.

The words had left her mouth in a tone far too cold. And

without meaning to, she'd struck him in a place she knew already held an aching wound.

"I didn't mean it like that, you know I love being your sister," Metztli clarified as quickly as she could.

"Just keep walking," he clipped in return.

Metztli didn't say another word.

She could try to redeem herself, but she knew success was an unlikely result. She would have to make it up to Acalan later, when their day of worship wasn't still looming over their heads. Until then she would be quiet. She would even pray for the both of them despite the fact that she knew her pleas would carry no weight.

She would do it for him because over the span of their lives, that had grown to be second nature for her.

ACALAN

Burden.

Acalan Amos was sure the word had been written across his forehead in some sort of ink that was permanently binding, defining who he was and everything he would ever be. The prince resented the notion that his sister felt like she didn't truly have a life of her own and instead lived only to protect him. He hated that more now that he'd grown to resent his position in life, though he would never confess that to another living soul, not even his sister who walked silently beside him.

Her smile had disappeared and was replaced by an emotionless blank stare. Acalan resented that as well. Unlike his sister Metztli, he'd never been able to master the ability to be so indifferent about these matters. His mother Xara had assured him from an early age that it was a blessing that he was so in tune with the gods, but he'd never been quite convinced, still wasn't.

Today, of all days, was important for that very reason. It would be one of the last opportunities that his family had to truly worship Nemiliztli. Everything had to go well on this day. If not, Acalan felt that it would be risking their victory in the Pyramid of Tributes. And they needed to win just as much as they needed to breathe air.

If they could just make it up this mountain and into the temple of Nemiliztli, if they could just get through the worshiping ceremony he'd been looking forward to and if he could show Metztli why this mattered so much to him, make her understand that their lives ultimately rested in the hands of the gods, then maybe, just maybe, there would be time.

Until then, Acalan would scale the mountain with only the

comfort of his own thoughts. Much like his sister, he found himself in a significant amount of discomfort. He was sure there wasn't a single muscle in his body that he hadn't utilized throughout their journey from their home in Tu'nethe to where they stood now at the base of the mountain.

Relief would come when they arrived, he was sure of it. Just like he was sure that Nemiliztli would see this sacrifice for what it was, and would help them survive and prevail over the other heirs inside the Pyramid of Tributes.

He just had to survive a little longer on his own, place one aching foot in front of the other, again and again until they arrived at the doors of the temple. Every drop of blood and sweat that was made until then, was simply another offering to Nemiliztli, another plea for the survival of his sister and himself.

They both needed to survive if they ever wanted an opportunity at living normal lives, or more so whatever capacity of normalcy that could be offered to them. Acalan was a first born son set to inherit his father's throne and Metztli...well, if she could simply start living for herself instead of others, Acalan would find himself quite satisfied with that.

Just like Acalan was sure that Nemiliztli would come to their aid when the time came, he was equally sure that there was more to life than this. But the tournament had split their lives cleanly in two. There was life before the tournament, and there was life after. That is, if they returned home.

He wanted the both of them to survive more than he'd ever wanted anything. Metztli had already given more than enough of herself to prepare for the tournament, and Acalan was sure that she would flourish if she was simply allowed to live without the burden of keeping him alive long enough for the tournament to end. If they won then she could truly come to be a person of her own. His sister could do things she liked instead of what had always been expected of her. That's what Acalan wanted for his sister the most.

Time.

As they scaled higher on the mountain, he couldn't help but feel an eerie sort of energy gathering around them. Looking over his shoulder, Acalan realized he wasn't the only one sensing it. Their people now bore a face of worry, some even wrapped shawls and thin blankets over their shoulders in attempts to fight off the cold feeling that was suddenly looming over them. But when he turned to his sister, she looked anything but affected by it.

Of course, she'd always had thicker skin than the rest of them.

"Father? What is this?" Acalan asked in a tone full of worry.

"What's what?" Metztli questioned, obviously confused as to why Acalan seemed concerned all of the sudden.

"Do not worry son, we're nearing the mist," their father said. "It's just a precaution the gods set in place to scare away any who may not seek the temple for benevolent reasons"

Still, Acalan was confused. He had read nearly all the scriptures and passages about the temple that were in his family's library, and none of them had mentioned this precautionary measure.

"Hmm…well whoever put it in place must have been weak because I don't feel a thing," his sister taunted, almost laughing.

That was a dangerous thing to do when they were so close to the temple of their god.

They couldn't have taken more than thirty or so steps since Acalan had first noticed the shift in the energy surrounding them, and even now he felt it growing, trying to consume him. He supposed it had been an intelligent move on Nemiliztli's part. Had he not been accompanied by his father, who'd made this journey twice before, he certainly would have retreated.

"The gods and our god are anything but weak," Acalan addressed his sister in a stern voice he rarely used.

"Right, well then, I must just be immune to Nemiliztli's will then, that's a perfectly sound and reasonable explanation," Metztli continued to mock, pressing her lips into a tight smile.

The gods must have really set out to test Acalan's patience. For all the love he had for his sister, he'd never be able to understand how she seemingly feared nothing, not even the very god who'd given her life. She was brave, yes, and strong when she needed to be. But her naivety was dangerous.

"Enough, both of you," their mother snapped. "Have you saved all your bickering for today? You may be entering thePyramid of Tributes in a few days but I will not hesitate to reprimand the both of you the second we return home if this feud between the both of you does not end this very second...Metztli, stop antagonizing your brother and the gods, now!"

"But I'm not, I truly don't-"

"Did I not make myself clear? I don't want to hear another word from either of you unless they are prayers. And you, Acalan. When you are emperor of our House will you allow just any antagonism from our enemies to become a war? I didn't think so. You must choose your battles wisely and know when they are worth pursuing. Do you both understand?"

Acalan couldn't recall the last time he'd seen his mother so upset. Of course, it wasn't often that he or Metztli did anything to warrant this sort of response. Surely it was just the tournament that had his mother on edge, he'd been feeling the same way for years now.

They both fell silent.

Unfortunately the silence only made the journey seem longer, more daunting. Even more so when they finally entered the mist. It restricted their sight even more than it had already been when the sky was pitch black before dawn. Now the sun shone high in the sky, cutting through the mist for brief moments but never burning it away.

It was nearly enough for Acalan to retreat, and truthfully if they didn't have a trail of people behind them, all depending on his family to lead the way, he would have considered making his way back down the mountain and back to their home in Tu'nethe.

Luckily, it wasn't much longer before the mist began to clear, giving way to a view of the temple. It was, in fact, far more beautiful than Acalan had remembered it to be.

Before it came fully into view, he'd used the word *heavenly* to describe it. But now Acalan knew the word did not come close to showing justice for the beauty before him. The temple was lined with gold that shimmered brightly against the sun. He could almost see the reflection of himself and his people through the pillars that were made of gold as well. There was no doubt in his mind that

Nemiliztli himself had a hand in building this structure. Only a god so marvelous could create something like this for his children.

As they finished their journey, closing the distance left between them and the temple, Acalan's pain and discomfort slowly dissipated as well. He was unsure if it was his own mind playing tricks with him, or if Nemiliztli had taken pity on him and gifted him with relief.

There was hardly a thought in his mind as they approached the pyramid, and it was impossible to not be completely and utterly drawn to its allure. It felt like the temple was pulling him in, pleading with Acalan to walk through its golden doors and worship the god who'd given him life.

Acalan knew better than to argue with these instincts, and he was even more relieved when he heard their people cheering behind him. Even his mother and father celebrated with them.

There was only one voice missing.

When Acalan turned to his sister. There was no smile on her face, no sense of relief or happiness. She seemed completely and utterly untouched by the magic that laid before them. He knew there was no point in questioning her about it. He'd only be upsetting his mother if he were to call out his sister's lack of emotion, and he was not at all intending on ruining this joyous moment for anyone, especially his mother who had never made the journey to the temple before.

He would need to wait until they returned back home to try and get through to her, and despite knowing that his pleas would likely fall on deaf ears, he would continue trying, even if they did only have a few days until the tournament started.

He'd do it for her, because over the span of their lives, that had grown to be second nature for him.

2

METZTLI

*C*ursed.

Metztli was convinced that was the reason why pain still gripped onto her limbs while everyone around her seemed to feel an overwhelming sense of relief. Hadn't they all gone the same way? Followed the same path to the temple of Nemiliztli? It didn't seem like it as she stood outside the golden gates, facing her people and waiting for her father to address them.

She recognized most of the faces in the crowd. Being an heir meant that she was often forced into attending events such as this one. While she thought their people's love for Nemiliztli was a bit heavy handed in all regards, it was somewhat comforting to take in the view of everyone waiting to hear from their emperor. Metztli found herself surprised at the amount of children and elders present but then again, the Tournament of Heirs only occurred once every twenty-five years. Even she hadn't been waiting as long as some had for this day to come.

As she waited with them, Metztli couldn't help but glance again at her brother Acalan, who looked like he'd just been renewed with a fresh breath of life. While he was relishing in this moment, she was loathing it. She wished time would pass by faster so she could return home and indulge in a hot bath, preferably followed by a hefty meal. But her thoughts of a tlaxcalli slathered in netl and mantecah were disrupted by her father's voice.

Metztli turned to face her father properly. Even after twenty years of life, she found it strange how quickly he could go from their father to an emperor. The change was tangible, and quite impressive in her mind.

"It has been twenty-five years since I last stood in this very spot, addressing the mighty people of The House of Life," he began, his voice echoing across the mountain. "Back then I was accompanied by my parents and brother Chimalli, who have now passed to a better life under the care of Nemiliztli. It is with great gratitude and honor that I stand before you all today, accompanied by my dear wife Xara, empress of our great house, and our children, the heirs to this empire. I present them to you all on this beautiful day as our chosen heirs. In the next few days, Acalan and Metztli will enter the Pyramid of Tributes and will fight to the death against other heirs, chosen just like them… in hopes of bringing our precious empire glory and power!"

The crowd roared at his words.

Metztli couldn't imagine having to do the same as her father did now. She had no doubt that her father loved her and Acalan, but she couldn't put herself in his position, having to offer his children to the gods as a form of entertainment.

The tournament was just another form of sacrifice, and if she survived, while managing to keep Acalan alive for the entirety of it as well, she didn't know if she'd be able to sacrifice her children.

But, of course, the responsibility to uphold the tournament and all its traditions lay mostly with Acalan, being that he was the first born son of the House of Life.

If their house had more heirs, maybe she would not be standing here at all, offered up to their people like so much cattle. It was not uncommon for other heirs to be chosen to compete. Choosing those who would be sacrificed was often strategic. The first born always had to fight, those were the rules…but their companion simply had to be blood bound to them, whether it be a sibling or more distant relative it did not matter, as long as they stood in the line of heirs, they could be used as sacrificial lambs.

Tenoch took a deep breath and repositioned his smile before speaking again. The sight was a reminder that the Tournament of Heirs affected her father as well, and for a moment, his carefully chosen words were at odds with the brief flash of pain that washed over his face.. Metztli couldn't imagine that even the strongest of men or women would be able to offer children without feeling an ounce of emotion.

"Inside the Pyramid of Tributes, they will not be alone…with them will be the spirits of our ancestors, those who fought before them, and the spirits of those who join us here today. My son and daughter have trained valiantly their entire lives in preparation for this moment, for our family, and for you all here today. They are the future of this empire, and they have taken this responsibility upon themselves in honor of their people.

"In anticipation of their sacrifice, we worship our god Nemiliztli, and ask him to aid Acalan and Metztli. We ask him to return the heirs of this great house to us, and we ask that they may find victory while remaining unscathed. We plead with Nemiliztli to return our children as noble as they stand before us now, and that their souls may remain untouched by the horrors they will face.

"We thank you all for joining us on this special day, and hope that you may find the kindness in your hearts to pray for our children, who will be fighting to keep yours safe. Every prayer whispered for my children will be heard by Nemiliztli today, of that I have no doubt.

"Now, let our worship begin!" her father announced confidently, so much so that for a moment, Metztli almost believed him too.

The princess had trained herself over the years to keep a straight face during these moments. It had taken an abundance of practice to look upon a crowd full of smiling faces and hopeful eyes and not let any expression take over her features. Her people cheered for her family as loudly as they could and while it was difficult for Metztli to believe any of them had malicious hearts, she could not deny that her people were naive.

She wouldn't fake a smile for the crowd before them, even if they were cheering her name. It was easy for them to do so considering they were not the ones who would enter the tournament, nor were they offering their children to the gods. Most of them were likely to die of old age, some of disease, and perhaps a few would meet an untimely death. But if Metztli or Acalan died in the tournament, it would likely be at the hands of another heir, and it would be anything but gentle.

Perhaps her father should have spent more time training her on these matters instead of perfecting her technique with the Tepoztopilli. Metztli reckoned that it was much easier to master a wooden spear than it was to master people. Luckily there wouldn't be any need for people skills inside the Pyramid of Tributes. In fact, she hoped she wouldn't need to speak a single word to any of the other heirs. It would be easier to take their lives if she knew nothing of them.

Her father stood to face the temple doors then. It seemed that he was taking his time, taking in the beauty that lay before him. Metztli didn't feel the same, not in the slightest. She wanted this to go by as quickly as it could so she could return home and take advantage of the little time she had left to prepare for the tournament. Anything other than this would be a more productive use of her time, she was sure of it.

Metztli was relieved when her father's hands finally wrapped around the golden handles and pulled the doors of the temple open. The crowd behind them erupted in enthusiastic cheers once again, this was a once-in-a-lifetime opportunity for most of them. There were very few in the crowd who'd been there when her father and his brother had been presented to the gods for their tournament.

One by one they were ushered through the door and inside the great temple of Nemiliztli. Within the structure there was a small fire being kept in the middle of it. It appeared there as if by magic, though, Metztli wouldn't be surprised if one of Nemiliztli's devout followers made the journey on a frequent basis to ensure it stayed well lit and fed.

The temple itself was vast, just as her father had described it to be. The stone walls reached high enough that it almost looked like they could touch the sun. None of it was very impressive in Metztli's eyes. The walk to the temple had been wildly more beautiful than the temple itself, but the princess did take interest in the paintings and carvings etched into the stone that surrounded them. The people of Tu'nethe had always been invested in the arts. Musicians, artisans and writers all lived among them, that much was obvious by the state of the temple's walls.

Tenoch instructed his children to stand before the fire and wait to be called on. Being that Metztli was no longer in the mood to argue or cause disruption for her family she obeyed and watched as the people of her father's empire filed in. The young were directed to find seats on the higher levels of the pyramid while the old, as well as the mothers with children, were directed to find seating on the first level. Soon enough the entire pyramid was filled to the rim and all their peering eyes were set on Metztli and Acalan. The princess could not say she was a fan of it but she would take this over having a conversation with their priestess any day of the week.

"Prince Acalan, Princess Metztli, I feel privileged to be holding service in honor of you both today," Azti declared softly as she approached them. "I only hope that I am able to do it justice as I did for your father and late uncle when I held service in their honor many years ago."

The old woman had always been among Metztli's least favorite people in her father's court. Despite the fact that she was meant to be a direct line of communication between Nemiliztli and his mortal children, all Metztli could think of when she looked at the old woman were the memories of being scolded as a child. Whether it be for forgetting to read her scriptures or getting lost in a daydream during one of her very long and very boring sermons, the priestess always seemed to find a reason to lecture her and she did so publicly without much remorse.

"We are grateful for your presence here today Atzi," Acalan bowed to the old woman, "and I have no doubt you have planned a beautiful service for my sister and I, truly we are in debt to you."

He'd always been much better with these interactions than Metztli was. Where Metztli struggled he flourished, and where he lacked, she compensated. Oddly enough it worked well for the both of them. Hopefully, it would continue to be this way for many years to come.

"Your sister is not grateful or honored, nor does she feel indebted to me Prince," Atzi responded, shifting her gaze to meet Metztli's. "There's no need to lie to me, I've known the both of you since you were mere babes."

Metztli fought back the desire to respond in the way that she wanted to. Everyone loved the old priestess and surely she could live on knowing Metztli did not feel the same, but it wasn't the right time to make that clear.

"Perhaps I've been sent by the gods as a test of your faith Atzi, I am here to worship amongst my people aren't I? It seems you've done your duty better than you give yourself credit for," Metztli replied.

It was a much kinder way of relaying what she truly wanted to say.

"Ahh, yes Princess I suppose you are right, let's just continue to hope and pray that the gods believe you have done your duty to them as well," Atzi responded in a clipped manner that made Metztli's blood boil.

She simply offered the priestess a curt smile and nod. There was no use in arguing with the old woman. Had anyone else spoken to her like that, they wouldn't have been offered the same kindness. Atzi was lucky that Metztli had been taught to respect her elders, even if they were bitter old women with delusions of the gods.

Atzi waited until everyone was silent to begin her sermon. In Metztli's twenty years of life, the priestess had never changed the way she started these things, always with a smile too bright and the request for a moment to pray in communal silence. Metztli just bowed her head, closed her eyes and filled her mind with the thought of dinner instead.

How long these moments lasted for all depended on the priestess and what she felt was right for the occasion. When Metztli had been younger she believed that Atzi had made their silent prayers extra long to teach her a lesson in patience. Maybe it would have worked on someone else, but it only made Metztli even more inpatient than she was by nature.

Metztli opened a single eye. She was squinting really but that did nothing to save her when she discovered that Atzi was already looking her way, prompting Metztli to sigh, close the eye and return to her thoughts. The old woman knew her well, that she could not deny.

It wasn't until a few minutes later that Atzi allowed them to come out of prayer. Having her eyes closed for even a few minutes had made Metztli sleepy, and she was sure that the feeling would only continue when the priestess began her sermon. That always seemed to happen regardless of the topics spoken about.

"While I know that most of us in attendance know the history of the Tournament of Heirs, I believe there are some children here who do not," Atzi began in a gentle tone. Though soft, her voice still managed to reach the entirety of the temple. "It is important that all generations remember the tragedies that came before the tournament so that we might not repeat our history and mistakes."

Metztli, of all people, did not need to re-learn the history of the Tournament. Nor did she believe that the children in attendance needed to know about the cruelties that came with it either. Metztli loved her parents, they'd both been kind and loving throughout her life, but the day she'd learned about the tournament and what was expected of her was the day that her childhood had ended.

The children sitting in their mother's laps, kicking their tiny legs, did not need to meet the same reality as she had. The princess rolled her eyes but stayed silent anyway, once Atzi started speaking, there was nothing anyone could do to get her to stop.

"You will all hear me speak more than enough for today, so why don't we have our prince explain how the Tournament came to be," Atzi said, turning slightly to offer a sweet smile as she beckoned for Acalan to take a step forward.

Now that was the perfect duty for Metztli's brother. Acalan had a fascination for literature and history. Sometimes it felt like he knew historical events far better than the people who have lived through them. His fixation was bizarre in some ways but ultimately special in Metztli's eyes.

"It would be my pleasure," Acalan said as he stepped forward, cracking his knuckles as if he were about to perform some difficult task.

Metztli had to stop herself from sighing again.

"It is said that a little less than a millennium ago, Mortals and Gods lived amongst one another," Acalan began. "You see, we were their children, not blessed with the magical abilities and immortality that the gods carry but their children nonetheless and they treated us as such as well. Mortals by nature can be quite temperamental. We are creatures who are never quite satisfied and so our ancestors became more and more demanding with the gods themselves, so much so that our people went to war with the gods. It is unclear what disagreement truly started this war but in the end mortal lives were lost in abundance."

Metztli often wondered if she would have paid more attention during their lessons if it had been her brother doing the teaching. Perhaps so, anything was better than listening to Atzi's slow paced phrases.

Acalan continued. "Mortals believed that all hope was lost until six men, all from different tribes came to the gods in search of their forgiveness. The gods, in their glory and fortitude, agreed to end the war at once and rewarded these six men for their bravery with positions of leadership throughout Mexica...but of course, they could not bring the bloodshed to an end without asking something of their children."

From experience, Metztli knew this was typically the part of the story with which Acalan struggled. It almost pained her brother to admit what the Tournament of Heirs truly was. Metztli felt quite the same, except, she wasn't nearly as afraid to voice it outloud.

"Eztli, the Goddess of Blood came forward with a resolution. The idea for the Tournament of Heirs was given as a sort of...of..." Her brother tried to continue explaining.

While Metztli hated the gods and what they'd done to her people. She did love her brother, and it was painful to watch him struggle through his explanation. Luckily this was one occasion where she had no doubt she could save him.

"Punishment," Metztli chimed in curtly.

Her brother turned to look at her briefly. Really he should have been grateful that she'd been listening enough to aid him in the moment, but instead she was met with a disappointed look.

"Well...I wouldn't say it's a form of punishment per say...more so..." Acalan said, turning back to the crowd.

"Retribution," Metztli said, interrupting once more.

Her brother sighed at her words but nodded softly at the crowd anyway. Metztli smiled slightly. Punishment and retribution were really and truly the same in this context but that didn't soften the angered look that Atzi threw her way. That was fine, Metztli would be lying if said she didn't find a little bit of satisfaction in pushing the priestess's buttons.

"Yes, retribution is a better way of putting it...And so, the Tournament of Heirs was given life. It serves as a reminder that we should never repeat our ancestor's mistakes and that even high-born families must pay a price for the sins committed by our people," Acalan quickly finished.

The crowd erupted again, clapping for her brother as he smiled and bowed slightly at their graciousness. Acalan was already beloved by their people so Metztli could only assume that love would grow when he became the emperor of their house. Deep within her heart, Metztli really hoped that he would and that she would live to see it.

"Thank you to the prince and the princess for their wise words and recollections of their histories," Atzi said curtly.

Metztli knew the woman didn't actually mean to thank her. If it had been up to Atzi the woman would have likely stood in front of their people and lectured them on why the Tournament of Heirs still remained. The princess would never find a way to agree, that much was certain to anyone who knew Metztli personally.

Atzi began her sermon then. She mostly spoke of how fragile mortal life could be. That too was not something that Metztli needed reminding of. If anything it seemed cruel to mention when they were about to enter a tournament to the death. Still, the princess still sang along to all the hymns and recited prayers she did not believe if only to please her family. That was, at the end of the day, all she wanted to do.

Metztli noted the mesmerized faces in the crowd, all joyous to be present with them on such a sacred day. It was easy to stand in awe of the gods when death wasn't looming above you.

From the looks of it however, Acalan seemed to be enthralled by Atzi's words as well. This should have burned irritation through Metztli's core, but instead she was met with a sort of happiness she hadn't experienced in a long time. Despite being twenty-two and nearly a full grown man, Acalan resembled a child much more in this moment, one that Metztli recognized well, having grown up with him.

She'd spent most of her life admiring her brother, he was after all, everything that a good heir should be. He was intelligent and far wiser than his years. He could improve on his fighting skills but that wouldn't really matter if he was crowned emperor of their house.

And above everything else he was kind. He never thought twice before giving to those in need. He'd make a good emperor someday, even better than their father had been and Tenoch was amongst the most beloved emperors of their house. She just had to keep him alive long enough to see his reign come to pass.

Acalan turned to meet Metztli's gaze, as if she'd been speaking to him though words that had never left her lips. She offered her brother a true smile, which he returned. Within the smile she found resolution. Yes, she despised everything that had to do with the gods, particularly their god, and the Tournament of Heirs. She'd never forgive her ancestors who'd agreed to such a horrendous tradition, but she would find a way to survive, and more importantly she would find a way to keep Acalan safe.

She would do it because her brother deserved to live. He deserved it more than anyone else inside the temple of Nemiliztli. Of that, no one would ever be able to convince her otherwise.

ACALAN

Relief.

That's what Acalan felt when he'd found his sister looking his way, even more so when she'd given him the first genuine smile he'd seen from her in what felt like forever.

There had been a time when smiles from her hadn't been so rare. Their childhood had been full of them despite the hours of training and academics they'd been forced to do.

It was believed that the House of Life was made up of the children of the God of Life, and when Acalan looked at his sister, he remembered all the times she'd dragged him into the forest and into trouble. She had been just that: a child full of life, a child of Nemiliztli.

Acalan couldn't read his sister's thoughts, but he wondered what he'd find if he could peer into her mind. He knew that she'd never been interested in the sermons, especially those given by Atzi, at least not in the way that he'd found himself fascinated by them, but perhaps, being that this one was special, dedicated to the both of them, she found herself as entranced as he was.

Everyone else in the crowd of people around them seemed to be under the spell of Atzi's stories. Even the babies that laid in their mother's arms were quiet, as if they were absorbing the histories of their people. Acalan's mother and father sat in the front row alongside the rest of their father's court.

But despite his father being the most poised man Acalan had ever known, it was quite obvious he was fighting sleep. Metztli was a bit like their father in that way, she always managed to snooze when Atzi gave her sermons too. Had Acalan not been in front of a crowd, he might have laughed at the sight.

His mother was doing her best to stay poised as well, but even from a distance Acalan could tell her eyes were beginning to water. He supposed he would have done the same if he was in her position, having to offer your children to the gods was not an easy task and he didn't want to even begin to imagine what he was to do when it was his turn to do so.

Atzi's sermon was quickly coming to an end. It had been so well prepared that Acalan hardly realized how quickly it was passing by. The priestess had a way with words, and they always managed to strike Acalan's heart. Even now, the prince was holding on to the ending of the sermon as if their success within the Tournament of Heirs depended on it. Everything that Atzi had taught the prince over the span of his life said it would, and while his sister did not believe the priestess, Acalan did. She'd never given him a reason not to believe or trust in her words. "Now, let us pray once more for Acalan and Metztli Amos," Atzi announced, beckoning for everyone to close their eyes and bow their heads once more. "Our heirs have a long journey ahead of them and while they carry the wisdom of every heir who has fought before them, no tournament is ever quite the same. It will be special, just as they are to us and to the history of our people."

Acalan did as he was told and found himself quite saddened that the sermon was truly over. That feeling was, however, quickly replaced with excitement as they began the next portion of their day of worship.

When they had first entered the temple of Nemiliztli, Tenoch had instructed both Acalan and Metztli to stand on either side of the fire. That is where the both of them stood now, arms behind their backs, knees slightly bent to avoid the embarrassment of toppling over in front of their people, or gods forbid, falling into the fire of life.

The fire itself was unlike anything Acalan had ever seen. While a regular fire offered an array of reds intertwined with orange shades, the fire of life burned golden and sparkled regardless of what angle you looked at the flames from.

Acalan wasn't entirely convinced that it was truly fire or could be used as such. It did provide warmth, but not the sort that one could feel on their skin. Rather, the warmth could be felt within a person's soul. The flames themselves were also large, not wide in the way a fire typically grew, but tall, nearly tall enough to hit the ceiling of the pyramid. Curiously, it never reached high enough to cause any harm.

It was certainly a sight to behold, one that Acalan was happy he'd been able to see and appreciate once more before his unavoidable fate…Unfortunately, it also served as a reminder of everything he had yet to see. Acalan was twenty-two and had never left their home in Tu'nethe. This was of course by his father's command, but it did leave the prince with an unceasing curiosity to know more.

If they managed to survive the Tournament of Heirs, perhaps Acalan would finally be able to fulfill this desire. But until then it was nothing but a hopeless dream for tomorrow.

"Now, Prince Acalan will do the honors of lighting the torch of continuity, which he will carry and keep alive on our journey home," Atzi announced in an authoritative tone. "Princess Metztli will follow closely behind as the second heir to the House of Life and together they will lead our empire into a new cycle. As they do so, I ask for all children of Nemiliztli, our god, the bringer and taker of life, to pray for the prince and princess as they leave behind their childhood, in sacrifice, for us, their people."

Acalan swallowed harshly, releasing a deep exhale. He'd known of his responsibility to the empire for a very long time. He understood it better than he understood himself sometimes. But as he was handed the torch, felt the wood riddled with splinters and understood the responsibility that lay before him, it all felt too real. They'd prepared for the trials ahead of them, but competing in the tournament had always seemed like something that would happen in the distant future. And now there was no running from what had to be done.

The logical part of his mind told him there was no reason to panic. For all he knew he would be the first to be slaughtered in the tournament. A quick death would save him from the responsibility of taking over his father's empire and would free him from everything his very existence promised their people.

Their eyes were burning holes into him now, Acalan pleaded with his body to move, to just light the torch and be done with it. He'd been breathing on his own from the moment his mother had brought him into this world, and yet he couldn't remember the way to do so now, such a simple movement and–

A soft hand on the back of his elbow pulled him back into the moment. It was Metztli.

"It's just a fire, nothing else, you've done this a million times before at home," she whispered to him.

Acalan nodded softly in return because she was right, it was just a fire, and he was just a young man. There was no need to be afraid, not yet.

With that thought, Acalan's grasp on the torch tightened, he welcomed the subtle pain that came from the aging wood and dipped the end of it into the golden flames before him. He'd half expected for the fire to reject him, a clear signal that he was not fit to rule or survive the tournament, but it did not. Instead the flames engulfed the torch and provided the most illuminating light he'd ever seen in his life.

Acalan turned on his heel to face his people and raised the torch, now beautiful with the blaze, over his head.

"ALL HAIL THE HOUSE OF LIFE!" Acalan declared with such confidence he didn't know he had within him.

The people before him, including his mother and father, responded with shouts of joy. Joy for him, joy for his unspoken promise for a prosperous future and a victorious win for their house.

"ALL HAIL, MY BROTHER, HEIR TO THE HOUSE OF LIFE, THE MIGHTY AND WISE ACALAN!" Metztli then shouted in a playful tone from behind him.

Acalan looked over his shoulder and smiled at his sister, his best friend, the only other person in the world who came close to understanding the pressure that lay on his shoulders and still found ways to make him laugh. Acalan was sure then that there couldn't be another person alive whom he'd rather have as a sister.

Metztli clapped from behind Acalan as the joyous shouting and cheering continued. He didn't think himself mighty or wise, but if his sister thought this of him, then Acalan knew there must be some truth behind her words. He bowed slightly at the waist, showing his respect for their people. They had all gathered here at the temple for them, and that, too, was something worth fighting for. Acalan tucked that thought into a special place in his mind. He'd think about it again when a moment arose that tried to convince him otherwise.

Their mother and father stood from their seats then, joining Acalan and Metztli beside the fire. His father rested his hand on Acalan's shoulder and gripped lightly, a gentle reminder that Tenoch was proud of his son and everything he'd accomplished so far. Acalan had needed that reminder today, especially after having almost frozen during the ceremony.

"We thank you all again for joining us today in prayer and worship for our children," he said to the crowd. "As a father, I have no doubt that the Prince and Princess will represent our house well and will return home victoriously. Now, if you will all join us in our journey home. As our beloved priestess Atzi explained earlier, it is Acalan's duty to keep the flames alive and well. Just as it will be, gods willing, his duty is to keep our empire prosperous and strong. I believe my wife, the empress, also has a few words she would like to share with you before we commence our journey."

He turned to his wife.

"As a mother I stand before you all today to ask that you may keep my children in your prayers. They are grown now as you can see, but in my eyes they will always be my children. It is not an easy sacrifice to willingly hand your children's lives to the gods, but in my faith, I know that Acalan and Metztli will prevail above the others… Now, if you will all rise for your heirs, the future of the House of Life, Acalan and Metztli Amos, my children and my greatest accomplishments in life itself."

She raised both hands.

Everyone stood from where they were sitting and bent at their waists, those who could bend at the knee waited for the Amos family to leave the temple. It was after all, time to return home.

Acalan led the way out of the temple, torch still in hand, though it did not feel nearly as heavy as it did before. Metztli followed closely behind him, and behind her followed their parents and the most important members of his father's court, including Atzi who was making her way towards them now.

"Well done, to the both of you," the priestess praised the both of them as she placed comforting hands on their shoulders and offered a bright, toothy smile.

The expression didn't last very long. Metztli's face wrinkled at the intrusion, and she quickly pulled away and shook the old woman off. Acalan shook his head softly in forced disappointment. What he really wanted to do was laugh, but the prince knew better.

"Thank you Atzi," said Acalan with a sweet smile. "You have prepared us well for the trials ahead."

"I hope I have Acalan…Do remember that every lesson I've ever taught the both of you was for a specific reason. It will take mental strength to survive the Tournament of Heirs." She pulled back to study the pair. "Strength that I know the both of you yield."

Acalan stared down his sister, forcing her to speak. He knew her feelings were less than favorable for the priestess, but being a princess meant that she still needed to mind her manners.

"Thank you Atzi, I will be sure to remember your wisdom when we are being chased through the Pyramid of Tributes," Metztli finally responded with a forced smile.

Acalan rolled his eyes at his sister. It wasn't nearly as mean as he knew she could be, but would it kill her to be nicer to the old woman?

"I hope that you do Princess," Atzi responded, her tone becoming cold as she stepped away to join the rest of their father's court.

Acalan simply shook his head once more before walking down the trail they'd come from.

The journey home was easier than the journey to the temple had been, this was to be expected considering it was mostly downhill now. The prince kept a close eye on the torch that had been entrusted in his care.

"What I said back there, I really meant it," Metztli said, noticing how close Acalan kept the flame. "It's just a fire, you don't have to keep looking at it like it's about to fall apart"

"But it's not really just a fire is it? It's magic straight from the gods," Acalan rebutted. "I've never seen anything quite like this before."

"You haven't been drinking have you? I know your eyesight has always been better than mine but all I see is fire, red flames, that's it…honestly, and I don't say this to antagonize you, I was just expecting… more," Metztli confessed.

"Are you saying it doesn't appear golden to you?" Acalan questioned in return.

"Is it supposed to be golden?"

"It is to me but…who knows, perhaps it just appears that way to the first born heir of our family, or maybe I'm losing my mind. Either would be a reasonable explanation," Acalan said playfully, enticing a chuckle from his sister.

"Yes well, I rather think it's the latter."

The rest of the journey home was peaceful. The thick mist they'd encountered before had dissipated completely now. When they reached the base of the mountain once again, the sun was still high in the sky, allowing them to fully enjoy the beauty of the forest that had caused them such pain and discomfort earlier. It wasn't long before Acalan and Metztli found themselves back in the comfort of Tu'nethe.

Their city was fairly small in comparison to others, but Acalan wouldn't have wanted it any other way. It was because of this that they were able to recognize so many faces in the crowd that followed them. They were highborn, but that had never stopped Acalan or Metztli from mingling with the others. Their father had built a beautiful community that strived to be the best for one another. Acalan only hoped that he could keep it that way when his time to reign came.

It had been a good day. Things had gone far better than Acalan thought they would go, and for that, he was grateful. It had never been more clear in Acalan's mind that he and his sister could win the tournament, and no one in this moment, would be able to convince him otherwise.

ACALAN

The prince found himself running through a forest, one he did not recognize and yet, somehow knew exactly how to navigate. Leaves crunched beneath his feet, trees came into view and then passed out of sight as he ran quickly from one edge of the forest to the next. He was searching for something or someone, but for what or whom he was not sure. The sun supplied just enough light for him to move freely, though admittedly, he could not feel the warmth it usually provided.

He was puzzled and did not understand how he could be so immersed in the path before him, yet know so little of what he was meant to do. The prince questioned how long he'd been running. He couldn't remember when he'd started, but his body did not ache. Perhaps that only meant that he hadn't been running for very long. That was the only plausible explanation he could come up with on his own.

When it all became too confusing the prince stopped abruptly, he'd been running so quickly that he felt his body nearly topple over from his sudden departure from movement. He'd expected to be winded, at least a little bit, but his breath was calm as he turned in a circle, taking in the forest. He was sure then he'd never visited this terrain, nor did he know how he'd made it there, or how long it had been since he'd left home.

Home.

Acalan brushed a hand through his curls as he tried to think of the best way to make it back home. He was sure that his mother would be hysterical if he'd gone missing and Metztli…He didn't want to begin to imagine the chaos she would start if she believed him to be in danger, so he had to return home and he had to so quickly.

Panic was beginning to boil within him, it would consume the prince shortly if he didn't find a way home. He didn't belong here. He was sure of it.

"I was not aware the son of an emperor could panic as quickly as you do now." A woman's voice rang through the forest.

Acalan turned, searching for the source of words. He reached for his blade at his hip but did not find it. This was just his luck: to be lost in the presence of someone hiding from him without a weapon. Yes, this was perfect indeed.

His gaze shifted to the ground, grateful when he found the branch of a tree. It wasn't sharp nor was it a blade, but he needed something to protect himself.

"Show yourself!" Acalan commanded, his tone colder than he was used to.

"And miss your panic?" the voice quelled. "No I think I would rather not, it is not everyday that I am able to witness such a thing"

Acalan moved again, flinging the branch in his hands viciously as he searched for someone, something.

"I don't want to hurt you but I will, I –I won't hesitate if you try to hurt me!" He was indeed beginning to panic, and he wasn't sure if he was trying to convince the hidden woman of his statement or himself.

"Naive boy…you cannot be hurt in your dreams, nor can you hurt me"

Dreams? Acalan questioned. But it couldn't be. This was all too vivid, too real to be a dream. Whoever was hiding from him was just trying to trick him, trying to fool him into dropping his guard, but he wouldn't. He was smarter than that.

"Acalan, son of Tenoch, I do not wish for you to drop your guard, you may keep your branch if you so wish, but I assure you it will not help you, not against me, not in your dreams."

She was reading his thoughts. That wasn't a thing a person was supposed to be able to do. Even the witches from his fairytales back home couldn't do such a thing.

"Who are you?!" Acalan questioned, still searching the brush for the mysterious voice. "What do you want from me?! Why have you taken me from my home?!".

"I do not have a name and I did not take you from your home. In fact, I can assure you that you are still sleeping peacefully in your bed. All I wish is that you listen to me, Acalan, Son of Xara."

"Perhaps it is just a dream," the prince thought to himself.

"It is Acalan," the voice assured him once more. "This is just a dream."

"If that is true then show yourself. You said I cannot hurt you. If that is so then there's no reason to stay hidden," Acalan pleaded.

"As you wish, my prince."

There was noise then, leaves crumbling and birds leaving their cozy homes in the trees. Acalan turned around to find whoever was haunting him and was met face to face with the largest panther he'd ever seen.

The prince was sure he was dreaming then. There had once been magic in Mexica, light and dark, but it had been gone for centuries. The only magic that remained was that of the gods, and none of them had the power to make animals speak, much less make them docile. At least, that's what Acalan believed.

"Am I not what you were expecting Prince?" the panther purred in his direction.

"It isn't every day that I meet a talking panther, not even in my dreams," Acalan said nervously.

"It is not everyday that I find myself with a message to deliver," the animal confessed.

Acalan felt his brow raise. Surely he could find a way to wake himself. Perhaps if he ran into a tree, or over a cliff…that would surely wake him, right?

"Do not be foolish, Acalan. I've brought you here. And I will deliver you back."

Acalan had forgotten his thoughts weren't safe around the animal. Knowing this, the prince stayed silent. He was afraid and confused but continued to hold his ground and hope that he would wake in the comfort of his room.

The panther circled around him as it purred. It was like she was testing him, seeing if he was worthy of her presence. She breathed in his very being, as if doing so would give her the answer she searched for.

"The scriptures do not speak of you, I fear I have called upon the wrong sibling," she said, sitting back on her hind legs.

Acalan didn't know what to think. Why he or Metztli would be spoken about in anything other than the histories of their house was a mystery. Even then, the histories were still being written and he'd already read everything that had been said about the both of them so far.

"Scriptures? There are no scriptures that speak of Metztli," Acalan responded, his voice betraying his panic.

"I'm afraid you haven't been reading the ones I speak of," the panther said without a second thought.

"Why don't you tell me which scriptures you are speaking of then? That is, if you are not lying to me," Acalan questioned harshly.

"Because the message I carry is not for you, child," the panther snapped. "I must go now, time is running out."

Just then the sun disappeared and the forest went dark. The panther turned in an attempt to leave him but she couldn't just leave Acalan with a million questions racing through his mind. She'd sought him out, pulled him out of his sleep, and brought him here. She owed him something, one answer at least.

"If one question is what you wish for, then I will give this to you," the panther sighed. Acalan had not said a word.

Acalan paused, thinking carefully about what to ask. There were a multitude of questions rushing through his mind, but he only had the opportunity to have one answer. That didn't seem like enough.

"The scriptures you speak about, do they refer to the Tournament of Heirs?" Acalan questioned.

"No, not directly…are you disappointed that they do not refer to you, Prince Acalan?" the panther questioned in return, tilting its head slightly in curiosity.

"No…I care about my sister's survival more than I care for my own," Acalan said as he lowered the branch in his hands. "Does it speak of this? Will Metztli survive the Tournament of Heirs?"

"Those are two more questions, Acalan. I'm afraid I only promised you a single answer but I will leave you with this: The answers you seek have always been at your grasp, you only have to look for them." And just like that, the panther was gone. Acalan was alone, left with only

the company of his questions.

"WAKE UP!" Metztli's voice echoed through his room.

Acalan lurched forward, surprised to find himself back in the comfort of his own bedroom. He swore he'd been in a forest a moment ago with…who had he been with?

"Breakfast was served nearly an hour ago. I saved you some but you need to get up quickly," Metztli commanded. "The other houses and heirs should begin arriving this afternoon and we need to train alone before then. I worshiped for you yesterday and now you must train for me today! If you're not at the training grounds in an hour I will return and drag you by the ear, do you understand?"

It was obvious to Acalan that his sister had woken up in a gracious mood. Definitely not the sort of mood that someone who had been visited by a talking panther in their sleep would be in.

"Is that all dear sister?" Acalan questioned as he pulled his lean, sleepy body out of bed.

"Yes that is all. See you in an hour, not a minute before and not a minute after."

Acalan was once again left alone, and this time he was grateful for it. He hadn't had a single drop of pulque the night before nor had he indulged in anything else that could have caused him to have such a wild dream. He didn't quite remember it as vividly as he wished he did, not vividly enough to find any of the answers he wished for.

Acalan tried to shake the thought of it. His dreams were usually peaceful, but perhaps they were simply being disturbed by the looming responsibility over his head. Even if he did wish to investigate the claims made by the panther who had visited him in his dreams, the tournament was only days away and there was still much to do.

Like training with his sister, who would indeed do good on

her promise and return to drag him by his ear if he wasn't on the training grounds when she asked him to be. Though he understood the importance of training, he was unsure why it was so important to train alone. The other heirs would see their abilities sooner than later, and why would they hide the fact that the both of them had practically held blades in their hands since they'd be strong enough to do so?

Acalan groaned to himself. It was foolish to add more questions to his overfilling list of them. The prince would simply have to be content with knowing that if his sister wished to train alone and before the other houses arrived, it had to be for good reason.

METZTLI

There was not much that a good night's rest could not fix. At least that's what Metztli was eagerly trying to convince herself of as she walked her aching and bruised body down the hallways of the pyramid she'd called home from the moment she'd been born.

Her home was busy and loud, filled with faithful handmaidens and stewards preparing for their guests. In truth, she'd always found it quite strange that the house who ruled the others was meant, or more so expected, to welcome the competing heirs and their families under their roof. Still, it wasn't her place to argue or share her opinion, it's not like anyone would actually listen to her at the end of the day.

Metztli's sore limbs were grateful when she finally reached the gardens of her home. Tu'nethe was a beauty unlike anything else, even more beautiful than the temple of Nemiliztli. *But* that was, of course, just her opinion, and she wasn't sure many shared it with her

She could thank her mother for the gardens, they'd been her idea many years ago when she'd first married Metztli's father. Being that by all accounts, her father had been irresistibly in love with Xara, he ensured the most glorious of gardens had been built and nurtured in her name.

"You're barefoot, why is that?" her father questioned from a nearby bench.

Metztli looked around and quickly found him; she made no effort to walk to him quickly. She needed to conserve her energy to train with Acalan.

"I'm in the comfort of my home father, am I not allowed to be barefoot?" she asked, taking a seat next to him.

He didn't quite resemble the emperor she'd known her entire life at this moment. Here, in the quiet of the gardens, he was simply her father, the man who'd sent for the gardens to be built for a woman he loved, and the man who was required to send his only two living heirs into a tournament of death.

"We've never expected guests before, not like today," her father said, offering her a knowing smile.

"Yes, well then when they arrive I will ensure that I have proper protection for my feet, wouldn't want them thinking we're some sort of barbarians now would we?" Metztli responded, though that's exactly what she would need to be a few days from now.

To be fearless, violent and uncontrolled, those were her duties once she entered the Pyramid of Tributes.

"You were a difficult babe, did you know that?"

"Yes, mother never fails to remind me," she sighed. "I think I've been an even more difficult daughter. I suppose I should apologize to you for that now while I can" Her own attempts at being playful were unsuccessful at best.

"You forget I was once in the very position you find yourself today. Young, afraid, with a legacy to protect and a disdain for the gods who made it so."

Metztli stayed silent, counting her breaths. She knew this conversation was bound to be had, there was no avoiding it, certainly not now that she sat with him.

"I'm afraid love is nothing if not violent Metztli," her father continued, his voice soft. "I've done my best to not shield you from this truth in the hope that when this day came, you'd be prepared for what you must do next."

He turned, surveying the garden. "Love can be light, and pure, like the flowers that grow in this very garden, but without violent demonstrations of said love, it can never really flourish. Your mother will deny this, but the first flowers we ever planted here died. No matter how much we cared for them, they simply did not take… and then, a single spring later they flourished, and grew into what they are today. There must be bloodshed in order for you and your brother to flourish, Metztli. It is not fair. It is cruel and unusual, but it is the way."

Tenoch turned to look at his daughter, but Metztli turned away.

She wouldn't allow him to see the tears beginning to form in her eyes. This truth was not one that had been kept for her, it wasn't a sudden realization that hit her in the form of a million lunges to her throat, but it was just as painful to be reminded of it.

"Acalan will return home, I'll make sure of it," Metztli responded simply.

She could make no promises for herself because her duty was to ensure he returned, if her own blood needed to be spilled to make sure of that, then so be it.

"In a perfect world, you both return home. You live out the rest of your days here, with your mother and I. You grow to be the wonderful people I know you two are capable of being. You grant us with the blessings of grandchildren, and you live in peace knowing you've done your duty to your people." He paused. "But this is not a perfect world…Acalan is my son, whom I love deeply but despite my continuous efforts he is not strong, not like you Metztli. Even now I question whether he will be able to kill when it is required of him."

He reached out, running his fingers through her hair.

"I'm sorry that this responsibility will lay mostly with you," he continued. "That is my own failing as a father, for not preparing Acalan the way I should have…Though, in knowing you, in being your father, I see that you, my daughter, are more than capable of ensuring that both of you return. That is my wish, my last command for you."

It was taking every bit of Metztli's strength to not weep like a child. She wanted to crawl into her father's arms like she had when she was little and things hadn't gone her way — when Atzi had scolded her, or she'd been pushed into Acalan's shadow.

Her childhood was gone, that much was clear. From this moment forward she was a woman, and she would need the strength of every woman who'd come before her to return home.

"And if I fail? What then?" Metztli turned, facing him despite the tears that spilled over her warm skin.

"Your uncle died in the tournament. He died saving me. Have you ever witnessed his name being shamed? Have you ever seen any disdain for him?" her father asked as he leaned closer to her.

Metztli shook her head softly in response. In truth, her uncle had never been anything short of honored, and she supposed that would be her own fate if she met an untimely death as well.

Before her father spoke again, he held her gaze with his own.

"You are stronger than him, stronger than he ever was. There is something inside you that I've never seen within anyone else. You are more than this tournament, and you will return home, as will your brother and it will be because of the strength you harbor within you…I am nothing, if not proud of the woman that I have raised, and in the unlikely chance that you must give your life for your brother's, do not for a single moment believe I was ever anything but proud of you."

Her hatred of the gods and the tournament they'd set in place would never change, she was sure of it. She would win out of spite, she'd return home to prove she and Acalan were more than just cattle to be led to slaughter.

She would spill blood, and when she did, it would be in the gods' names.

There was no need to respond to her father. The both of them understood what came next. She simply wrapped her arms around him and relished in the warmth he provided.

They sat in comfortable silence for a little longer, enjoying their last moments of just being a father and daughter and not an Emperor and Princess.

"When the heirs and their families arrive this afternoon, you must be on your best behavior," her father said, seamlessly going from a father back to an emperor again. "They'll be watching closely for anything they can weaponize against you once the tournament begins."

"Acalan and I will train away from their eyes," she said, pulling away from him. "I don't think we'll get another opportunity to do so before the tournament begins. I'm not sure what to do after their arrival. We have tomorrow and the day after to train as well, but I don't find it advisable or intelligent to show our strengths."

Her father took in her response, analyzing it just as she had when she'd thought of the strategy to begin with.

"Are you not afraid that the other heirs will think you are weak? If you do not show your strengths?" he questioned

It was a good question, luckily Metztli had an even better answer.

"No, I quite hope that they do actually," she said with a smile. "If they think I'm weak they'll come for me first."

"I trust your judgment. We should speak again, with your brother, once the heirs are presented, until then I'm afraid we don't know much of what you will be going up against."

It was cruel, leaving everything to be declared and announced until a few days before the tournament began. But Metztli supposed the gods liked seeing them like this, scared and scattered.

"Go, fetch your brother to train. Your mother will be expecting you after, for your garb fitting. Do try your best to be kind and understanding of her, these are difficult times for all of us," her father added, offering a warm smile as he gently rubbed her back.

Metztli understood that. She was sure her mother had already begun mourning the both of them even though the tournament itself hadn't even started. In a way, she was grateful to be on this end of it. She imagined that fighting was perhaps a bit easier than offering your children as sacrifice.

"And what will you do father?" She asked curiously as she stood from the bench, wiping away remnants of her tears.

"I have an empire to look over, I will do what I do best: observe."

Metztli chuckled softly, though she knew there was truth behind his words. For the first time in twenty-five years, all six houses, their people, families and heirs would be within the city walls of Tu'nethe, which surely required close observation from her father.

"Right well, have fun with that I suppose," Metztli responded playfully as she turned her heel and made way for the training grounds.

Though the princess wore a smile on her face, the reality of how she felt was different. It didn't seem fair that everyone else would be allowed to move on with their lives, believing that love was sweet and gentle while she knew the truth.

If violence was what was required of her then that's exactly what she could give her rivals. If that's what she needed to do to prove her love for her brother and the House of Life, then she would do just that.

The knowledge of this weighed heavy on Metztli's heart and soul as she walked through the palace and towards the training grounds. The princess knew that even if she returned victorious, she'd never quite be the same. The Tournament of Heirs would change her in more ways than one but maybe, just maybe, that would be a good change or at the least, a change she was willing to make in order to save her brother.

METZTLI

Acalan was nowhere to be found when she arrived at the training grounds, but she couldn't blame him. She'd told him to arrive there in an hour, no earlier and no later. As long as her brother wasn't late like he typically was, then everything would be fine.

If anything this worked to her advantage, after yesterday's trek, she needed a little longer than normal to warm her body and muscles, and she needed as much time with a spear today as she could get. It was likely that she wouldn't get another opportunity to train with one properly, not before they entered the Pyramid of Tributes.

The training grounds of her home had always been Metztli's safe harbor. While her brother found solace in visiting Atzi in her sanctuary of prayer, Metztli had never felt more safe than she did here. She relished in the feeling of the sand underneath her bare feet and loved the way the opening in the ceiling of her home allowed the sun to shine directly on her skin. She wished she had more time to just enjoy it without the stress of the tournament weighing on her shoulders.

Relief filled her body the moment she started her routine, the same one she'd followed from the moment her father had begun training her many years ago. She rolled out her stiff shoulders and neck. The resulting ache from moving her body this way was blissful, exactly what she needed to make it through the rest of the day.

Metztli retrieved a dull training spear from its place on the equipment wall. The one her father had gifted her on her fifteenth name day was back in her room, carefully stored away and ready to use when the time came.

She preferred training with her own spear, but recognized that there was the possibility of losing it once the tournament started. It was a beautifully crafted weapon that had been designed to withstand during battle, but it could break. They all could.

Metztli began by going through the basic motions she'd first learned as a little girl, lunging forward with the sharp end leading the way, passing it from one hand to the other and swinging it over and above her head, slicing through the air in front of her.

The princess knew far more technical movements – like spinning the spear in such a way that it could easily take out two opponents at once, even if they came from completely different directions – but the basics were important. Her father had never failed to remind her of this when he'd been in charge of her training, and even now that she trained alone, that knowledge stuck.

She continued in this way for a while, slowly increasing the technicality of the movements she repeated until she'd practiced enough that her breaths became ragged and sharp, pressing an ache into her chest.

Typically when she started feeling like this, she pushed even harder, promising her body they would only go through one more movement. But one movement became two and two became three. This repeated until her body could simply do no more.

Today wouldn't be any different. Above anything else, Metztli needed to train to the best of her ability. If the option was between pushing her body to a new limit or to risk losing the Tournament of Heirs, there was no question which the princess would choose. She'd find time to rest later, perhaps indulging in a hot bath full of salts and oils that could help her body replenish. But until then, the princess was ready to welcome the pain that her body would endure.

Metztli was grateful that at least she didn't have to travel like the other heirs did. Some of them were only a day trip away, but the others had likely been traveling for the last week or so to reach Tu'nethe. That certainly had to work in her advantage somehow.

The princess allowed herself a quick drink of water from the fountain in the middle of the arena before returning to the task at hand. She was still panting slightly when she began spinning her spear and throwing it upwards in sporadic movements, always catching it and making sure to grip the wood beneath her fingers tightly. The last thing she needed was to accidentally drop her weapon in the middle of an encounter with a competitor.

While Metztli had never met any of the heirs from the neighboring houses personally, she had listened closely enough to her father's lectures to believe she knew enough about them.

The House of Flor was the nearest to Tu'nethe and would likely arrive first. From what Metztli understood, they'd provided strong competitors in the past, but their downfall always came when the heirs of their house became uncomfortable with their circumstances within the Pyramid of Tributes.

After all, it was difficult to go from being bathed in riches to being nothing but a dirty sacrificial lamb.

She lunged toward the ground, catching the spear before it hit the dirt. It never hit the floor, not while it was in her hands. Now, she caught it mid air and still managed to position her body in a way that made it easy to regain her composure. From this angle the princess could do a number of things, whether that be to slash through her enemies ankles or angle her blade upright and aim straight for their necks, either would end in a fatal injury.

That is, if she was fighting an heir who was dull enough to drop their guard long enough to allow her to do so and while that would be nice Metztli knew that they were all well prepared in their own regard. The House of Wind, for instance, wasn't known to be strong or technically skilled in the art of violence, but they always came with some sort of new invention, something never seen or heard of that could easily catch their competition off guard.

Still, in all the years the Tournament of Heirs had been in place, they'd only won a handful of times so that brought Metztli some comfort as she brushed the sand off her hands, took a deep breath and prepared herself to start again.

Being that her body remained tired and bruised from the day before, Metztli's muscles had begun to ache far quicker than they normally would. The princess paid no mind to this, however, not as she threw her spear again and certainly not as she caught in a defensive stance and hurled it towards one of the targets before her.

Violence would be required from her in just a few short days and while she felt confident that she would be able to provide an ample amount of it, there was still a deep-seated fear in her chest that she would somehow fail miserably and, in turn, prove to be unfit for the only responsibility she'd ever been given.

She tried to shake the thought out of her mind as she walked over to the target to pull her spear from it. She'd hit the center as she normally did but that did nothing to ease the anxiety building up within her.

She'd never killed a person, much less come close to doing so. Metztli had hunted animals before and while she hoped it would be quite the same she knew it couldn't be. The two experiences had to be wildly different.

She was at a disadvantage in this. Her father had warned her to avoid the heirs from the House of Serpent and the House of Blood by all means possible. Both were incredibly hungry for power and would likely ally together just as they had done in the past.

Facing allied heirs didn't scare Metztli as much as knowing what some of the heirs from those houses had already done.

The House of Blood was known for their macabre traditions. While Metztli and Acalan had enjoyed festive celebrations on their fifthtenth name days, the heirs from The House of Blood were forced to commit great tragedies in order to enter adulthood.

Sacrifices used to be a common practice throughout Mexica, that was true, but it had been centuries since the act of ritual sacrifice had been abandoned. The House of Blood did not care, they'd never stopped massacring their own people as offering to the gods. To say this made them dangerous was an understatement.

Metztli would have no choice but to kill during the tournament, even if it pained her, she knew her brother was unlikely to look past his morals and plunge a blade into someone's chest. The responsibility would almost certainly lay with Metztli, and she had to be capable of killing. Metztli understood this as she walked away from the target with her spear tightly gripped in her hand.

As much as she wanted to frown upon the House of Blood and their heirs, she couldn't help but wish she was a little bit like them in regards to killing. It would have been a relief to know she could take someone's life instead of simply hoping that she would be able to.

Regardless, Metztli knew there was nothing she could do to remedy that fact now, so she raised her spear above her shoulder and launched it into the air and towards the target again. The only thing that comforted her now was knowledge that her aim continued to be perfect.

"How long have you been training for?" Acalan's question, full of worry, broke through her concentration.

Metztli jumped at the sudden intrusion. She'd been so focused on her own thoughts that she hadn't heard him enter the training grounds, nor did she understand why he looked at her like there was something wrong.

"I don't know…not very long I suppose," she replied, trying to catch her breath. "My options were to come here or to visit mother for my garb fitting. The choice was easy, don't you think?"

"Well, you look like you've been training for much longer and that is not a compliment," Acalan responded, equally playfully.

Metztli had no doubt that she looked terrible, her body felt that way too.

"I just came from my garb fitting actually, and I can confirm, it was easily one of the worst experiences of my life," Acalan continued, tilting his jaw slightly as he seemed to recall the experience. "The designs they came up with are very…extravagant, certainly not what we were expecting so there's little to no hope that we won't stand out amongst the other heirs."

Metztli whimpered and faked a sob. She'd been very clear when she'd asked her mother to not go overboard with this. It was important that they, as the heirs of the House of Life, stayed out of the spotlight as much as they could. Being that their house currently ruled over the others, they already had targets on their backs, and outrageous garbs wouldn't make that any better.

"Did you see mine? How horrible is it?" Metztli asked.

It's not that she didn't enjoy dressing up. In fact, she quite enjoyed looking beautiful. It was a satisfaction like no other to find a dress that perfectly accentuated her toned features while still remaining feminine. Feeling beautiful was a wonderful experience, but it was not a skill that would aid her in the tournament.

"Oh it's dreadful, worse than mine by all accounts. They've sown all sorts of feathers and bells into your gown. I wish you the best of luck trying to walk an inch without being noticed or heard," Acalan responded with a sly smirk.

"You're a Prince not a jester, that wasn't funny I was truly beginning to panic! You're here to train, not practice your comedic abilities. Now go grab a bow, you should have brought yours to train with," Metztli scolded.

"Apologies, I saw an opportunity and I had to take it. You don't have your spear…is there a reason I would need my bow?" Acalan asked with the curious head tilt and raised brow.

"I've been training without it, just in case it's misplaced or broken during the Tournament. Spears are easier to replace than bows. So, when we're in there your bow needs to be on you at all times, I can always make another spear but we won't be able to make you another bow."

"Of course, whatever you say," he said as he raised his right hand to his heart, pounding it against his chest twice.

That movement was how one saluted a general in the society of warriors, and Metztli was no general, so she simply rolled her eyes as she watched her brother walk away to retrieve a training bow from the wall.

While Acalan wasn't nearly as imposing in hand to hand combat, Metztli couldn't deny that her brother was quite impressive with his bow. Even though their father had been adamant that they try all sorts of weapons before settling on one to specialize in, this weapon had always been best suited for him.

She still recalled Acalan's fifthteenth name day and the ceremony in which he'd picked the bow to be his weapon of choice. Everyone present seemed to have been confused as to why the prince had picked it. Even those who had watched him train with it and knew he never missed a shot wore expressions of confusion. To Metztli however, it had made complete sense, she knew her brother was going to pick it long before even he did.

The bow had practically called his name from the very beginning. Wielding it was a gentle art, and Acalan was a gentle soul. It was also the least violent weapon offered to them so it made perfect sense that he'd picked it. Seeing Acalan hold it in his hands, even back then when they were children, was a sight that made perfect sense to Metztli.

It was, however, obvious that Acalan's decision had been disappointing to some of the men in their father's court. Metztli was sure that they would have much rather seen him pick a spear or perhaps the very Macuahuitl that their father had once used, but their opinions didn't matter. When a weapon calls to you, you have no choice but to accept it and that's exactly what Acalan had done. Even now, Metztli remained proud of her brother for choosing to follow his heart.

Two years later, on her own fifthteenth name day, Metztli didn't think twice before placing her hand over the spear, and that seemed to surprise the crowd as well. She began to realize from that day forward that regardless of what her brother and she did, they couldn't make everyone happy. There would always be someone in the crowd who would be displeased with their actions. Someone who found their decisions inappropriate, too feminine, too masculine. Or perhaps not masculine enough.

While Acalan resented this truth and did everything that he could to be exactly what everyone needed him to be, Metztli embraced it. So, the princess did as she pleased, when she pleased. Always within reason, of course. She was masterful in this art, and perhaps that's what allowed her to grow so lethal over the years.

"Okay that was…better," Metztli announced half enthusiastically.

They'd been training together for a little while now but as her brother became bored with her commands, his aim had begun to falter too.

"When we train with the other heirs tomorrow, make sure you don't miss a shot…and don't speak to any of them okay?" Metztli added. "I know we're expected to be pleasant hosts, but this isn't the time to make friends. It will be harder to aim for them if you think of them as people."

"But they are people," her brother rebutted, letting his shoulders drop slightly.

He was right, they were people just like them, but that didn't make the responsibility weighing on their shoulders any lighter.

"They are," she said as gently as she could. "I know they are, but they will be coming after us. They all have debts to settle with our family. I know it's not fair that we have to pay for the sins of those who came before us, and I'm not saying that we will be hunting them, but they will be hunting us whether we like it or not."

"So that's all we are? Predators and Prey? The other heirs have hopes and dreams just like us,"

Acalan replied bitterly.

"You're directing your anger at the wrong person!" she snapped. "My duty is to you, not the gods, not mother or father or the entirety of their empire. My duty is to keep you, my only brother, safe. And if I can, by whatever miracle it takes, return home as well, then I will spend the entirety of my life being grateful for it. But I did not decide to send you or I into the Tournament of Heirs, the gods decided that, and I reckon it would do you well to remember that."

She moved then to replace the worn out target. Acalan had been doing quite well until he started missing the center. Metztli knew this was on purpose. He always did this when he was beginning to get bored and wanted to be done with training. Unfortunately for the prince, his antics would do very little for him today.

Still, Metztli knew they shouldn't be arguing, not so close to the start of the tournament and certainly not when the other heirs would begin arriving soon. Both of them would be watched, every one of their moves would be analyzed, and they had no room to appear weak, not unless of course, it was part of a well calculated strategy to deceive.

"We will not kill unless we are prompted to," she said, fiddling with the board in her hands. "I can't promise you much but I can promise you that…In fact, just leave the killing to me if you must, that's a sacrifice I'm more than willing to make for you."

Acalan shook his head in response. There was an eerie silence between the both of them, but Metztli couldn't understand why. What more could she promise him other than this? If he was worried about branding his soul with the blood of the other heirs, then she would take the brunt of it without thinking twice.

"What sort of man will I be, if I allow my younger sister to kill for me?" Acalan, questioned in a tone that made it clear he was hurt by Metztli's suggestion. "What kind of emperor does that set me up to be?"

Once again Acalan resembled a boy — the one who had been too scared to pick up a blade when they were little, when they barely understood the meaning of being heirs.

Before responding, Metztli beckoned for brother to raise his bow. If he was insistent on having this conversation that was quite fine, but they would need to continue training at the same time. She watched closely as her brother rolled his eyes before aiming and letting an arrow fly. He'd missed once again, this time even worse than before.

"Seriously?" Metztli questioned, her brows arched in confusion.

Acalan didn't respond. Instead he raised his brow and remained silent. It only took Metztli a few seconds to realize what he wanted a response before he'd begin actually trying again. This realization made Metztli huff in frustration but if that's what Acalan wanted, she'd give him that.

"You'll be the kind of emperor the House of Life needs. We just need to get through the tournament, and then when we return, you can change things. You'll have the power to change things, Acalan. Until then we're just pawns to be moved in this game." She paused. "And the only way we return home safely is by playing this game better than them. Not by missing targets on purpose."

"I do understand, I just…I wish things were different. I don't want your soul to be tainted just as much as I don't want mine to be marked," Acalan said with a heavy sigh.

Metztli took a step forward, placing both of her hands on her brother's shoulders, doing her best to keep his gaze locked with her own.

Though she respected that Acalan wanted to keep her safe, she knew there was nothing either of them could do to assure this. No one was truly safe in this tournament they were about to enter.

"My soul will be just fine. In fact, if anything it will be an honor to serve as your protector in the pyramid," she said, offering him a small smile. "We're not the first heirs to compete in this, and we won't be the last. Father competed with his brother, and his soul remains intact… Besides, I have a plan, father approved of it, so I just need you to play your part in the coming days."

Acalan listened, absorbing his sister's words. His shoulders seemed to relax just enough for him to speak again.

"What is it?" her brother questioned softly.

Metztli took a deep breath of her own before she started explaining, she knew her next words would be a calculated risk, one that she hoped would pay off.

"The heirs will be arriving today," she explained. "Some of them will train as soon as they arrive and some of them won't, but tomorrow everyone will train together. I have no doubt about that. I need you to train as well as you can when we're in their company. As I said before, they'll be watching and they need to fear you, you need to be a threat like none other.

She paused, gazing at her brother as if measuring whether she could trust him with what she was about to say. "I, on the other hand…father and I thought it might be beneficial if I make myself appear…weak. That way, when they come for us, they'll come for me first because they'll assume I'm the lesser threat."

Acalan hardly let either of them breathe before he responded. "Absolutely not! Under no circumstances will we trick them into coming for you in my place. If I die as a result of rejecting this strategy then so be it! At least it will be an honorable death."

It was in moments like this one that Metztli wished she and her brother were more alike, that they could understand each other better.

As she thought of what to say in response, her father's words echoed in her mind.

Love is nothing if not an act of violence.

"I apologize, it seems I haven't made myself clear," she said. "This is the plan, I wasn't asking for your permission or opinion. You either follow along and do as you're told or you die, and it won't be an honorable death, it will be a foolish one. The Tournament of Heirs isn't about honor, it's about spilling blood, and I won't have it be yours."

The silence that settled around them was suffocating. It was all consuming and too much to handle.

She waited for her brother to respond, but he said nothing for what felt like minutes if not longer. His eyes seemed to cut into her. It was an intrusion that she did not welcome, but there wasn't much else that she could do except stand there and let him in.

"You pride yourself on being so different, but you're just like them," Acalan spewed bitterly. "It's a shame it's taken me this long to realize the truth." His words were daggers, and before him, she remained armorless.

It wasn't fair, none of this was.

Metztli didn't move, much less speak as she watched her brother drop his bow, turn, and walk away. He was gone before she could muster the courage to speak. He'd left her there, alone with nothing more than her thoughts and those were perhaps the most dangerous of company.

ACALAN

Acalan stormed out of the training grounds as quickly as he could. He'd never felt so frustrated, and he'd most certainly never said such hurtful things to his sister who was the only person who had ever truly been there for him, who had cared for him as a person and not just because he was the heir to the empire that was House of Life.

The prince immediately hated himself for it. He knew he shouldn't have been so cruel but he couldn't bring himself to go back and apologize. Even if he did, he wasn't sure that he could come up with the appropriate words. Nor did he think that Metztli would let him explain himself.

Instead, Acalan just walked in the other direction, passing the kitchen and library as he made every attempt to get far, far away from her. He had no true destination in mind. He just needed to be alone for a moment.

It was, however, a terrible day to want to be alone. The palace was brimming with people. For a brief moment it started feeling like the walls were beginning to close in on him, like the hallways were no longer wide, and he no longer fit within them.

Acalan walked faster then, earning a few confused and concerned glances from the passing handmaidens. In an attempt to not alarm anyone, Acalan turned quickly and made way for the only place in the entire palace he knew would be somewhat peaceful.

Atzi's sanctuary was always quiet, and if he was lucky, Atzi would be there. She would surely be able to advise him on what to do about his sister. When they were children, Atzi had always mediated their brawls, even if they were simply over who would get the last cookie or piece of chocolate. The priestess had always been happy to aid him in the past, today shouldn't be any different, even if the circumstances were much heavier.

Acalan was walking so quickly he nearly stumbled into the door when he finally reached the sanctuary. Atzi didn't flinch or even look up at the prince when he entered. She simply kept her position, kneeling before the statue of Nemiliztl, and continued to whisper what Acalan knew to be a prayer.

The prince made quick work of composing himself. He knew the woman before him would be able to sense that something was wrong, but he didn't want to give off the impression that he was too disgruntled. Atzi was wise, yes, perhaps the most wise of them all, but she was deep into old age, and he didn't want to worry her too much.

"You come to me troubled prince?" Atzi questioned in a sweet motherly tone when she finally finished her prayer.

Acalan nodded in response as he approached the woman, offering a hand to help her stand.

"It's been a difficult day, from my dreams to now, I've felt… troubled as you say. I thought you might have some wisdom to share with me."

He had had no intention of mentioning his strange dream before coming in, but being in her presence always made him open up about matters he didn't even know were an issue to begin with.

"I see… your spirit weighs heavy Acalan, take a seat, recite a prayer while I go retrieve something," she said, offering a comforting smile. "And when I return perhaps you can share with me what it is that has brought you to me so troubled."

As she stepped away into her own personal library, Acalan did as he was told. The prince found himself a seat on the closest bench to the statue of Nemiliztl. He'd done this a million times before, so it felt like slipping into a memory as he bowed his head and prayed.

Divine God of life,
Grant me the breath of your wisdom,
Envelop me in your boundless love and light,
Guide me in the direction of peace and harmony,

Bringing forth renewal and strength.
In your sacred name, I honor the gift of life.
Amen.

He recited the words over and over in a soft whisper until he started believing them again. Acalan knew it wasn't uncommon for one's faith to diminish in stressful moments like this one, but with a little effort, he swore he could feel the spirit of Nemiliztli flow within him. It put him at just enough ease that he was able to at least list everything that was bothering him in his mind.

"Feeling better, my prince?" Atzi asked as she approached him.

Acalan was surprised to find she only carried one book in her hands. She'd been gone for so long he thought she might return with more. It wasn't exactly encouraging that he didn't recognize the book either. It was small and thin, but worn out and hardly in one piece. As far as Acalan was aware, he'd read everything in the sanctuary and in his family's library, but not this book that she held with her wrinkled hands.

"To an extent, yes, prayer always helps clear my mind...I'm afraid I'm still quite troubled though," Acalan said honestly.

He knew nothing good could come from being dishonest.

"It is not abnormal for someone in your position to feel this way, Acalan," she said, taking a seat next to him "Stress can manifest in many ways, but in order to help you, I must know what it is exactly that troubles you"

Acalan stayed silent for a moment as he collected his thoughts and decided what to speak about first. Even thinking about his dream from the night before made him feel like he was going mad.

"I had a dream last night," he confessed with a deep sigh. "I was in a forest I did not recognize, and there was a voice. I thought it was a woman at first, but then a panther appeared before me...It felt so real, that's what bothered me the most."

He watched as Atzi took in his words almost as if they had a double meaning, but he truly had no intention to mislead her.

"Yes, I imagine that dreaming such a thing could be disorienting," she said. "And what did the panther tell you? I'm curious if perhaps what it said was simply just your stress manifesting through a dream?"

That was what Acalan had determined on his own as well. He was afraid to repeat what had been said in his dream though, as if saying it outloud would somehow make it real.

"The panther, she spoke of a prophecy and a message she had to leave with the chosen heir," Acalan started explaining hesitantly. The act alone of speaking these words made him feel like he was betraying the very gods he loved.

"At first I think she believed it was me," he continued, "but then she said she had visited the wrong sibling... It didn't make any sense then and it still doesn't make any sense now.

"If there was a prophecy that spoke of my sister we'd know about it...This dream, it left me with questions but now I feel guilty that I've even questioned if it could be real," Acalan concluded. The prince was far more confident in these words than he'd been in the others.

Atzi smiled towards Acalan, which confused him, nothing about his dream had made him smile.

"Metztli is a strange creature, more beast than woman.

"It seems to me that perhaps, her crude nature has formed some sort of insecurity within you," she continued "You must remember that dreams are nothing more than just that, dreams... You are the heir of this house Acalan, you must believe in yourself, as much as you believe in Metztli, if not more."

Atzi was so confident in her words that it was easy for Acalan to believe her. His dream didn't hold anything that he didn't already know, and he did need to start believing in himself if he wanted to survive the tournament.

"What else troubles you today?" Atzi asked, brushing aside his dream.

"I argued with my sister just now," Acalan confessed as he looked down at his hands, playing with the heir ring that sat on his finger. "I allowed my emotions to get the best of me and I said something I shouldn't have."

This wasn't the first time he'd argued with his sister of course, nor was it the first time Atzi had heard word of such an argument, but it was the first time he felt so ashamed over it.

"What was the argument about?" Atzi asked softly.

"The tournament of course, she believes me incapable of killing, and she's right," he explained, feeling lighter as each word slipped from his lips. "The thought of it makes me want to crawl into my own skin…

"She advised me not to think of the other heirs of people, but they are people, just like Metztli and I… I don't want to kill anyone, but I know I must. It is a duty that conflicts with everything you've ever taught me…Nemiliztli, our god, he worships life, and I'm meant to take it for what? A tournament?"

"The gods envy us you know," Atzi responded rather quickly.

Her statement confused Acalan. What could they have that the gods could possibly envy? They were gods after all.

"Do you know why you value life so much, Acalan?" Atzi questioned before he could respond.

"Because you taught me to, of course," he said without a second thought.

"Well yes, but why else?" Atzi pressed.

Acalan thought about it for a moment, but he couldn't come up with an answer. For as long as he remembered he cherished life, but there wasn't a specific reason why, at least not one that he could recall.

"You value life because it's so fragile." She smiled, clutching the book to her chest. "Unlike the gods, we are not immortal, we won't live forever like them…Your mother lost a child, and with it almost lost her own life as well. I still remember how devastating it was for her and your father, but in that tragedy I saw a love for life bloom within her. I don't believe there is a woman in the entirety of Mexica that loves their children the way Xara loves the both of you.

Atzi paused, looking over Acalan knowingly. "So you see, the gods envy knowing that we are fragile, because they are not fragile at all."

Acalan shifted his gaze from his hands to the woman who sat next to him. He'd never thought about it in that way. He'd never considered that they had something that the god's envied, but this made perfect sense, he didn't question it at all because he saw it for what it was: the truth.

"The tournament is a punishment then, for what they envy in us?"

Atzi stayed silent for a moment, calculating what was appropriate to say next.

"In a way yes, but it also serves as a reminder of the war and of our standing with the gods. They may allow one family to rule amongst the others, but ultimately they rule over all of us, we are under their will."

Atzi spoke with such conviction that it was easy to believe her. "I know this all might feel conflicting or contradictory to our beliefs, but you must understand that we all have a role to play in this empire. It is unfair that a soul like yours should be chosen to compete in this tournament, but you have been chosen for a reason. And when the time comes, whether you choose to kill or not, that will be your decision to make, and I know you will make the right one, just as I know that Metztli will make the right one as well."

It helped that most of what she said were things Acalan already knew to be true. He'd just needed to hear her say them, something to remind him he wasn't going mad for feeling the way he did.

"Apologize to your sister when you can," she said with a soft smile. "I will not ask you to repeat what you said to her, as I can see it pains you deeply…Metztli can be terribly stubborn but she loves you unconditionally, and there is no doubt that a simple apology will mend the wound between the both of you…I would like for you to read through the history of the Tournament of Heirs on your own, as well. I find that reminding oneself of the origin of these things often reignites a deep appreciation for them."

Acalan remained silent. He didn't really want to re-read the history of the tournament. Much of it was morbid and would surely put him in an even more foul mood, but if Atzi thought it might be beneficial then he wouldn't argue.

"Thank you Atzi, I hope that all of the wisdom you have shared with me throughout my life will be present with me inside of the pyramid…"Acalan stood from his seat then, offering an arm to help Atzi stand as well. The woman took it with a brief smile, while she still clutched the worn book in her other hand.

METZTLI

For the first time in what felt like her entire life, Metztli couldn't stand the thought of being alone.

On any other occasion she would have savored the opportunity for some solitude but it felt more like a punishment now that she couldn't stop replaying her brother's words in her mind.

"You pride yourself on being so different, but you're just like them. It's a shame it's taken me this long to realize the truth."

Metztli wondered if it was true.

She'd never despised anything more than she despised the gods. They were cruel and selfish, always taking for themselves and never considering how their actions would affect anyone else…Surely she wasn't just like them. Her entire life up to this very second had been dedicated to becoming the sort of person who could protect her brother when the time came. The gods were wicked, and she could not find it in herself to believe that she was too.

Metztli tried to shake those thoughts from her mind, earning a few curious glances from the palace keeper's as she passed them on her way to her mother. She'd been planning on avoiding this garb fitting for as long as she could, but now it was an opportunity to be in comforting company.

For as long as Metztli could remember, her mother Xara took her duties as the empress of the House of Life far more seriously than she could imagine herself doing if she was in her position. Often, it felt like her mother had been born for her role, and that was admirable to anyone who encountered her, Metztli included.

"Mother?" Metztli called out as she opened the door.

Her voice echoed through her mother's beautifully adorned quarters. Although they lived in a palace, it wasn't necessarily as lavish as it could be. More often than not, her parents chose to give to those in need rather than taking their riches for themselves. This, too, was something that Metztli admired about her mother and father.

The room itself was quiet, like it had always been. Paintings made by local artisans were hung on the walls alongside drawings that she and Acalan had made when they were children. Their interpretation of art wasn't nearly as beautiful, but her mother kept them hung anyway. She always had.

"She's here!" Xara beamed as she came into view.

Metztli pouted as she noticed her mother's excitement fade when she actually caught sight of her daughter. Was Metztli incapable of doing anything right?

"Did you really think it wise to come to your garb fitting a sweaty mess?" her mother asked in a scolding, yet loving tone.

On any other occasion Metztli would have rolled her eyes and responded sarcastically, but she simply didn't have it in her today, not after what had just happened with her brother.

"I apologize," she said, offering an exhausting half smile. "I was just training with Acalan, I should have come beforehand just as he did."

"That's alright darling, let's get you fitted and then you can take a hot bath…We'll have to be quick though, I'm afraid the other heirs and their families will begin to arrive soon," her mother said as she reached her, rubbing a warm, comforting hand over Metztli's bare shoulder and pulling her towards the parlor where Nenetl, their seamstress, was waiting.

This wasn't the most ideal situation by any means, but at least Metztli wasn't alone. Her mother and Nenetl would keep her busy and distracted, and right now that's all that Metztli could really ask for.

"Oww!" Metztli whined for what felt like the thousandth time since Nenetl had draped the gold silk over her chest and fitted the teal skirt around her waist.

She'd come here to be distracted and to be in good company, but she hadn't come seeking to be poked and prodded by the seamstress's needles. Her mother had promised that this would be quick, but she'd been standing in front of the mirror for at least an hour.

One would think that this was more than enough time to perfect the way the teal silk wrapped around her hips, but apparently it was not.

"My sweet winter child, you must understand that beauty is pain. Now stop complaining so Nenetl can do her duty!" Xara scolded her daughter once again.

"I barely nicked her that time…you would think such a strong girl would have better tolerance for pain," Nenetl said sarcastically.

Both women giggled.

Metztli couldn't help but roll her eyes at that comment. The thing about their seamstress was that she just so happened to also be her mother's best friend and an aunt of sorts to Metztli and Acalan. So while Nenetl could poke fun at the princess, Metztli had to stay reserved with her responses.

"I apologize, I would just much rather not enter the Pyramid of Tributes all bruised if I can help it," Metztli said in the most courteous tone she could muster.

"I think that's enough for now, Nenetl. I trust you can make all the alterations before tomorrow?" Metztli's mother asked.

Nenetl scoffed at the task before brimming with confidence.

"Of course I can, Xara," she replied. "Though if I could, I would like to adjust the shoulders. I didn't account for Metztli arms being so…*muscular.* Perhaps we should drape more fabric here to hide how *broad* she is?" Nenetl demonstrated what she intended to do with the fabric.

Metztli turned to her mother, trying to convey a million words with her gaze. There was only so much she could take in a day, and after Acalan's verbal attack on her pride, she wasn't sure she could take any more of Nenetl's criticism. Not without it ending in an outburst on her end.

"No," Xara said, rising from her seat to stand behind her daughter in the mirror. "My daughter has trained a lifetime for the honor of walking into that pyramid. Let the other heirs see her strength for what it is." She admired Metztli's reflection before her.

"As you wish, Xara. Mothers always seem to know best." Nenetl began to help Metztli out of the misshapen silk, and gathered her things. The woman excused herself shortly after, leaving Metztli and her mother alone.

"Did Acalan's fitting take as long?" Metztli asked as she slipped back into her own clothing.

"It did not. It's much easier to dress a man though." Xara paused. "You know Nenetl never means harm, she just wanted to ensure you looked beautiful for your presentation."

Metztli scoffed at that. She had nothing against looking and feeling beautiful, it was just the ceremony of it all that bothered her.

"I know, but I need to look scary as well, mother. I can't exactly kill the other heirs with beauty, now can I?" Metztli asked with a raised brow.

She expected her mother to scold her again, but she did not. Instead Xara stood in front of her, placed two gentle hands on Metztli's shoulders, and looked her directly in the eyes.

"What could possibly be more dangerous than a beautiful woman?" Her mother asked in the most serious tone Metztli had ever heard her mother use.

Metztli nodded softly as she pondered her mother's statement.

"Men might think they rule this world, Metztli, but it is beautiful and intelligent women who truly do. Otherwise all of the gods would be men, and they are not…being a woman is a skill in itself, and you must remember to use every skill you have within the Pyramid of Tributes. Understood?"

"I hardly think the art of seduction will come in handy when the tournament starts," Metztli responded, a soft chain of laughter enveloping her words.

"And why not?" Xara said, pouring herself a cup of pulque. "You must do what you can to keep your brother and yourself alive...Men are easily swayed, Metztli, under the right circumstances of course."

Metztli was shocked to say the least. She'd never heard her mother speak this way. Xara, much like Atzi, had always preached about purity amongst other things, but never about this. She didn't know how to respond or if she should, so Metztli stayed quiet and came to the conclusion that the tournament was simply starting to get to her mother's head as well. That had to be it.

"Right, well I'll keep that in mind." Metztli began to back towards the door. "I should get going or I'll be late to greet the other heirs. I'll be in my room until then if you need me." The princess accidentally stumbled over her feet when she finally turned to leave but managed to keep her body from tumbling towards the floor.

She was simply not at her best today.

"Don't forget what I said!" her mother shouted after her.

The moment Metztli was back in the hallway she had to squeeze her eyes shut and shake her head to ensure she was awake and that this wasn't just some terrible dream. When that wasn't enough she pinched herself as she made her way to her room.

Despite all of her attempts though, she did not wake and came to the conclusion that this was real. Everyone around her just seemed to be going mad.

Metztli walked quickly in an attempt to avoid any chance of seeing Acalan. While her garb fitting had been quite the distraction, she had no choice but to be alone now, and when she finished bathing and dressing herself, she would have to face her brother. The thought of doing so made dread settle in her stomach.

As she entered her bathing chambers and set upon finding the salts infused with lavender that she'd set aside for a particularly difficult day, she couldn't help but wonder if there was anything she could do or say to make the situation at hand any better.

It was quiet as she waited for the water to cool down enough that she could submerse her body without hurting herself. The silence, however, only gave the princess more opportunity to think of ways to remedy her mistakes, even if she did have to hurt her pride in the process. The thought of apologizing to her brother made her irritable enough that she gave up on waiting and instead slid into the water, welcoming the subtle pain that came from the water being too warm.

If she really had been like the gods, then the act of doing so wouldn't have brought her no pain at all. Metztli wondered if it would have been better to live that way, feeling nothing.

She did feel an abundance of emotions though. If anything she felt too much. It was for that very reason that she was trying to come up with a solution as she massaged through the knots that had settled in her shoulders and neck. If she had felt nothing then she wouldn't have cared to reconcile with her brother nor would she have spent her entire life preparing for this tournament.

She'd done that for him, not for the opportunity of glory.

She was nothing like the gods. She was simply making the best of the situation they'd been handed. Killing was an unfortunate outcome of the tournament and they couldn't possibly survive the entire thing without at least harming one of the other heirs.

She just wished her brother would see the tournament for what it was.

Metztli determined that all she could do was resign to her feelings. She would apologize to Acalan in an attempt to keep peace between them, but the fact that she would need to kill when the time came remained, and nothing could stop her from doing that. Not her morals, and certainly not her brother.

After all, her duty was to kill in order to keep him alive.

When Metztli was finished with her bath, she dressed quickly, refusing to create any more embarrassment for her family. She opted for a pale yellow and teal dress she knew fit well and accentuated her figure enough that she felt beautiful when she looked in the mirror.

She made sure to don a pair of sandals as well, recalling how her father had questioned her earlier when he'd seen her barefoot. Her wet hair sat nicely on her shoulders, it would dry quick enough once she was under the summer heat, though she did add a few braids here and there so it at least looked like she'd put some effort into her appearance. It felt silly considering she was in her own home, but she was well aware that first impressions mattered, even if most of the competing heirs would be dead before the end of the week.

By the time she left her room Metztli knew she was running late. She was quite surprised nobody had been sent to find her yet, but perhaps that was a good thing. At least that's what she believed until she turned the corner and walked straight into Acalan, knocking the both of them off of their feet.

"Sorry! I was rushing so I wouldn't be late…Are you alright?" Metztli asked, making every attempt to not make eye contact with her brother as she got back on her feet.

She figured it was likely that he was still upset with her after their argument from earlier.

"I'm fine…and there's no need to rush," Acalan responded quite plainly, which confused Metztli to her core. "The House of Flor's banner was only just now spotted so we have some time before we need to be present."

"Where were you going then, if not to fetch me?" Metztli questioned, curious as to his intentions now that she realized they weren't on the brink of entering another screaming match.

"Well, I was looking for you of course…I thought we should clear the air."

Metztli simply nodded in response as she gathered the apology she'd prepared for him.

"Right…well I apologize for push-"

"No! No…Sorry, what I meant by clearing the air is that…that I came to find you to apologize, not the other way around," Acalan clarified tenderly, offering an empathetic smile.

"You have nothing to apologize for Acalan…I pushed too far earlier. It's my fault. If I hadn't done so…you wouldn't have said what you did." Metztli played with her house ring on her finger. "I know how difficult all of this is for you and I just…I just want to make sure the both of us make it out of there alive. If anyone has to apologize for their actions, it's me."

It wasn't often that she was put in a position where she needed to apologize. Her pride did ache but she knew this is what she needed to do.

"While I do appreciate hearing that, it's not true, Metztli." Acalan paused, taking a deep breath. "You know that…even if you did push too far I had no right to say what I did."

Metztli waited for her brother to regain his composure. A part of her wanted to interrupt him and tell him he was wrong but she couldn't bring herself to speak or stop him from going on.

"I don't know what overcame me," he continued. "I've never been cruel with you and I knew what that comparison would do to you, so I must apologize for allowing my emotions to get the best of me."

This time he was the one avoiding eye contact by fidgeting with the ring on his finger.

"The comparison was a bit…harsh, I suppose." She offered half a smile. It was the best she could do for now.

"Yes it was and I truly feel terrible about it…I can't guarantee that I'll be able to kill when the time comes but I will try…What kind of brother would I be if I allowed my little sister to do all the work?"

From where Metztli stood in front of her brother she could see small tears form in the corners of his eyes. He truly meant what he was saying. Out of all the outcomes possible, Metztli hadn't planned for this one.

As she wrapped her arms around him, she couldn't remember the last time they'd hugged each other, but she could remember numerous occasions when her brother had comforted her in a time of need and now it was time for her to do the same with him.

"I don't care what kind of brother you are as long as you let me keep you alive," Metztli confessed.

They could deal with the aftermath of this tournament when and if they returned home, but there was no point in doing so now.

They'd both return changed, of that she was sure.

Acalan wrapped his arms around her shoulders, resting his head on her own. They didn't resemble heirs in this moment, more so the children they used to be before they were handed the responsibility of upholding the legacy their father had made for his people.

"We'll be fine, Acalan," she said as she pulled away. "Let's not dwell on this for longer than we already have…C'mon, let's go before mother and father send someone after us."

With that, Metztli and Acalan made their way to their parents. It was time to greet the House of Flor.

ACALAN

Though there was a mixture of grief and regret that remained in the pit of Acalan's stomach, he could not deny that he did feel better after apologizing to his sister. Metztli had been far more understanding than Acalan had expected her to be, but he knew he had made a mistake in speaking to her in the way that he had, even if Atzi had played it off as a simple dispute between siblings and nothing else. Acalan was determined to make it right though, even if Metztli claimed everything was okay between them.

"There they are! No need to panic, Xara," Tenoch said at the first sight of his children.

Acalan smiled towards his father, Metztli had been right, if they had waited a moment longer to make way to their parents, their mother would have sent for them, and surely a small scolding would have ensued, but they'd crossed the palace and made it to the entry gates just on time.

Another crisis defused.

"And they look presentable! I believe it is our lucky day, my love," his mother said as she looped her arm through her husband's and smiled brightly at her children.

Acalan had always admired how in love his parents seemed to be despite the amount of time they'd been together. He dreamed of being able to experience that sort of love as well, but it was difficult to pursue when he was unsure if he'd be alive to see the next week pass by.

"I even wore sandals! See!" Metztli teased her father, pointing towards the shoes on her feet. This caused Acalan to raise a brow in confusion, but he ultimately laughed at the sight too.

"I do see." Their father laughed. "Very lady like of you Metztli, a true princess through and through"

"Now, if we can only get her to keep them on!" their mother then said, joining in the banter.

"Unlikely… but I will try my best. Acalan keeps his shoes on at all times. That should be more than enough"

"Yes, well some of us are a bit more refined than others," Acalan teased, causing his sister to throw a playful jab towards them, which he skillfully dodged.

"Did I not just praise the both of you for looking presentable? Don't make me take it back," their mother scolded in a familiar tone that made warmth spread across Acalan's body.

Just then a messenger arrived, letting them know that it would only be a few minutes before the House of Flor made their introductions.

Acalan could see them more clearly now that he stood on the steps leading up to the entrance of their home. There were a few carriages that he assumed held the Empress and Emperor, as well as the heirs of the House of Flor, and those carriages were followed by far more people than Acalan had expected, some on horse and on foot while others were in makeshift carriages on their own.

The thought that they'd all traveled to Tu'nethe for the Tournament of Heirs left a bitter taste in his mouth, but it was their duty, just as it was his. Acalan knew it was wrong, but it almost felt like their presence alone was tainting the loving home and palace that he and Metztli had grown up in.

"Acalan, I know we disagree on this but please, just greet the heirs and move along," Metztli whispered as they got into position, forming a line depending on their rank in the family. "These people aren't our friends…they're here solely for the entertainment of it all and nothing else"

"If we survive this tournament I have every intention of making you my second in command. Who else will keep me in check as well as you do?"

Metztli responded with a burst of laughter that warmed Acalan's heart.

"When we win this tournament, I will be honored to do so…I won't work for free though, you should know that before you make any decisions."

Acalan was somewhat surprised by the confidence in Metztli's tone, but if his sister believed they could get through this tournament, then he had to believe that they could as well.

Time seemed to pass by slowly as they waited for the Flores family to leave their carriages and make their way to the steps of Tu'nethe. The House of Flor was known for a number of things, but the most renowned was their beauty. Acalan could see those claims were true now that he watched them from afar.

From the looks of it they were a plentiful family as well, they had what seemed like two carriages full of heirs, all women, aside from one boy who appeared to be too young to compete in the tournament. It was going to be impossible to determine who would fight for their house until it was announced the next day during the celebration of tributes.

This should have made Acalan nervous, but when he turned to look at his sister, he noted how she looked anything but frightened. If they didn't scare her, then Acalan had no reason to be afraid either.

It was, however, very particular how all the women in the Flores family resembled one another. Perhaps this was normal for a family as large as theirs, but it still brought goosebumps to Acalan's skin as he watched them walking towards and up the steps.

The prince also felt slightly underdressed in their presence, but how could he or Metztli have been expected to know that this family would arrive in the finest of lavender fabrics and gold embellishments. It was almost as if they had prepared to greet the gods themselves.

"They look tacky," Metztli whispered softly enough that Acalan had to lean in to fully hear her words.

While his sister's comment had not been kind, it did bring a smile to Acalan's face. She always knew how to make him feel better in moments like this.

"Tenoch! I see why you never leave your home now," the emperor from the House of Flor bellowed. "Tu'nethe is beautiful…humble but beautiful nonetheless."

"Why leave when I have everything I could ever want here, Ohtli?" Tenoch responded, seemingly unscathed. "But thank you, I do appreciate that you find my city to be humble and beautiful nonetheless."

Acalan had always admired this in his father. Tenoch was always poise regardless of the situation. Acalan only hoped he'd be a ruler much like him. That is, if he lived long enough to sit the throne.

"And these must be your children? There are so many of them!" Xara exclaimed in a curt tone. Acalan smiled at that, it was so rare when his mother showed anything but genuine kindness, but it was obvious that she understood these people weren't their friends. That realization made Acalan fill with shame. Why hadn't he realized this on his own?

"What can I say? My womb is blessed by our goddess Xochitl," said Ahuic, the empress of the House of Flor.

That didn't sit right with Acalan.

The House of Life did have a shortage of heirs, that was true, but it wasn't because his mother hadn't been blessed.

On the other hand, the House of Flor had an abundance of them, all pristine, standing straight with their hands behind their backs and their lips tightly closed in straight smiles. They resembled soldiers more than people and that was not a compliment in any regard.

"My mother was blessed as well," Metztli spoke before Acalan could even think about defending their mother. "Enough that she felt she could stop after birthing two heirs...It's a shame you didn't believe your first two children were perfect enough to stop as well."

He was grateful for Metztli's wit now. It was a good thing that she didn't care what any of these people thought of her. Acalan wished he could be that brave, too.

The woman lunged forward then, as if she were about to scold the Princess for her words. However, before she could, her husband grasped her wrist, keeping her in place.

"The gods have blessed us all in our own way," Tenoch said, attempting to calm the situation. Acalan was surprised to find that neither of his parents scolded Metztli, nor did they send her warning glances.

"Ever the wise Tenoch," said Ohtli, cutting through the tension between both families. "Now, let me introduce my plentiful children. Our first born, Xochitl, named after our goddess of course, Atlatonan, our second born daughter and then there's our son Xochipilli, also named in honor of our patron goddess…" Ohtli continued, naming each of his children until they reached all seven of them.

Acalan kept count, but it was unlikely that he would be able to repeat the names in the correct order and it didn't help that they all looked nearly identical to one another. All seven of them bore warm brown skin and long black hair that spiraled into nearly perfect curls. This family was beautiful to the eye, but the prince had a feeling they were not so beautiful within.

He also found it curious that none of their children spoke. Metztli had spoken so freely just now and though their children offered curt close lipped smiles and slight nods that were supposed to indicate their respect for their hosts, they said nothing. Perhaps they had been instructed to keep quiet as well.

"A plentiful family indeed…It is of course an honor to host your family and people, Ohtli," Tenoch said before presenting his children.

It was almost laughable how short the introductions were on their father's end.

"It is an honor to meet you both…they look strong, don't they, darling?" Ohtli turned to ask his wife after appraising Acalan and Metztli.

Acalan held his breath while the woman took a second a size the both of them up.

She showed no emotions as she analyzed Acalan, but a vicious smirk settled on her lips when she turned to look at Metztli. In that moment, Metztli demonstrated more self control than Acalan had ever seen from her. He was proud of her. It was obvious she was well suited to play this game.

"Strong and beautiful," the empress from the House of Flor responded coldly. Whether the woman actually believed what she'd just said, Acalan wasn't sure, but she should believe it because if anyone was going to win this tournament, it was Metztli. Sometimes it felt like that was his sister's only purpose in life, which both saddened Acalan and gave him hope, all at once.

Acalan was relieved when the Flor family were finally escorted by guards into the palace to be shown to their quarters. The prince counted nine handmaidens following closely behind, one for every member of the family. His family only had a few handmaidens, and they were more like family than employees.

By all accounts the rumors had been true, the House of Flor lived lavishly, regardless of where they were staying.

Acalan took a deep breath once they were gone. He'd known it was going to be difficult, but he hadn't imagined it would be this bad. The prince had thought the animosity would start later, maybe even after the tournament was all said and done, but he'd been wrong. These families weren't here to make friends. They were here to settle debts they believed they were owed by the House of Life.

"Well that was lovely! We only have to do that what…four more times?" Metztli asked sarcastically.

Acalan turned to her, assuming he would find his sister in a similar distress that he was in, but she was not. If anything she looked excited to do this all over again.

"Settle down, Metztli," their father warned. Metztli scoffed but found her place in line again.

Soon, House of Wind arrived. They were a smaller family in comparison to the House of Flor, but five heirs was still more than the House of Life could say they had. None of them seemed physically imposing, but Acalan knew physical strength wasn't where they shone. The House of Wind was known for their intelligence. Unfortunately for them, they would need a lot more than just that to win the Tournament of Heirs.

The House of Rain followed closely behind. They were a curious family that consisted of six male heirs and a slew of others that were self-proclaimed bastards. The notion of that had made Acalan gasp slightly without meaning to. It wasn't that bastards were unheard of within the houses, it was just the idea that perhaps the emperor had so many in order to save his true-born heirs that made Acalan's skin curl.

Bastards were dangerous, they had far more to prove then true-born children.

The prince was glad that at least his father hadn't committed such a betrayal against their mother, even when she could only provide two heirs.

The sun had begun setting by the time the House of Serpent arrived. By now, Acalan had grown bored and tired of introductions, and it didn't help that they were exactly like all the others. They all had far too many heirs to keep count of, and they all looked at he and Metztli as if they were something to sink their teeth into.

That was not a comforting feeling.

Not long after, Acalan's eyebrow raised curiously when he noted there was only one carriage with the House of Blood banner flying high in the sky. The banner bore the etching of a warrior wearing a head-dress adorned with feathers. The other houses had similar banners as well but none of them were in the color of blood.

"You said the House of Blood was the most vicious…right father?" Acalan asked, turning to give his father a curious look.

"Yes. Be most careful with them. Their goddess, Eztli, requires things of them that no other god does," Tenoch explained. "They're not nearly as fortunate as we are either, and they've won in the past. They're vicious even if they don't seem like it so the both of you should watch what you say and do in their presence."

There was a slight hint of what seemed like fear in Acalan's father.

"They're a small family like us. That's strange," Metztli said, causing Acalan to turn his gaze back onto them.

Acalan's breath caught slightly in his chest. Metztli was right, there was the older man who must have been the emperor, two young men who Acalan assumed were heirs, and a young woman. Her skin was golden, hair neatly pulled back in the most alluring braid he'd ever seen. She was stunning, an absolute masterpiece, and none of the words that came to mind could truly describe how Acalan felt.

She moved so swiftly and with such ease that Acalan's gaze remained fixed on her and her alone.

"Snap out of it," Metztli whispered harshly as she lightly kicked her brother's leg. He didn't realize he'd been in a trance until then, but he had been. "You're drooling like a dog, it's embarrassing, you've seen beautiful women before, act like it."

Acalan quickly tried to shake his thoughts away.

Metztli was right, there were far more important things to do than lust over a princess he knew he could not have.

Metztli

If this moment wasn't as important as it was, Metztli would have found herself laughing at her brother for having such a strong reaction to a woman. Admittedly she'd never seen him react this way before, at least not since they were children. It was comical in every way that it could be, but Metztli had to keep her emotions in check.

The woman was beautiful, Metztli could not deny that as she watched the family approach. The men were also intriguing, but unlike her brother, Metztli was able to keep her thoughts from being read on her face.

At the end of the day, it was still likely that the heirs from the House of Blood would be the strongest of their competitors. Not only because they had resources that Metztli and Acalan did not, but because they had a life debt with the emperor of the House of Life, one that could only be settled in blood.

"Yaotl…I do hope your travels were pleasant," Metztli's father said when the emperor and his children neared.

She noted how her father spoke to the man like they were old friends, though from everything that Metztli knew, they were anything but.

"We're exhausted and hungry. Hopefully the feast that awaits will be everything that was promised," Yaotl replied.

Metztli had to stop herself from scoffing at the remark. Of course there was a feast inside, her father was nothing if not a gracious host, but the emperor of the House of Blood could have returned her father's courtesy instead of responding with demands.

"That's unfortunate…but yes, there will be a feast this evening, you're welcome to take it in the comfort of your quarters or in the dining hall. Whatever you see is best for your family," Tenoch responded, still displaying kindness in his words.

"Take our feast in privacy? I think not. How else would I be able to display my heirs?" Yaotl quipped in return.

"Absolutely, it was just a suggestion Yaotl, I meant no disrespect of course…perhaps you may do us the honor of introducing us to your heirs before you display them for the other houses. These are my children, Acalan and Metztli, and I'm sure you remember my wife, Xara."

"Hmm, right well my heirs can speak for themselves. Isn't that right Necalli?" The emperor beckoned for his son to speak.

"Of course father," said the young man by his side, stepping forward with an obvious confidence that infuriated Metztli. "Necalli Cruz, first born son to the House of Blood and my father's soon to be champion."

Who did he think he was besides being a guest in her home and in her city?

What Necalli did next surprised Metztli even more. The young man reached out and grasped her father's forearm to shake it. Such a ceremonial way to greet someone when they'd shown no manners until now. Necalli didn't stop there though, he reached for her mother's hand and gently placed a kiss upon the back of it. The gesture made Metztli recoil, but she was well aware of his intentions.

The prince of blood wanted a reaction from them. For him, the tournament had started the moment they stepped onto the grounds of their palace.

Unfortunately though, for Metztli the tournament had started the day she learned how to hold a blade in her small hands.

Necalli turned to Acalan next, shaking his forearm as well before turning to Metztli. She reached out her hand quicker than him though, grasping his forearm tightly. The last thing she would allow was for him to treat her like she was just another maiden who would swoon at the feeling of his lips on her skin.

"It's a pleasure to meet you, Necalli Cruz," Metztli said, mimicking the same arrogance Necalli showed in his own words.

She expected for the man's gaze to fill with fear, but instead it filled with something else she couldn't recognize. A smile crossed his lips.

Necalli Cruz was amused.

"Your daughter reminds me of Chimalli," Yaotl interjected. From the tone of his voice Metztli could tell he was amused too. "She'll make for an interesting tournament, just as your brother did, Tenoch."

This wasn't the first time in Metztli's life that she'd been compared to her uncle. She didn't mind the comparison. Her uncle had been a warrior, he'd died in the Tournament of Heirs but the memory of his name, playful mischief, and kind heart was still well known in Tu'nethe.

If anything Metztli welcomed the comparison, she just hoped that her fate would be different from his.

"It's funny you say that, Yaotl," her father said. "She reminds me of my brother as well, Metztli is better though, and an interesting competitor indeed, as is my son Acalan."

He turned to look at her. In his gaze, there was a certain admiration that filled Metztli with confidence.

There were a few moments of awkward silence then. That was not something that had occurred with the other houses. Metztli eyed all of the Cruz family before landing on the woman from before. She wore a sweet smile and fiddled with the rings on her hands. It looked like she was anxious to speak.

Metztli was unsure of what overcame her then, but she found herself smiling at the princess and that simple act seemed to brighten her eyes and boost her confidence enough that she spoke next.

"Citlalic Cruz, second born heir to the House of Blood," the princess explained brightly as she took a slight step forward. "Your home is beautiful, I quite like all the gold accents, I wish we had more of that back home…and you both are so beautiful! I was a bit stunned upon arriving. Thank you for hosting my family."

Metztli's eyebrow instantly furrowed in confusion. This woman was nothing like Metztli had expected her to be, nor did she believe her demeanor was an act.

Then again the most beautiful of flowers bloomed in the most treacherous of environments. Citlalic seemed to be proof of that.

"Thank you Citlalic, that is very kind of you. You are a very beautiful young woman as well…and no need to thank us for hosting you all, it's our pleasure." Xara offered the young woman a sweet smile before she turned to look at Metztli, urging her to respond as well.

"As my mother said, you are very beautiful. We all think so," Metztli responded with a tight smile as she nudged her brother in the ribs.

The opportunity to tease her brother had been too tempting not to take, though she was sure she would pay for it later.

Citlalic simply smiled and bowed slightly at the compliment. The noticeable blush on her cheeks was sweet and made Metztli question how she'd remained so innocent when being surrounded by these men.

"And you must be Coatl?" Her father asked as he turned to the last man. The tinge of hesitancy in her father's voice was obvious and Metztli knew exactly why that was.

"Yes I am, your Majesty…I've been told I'm the spitting image of my father, that must be why you recognized me," Coatl said before reaching out to shake hands with everyone.

It was much less formal but Metztli could tell the gesture had been genuine.

"There was only one man in the entirety of Mexica with the birthmark you bare," Tenoch explained as he pointed towards the mark on Coatl's arm.

Metztli had noticed it as well but hadn't given it much thought. Then again, she didn't have the history with Coatl's father that Tenoch did.

"Your father was a great man, amongst the best that I've ever known," her father said, keeping his sentiments short even though they were sincere.

During the entirety of her father's tournament he'd only taken one life. It had happened at the very end of the tournament and after his own brother had died. That man had been Coatl's father.

Metztli only knew this from the stories that her father had told her of his time within the Pyramid of Tributes. They'd all been friends back then, separated by the need to keep their lives. That was just another reason to hate the tournament even more.

Knowing this, Metztli understood her father's hesitancy, she couldn't judge him for the shame he felt, if anything she imagined she would feel shame too if she returned home.

"I'm told quite the same, I hope to honor him by competing alongside my cousin in the Tournament of Heirs," Coatl explained.

There was no animosity in his tone, he was simply stating his intentions. Metztli could have guessed on her own that he would be the second heir competing. After all, Coatl resembled a warrior. He was tall, broad and bore more muscles than she knew was possible for a man. He didn't seem vicious by any means, but he was on a mission to honor his fallen father and that was perhaps more dangerous.

"Your father would have been proud," her father said, bowing his head in respect. "I knew him personally, you and your mother were the light of his life. I wish you and Necalli luck, just as I do for my own heirs."

They were all silent for a moment before Yoatl complained once again about being tired and hungry. Metztli found herself in the same state. She was absolutely spent and wanted nothing more than to stuff herself with Tlaxcallis and whatever else the kitchen staff had prepared. Most of all, she wanted to be alone for a little while.

Luckily there was a guard and handmaiden nearby, ready to take the small family to their quarters where they could rest and eat if they pleased.

Metztli and her brother were alone once again, their parents disappearing after the Cruz family to attend to their hosting duties.

"They don't seem that viscous," said Acalan once the Cruz family was out of sight.

Her brother's declaration made Metztli laugh. Acalan was far too naive if he actually believed that. She didn't need to see Necalli train to know he could fight. And Coatl had purpose, which only made him more dangerous beyond his massive stature and build.

Metztli hadn't been fearful of any of the other families or heirs, but the House of Blood made her nervous. They clearly knew how to play this game far better than the other houses, and they'd won the tournament before, which could only make them more eager to reclaim the victory they'd once known.

"You mean Citlalic doesn't seem vicious, but her brother and cousin certainly are. They're here to win Acalan, don't forget that… Especially Coatl, did you miss the entire speech about his father?" Metztli was genuinely curious if her brother had been listening at all, or if he'd spent the entire conversation admiring the young princess.

She couldn't blame him if he did, the woman was truly a sight if she'd ever seen one.

"Of course I did…It's a shame his father died in the last tournament. I didn't realize there were living heirs of those who passed back then."

Metztli hadn't realized this either, not until now anyway. It was difficult to fathom that there had once been an heir irresponsible enough to bring a child into this world before winning the tournament. That was completely unheard of. Now, everyone waited for their lives to start after the tournament and never before.

"Certainly a shame," she murmured. "But it was his father or ours. I'm just glad our father won that fight." As unfair as it was, that was just the truth.

Acalan pulled away for a moment. There was a look in his eyes that was a mixture of judgment and genuine surprise. Metztli had seen this look on her brother before but not since they'd been children and he'd learned that the world didn't always spin according to his books.

Had he truly not listened to all the stories their father had told them throughout their lives?

"You don't mean that…no certainly father didn't kill his own friend?" Acalan asked half frantically.

Metztli found it just a little bit entertaining to watch Acalan try and keep his composure at the realization.

"Well of course he did, he had to. It's a tournament to the death Acalan, friendships don't exist within the walls of the Pyramid of Tributes. I keep trying to tell you this."

She tried to make her words sound comforting. After all, she understood how difficult these matters were for her brother.

This reminded her of how much she hated this tournament to begin with. It was just entirely unfair that such kind souls like Acalan had to suffer with these truths. She could handle them, but her brother struggled with them far more than he should. It both saddened and frustrated her. He needed to understand their reality before the tournament started, that much she was completely certain about.

"It's likely some of the heirs know each other, but I think father kept us away from everyone for that reason," Metztli said, taking her brother's hand in her own. "It just makes the tournament more conflicting if friendship is entangled with everything else…we'll be fine, Acalan. Every decision in our life has been made to prepare us for this. Father won, he knows what's best, you just have to start believing that too."

"I do know Metztli, I do…it's just difficult to imagine that father competed in this tournament when he was our age. He's so… gentle now, you know?"

Metztli quite agreed. It was difficult for her to imagine her father as a warrior, too. He was strong and had the build of a warrior of course, but he was gentle as Acalan had said.

It almost felt like he'd put that viscous side of himself away the moment he'd won. She couldn't blame him for doing so. She was planning on doing quite the same if she won.

"Now that I can agree with…Time just changes people I think, though I wouldn't know. I'd wager I've been the same since what? My tenth name day?" Metztli responded playfully.

She was done with serious conversation for the day, and could hardly imagine she'd have energy for it even after she filled her belly with supper.

"Ahh yes, you're quite right. That was the first year I noticed a mischievous glint in your eyes, and it's been present ever since, won't leave no matter how much I pray for it to go!" Acalan teased, causing Metztli to throw a jab which he masterfully dodged.

Metztli hoped he would be able to do the same when it was a blade and not her fist.

"You and Atzi both, trust me. I hear it everyday from her! She can go on and on about her prayers for me never reaching the gods…I mean truly, has she never stopped to consider that perhaps there's nothing wrong with me? You'd think the gods would have delivered a handwritten manual stating how to fix me otherwise."

She stopped herself before her little rant went on for too long though. Just like Atzi could complain about Metztli all day long, Metztli could do the same when it came to the old priestess.

"She means well though, you know that right?"

Metztli sighed audibly. Not because she was annoyed with her brother's question, but because she knew what he was saying was true. As frustrating as Atzi was, she did want the best for the both of them. They only disliked each other because of how different they were, but that didn't mean that Atzi was trying to hurt her.

Metztli knew that to be true.

"I know Acalan, I do. Sometimes I wish she didn't mean well so my disinterest for her could be more appropriate," she said. "She'll have no choice but to praise me when we return home victorious, and that will certainly be something to look forward to."

After such a long day, all she wanted to do was sleep. But even rested, she wasn't sure how she would face the celebration of Tributes.

Metztli pulled on her brother's arm, dragging him up the steps and down the hallways of their home. It had been a long day for both of them and what they needed now was full bellies and rest.

Both siblings made their way to the dining hall, which was far more empty and quiet than Metztli had expected it to be. It seemed that most of the houses had chosen to take their dinner in the privacy of their quarters. Smart move, Metztli couldn't deny that. It felt strange though, their home had seemed more lively when they weren't in the company of strangers.

They both joined their mother and father and ate with them. It hadn't been the most ideal of days, and Acalan's words from earlier still stung quite a bit when she recalled them, but they were enjoying dinner as a family, and that was more than enough to get Metztli through the rest of the night.

They were going to be alright, she was so sure of it that it frightened her. But only time could truly prove her to be right and the clock was starting to count down, whether she liked it or not.

ACALAN

Dinner with his family went as well as it could considering how close the beginning of the tournament was. The prince couldn't deny that he felt better now that he had a solid meal in his stomach and had been left to rest alone in the privacy of his room.

The argument he'd had with his sister earlier still irked him though. He couldn't recall a single time he'd been that cruel with anyone, let alone his sister. He was relieved that at least his apology had gone over well.

The prince only hoped that in the coming days his sister wouldn't hold his words against him, not that she ever had in the past. But their arguments had never been as extreme as this one.

The Tournament of Heirs was beginning to feel far more real than it ever had before. It was frightening, allowing these prying eyes and families into his childhood home, but he found some solace in knowing all this was just temporary. In just a matter of days the tournament would begin. He would enter the Pyramid of Tributes with his sister, and whether they survived or not, the palace he called home would go back to being as he remembered.

Tranquil and comfortable – that's how it had always been.

Acalan tried not to think too much about the coming days. There was nothing he or anyone else could do to stop destiny.

This thought was both comforting and painful.

The young prince debated whether he should climb into bed early and rest as much as he could before the next day arrived. It was probably the smart thing to do considering the events planned for them. Instead however, he found himself sitting by his desk, eyeing the book of tournament histories that Atzi had handed him earlier in the day.

Had it been any other day Acalan wouldn't have thought twice before picking up the damn thing and reading through it, but there was something about this book that made him want to crawl into his own skin.

It was a conflicting feeling, he'd read the history of the tournament before. He knew what would be written within the pages of the book, but the priestess had been clear when she'd sent him away with her personal copy, even though she knew very well he had a copy of his own back in his quarters. That had to mean something and Acalan was afraid to find out exactly what it was.

Acalan spent what felt like hours looking at the worn leather cover, fiddling with his hands until he'd mustered enough courage to open it. That was after all, the only way he'd find the answers he sought.

Dust filled the air as he opened the book to the first page. Enough of it had caught in his throat that he found himself coughing and gasping for air.

The prince gathered his composure before he really started reading. He was happy to find that much of the first pages were the same. They recounted what life had been like for mortals before the war between men and gods. Acalan knew these histories like he knew the back of his own hand.

Their people had been rather uncivilized back then. Violence, famine, and poverty used to run rampant in all parts of Mexica, but the gods loved their children and hated seeing them suffer. They'd tried to help by setting standards to live by, but the mortals were defiant, and so the war between mortals and gods started.

Acalan read through every single word despite knowing that he knew these histories better than anyone. While Metztli had spent an extensive amount of time training outside of their expected hours, he'd spent those same hours here in the comfort of his room, nose deep in the histories of his people.

For as long as Acalan could remember, he knew he was the heir to his father's empire, and he understood the responsibilities that came with that title. He'd always been determined to be a fair ruler like his father, so he learned as much as he could, hoping that someday he would be.

After so many pages Acalan was truly beginning to question why Atzi had wanted him to read her version of the histories. She'd said this would perhaps inspire him, help him remember why it was so important for him to fight in the Tournament of Heirs alongside his sister, but instead he was left confused.

Everything written in this book were things he already knew.

Until they weren't.

His eyebrow raised slightly in confusion as he frantically got up from his seat, heading straight for the wooden bookcase that framed the back wall of his room. He didn't have to think twice about where his copy of the histories would be. He had organized the books himself, never allowing the handmaidens to help in doing so.

The moment he found his own copy, wrapped in brown leather and in far better condition than the one that sat on his desk, he turned to the section of it that correlated with Atzi's. His eyes searched quickly for the specific sentence.

"And so, in the aftermath of the great war between mortals and immortals, Eztli, the goddess of blood and sacrifice suggested the Tournament of Heirs as a form of punishment for the wrongdoings of men against their gods."

Once he'd confirmed what was written in his copy, Acalan returned to his desk. He was trying to convince himself that he'd simply read the sentences wrong. His eyes were tired from the long day that had just passed. That had to be it, there was no other conclusion he could come to on his own.

Acalan quickly cleared enough space on his desk so that he could place both histories side by side. He knew he would hate himself later for making such a mess of his usually neat space, but that didn't matter right now, not while he searched for clarity in Atzi's version of the histories.

His eyes roamed the pages again until he found the paragraph he was searching for. But once he located it, he did not find clarity, but rather more confusion.

"And so, in the aftermath of the great war between mortals and

immortals, Nemiliztli, the god of life suggested the Tournament of Heirs as a form of punishment for the wrongdoings of men against their gods, and so that the prophecy may never truly come to complete fruition."

Acalan's throat ran dry as he read the passage over and over again. This was now the second mention of a prophecy he knew nothing about. Even worse, this time the mention of it came from a much more reliable source than his dreams. Atzi was perhaps the most honest person he'd ever known. She was holy and wise and… and she would never lie to Acalan.

Acalan sat back down in his chair, hands raking through his hair as he set his head between his knees. For a moment, it felt like the walls of his room were beginning to close in, suffocating him to the point where he couldn't breathe.

A million possible explanations ran through his mind. There had to be a mistake in the writing. It didn't make sense for Nemiliztli, the god of all living things, to want to end so many precious lives.

Aside from that, Acalan was still battling with the thought of a prophecy. He'd never heard of such a thing, and Atzi herself had told him she'd never heard of one either, at least not one that spoke of him or his sister… and yet, it was clearly written in the very history she'd handed him. He'd read the sentence over and over, just to make sure that his eyes weren't fooling him.

The prince was unsure what came over him then, but in his despair and confusion he lifted his head and started reading again. He needed answers and he needed them now.

Acalan read for as long as his body allowed him to, he took note of all of the discrepancies in each of the histories in a neat list with a pencil and parchment:

1. Eztli did not suggest the Tournament of Heirs, Nemiliztli did.
2. A prophecy had been the catalyst for war.
3. The Tournament of Heirs was not retribution but a punishment.
4. Mortals had not been uncivilized before the war against gods.
5. Anyone found with magical gifts had been massacred in the days after resolution.

The prince couldn't help but wonder how it was possible that he'd gone his entire life without hearing the mention of a prophecy or any other of these discrepancies. If they'd been important then they would have been mentioned somewhere else. He would have known about them. They would have been prepared for the prophecy, but they weren't, not in the slightest.

At some point in the evening, Acalan's mind and body finally gave in to his need for rest. The poor prince didn't even make it to his bed. Instead, he simply fell asleep with his head laid upon the histories, drool spilling from his mouth onto the delicate pages…

It was late into the morning when a soft knock on the door rang through Acalan's room. Not that he was aware of it, the prince was still deep in his uncomfortable slumber. It wasn't until the knocking grew louder that he began to regain consciousness, not nearly quick enough to avoid his sister barging in on him though.

"ACALAN!!! I've been knocking for–" Metztli stopped, taking in the sight before her.

In the midst of the chaos of books and loose papers, the half-conscious prince managed to close the books in front of him. The last thing he needed was for his sister to be in on this confusion as well. Luckily she didn't seem too concerned, this was far from the first time she'd walked in on him asleep at his desk.

"Do you know what time it is?! All the other heirs are training AS WE SPEAK Acalan! You've missed breakfast to what? Read your little books?!" Acalan pondered for a moment if she was going to slap him upside the head like their mother had done when they were children.

Truly he had no idea what time it was, nor did he care about the fact that the other heirs were already on the training grounds. That was all for show, to intimidate each other and nothing else. He had much more important things to worry about now, and his sister wouldn't be able to convince him otherwise.

"Sorry," Acalan responded plainly. He knew it would have been far wiser to respond differently but he couldn't find the words, not with the memories of what he had read the prior night still fresh in his mind.

The prince pondered for a moment if he should perhaps share his findings with his sister. It would at least help him clear his mind but if he did. He knew Metztli was likely to throw this newfound knowledge in his face. No one hated the God of Life more than his sister, and she'd always had a particular love for being right.

"Sorry? That's all you have to say?!" Metztli snapped, taking a step closer.

Acalan couldn't blame her for reacting this way, but if she knew about the prophecy, then she would be acting much the same. He was sure of it.

"Yes sorry, I'll make it up to you later I promise," Acalan stammered as he rose from his chair, collecting his things into a neat pile before he took a look in the mirror.

Gods, he looked like a mess. His hair was unkempt and he now had dark circles underneath his eyes. On top of all this, he was completely unsure how long he'd actually slept for. This day was already turning out to be terrible and it was only the start.

"Give me an hour to run an errand with Atzi and I'll come train with the other heirs, I promise, I just need an hour" he pleaded.

He knew he was asking for a lot, especially on a day where they didn't have time for distractions, but he needed to speak to the priestess before it was too late.

Metztli glowered in anger as she pretended to strangle the air in front of her.

"You're lucky I have enough intelligence not to strangle you right here in your very room!" she fumed. "An hour, that's all I'm giving you, after that I'm sending mother after you and we both know she's worse to deal with than me. Understood?"

She was right, his mother was much worse to deal with when it came to punctuality, but he'd make it back on time, hopefully with the answers he'd been searching for all night long.

Acalan nodded as he gathered his things in his arms, not even taking a second to properly respond before he made his way to Atzi's sanctuary.

He left his sister confused, but Acalan would explain later when he understood what was happening. Until then he didn't care about anything but speaking to the old priestess. She owed him some answers and he was determined not to leave her sanctuary until that debt was paid in full.

"Atzi!" Acalan exclaimed as he barged into the sanctuary, disturbing the peace that resided there.

He'd never done that before but then again he'd never been in this situation either. He was relieved to find the woman sitting at her own desk, though he noted there was nothing on it. She simply sat there, hands intertwined and resting on her desk as if she had been waiting for him to arrive with his questions.

That was it, he was finished playing these childish games. He needed answers and he needed them now.

"Why have you given me a book of lies? If this is some test of my loyalty to the gods then I have no choice but to inform you of how cruel that is. You have no right to do this when I've shown nothing but an abundance of loyalty and respect for Nemiliztli and the rest of the gods!" Acalan shouted as he laid out everything before her.

His arms flew through the air as he spoke, expressing every emotion that had built up within him. This felt like a betrayal that he could have never expected, and he was even more frustrated to find that Atzi seemed unaffected by all of it.

"Sit," Atzi commanded in a gentle tone. "We have much to discuss,"

Despite his anger, Acalan did as he was told. He would do anything at this point to get the answers he believed he deserved.

Even if that meant obeying the commands of a woman he wasn't sure if he could trust anymore.

METZTLI

etztli wanted to throw a fit.

It was her right to do so after how irresponsible her brother had been that morning. She'd asked so little of him. All he had to do was wake up on time, eat, and train for a few hours before they were pulled away for their duties as heirs. But instead he'd stayed up for what Metztli assumed was far too late into the night, reading.

If he was going to lose sleep so close to the tournament, it would have been better to do so for something worthwhile.

Regardless of what she thought, there was nothing she could do. If she scolded him the way she wanted to, she'd be embarrassing her family, and she couldn't do that to them, not when the celebration of tributes would take place that evening. They had roles to fill, parts to play, and Metztli was determined to represent her house well.

Aside from dignity and honor, Metztli simply did not have the energy to deal with her brother this early in the morning. She'd settled into bed the night before in hopes of gaining a few extra hours of slumber. Instead, she'd found herself tossing and turning. For the first time in her life she didn't feel safe in her home. It was impossible to feel safe knowing the other ten heirs who would be competing against Acalan and herself, were under the same roof.

There were rules of course. It was forbidden to physically harm a fellow heir before the trumpets sang their death song announcing the beginning of the tournament. Any act of that sort was treason and could be punished as such.

From what she'd gathered about the other heirs she'd met, she didn't think any of them stupid enough to attack her in her quarters, but not all attacks were physical. Metztli knew this very well.

In fact, Metztli recalled a story she'd once been told by her father about his Tournament of Heirs. He and his brother had purposely flirted and danced with women from the other houses in order to sew jealousy amongst the men competing. It was smart, doing so made for a very entertaining tournament, they all knew that.

There had been a few times throughout the night where Metztli swore she could hear footsteps outside her door. She'd been so certain that she'd gotten out of bed at one point, blade in hand just in case there was someone trying to mess with her. But she didn't find anyone outside in the hall, nor did she find anyone down the passageway that led to her quarters.

When she settled back into bed though, the footsteps continued, and she didn't manage to sleep at all until she propped a chair against her door. It wasn't the most intelligent precaution, but it gave her enough peace that she was able to sleep for a few hours at least.

Perhaps that's why she was so willing to give Acalan another hour to do whatever he needed to. She couldn't even begin to guess what his errand was, but she was secretly grateful for it. At least now she could relax a little bit before training by going to the garden, sitting in the sun and absorbing its rays until she felt like herself again.

Yes, that was exactly what Metztli needed.

She managed to walk through the palace without bumping into any of their guests, which was a relief to say the least. The palace itself was quiet aside from the soft chatter coming from all the handmaidens and stewards preparing for that evening's festivities. It was nice to at least know the heirs were keeping to themselves, even if that would only be temporary.

The gardens of her home were fairly empty aside from a few groundskeepers who were working diligently to ensure they remained as beautiful as they could be. That was fine. They wouldn't disturb her nor would she disturb them. Metztli respected their work, it was because of them that all sorts of flowers and plants bloomed there, from roses to agave plants. They all grew happily underneath the warmth of the sun.

Metztli planted herself on one of the benches. Underneath the sun she could feel her body practically melt into comfort. Her muscles relaxed and she felt refreshed. It wasn't long before a yawn slipped out of her. She realized then that she was far more tired than she'd first believed.

There was no time to sleep but that didn't mean she couldn't rest. And resting would only do her good, or at least that's what she was trying to convince herself of as she laid down on the bench, closed her eyes and absorbed the warmth around her.

She stayed like that for a little while, unsure of how much time had passed or how long she had before she would have to go find her brother to force him to train. It was rather important that they trained today, as tomorrow was reserved for mourning and remembering past heirs who had lost their lives to the tournament and the morning after that they would be woken up before dawn to march towards the Pyramid of Tributes with the other heirs.

Nobody could tell what would happen once they were delivered into the hands of the gods. Each tournament was different, unique to whatever the gods thought they'd find most entertaining.

If the gods really wanted to be entertained then they should enter the damn Pyramid of Tributes themselves. Given the opportunity to spend at least a couple minutes with any of them, Metztli was confident she could at least cause some damage.

Would she lose her life? Most certainly.

But it would be worth it to strip them of their infinitely large egos for even a moment. She thought it might hurt them to be reminded of their duties. They were meant to help their children, not punish them every twenty-five years by hosting the death of at least ten young heirs.

None of it was fair, but she didn't have the power to change anything, at least not yet.

Metztli must have been deep in thought because she didn't

realize she had a visitor until a shadow fell over her, shielding her from the rays of the sun. Naturally the princess assumed it was her brother messing with her. Perhaps he'd finished his errand and had come to find her to train.

"Move, you're blocking the sun," Metztli sneered before opening her eyes, expecting Acalan. Except, instead of finding her brother, she found it was two young women. She recognized them as the heirs from the House of Flor. Immediately she felt shame for having spoken to them the way she had.

Metztli waited for a moment, expecting for them to respond but they never did, instead they just stared at her through their big brown eyes.

The rumors were true about the House of Flor, these women were stunning, perfectly toned. Their hair curled perfectly down their backs and spirals framed their already beautiful faces. Metztli had thought she was a sight but she was nothing compared to them. Luckily, The Tournament of Heirs was a battle of strength, not beauty.

"I apologize I assumed you two were someone else...Is there something I can help you with?" Metztli asked curtly.

She knew better than to taunt either of them, she'd be competing against at least one of them, and it was better to not enter the tournament with enemies already made.

She waited for a response,but the pair said nothing. There was no better word to describe this other than eerie. They were just staring at her. Now that she really thought of it, she hadn't heard either of them speak since they'd arrived. That realization left her with an odd feeling in her stomach and she was suddenly aware of the fact that they were alone.

Two against one.

"Alright then...I better get going. Enjoy the gardens I guess," Metztli stammered.

The rules were clear but she wasn't going to risk it. She was confident in her fighting abilities but two against one was hardly a fair fight. She tried to rise from where she lay and slide past one of them to escape, but they had her cornered. This was the complete opposite of what she'd come to the gardens for. She had wanted peace but instead she found herself in the midst of something she didn't understand but knew couldn't be good.

Metztli moved again, trying to slide past without causing any trouble, but the younger of the two, Atlatonan, followed her movements and blocked her path.

Fine, if they wanted to do this the hard way then Metztli could do that too.

"Need I remind you both that you're in my home?" Metztli questioned harshly.

Both sisters turned their gazes towards each other. Xochitl, the sister who Metztli recognized to be the oldest between the both of them nodded, almost as if she was giving her younger sister, Atlatonan, permission to do something.

They'd planned this, Metztli was sure of it. The footsteps outside her door the night before – it must have been them.

Metztli stood her ground, shifting her feet slightly into a fighting stance. She had a blade carefully strapped on her thigh, hidden beneath her skirt. It was in reach, but she wouldn't move to grab it until she needed to.

It was then that the younger of the two moved, taking a slight step forward. Her lips shifted into a close-lipped smirk. She was trying to intimidate Metztli, but the princess had seen scarier things than the young woman. She'd prepared for moments like this.

What she hadn't prepared for though, was the sight of Atlatonan shifting her lips once again, this time forming the most horrifying wide smile Metztli had ever seen.

Metztli swallowed harshly when she looked over to Xochitl. The older sister was now smiling, too. Whatever beauty they'd displayed before was gone now. They were nothing but beasts looking down on their prey.

Metztli had heard of the extremes heirs would go to in order to help their odds in the tournament, but seeing it for herself was so utterly different. Nothing could have prepared her for this.

Both sisters had mutilated themselves. Their teeth were shaved into pointy peaks, and despite the fact that they were a pearly shade of white for now, Metztli somehow managed to imagine blood dripping down the peaks. They weren't just here to kill for honor, they were here to kill for sport, and that simple fact was terrifying.

"I told you she'd be scared. They always are," Atlatonan hissed, allowing her smile to widen enough that Metztli realized most, if not all of their teeth had been shaped that way.

She didn't say anything in response, purely because of the shock running through her body.

"Do you think her blood will taste sweet or sour?" Xochitl turned to ask her sister.

They were insane, surely driven to madness by the desire to win a tournament put in place to punish the sins of their ancestors.

"I reckon it will be spicy…but her brother's – mhmmm his will be sweet," Atlatonan beamed.

The girl seemed eager, excited even to taste blood. They could threaten Metztli all they wanted but she drew the line when it came to Acalan. It was her sworn duty to protect him, not only within the walls of the Pyramid of Tributes but in their home as well and she wasn't about to let two foul bitches to make her fail in that.

"And what does your blood taste like?" Metztli asked in return.

She was done playing the role of prey. She needed them to understand she could be a cold-blooded killer just like them.

"I'll let you know when my blade is so deep in your throats, that you're both begging for a merciful death." Metztli spat her threats out like poison. "Let it be known that I won't give either of you that, I'll remember this moment when you're pleading for your lives. Now move, or would you rather the tournament start now? It would be a shame to stain my family home with your putrid blood."

She was the second born heir of the House of Life, daughter of Tenoch and Xara Amos, and she would be damned if she let herself be intimated in her own home.

The younger of the two lunged forward with every intent to harm, but her older sister stopped her. Metztli smiled teasingly. They were revealing much more than they realized. She now knew that if she killed the older sister first the younger would be lost. She'd be so rageful that it would be an easy kill, and so Metztli's lists of potential victims in her mind began, and with it the names of these two landed at the very top.

"Let her go sister," Xochitl commanded, stepping aside to allow Metztli to pass. "Her threats are empty. She's never killed before, I can smell the fear off of her, can't you? There's no use in wasting our time with her…"

At least now she was free. They could think she was weak, she didn't care, Metztli knew that was far from the truth.

"Watch your back, Metztli, and your brother's. I'm going to enjoy killing you both." Xochitl threatened as Metztli started backing away.

"Likewise," Metztli replied.

She disappeared in between the rows of agave plants that were taller than her. The princess was quick but not quick enough that her actions displayed fear. She just needed to get away, and she needed to find her brother before they did. While she could handle intimidation like this, she was unsure that Acalan could, and it wouldn't do either of them good if these heirs got into his head before the tournament even started.

Once she was out of sight, Metztli rushed through the hallways of her home. She earned concerned looks from several handmaidens and a few guests along the way but she paid no thought to it.

Acalan had said he needed to run an errand with Atzi, so she made way for the woman's sanctuary. Metztli hated that part of the palace. She'd been forced to spend far too much time there as a child, and always left with at least one scolding that made her question if she was a reincarnated demon while her brother was praised for being perfect.

Still, regardless of her hesitation, the urgency to find her brother beat back any ill feelings she felt towards the priestess or her sanctuary. She turned to look over her shoulder for a single second while turning the corner, just to make sure she wasn't being followed. That had been a mistake because only a second later she was met with what felt like a hard fleshy wall.

DAMIT! Metztli thought to herself as she went tumbling down onto the ground. This was the second time in the last two days that she'd accidentally stumbled into someone while being distracted.

She felt fine, uninjured, but she couldn't risk getting hurt, certainly not after her encounter with the feral sisters from the House of Flor.

"You alright?" Necalli Cruz asked from above her, reaching out his hand to help her up.

"Great," Metztli mumbled.

Hadn't she suffered enough for one day? She wasn't in the mood to deal with another crazed heir.

"You don't look great," he said in return.

Metztli rolled her eyes at his response. It wasn't that she cared what he thought of her, but it did sting just a little.

"I think I look much better than some of the other heirs," Metztli argued as she pulled herself off the ground and brushed the debris off her hands.

"Let me guess, you've met the sisters from the House of Flor?" Necalli questioned, seemingly unphased by the fact that she'd refused to take his hand and instead picked herself off the damn floor.

Metztli gawked at him. How could he possibly know that? Had he been watching from afar?

"What makes you say that?" she questioned.

She didn't exactly want to entertain this conversation, but she'd already made two enemies before the tournament even started. It would be unwise to add another to her growing list.

"I've known them my whole life. They tend to have this effect on people," Necalli explained. His response was enough to make Metztli anxious, but she kept her composure. She believed her father had done the right thing in keeping them isolated from the other houses, but in the years she'd spent isolated, friendships had formed, perhaps even alliances, and she and Acalan only had each other.

"Great, well your friends are in the garden if you'd like to see them. Sorry for bumping into you. Would love to chat but I'm busy with…with heir duties," Metztli stammered, trying to move past him without turning her back to him.

Necalli kept his gaze steady on her own. He was so fluid with his movements that it was both equally concerning and impressive.

"I think you're forgetting something," he said before pulling her blade from behind his back.

Instinctively she patted her thigh. She hadn't felt it fall or heard it tumble from her body. She was truly starting to fall apart when she couldn't afford it.

"Thanks, I owe you one," she responded, reaching out for her blade. She expected to be met with some sort of resistance but he handed it over with ease.

"I'll keep that in mind, Metztli Amos."

Metztli immediately regretted what she'd said. She was in no position to be offering such things, nor would she be able to keep to her word. That was fine, there were far worse things that she could be than dishonest.

The princess didn't trust herself to say another word, instead she simply tucked her blade back into its holster and walked away. She'd wasted too much time conversing with Necalli, and she still needed to find Acalan. They needed to sit down and strategize together, because the tournament was real and it was happening whether they liked it or not. Returning home required one thing and one thing only.

Killing.

Acalan

Acalan couldn't find the way to comprehend what he now knew.

His entire world had been spun on its axis. He was on the verge of being sick, but his stomach was empty and his heart felt the same way. Everything he'd thought he knew was a lie. His beliefs were just fairy tales put into place to make him trust that the gods were good.

A part of him still believed that they were. That belief had practically been molded into him, and even if it was Atzi telling him otherwise, it would take time to separate fantasy from reality. Unfortunately for him he was out of time.

There was a knock at the door, pulling Acalan away from his thoughts. He turned quickly to look at the priestess. The look on her face was somber, but there was no regret. He would give anything to go back to that morning and stop himself from visiting her, at least then he wouldn't have to deal with the tangled mess of emotions coursing through his body and mind.

"It's important that you do not share anything we've discussed today with your sister…or anyone else for that matter. Understood?" Atzi asked, reaching out to place her hand on top of Acalan's.

She squeezed it gently, a comforting gesture that did little for Acalan now. He nodded in response anyway. She'd already reminded him of this a million times, so he knew it was important. At least that's what Acalan was trying to convince himself of as he mourned everything he thought he knew.

"Come in!" Atzi shouted to whoever was behind the door.

Acalan didn't have to turn around to know it was his sister. He was likely running late for their scheduled training but that seemed like the least of his worries now. He found it unlikely that he would be able to train adequately under these conditions. If anything he would just make a fool of himself if he did.

With his mind cloudy there was no doubt within him that he would miss every target. His bow would be just as useless as he felt.

The door creaked open, footsteps echoed within the sanctuary, but Acaclan couldn't force himself to turn and look at Metztli. She knew him too well. She'd be able to sense that he was harboring something terrible within him and then what would he do? Lie to her?

No, he'd always been terrible at doing so.

"Is everything alright Metztli? You look…disturbed,"Atzi questioned with genuine concern in her voice.

It was enough that Acalan forced himself to turn and look at Meztli. The priestess was right, his sister did look out of sorts. He couldn't recall a single time during their lives that she'd ever looked this scared.

"Yes, I'm fine," said Metztli, brushing a frantic hand through her hair to smooth it down. "Could I steal my brother? I have something very urgent that I need to discuss with him."

Her response left Acalan curious.

For a moment Acalan thought back to the first time they'd been taken into the forest as children. They hadn't been allowed to come home until they caught and killed something. It had been the first test of many. But even then Metztli had not looked scared when she stared down the boar that she eventually caught and killed. Acalan had always known that his sister was different, but he could have never guessed to what extent.

"Of course, we were just finishing up here. Do be kind to him today, it's a difficult time for everyone," Atzi replied, practically pleading with the Princess.

That was a sight that Acalan had never seen either, but he didn't find it amusing. It was impossible to with the truth he was holding in his mind.

For the slightest of a moment the priestess turned to look at Acalan. The look in her eyes was enough of a reminder of what she'd asked of him. It was a simple request really. All he had to do was keep what he knew to himself, but he doubted it would be as simple as it seemed now.

"Of course…Acalan, we're skipping training for today, I'll explain once we're alone." Metztli beckoned for him to join her.

It was a relief, of course, to know training was off the table, but he hardly felt it in his body as he stood from where he was sitting. Whatever it was that his sister wanted to discuss with him, it had to be important if she was willing to skip training for it, especially this close to the tournament starting. He wasn't sure how much more he could handle though. He felt unstable even as he stood.

Somehow, Acalan found the strength to collect his things, say his farewells to the priestess, and join his sister. He was stronger than he believed himself to be, he just needed to embrace that before it was too late.

"Are you alright?" Metztli questioned, placing a comforting hand on her brother's shoulder. He'd never kept anything from her, but now he was being forced to.

"I'm just stressed about the tournament and needed to settle my mind with Atzi…Are you okay? You've never skipped training before," Acalan responded, doing everything he could to change the subject from his well being to hers.

"I'm okay. I'm afraid this is about the tournament though so it might not help. We need to go somewhere private. Maybe Father's study? I doubt he's in there when he has a palace full of guests."

Acalan nodded softly in response, and they started making way for their father's study. He'd always admired how prepared his sister seemed to be. Metztli was unconventional in her ways, Acalan couldn't deny that, but she always took care of her responsibilities, especially when they had to do with him.

Acalan noted how careful she was being, looking over her shoulder every so often to ensure no one was following them. With a bit of distance from Atzi, Acalan was finally able to think. It was truly unfair that he'd received this information so close to the tournament starting.

There was nothing he could do with what the priestess had revealed to him now. Maybe…if he'd just known sooner then maybe he could have done something. It was his own damn fault for being so complacent with the gods, but that had ended today.

Acalan stepped into his father's study right after Metztli. He took notice of how she locked the door behind them.

"Sit," Metztli commanded in a gentle tone.

Luckily for her, Acalan was more than happy to do so. In fact, he would be even more happy if he could return to his room and sleep through the tournament. That was just a dream though, and even if he could he wouldn't leave his sister to fight in the tournament alone, not with what he now knew.

He watched as Metztli took their father's seat behind the large wooden desk. There were pieces of parchment scattered here and there. Nothing that sparked either of their curiosities though. It was pointless to worry about their empire when they were unsure if they would even return home.

His sister practically melted into her chair. Her shoulders dropped, hands tangled into her hair while a desperate sigh escaped her chest. He could tell that she'd had a rough morning too.

"I know that you're capable of taking care of yourself, Acalan, but I can't have you leaving my sight," Metztli finally said, avoiding eye contact with him.

Acalan found the request just a bit strange. He didn't believe that they were in danger. There were rules in place that ensured this before the tournament started, they both knew that.

"Why?" he questioned. "We still have the rest of today and tomorrow before the tournament starts. Father said there was no need to worry until we stepped foot in the pyramid."

Surely their father wouldn't have lied to them. They were his children, and that was more than enough of a reason to want them to return home. Aside from that, they were also his only heirs, so if he believed that there was any danger, he would have warned them.

Even knowing all of this, there was no doubt that his sister's concerns made him feel even worse than he was already feeling. If it wasn't for the fact that he'd skipped breakfast that morning, Acalan was sure he would have already made himself sick with worry.

"No I know it's just..." Metztli sighed. "You're right. The

tournament doesn't officially start until the day after tomorrow, but for the other heirs it started the moment they stepped foot in Tu'nethe. They're plotting, waiting for any moment to strike, not physically, perhaps, but they'll do anything to make us weak before the killing starts." She shifted her eyes from the ground to find his.

Acalan knew there was more to this, something she wasn't saying. It was frustrating, they had two days until they were handed to the gods, and she still didn't trust that he was capable enough to handle her truth.

"Stop speaking in half truths, whatever it is you're trying to say, just tell me outright," Acalan ordered with a furrowed brow. Now was a better moment than any to prove that he could handle whatever it was that she felt the need to hide from him.

"I'm not purposely hiding things from you. I'm just trying to protect you." Her voice sounded weak, almost as if her will was beginning to falter.

"I can't protect myself or you if I'm not aware of what's going on," he said, and it was the truth. He knew his sister was carrying the burden of keeping the both of them alive, but it didn't have to be that way. After all, he'd trained his entire life for the Tournament of Heirs just as she had.

His sister sighed again, though he could tell her anger wasn't directed toward him. She was just frustrated with their reality, and he couldn't blame her. He felt much the same. He loved his family more than anything, but the tournament and all of the responsibilities they were expected to uphold — it just felt like too much.

"The sisters from the House of Flor just cornered me outside in the garden…" she finally admitted. "Did you notice how neither of them spoke yesterday?"

He thought about it for a moment and did, in fact, recall how he had found that strange about them. Mostly he'd just thought that they'd been scared, a little bit shy perhaps.

"I guess I didn't think much of it," he said, hoping that after this he would get some sort of clarity as to what she meant by being cornered. If something physical had happened then they needed to inform their father.

"I didn't think much of it as well, until they had me face to face. They've sharpened their teeth into peaks." She shuddered. "I can only imagine it's so that they can rip out throats, maybe worse. They're hungry for blood, Acalan, and I don't mean that metaphorically. They talked about what our blood might taste like. Both of them are absolutely vile. Worse than me."

Of everything that Metztli said, the last three words shocked Acalan the most. Their argument from the day before was still thick in the air, even if it didn't seem like it. Otherwise she wouldn't have compared herself to them.

Acalan didn't think that she was vile though. They didn't completely see eye to eye when it came to the tournament but he knew that Metztli would never kill the way that these sisters were planning to.

When Metztli eventually killed someone, it would be quick, merciful even.

"So they threatened you? We could tell father, I'm sure he would want to know that something like that was happening in our home," he said, tone full of concern.

Perhaps he wasn't sworn to protect her the way that she was sworn to protect him, but she was still his little sister. There were unspoken duties that came with that.

"Absolutely not! I won't be speaking a single word of this to father and I don't want you to either. If we do, we'll appear weak and you know we can't appear that way to them" Metztli argued. She sat a little straighter now, indicating that she meant what she was saying.

"Some of the heirs have alliances already formed and we only have each other," she continued. "We might not have sharpened teeth but I know we're connected in the way that they are not. I still think we can win, we just have to play our cards right. I need you to trust me."

Acalan could see in her eyes that she meant it. She truly believed that they could be the last ones standing in the tournament, that they could win and return home.

And for what felt like the first time since they'd known about this damned tournament, Acalan felt like they could win, too. Before he only felt that way in fleeting moments because it was expected from him. But with what he knew thanks to Atzi, and seeing this spark of confidence in Metztli, he now knew that it was possible.

They could win this entire thing. They could put an end to the bloodshed.

"I trust you, I always have," he said after a moment.

There was nothing else that needed to be said. If they were going to enter the Pyramid of Tributes, then they would leave it too. Metztli had to, according to Atzi, and she needed him to survive as well. Acalan would put his morals aside for Metztli, not because it was expected of him, but because he wanted to. It was a sacrifice worthy only of his sister.

Metztli's brow furrowed before a laugh finally slipped out of her. It was so unexpected that it caught Acalan off guard and made him laugh too.

"Okay? That's it? No arguments or objections?" she questioned, bits of laughter still enveloping her words.

"No arguments or objections. If the tournament has already begun the way you say it has then we need to play our cards right. You've prepared for this better than I have, so we'll do what you think is best. I want the both of us to come home, and we will," he continued, suddenly serious again. "We have to, it's not a choice for us the way that it is for the rest of them."

For Acalan, the sentiment had a double meaning. The tournament was different for the Amos family, simply because they had no other heirs. Metztli and Acalan were all that was left of the House of Life…but they also had to win because Metztli had a destiny to fulfill, and Acalan wanted to be there to see it come to fruition.

He watched carefully as she absorbed his words. It was almost like she'd been waiting for this to happen, for him to accept her. It made Acalan feel guilty in a way but there was nothing he could do to change the past. All he could do was ensure her future played out the way it was supposed to.

"We're going to win this tournament," Metztli declared then, more sure of her words than she had ever been.

"Together," Acalan added, matching his sister's tone.

"Together," Metztli repeated after him.

METZTLI

"Do you remember that time you fell down the hill? Mother was so angry with me because you claimed I pushed you!" Metztli questioned as she laughed.

Metztli and Acalan had spent the last few hours strategizing in their father's study. Or more so half of the time had been spent strategizing and the other half of the time was spent laughing and recalling memories from their childhood.

"You did push me! I remember it clearly!" he argued while trying to catch his breath. "I was enjoying the view of Tu'nethe from on top of it when you totally pushed me and I went rolling down the entire way. I stumbled into that tree truck at the bottom and I was bruised for weeks. I even have a scar from it!"

Acalan pulled down his shirt slightly to reveal the pale pink scar that had never faded completely.

"First of all, you stumbled over something because you had a book in your hands," she countered." You weren't enjoying the view of Tu'nethe at all. You were reading about constellations. I still remember it very vividly. Mostly because mother forced me to spend the next month visiting with Atzi to repent for my sin."

Metztli watched as her brother thought about it for a few moments and then, suddenly, it was like everything came back to him. He covered his face with his hands in embarrassment which was well deserved considering the punishment that Metztli was forced to endure as a child.

"Okay. I think you may be right, but to be fair, I did think you pushed me in the moment, and you know how stubborn mother has always been with us about being careful not to injure ourselves."

"Oh! I remember! We were hardly allowed to do anything out of her sight. I can't blame her though." Metztli relaxed back into her chair.

"What do you mean?" Acalan questioned with a curious look in his eye.

The curiosity that lived within her brother was something that Metztli had always admired. She was sure it was why he was always so eager to read and learn more. That wasn't something that she shared with her brother but that was okay. In her eyes, they were each special in their own way.

"Well, mother lost a baby during birth, father has no living family aside from us and we were trouble when we wanted to be. I imagine she was just afraid of losing us to mischief," Metztli started explaining before a soft sigh escaped her.

She continued, "You know how the women speak of her for being unable to provide father with more heirs. I'm sure that the combination of fear and shame just made her extra precautious." The words left an extra bitter taste on her tongue.

The day before, the empress from the House of Flor had made a not-so-kind comment about her own womb being blessed. Metztli had heard enough talk amongst women to know that her words had been a personal attack towards their mother. She never understood why though. Women were meant to empower one another in a world full of powerful men, but it never seemed to go that way.

"Hmm, well I suppose you're right," Acalan said, a somber expression taking over his features. "I can't bare the thought of mother losing either of us to the tournament and if I can't bare it, then I'm sure mother feels even worse."

"We'll just have to make sure that doesn't happen then," she said. "For mother and father's sake and for the sake of Tu'nethe as well… Can you imagine what it would be like if the House of Flor or, gods forbid, the House of Blood had to reign over our people? It would be terrible. We have to do this for them."

The idea of her people being treated less kindly than her father had treated them during his reign made her blood boil, but she tried to push the feeling away. It was better that she save it for the tournament itself.

"Well, when you put it like that then, yes," he said, a soft smile replacing the frown that used to cover his lips. "We absolutely have to win."

Metztli nodded in response. She couldn't agree more. Winning was simply their responsibility.

It was only when a comfortable silence fell upon them that Metztli felt safe and composed enough to leave their father's study. That — combined with the fact that she was sure their mother would come looking for them any moment now with a scolding regarding how it was improper to ignore their guests — was more than enough for her to find the strength to rise from her seat.

They'd both agreed to keep their interactions with the other heirs to a minimum. Nothing more than necessarily. The sisters from the House of Flor had been quite forward with their intimidation, but Metztli knew all the heirs were thinking the same thing. It was almost like the rest of the heirs had forgotten that there were twelve of them competing against one another, and instead just viewed Metztli and Acalan alone as their enemies.

For a moment Metztli allowed herself to consider what life could have been like if the tournament was a work of fiction and not their reality. Perhaps she would have enjoyed the company of Xochitl and Atlatonan. Both women seemed to be made of the same fire that Metztli was. In another life they could have been great friends, but in this one they were sworn enemies. And it was likely that somehow, someway, they'd be the reason for each other's death.

She only allowed herself to think about it for a moment though. Just as she had told Acalan many times before, there was no use in spending their time contemplating what their lives could have been like if they hadn't been born into the world they were. There was nothing they could do to change what had already been decided for them. But perhaps they could bring change if they managed to win this tournament.

Until then, they simply had to do whatever it took to survive. Which, in this case, meant being able to get across the palace without being spotted or interrupted by any of their guests. Regardless, if it was an heir, their parents, or other members of the foreign families. Metztli wanted nothing to do with them. They'd all developed a distaste for the Amos heirs anyway. The princess knew this from the way all their guests looked at them like they were a meal to devour. But if Metztli and Acalan were only a meal to them, what the other heirs didn't realize was that they were poisoned with the responsibility to win the Tournament of Heirs.

"It's a little early…but perhaps we should go see mother? I'm sure she'll be happy to pamper us for as long as she can," Metztli said as they walked through the corridors of their home.

Despite the fact that they'd lived within these palace walls for their entire lives. It looked different now. The hallways were busy, full of handmaidens, and groundskeepers preparing for the celebration of tributes that would occur later that evening. Metztli thought the whole ordeal was overblown. She would have rather just received a scroll with every heir's name instead of having to be presented to the gods formally.

"That's a good idea," Acalan replied softly. "It's been a while since we got ready together for something like this." Acalan responded softly.

There was a glint in his eyes, something that Metztli recognized because she was feeling it, too. Though she believed that this tournament would end with the both of them returning home, she couldn't deny that everything they did now felt like it could be the last time.

It was a dreadful feeling, wanting to experience what could be the last days of their lives fully, while also being careful under the watchful eyes of their enemies.

"You helped me get ready on my fifthteenth name day. That wasn't that long ago you know," Metztli remarked idly.

Even five years later that day held some of her most favorite memories. Nenetl had made her the most beautiful teal gown, embellished with pieces of real gold. It had been the day she formally picked her weapon of choice and the day she had been named an heir to their empire. At the time, she didn't quite understand the responsibility to its full extent. Not like she did now.

"No it wasn't…just a few years really but, we're different now, then we used to be," Acalan replied.

Metztli couldn't find the words to respond, nor could she argue with that. They were different now than they had been. She was just unsure if that was a good thing. She remained tight-lipped and nodded softly as they cut through the open ward of the palace. It was the shorter way of getting across the palace and to their mother, but Metztli hadn't realized that the courtyard of their home would be so full of people when she'd guided them that way.

From the looks of it, some of the male heirs, including Necalli, his cousin Coatl and the men from the House of Serpent were busying themselves by playing ōllamalitzli.

The game was a bit barbaric and childish in Metztli's mind. She'd never been interested in it even when she was a child. After all, there were much better things to do than chase a ball around for hours on end. Luckily her brother had been much the same. Unlike most of the boys in Tu'nethe, Acalan would have rather spent his free time with his nose in a book instead of chasing a ball. It was comforting knowing that they were at least similar in this.

"Oh no," she sighed. "Okay just smile and walk by. Remember, these people are not our friends."

They continued through the courtyard, not necessarily going unnoticed but at least no one was making any effort to speak to them. That is, until Metztli heard a familiar voice call out her name.

"Metztli! Wait up!"

By the time Metztli and Acalan managed to turn around Necalli was already pacing towards them, leaving the game behind. Necalli was starting to get on Metztli's nerves. Had anything from their brief conversation earlier led him to believe she had any intention of being friendly?

"Are you sure I can't just start killing them now?" Metztli whispered to her brother, only half joking. She waited for her brother to respond, but when he didn't after a few seconds she grew confused. She turned to him, only to find he was distracted by something. Or, rather, someone.

Acalan was completely dazed by Citlalic Cruz. The young woman was sitting in the grass, reading a book.

Metztli wanted to slap her brother upside the head. Now was not the time to admire a woman who would surely hate them if they returned victorious and her brother did not.

Before Metztli could kick him though, Necalli was in front of them. His breath was heavy and beads of sweat dripped down his forehead to his jaw and chest. Metztli's breath hitched slightly at the sight of him. A natural reaction certainly. Even if he was a sworn enemy, Metztli was only human.

His gaze followed Acalan's, and while it was obvious that Acalan was gazing upon his sister, Necalli didn't say anything about it. That was strange. Had Metztli been in his place, she would have surely said something.

"We have room for two more if you guys want to join," Necalli offered, as he turned back to look at Metztli. She raised a brow and kept her features unamused. Mostly she was just confused about why everyone was so keen on being friendly when they'd be at each other's throats in the matter of days.

"Not our thing, sorry," she said, waving away the offer.

"Do you know what book your sister is reading?" Acalan then asked, earning confused looks from both Necalli and Metztli. "It looks familiar."

Her brother was perhaps the most intelligent person she knew, but right now he was acting just plain stupid. She would have to speak to him about this later when they were alone. Perhaps it hadn't occurred to him that they could never be. Even in the wildest of his dreams.

"Not really my thing," Necalli responded before turning to face Metztli again.

Admittedly, his response did make her want to laugh, but she held it in. She didn't want to further the notion that friendship was on the table between the both of them.

"Ōllamalitzli can be really fun if you play it with the right people," Necalli added with a sly smile.

Metztli's brow furrowed. If he thought that would be a convincing argument then he really was incompetent.

"I'm sure it is, but shouldn't you all be getting ready? I heard the gods might make an appearance tonight," Metztli snapped, almost like she was scolding him and his playmates for not being up to par with her.

"They won't be," Acalan said offhandedly, still eyeing Citlalic. "They haven't made an appearance at the celebration of tributes for at least ten documented tournaments, so I doubt this one will be any different."

"Right, thank you Acalan for that very needed piece of information." She turned again to Necalli, offering him a sarcastic smile. "I'm afraid we're too busy to play games though, but good luck!"

Necalli seemed quite amused, which only infuriated her even more.

"Is your sister always this rude?" Necalli asked Acalan.

While her brother did seem distracted by Citlalic, the notion of someone insulting his sister pulled him back into the moment. He stood tall now, keeping his gaze locked on Necalli. This was a line that Metztli knew her brother would not let Necalli, or anyone else for that matter, cross.

"Rude or not, she's still an heir of the empire you're in right now," Acalan hissed, taking a step forward. "I would be careful how you speak of her in our home."

Necalli seemed amused by that, too, so much so that he let a bit of laughter slip from his lips. And there it was. The switch from friend to enemy happened so quickly it could have been easily missed if one was not paying attention.

"Strange, for a moment there I thought you'd be able to fight your own battles, Princess. It's a shame I was wrong. You were far more intriguing when I was under that impression."

Acalan's movements were so quick that Metztli almost didn't have the time to respond. Luckily, she managed to step between them just before her brother took another step forward in an attempt to close the gap between his fist and Necalli's jaw.

"You lay a hand on my brother and you'll be the first person I kill inside of the pyramid. Touch him and you die, it's as simple as that," Metztli sneered.

She wanted her words to place some fear in Necalli, and they did, even if he was trying to mask the emotion with a ridiculous smirk on his face. But the way that his eyes avoided hers told a completely different story.

"Rage is a good look on you Princess," Necalli responded, his voice a little softer than it was before.

She scoffed loud enough that it earned her a few looks from the other heirs.

"Let's go Acalan, we have better things to do then waste our time meddling with those who don't deserve it," Metztli spewed, daggers and thorns engraved into her words.

She backed away, resisting the urge to really show the prince who he was messing with. Necalli — or any of the other heirs for that matter — were not worth her time or energy.

Both Metztli and Acalan made their best attempt at leaving the courtyard as quickly as they could. They'd already wasted more time than they could afford to, and while Metztli was slowly growing used to prying eyes, she would prefer to be away from the other heirs until it was absolutely necessary.

"Metztli!" Necalli called as they walked away. She wanted to keep walking and avoid Necalli for the rest of the day, but curiosity got the best of her. She turned with a menacing look on her face.

"You still owe me one, Princess," Necalli shouted loudly enough for everyone to hear. "I'll be in my room later if you want to go ahead and get that over with."

Rage fueled her movements as she sprinted towards him. To hell with the rules, she was going to hurt him. And if she had to face consequences for it, then so be it.

She could hear Acalan just a few steps behind her, shouting something, but she was too enraged to comprehend his words. She lunged forward pushing Necalli.

"You're a prick Necalli Cruz!" Metztli shouted loud enough for everyone to hear as she pushed him again and again until he stumbled backwards.

Despite her brother's efforts to stop her, Metztli still found the strength to climb on top of the Prince of Blood. She was well aware of the fact that they now had a crowd surrounding them. Some cheered for her while others cheered for Necalli. None of this stopped her from clawing at him though. She wasn't going to stop until she drew blood.

"Yeah? I think you like it though, don't you?" Necalli taunted from underneath her.

There it was again. Necalli had perfected the art of being arrogant, and hearing him suggest that she favored him in any way only filled her with more fury. Metztli opted to not respond with words, continuing clawing at the prince beneath her until he managed to restrain both her arms.

"LET ME GO!" Metztli shouted frantically.

She was blind with anger, so much so that she didn't hear her brother's pleas for her to stop. All the princess knew was that she had to get out of Necalli's grasp and aim straight for his face.

Metztli's anger got the best of her when she felt a hand on her waist, attempting to pull her away from Necalli. The princess didn't even stop to think about who it could be before she pulled all her body weight backwards, escaping Necalli's grasp and elbowing whoever was behind her all at once.

"Talk about bedding me again and I'll slit your throat," Metztli spat as she climbed off Necalli's body.

She turned, only to find that Acalan had fallen victim to her anger. He lay unconscious with blood pouring from his nose. It had, of course, never been Metztli's intention to hurt her brother, but she had.

Guilt coursed through her body. He'd only been trying to help and in the process she'd knocked him unconscious. Someone in the crowd must have alerted the guards because the next thing she knew Acalan was being carried to the medical ward, and all she could do was chase behind them silently, full of regret and shame. She'd made a fool of herself and in the process she'd hurt her brother.

ACALAN

In all the years that Acalan had trained with his sister, he'd never seen her so rageful. It was like Metztli had been possessed by her anger. She was no longer a woman but a beast with every intention of hurting Necalli. He couldn't blame her for wanting to do so. He wanted to hurt the heir from the House of Blood, too, for speaking of his sister how he had.

Their father had warned them that the people from the House of Blood were unhinged, but this was something else. Necalli had taunted Metztli publicly, he'd made her look weak in front of the other heirs.

Still, as her brother, and as the only one between the both of them who still had the ability to think clearly, Acalan knew that it was his responsibility to make sure she didn't do anything she would regret later.

He'd struggled with her, trying to pull her off Necalli while Coatl shouted for Necalli to let her go.

And then, suddenly, Metztli's elbow crashed into Acalan's face. It happened so suddenly and quickly that he hardly felt any pain. Instead he just felt the world around him start to spin. He saw stars despite the fact that the sun was shining high in the sky, and before he knew it, his eyes had rolled back into his head. The world around him went dark and he was gone, taken somewhere unknown.

Acalan gasped as his eyes opened. He was expecting to find himself somewhere familiar in his home, but instead he found himself in a field he did not recognize. He immediately knew this was a dream of sorts, it couldn't be real, because one moment he'd been elbowed by his sister and the next he was here, and that didn't make any sense.

He felt something warm covering his body. The atmosphere around him was cold, but his body was warm. His hands were covered with blood.

Frantically he stood from where he lay on the ground. He was covered in it, and he searched his body for an injury but found nothing. His breath quickened with fear, and it only worsened when he looked around and found bodies on the ground. None of them were people he recognized, but they were all covered in blood.

Acalan screamed, but he couldn't hear himself make any sound. He needed to wake up from this horrible dream. He tried to move but he couldn't, he was stuck, unable to wake himself and return to what he knew was real. Panic flooded through him as he was left to look over the bodies that surrounded him.

"Acalan..." his sister's voice whispered.

It should have been comforting but he couldn't find her no matter where he turned to look. The whisper continued, each time the tone of his sister's voice became more and more eerie. Her voice lowered and turned into something far from human until he hardly recognized it to be her.

Suddenly, The bodies around him began to multiply, piling up on each other. He was drowning in them. He could feel himself suffocating underneath the weight of the bodies around him. He pleaded with his mind to simply wake up. It was such a simple task but he couldn't bring his consciousness to obey.

"This is the way" Metztli's voice echoed through his mind. He turned his head quickly but wished he hadn't because there he found his sister, blood soaking every inch of her body, her spear in her hand. Acalan frantically searched for injuries on her too but found nothing...it was then that he realized it wasn't her blood, but the blood of all the bodies swallowing him alive.

"This is the way," she said again and again. Every time Acalan tried to shout and tell her she was wrong, but the sound of his words never left his mouth. He was stuck in an endless loop of terror that he could

not escape.

All the prince could do was close his eyes in an attempt to wake himself, but he could still hear her voice echoing in his mind until it suddenly stopped.

Acalan gasped as his eyes opened and his body jolted forward. Any bit of relief that he should have felt was swept away at the sight of Metztli standing at his side. His parents were there too. They tried to calm him, but his gaze was fixed on his sister.

His dream must have been some sick warning of what was yet to come. Atzi had been clear in her explanation of the prophecy. Letting his sister lose control was far more dangerous than the Tournament of Heirs itself. After what Acalan had just seen, he didn't need any further evidence to know Atzi's claims were true.

"Acalan…" she whispered, taking a step forward.

The prince knew his sister better than anyone, he knew she wasn't the vicious killer she had been in his dream. But he couldn't stop himself from pulling back as she reached out to touch him.

Confusion and shame washed over Metztli's face. In his dream she appeared as she did now, except for how prideful she'd looked as she stood over the dead bodies. As Acalan continued to study her expression, he couldn't help but wonder how anyone could be proud of massacring a crowd of people.

"I'm sorry Acalan, I-I didn't m-mean to hurt you," Metztli apologized, pulling her hands back.

He tried to calm himself. This was his sister. The version of her that he'd seen in his dream wouldn't have apologized for the bodies she'd slayed.

Of course.

Because the sister who stood in front of him now apologizing as tears formed in her eyes, and the version of her that he'd seen in his dream, were not the same, nor did they ever have to be.

"See what you've done?!" Xara scolded Metztli. "We asked one thing of you Metztli, one thing! You simply had to behave yourself, and instead you disgraced this family and in the process knocked your brother unconscious!"

Their mother's words brought even more tears to Metztli's eyes, and while he would have much rather not been elbowed in the face or dragged into the dream he'd just escaped from, his parents had not been there to bear witness to what Necalli had done.

"I already said I'm sorry a million times! What more do you want from me?!" Metztli shouted.

Acalan wanted to say something but the shouting continued and aside from feeling weak, slightly nauseous and his face feeling sore from Metztli's assault, he was also nursing a headache unlike any other he'd ever felt before.

"Don't you dare try to make yourself the victim when your brother has been lying here unconscious for the last hour!" Their mother's tone was violent.

This all felt wrong. They shouldn't be arguing so close to the tournament, not when there was still a chance that the both of them could die within the Pyramid of Tributes.

"What are you going to do?" Metztli snapped, a flood of tears pouring down her face. "Punish me? I enter the pyramid in less than two days! Isn't that punishment enough?!"

Acalan felt worse for her than he did for herself.

He turned to look at their father who stayed silent, simply observing his wife and daughter scream at each other. He had a god given gift for telling the truth from lies, so Acalan was certain that his father knew Metztli was being genuine. He just wanted the shouting to end, he didn't want the last memories of his family to be of them arguing.

"Enough!" Tenoch finally commanded. The room went silent. Metztli and their mother continued arguing through their eyes, but no more words were spoken or shouted.

Tenoch turned on Metztli. "Metztli, you were wrong in attacking Necalli. Regardless of what was implied or said, you've been taught to control yourself."

His sister stayed quiet. It was strange, he'd never seen her back down from an argument, but she said nothing as she turned her gaze to her feet.

"Xara," Tenoch turned to his wife, "my love. I understand you're frustrated and disappointed in Metztli but you must remain calm… Our daughter is right. It is only a number of hours before we place their lives in the hands of the gods. Do not let this be the last memory our children have of us."

Xara stayed quiet as well. Shame took over her features, and the sight made Acalan's heart ache. But the argument was over now and that was something to be grateful for.

"Now, back to what's most important…Acalan, son, how are you feeling?"

The room was less chaotic but he was still hurting physically. He just wished they could go back to an hour ago so that he could have stopped Metztli before she even took a step towards Necalli.

"I'm fine, I promise, just feeling a little bit weak is all." Acalan forced a smile. "Perhaps I could have something to eat?"

"Of course…Come Xara, let's get a bit of air my love, we'll be right back with a meal. I trust that the both of you will remain calm until we return." Tenoch beckoned for his wife to join him.

Their mother seemed to relax in his embrace. Acalan was grateful for that. Just as he was grateful when his parents left the room and gave both him and his sister a little space to breathe.

"I'm sorry Acalan, I really am…" Metztli said softly, looking down at her feet as she tripped over her own apology. "I didn't mean to lose control like that and I certainly didn't mean to harm you."

He'd never seen her look so small. Metztli had always been this larger than life figure and now she was helpless and ashamed. Prophecy or not, they were family, brother and sister, and she had to know that.

"It's alright Metztli. It's probably my own damn fault for getting in your way. I was just scared that you would hurt him and get in trouble for it. I don't blame you for wanting retribution for what he said."

"No, don't try to take the blame for this. It's my fault, it was my elbow that knocked you unconscious," Metztli confessed in response. "All of this is my fault and I'm sorry, I can't seem to do anything right no matter how hard I try."

It wasn't easy watching his only sister fall apart right in front of him. Even if the memory of his dream and Atzi's words were still vivid and clear in his mind, nobody knew Metztli the way that he did. And it was because of that simple fact that he knew that she didn't have to become the version of herself that he'd seen in his dream. Someone who was truly cruel wouldn't fall apart over a simple accident like this one.

She just needed someone to keep her on the right path, to protect her from herself, and if that was Acalan's duty in all of this, then that was a responsibility he was more than willing to bare for her.

"Mother is just upset because of what the other families will say. You know she's never been good at accepting criticism. Everything will be okay, and if anything now the other heirs know just how vicious you can be."

"But we had a plan!" Metztli argued. "They were supposed to think I was weak, not feral!"

She resembled a child much more than she resembled herself right now. Perhaps that should have worried Acalan, but it didn't. He'd had his fair share of outbursts like this. He thought back to their fight just a day ago and laughed.

"That plan was never going to work, Metztli. I think you're intelligent enough to know that you're anything but weak, and you wouldn't know how to pretend to be weak even if I wrote you a step by step guide." Acalan reached out for her hand. He knew that he'd likely wounded her even further when he'd pulled away earlier.

"Embrace your strength," he continued. "I saw the looks on their faces when you were attacking Necalli. Even the sisters looked scared of you, that's a good thing, they'll think twice before they come for us."

A familiar spark appeared in her eyes.

"Did they really look scared?" Metztli asked as she wiped away the tears from her face.

Acalan laughed once again, he was happy to see a slight smile in her expression.

"Terrified, even Necalli looked scared. I think he saw this life flashing before his eyes," Acalan teased.

A comfortable silence fell upon them again, but Acalan welcomed it. He was still nursing a headache, and his entire face hurt from where she'd hit him, but he felt infinitely better when he heard her laugh. She was good in her heart, regardless of whatever anyone said or thought.

"Acalan?" She questioned after a few minutes of silence. Her tone was soft, once again resembling a child.

It reminded him of when she used to come knocking at his door late at night when they were children after having awoken from a nightmare, begging him to let her in or to check for monsters in her room.

At some point in their lives, their roles had switched. He'd gone from her protector to the one she protected. That was unfair much like a lot of other things in their lives. He regretted that he had allowed it to go on for so long. He'd do things differently if he could go back but he couldn't so instead he decided right then and there to make things right while he could.

"Yeah?" Acalan responded mimicking her tone, because in this moment he wanted to resemble the boy who used to open the door to his sister and let her crawl into his bed, or who would follow her to her room and reassure her over and over again that there were no monsters hiding underneath her bed.

"I'm glad you're my brother," she said simply.

He allowed her words to sink in for a moment. He hadn't done anything to deserve the sentiment, but he welcomed it anyway.

"Well there's no one else I'd rather have as a sister," Acalan replied, a warm smile spreading over his lips.

They would be okay, because they had a bond he was sure the other heirs couldn't come close to having. Despite their lives and roles they had never seen each other as competition for their father's throne.

They were just siblings.

Brother and Sister.
Best friends.

METZTLI

Metztli was happy to see that her mother and father were much calmer when they returned. Though, whether they had truly forgiven her, or were just pushing their emotions aside to enjoy the last moments they had with their children, was a mystery.

She was even more relieved when she realized that they'd brought a tray of fresh tortillas and beans all ready to be made into lunch. It wasn't the grandest of meals, but Metztli didn't mind. If anything, the sight of the food made her remember all of the days her mother had fed them the same things when they were small and could barely walk on their own.

"I do not want to rush either of you but we must make haste," their mother announced as began spreading the beans over the tortillas, rolling them perfectly and passing them to everyone. "We still have a ceremony to get ready for, and I will not let either of you be presented to the gods looking anything but perfect."

Metztli nodded in agreement before taking a bite of her taquito. It tasted like heaven despite being made from the simplest ingredients.

The princess had another, followed by a couple more before her mother looked at her with a raised brow. That was Metztli's cue to know she'd had enough unless she wanted to squeeze into her dress when it was time to get dressed.

"I'm feeling much better now that I have food in my stomach," Acalan announced.

His words were more than enough to bring a soft smile to their mother's face. Metztli couldn't deny that it was much better than seeing her filled with worry.

Acalan slowly stood with the help of their father. It could have been a lot worse. Metztli had been uncontrollable in the moment and she could have caused some real damage to her brother. The thought of that made the food in her belly threaten to make its way out, but she reminded herself that Acalan was okay. The sight of him walking slightly ahead of her as they made their way to the dressing parlor helped too.

Even if their parents wouldn't admit it, Metztli knew what they were doing. They were escorting the both of them to get ready, and they did so in fear that if left alone, Metztli would find herself in another altercation.

But Metztli would rather die untouched before considering Necalli as a suitor.

It wasn't long before they reached the fitting parlor. Metztli was prepared to suffer through being pampered for a few hours. She would do anything to not disgrace her family any more than she already had. If it would please their mother to have the both of them looking absolutely perfect for their presentation to the gods, then she would sit through all of it.

Acalan had said the gods would not make an appearance that evening, but she needed to be prepared just in case they did, so that they might remember the beautiful young woman from the House of Life.

The one that hated everything they stood for.

The one who would do anything to make people see them for what they really were.

"Can I speak to you for a moment?" her father asked in a hushed voice right before Metztli entered the room.

"Are you going to scold me again?" Metztli asked as she stood back, letting her mother and Acalan enter the dressing parlor.

Xara was busy doting on Acalan and tending to his every need, so she wouldn't notice if Metztli was gone for just a few moments.

"Actually…I wanted to tell you that I am…that I'm…Well I'm proud of you for defending yourself," her father explained with soft eyes and a gentle voice. "Your timing could have been a bit better, of course, but you should never let a man disrespect you. Not in our home, and not anywhere else."

It took her a second to realize he was really praising her instead of reprimanding her for what she'd done. His words made the remaining stress in her body fade away. Maybe she had done the right thing… Well, aside from accidentally elbowing her brother unconscious.

"Oh…well, thank you father…I mean, Your Majesty," Metztli responded, offering her dad a playful wink that made both of them smile.

Sometimes, when life was really good and peace surrounded her family, she would forget about the titles that followed them. In another life, they could have just been a family that loved and cared for one another.

But in this life, there was no use in wishing for things she knew she simply could not have.

"Of course…now go in there and listen to your mother please. Let her pamper you until she thinks you look perfect. It will make her feel better about this whole ordeal."

Metztli could tell from the glint in his eyes that he was pleading with her. He didn't have to though, just knowing that her mother had been feeling anything other than happy was enough for Metztli to agree to keep her mouth shut and let her mother be a mother for the next couple hours.

"I will, I promise," she said, turning her slight frown into a tight smile.

With the reassurance that his daughter would behave, her father left to take care of all of the duties he'd been ignoring to take care of his family. It wasn't easy reigning over Mexica, but there was no one better suited for these duties.

Metztli was sad to see him go. Really, right now all that she wanted was to be able to enjoy as much time with her family as she could. But duties were duties. Her life was a constant reminder of that.

She managed to slip into the dressing parlor without much notice. Her mother was in the midst of playfully scolding Acalan for his messy hair when she walked in.

It was a sweet sight, one that she wasn't quite used to, but welcomed nonetheless. When they were little, their mother would come to their rooms every evening to brush their hair. At the time Acalan's reached down his hip. It wasn't until his tenth name day that he'd requested to cut it so he fit in better with the few friends they were allowed to have.

When Xara was done with Acalan's hair she would slip into Metztli's room to brush hers next. She had so much of it that it would hurt sometimes when the brush caught a knot or two. Metztli remembered that her mother used to be gentle when she did it though. Trying her best not to hurt her little princess. So much had changed since then, but perhaps, just maybe if she and Acalan returned, they would have enough time for things to go back to what they used to be before the tournament and all its responsibilities had gotten in the way of their lives.

"Do you need me to bathe mother? Or will a quick rinse do?" Metztli asked as she stood behind them. "I'm afraid if I get my hair wet it won't dry for hours."

Her mother turned and took a quick look at her. Both Metztli and Acalan had slept very little the night before, but Metztli looked far better than her brother did. Probably because she had at least fallen asleep in her bed and not seated at her desk.

"You look perfectly fine darling, no need for either. Your brother on the other hand needs to be dunked in ice cold water. Just look at these dark circles under his eyes!" her mother exclaimed, turning her attention back to Acalan.

Her words made Metztli giggle. It was so rare when her brother was scolded in her place, and she couldn't deny that she quite enjoyed being on this side of things.

"You should have seen the state of him when he rushed out of his room this morning to see Atzi. Which reminds me, what was that all about Acalan?" Metztli asked, trying to hide her true motive behind the laughter entangling her words.

Acalan's gaze became panicked.

"It was…It was…Well it was nothing. I just asked a question that needed answering."

"But you had books in your hands, what was that about?" Metztli continued to press.

This wasn't the most opportune of moments, but she wouldn't let the conversation go until he revealed the truth. He was a terrible liar, amongst the worst she'd ever known.

"Did it have to do anything with the princess from the House of Blood?" their mother interjected before Acalan could respond.

His cheeks immediately flushed, which was a sight Metztli had never seen.

"I haven't been that obvious have I?" Acalan asked with a look that was a combination of panic and embarrassment.

His response made her chuckle. It wasn't just that he had been obvious about his attraction towards the young woman, it was that he didn't notice he had been. You could only stare at someone for so long without causing suspicion.

"Obvious is an understatement, Acalan, your pupils practically turn into little hearts when she's near," Metztli teased, causing her brother to cover his face with his hands.

He couldn't escape this though, their mother was giddy about the notion of her son being pulled towards a woman, even if she was the heir to an opposing house.

"I must confess she caught my attention as well, she was so kind and well mannered!" Their mother beamed as she beckoned for Metztli to take a seat. "So much better than the other heirs, and certainly better than that brother of hers. I wonder what she'll be wearing tonight, something absolutely stunning no doubt!"

Metztli suddenly felt a brush going through her hair, followed by her mother's hands starting to braid a piece of her hair away from her face. She melted into the chair, perfectly content with allowing her mother to take care of her.

This could be the last time she ever got to experience this.

The thought made her heart drop to her stomach, but she

pushed away the sick feeling so she could just enjoy this moment.

"She won't be competing, Acalan," Metztli said lazily. "You could ask her to dance tonight. I wouldn't do anything more than that though. I hate to be the bearer of bad news, but our lives are on pause until we return. And even if we somehow make it out alive, who knows how she will feel then."

She instantly knew she had said the wrong thing. Even if her sentiment was meant with good intentions, that didn't stop her mother and brother from gawking at her.

"Oh nonsense!" their mother chimed. "I loved your father despite knowing what he'd done to survive. Love conquerors all at the end of the day so you must ask her to dance! I bet she's quite smitten with you already as well."

Metztli had never really thought about it. Perhaps her mother was right and love did conqueror all. If that was the case then the love that she had for her brother would be enough to push them through the end of the tournament, and when they returned, Metztli would be more than content to sit by and watch her brother fall in love.

"Mother's right, and if it so happens that she has an interest in men who keep their personal libraries so well organized they won't even let their sisters borrow a book, or those who drool in their sleep and snore, and have a weak left—"

"That's enough, Metztli." Xara warned. "Acalan is perfect in my eyes, as are you. I have no doubt that when you return home, you will find a suitor rather quickly as well. Especially after how beautiful you will look when we're finished here. You'll have a line of men just waiting for the opportunity to have your hand."

It seemed that she was finished with the braid. It hadn't lasted nearly as long as Metztli hoped it would, but she was glad it even happened in the first place.

She scoffed slightly at the mention of marriage. If she returned home, she would not be spending her time pursuing a spouse. Metztli was planning on enjoying her freedom and nothing else. If anything, she wanted to avoid love for as long as she could.

"Sure, and then I will have a million children and fill the home with as many little heirs as I can!"Metztli responded quite sarcastically.

"It's like you read my mind! Oh just the thought of it is so lovely!!" Xara exclaimed with a bright smile on her face.

Acalan gave Metztli a knowing look, and while she considered correcting her mother, she was quickly reminded of her father's request from earlier. She was to be kind and nothing else. If the thought of having many grandchildren made her mother happy, then she would let it remain for now.

"So that's what you spoke to Atzi about then? About the princess and nothing else?" Metztli said, turning to question her brother.

Panic filled his eyes again, which was enough of an answer for her to know he was keeping something from her, even if he wouldn't openly admit it now.

"Yup, just needed assurance about Citlalic and nothing else," he responded.

Metztli was unsure if he noticed his movements but he had sunk into his chair slightly. Another indicator that he wasn't being entirely honest with his sister.

"Alright, enough chit chat," their mother announced, ending Metztli's line of interrogation. "Acalan needs to bathe, and we need to start getting you dressed! You are both going to look so beautiful! If the gods do show then they will be in for a real treat!"

Metztli wasn't quite satisfied though, and whether it be tonight or tomorrow, she would get her answers before they entered the Pyramid of Tributes. Still, she turned away and watched from the corner of eye as her brother practically leaped out of his chair and slipped into the bathing chambers.

He was lucky that their mother had given him the opportunity to escape, but that wouldn't last forever. She would catch up to him eventually.

"Now, don't make me look too good, I wouldn't want to outshine the other heirs," Metztli teased as she stood from where she'd been sitting.

She roamed over to the rack of dresses she recognized from the day before. Nenetl had done her job well, everything looked beautiful, and she especially favored the gold embellishments the seamstress had added to her gown.

"Impossible, you would outshine them regardless darling. Embrace your beauty, it's a strength."

When she put it that way, Metztli was more than prepared to be pampered to perfection. If beauty was a strength, she wanted to look as beautiful as she could possibly be tonight.

ACALAN

Acalan was glad for the opportunity to escape his sister and mother. Even if it was only for a moment. He hadn't yet considered that his sister would be able to see through him, making him feel like he was somehow made of glass and not flesh and blood.

Between the Tournament of Heirs, a prophecy he still didn't know what to make of, and the need to protect his sister, it was all too much. For a moment it felt as if he was drowning in his worries. Which was not a very comforting feeling to have in the middle of a bath.

He'd always been a terrible liar. There was no need for that skill when their father had been given a gift to tell the truth from lies. It had been a strange gift to receive from the gods upon winning the Tournament of Heirs, but it had served his father well.

He had to lie now though. It was that, or try to explain something to Metztli that he didn't quite understand himself. It didn't help that Atzi was willing to tell him so little.

When she'd explained it to him, she'd been so short with her words. It was almost as if she was worried there was someone listening to them, waiting to pounce from the shadows and punish them for even speaking of the prophecy.

However, there had been relief in her eyes, too. Acalan supposed that it felt good to finally share her secret with another after having held it for so many years alone.

Citlalic was admittedly a nice distraction from all of this. Acalan knew it was wrong to think of anyone outside of his family, especially with the tournament nearing, but he couldn't help it. He felt an utter pull to the woman.

It was silly really, they'd only spoken once, and on that occasion Acalan hadn't even actually spoken. Instead he'd just stood by, admiring her from afar, wishing the tournament was just a bad dream instead of a reality that cast them worlds apart.

A dance couldn't be of harm though, not if his mother and sister had both encouraged it.

The prince allowed himself to be somber about the whole situation for a minute more, sinking into the water and letting it cover him entirely. He held his breath for a little while before letting it go slowly, watching the bubbles rise and disappear at the surface of the water.

Time seemed to go by slower when he was beneath the water instead of above it. That was comforting but the sudden burn in his lungs from the lack of oxygen in his body was not, so he rose back to the surface to face his reality.

Once he was thoroughly clean and prepared to face his mother and sister again, Acalan quickly dried himself before throwing on a fluffy robe and making his way to open the door.

He only stopped because the strangest of sounds halted his movements. Acalan pressed his ear against the wooden door, to make sure he was hearing things correctly.

His mother and Metztli were *laughing* together. It was sweet, he couldn't remember the last time he'd heard such a thing.

Acalan enjoyed the sound for a little while longer before he finally opened the door and stepped through it.

Metztli was fully dressed in a teal and gold gown cut into two pieces. She looked beautiful and lethal all at once, which was a strange sight but, then again, he did suppose that the most beautiful things in life were often the most deadly. Metztli seemed very happy, so he supposed that was a win in itself.

"Sounds like you two are having fun here without me," Acalan teased with a slight pout.

He was only feigning jealousy of course. In fact, for many years Acalan had wished that his mother and sister would spend more time together. It seemed like the right thing to do when their time together was so limited.

He wasn't quite sure, but after meeting the heirs from the other six houses, he was willing to wager that Metztli was among the youngest who would be competing.

"Mother is letting me drink pulque! But not too much though or I'll tip over walking up the steps of the great hall if I do!" Metztli beamed. By the sight of her he could tell his sister had already had enough of the sweet alcoholic beverage for one night.

It was tradition though. The beverage itself was fermented from agave plants nurtured and grown in their very home.

"Oh? Is that so? Well then, perhaps you've had enough for now."

He almost giggled when Metztli's expression changed. Her eyes narrowed and she lifted the drink above her head, unwilling to give it up.

"Absolutely not! I've barely had any!" Metztli argued, getting up from her seat.

She was in no way planning to give it away without at least a little bit of a fight. Acalan had a better plan, though, and it would surely resolve this all much quicker than fighting would.

"Hand it over or I'll tell mom that you're already half drunk and then she'll take it away!" Acalan threatened in a whisper.

They were bickering like children. It wasn't a useful way to use their time, but it was fun. Acalan supposed that they needed a little of that right now considering the situation they were in.

Unfortunately the bickering was over before it really ever started. His mother snuck behind Metztli and took the cup out of Metztli's hands herself. Metztli whined like a child, but it was okay, she could have some later when the pressure of being presented in front of the masses was over.

"You wouldn't want to spill any on your dress now would you?" Xara spoke softly.

Metztli pouted once again before sitting back down in her chair and crossing her arms over her chest like a child who had just been scolded for eating too many sweets in one sitting.

"Now you!" His mother turned, scolding him next. "Go get dressed, we're running late and we still need to paint heir markings on the both of you!"

Acalan raised his arms in defeat before taking the clothing his mother handed him.

He dressed as quickly as he could and was able to slip into his skirt without any issue, but found himself tangled in the gold sash.

Yesterday he'd been given an extra layer to wear underneath the sash but today he was going bare chested. If they were trying to stand out this would certainly do the trick. After a few more minutes of trying to properly place the sash on his body, Acalan gave up and slipped out of the dressing room in search of his mother.

"Help?" Acalan's voice rang through the room, causing both his mother and Metztli to turn around in unison.

Metztli whistled and clapped at the sight of him, taunting him for how little clothing he was wearing. If it had been up to Acalan he would have chosen something far more modest, but he trusted his mother with these sorts of things. And from the quick glance he got in the mirror, he couldn't deny that he did look quite remarkable.

"You can hit birds straight between their eyes with your bow but you can't figure out how to wrap your sash?" his mother asked teasingly as she approached him to fix the fabric twisted over his limbs.

He didn't take the comment seriously, of course. If anything he knew that his mother enjoyed doing things like this. It was so rare when they had occasions where she could pamper them. Most holidays were celebrated at home, and the ones that were not, did not require elegant clothing like this.

He wondered how different he and Metztli's experiences were to the other heirs, and hoped that their isolation would somehow work in their favor in the end.

"That's not fair, I've been doing that my entire life," Acalan argued in return. "This is the first time I've ever had to wear something like this. Is this even appropriate for the celebration? I feel a bit…naked."

Metztli laughed, which caused Acalan to give her a knowing stare. Tipsy or not, she needed to control herself. Metztli was safe to be herself in the privacy of the dressing room, but once the celebration started they would need to be very careful about how they presented themselves.

"I assure you this is quite appropriate." Xara said. "When your father participated in his own tournament, most of the male heirs were presented completely bare from the waist up. If anything this is a bit reversed…perhaps we should take it off?"

"No!" Acalan responded quickly. "No need, it's umm…it's nice I think…It might be chilly tonight so we best not risk it. Wouldn't want to catch a cold right before the tournament!"

Metztli raised an eyebrow at him, which reminded the prince once again that he could hide nothing from her — at least not for very long.

"It's the middle of summer, Acalan. It will not be chilly. And besides, what if Citlalic wants to see a little skin?" Metztli asked, wiggling her eyebrows suggestively.

Now Acalan was the one raising an eyebrow in confusion.

"Well in that case perhaps you should go topless as well! Necalli seemed very much interested in you. I've never spoken to Citlalic, so she could very well hate me for all I know" Acalan

responded, the latter of his words left a bitter taste in his mouth.

He continued, "Necalli on the other hand — terrible intentions I'm sure, but there's no denying he would enjoy the sight."

It was still a little difficult to believe that Necalli had truly been so bold to taunt Metztli the way he had. Perhaps it was acceptable to speak to women in the House of Blood like that, but it was not in Tu'nethe. Acalan just hoped that Necalli would be able to keep his mouth shut for the evening.

"You think that low of me brother?" Metztli asked with an exaggerated gasp.

In this tipsy state she was so animated that he couldn't help but laugh at her.

"That boy is trouble, I could practically smell it on him!" Their mother said as she finished laying the sash over Acalan's chest. "But he is very handsome. I fear I would have been very intrigued as a young woman."

He'd forgotten that it was supposed to form a cross over his upper half. It wasn't the most ideal garb, but he was quite happy with it. Besides, it was better than being bare chested for everyone to see.

"Well I am intrigued, mother. Don't get me wrong. It's just that I'm intrigued to stab him with the pointy end of my spear and nothing else!" Metztli said, followed by a deep laugh.

"Very funny Metztli, but I'm afraid it's that very attitude that intrigues men like Necalli. The more dis-interested you are, the more they want you," their mother explained.

Hearing their mother speak of men in general was a bit strange. Their mother and father had been hopelessly in love for as long as Acalan remembered. He supposed that he'd just never considered that perhaps his mother had lived an entire life before marrying their father — one that might have taught her all these little things about how men behaved.

"Well he'd be terribly mistaken if he actually believed I would willingly give him any of my time." Metztli replied. "Besides, he's a rival, nothing else, it would serve him well to remember that."

"Oh I think you did a very good job of reminding him of that earlier, darling. He's got a big long scratch on his left cheek to prove it." Their mother turned, beginning to prepare the turquoise paste that would paint their skin in just a few moments.

Acalan smiled softly as he noted the soft blush on his sister's cheeks.

"You should have seen her, mom! It was like she turned into a predator, fully committed to catching her prey! Seriously, Metztli you went ballistic. You might not be proud of how you behaved but you did us a favor. The other heirs and the few members of the families who were present were terrified of you."

Metztli's smile got even brighter, which in turn made Acalan smile, too. Their day hadn't started out very well. In fact, it had probably been the worst morning of his life, but he would experience it all over again if he could have these moments with his mother and sister.

"Alright, alright, enough talk about predators and prey. It's time to start painting. Do you both want something unique or would you like to match one another?" their mother asked.

It wasn't something that Acalan had considered before this very moment, but the answer seemed obvious.

"Match." Both Amos siblings responded quickly without second thought.

They were in this together, until the very end, until they returned home to their mother and father.

Metztli

Metztli was not tipsy or drunk, despite her brother's claims. It was, however, entertaining to watch Acalan keep a close eye on her while they waited to be called upon in the comfort of the dressing parlor.

It had been at least an hour since their mother had finished painting the heir markings on their skin with a careful hand. A hundred years ago these markings would have been placed on their skin with bone and ink.

Metztli thought that was slightly barbaric, and it sounded painful. Besides, in her mind she didn't deserve to be permanently marked until she returned home with Acalan by her side. It was only then that she would consider taking true markings, much like her father's to show her standing in their family.

Still, she'd happily sat down while her mother painted a turquoise peak down her forehead, followed by similar triangular markings on both of her cheeks. Lastly, Xara drew a long stripe from her bottom lip to where the fabric of her dress covered her chest.

These were temporary and ornamental, but the markings she would take if she returned home victorious would be forever.

Markings were intended to demonstrate one's achievements. Her father had more than a few from all the time he'd spent as an emperor. Their mother had three of her own — one for each of her children.

The marking she'd taken when Acalan was born was displayed on Xara's right shoulder. By all accounts, Acalan's birth had been easy and smooth. It had happened in a river near their home. This was most traditional for high born women in Mexica. In honor of her first born son, Xara had waves inked into her skin. They were beautiful, and meant a great deal to their mother.

The one for Metztli was slightly bigger than the one Xara had gotten when Acalan was born. Only because by all accounts Metztli's birth had been far more difficult. She'd been born in the middle of the night and during a great winter storm, so naturally her parents had named her after the goddess of the moon and night. The marking itself indicated this —a moon with twinkling stars surrounding it. Her mother wore it with great pride.

The last birth had ended in tragedy, but Xara had memorialized it on her body as well, marking her left wrist with a pair of wings. It seemed fitting considering that she'd nearly died before springing back to life.

Metztli didn't feel like she'd done enough to earn any true markings yet though. Some heirs were marked simply because they'd been born into their position, but that couldn't be enough to justify receiving a mark.

Necalli had more than a few on his body, for what exactly? Metztli didn't even want to start imagining what the vertical messy lines on his right arm were meant to represent. They weren't beautiful, not like the markings on her mother's body, but the princess couldn't imagine that what he'd done to receive them was beautiful either.

The House of Blood was known for all sorts of things, but most of all they were known for their blood sacrifices and rituals. One had to be some level of cruel in order to take part in such things. At least, that's what Metztli believed.

"Don't touch your face!" Acalan snapped, stealing her away from her thoughts.

This wasn't the first time in the last hour that he'd had to remind her. His raised tone still managed to catch her off guard though, causing her to jump slightly in her chair.

She didn't even realize she was raising her hand to brush her cheek, all that she knew was that it was itchy, and she was getting sick of waiting to be called upon. Hadn't their mother said they were in a hurry?

"Do we really have to be presented last? Seems a little unfair considering the celebration is being held in OUR home." Metztli complained with a huff as she slumped in her chair and crossed her arms against her chest. "This paint is starting to get itchy, and I'm tired and hungry."

She could tell from the look on her brother's face that he agreed — he just wouldn't say so out loud. It was moments like this that made Metztli grateful that she wasn't the primary heir of the House of Life. She still had to be respectful, but for the most part she could get away with saying all sorts of things.

Hell, she'd gotten away with attacking one of the competing heirs just that afternoon. She wouldn't trade that freedom to be closer to her father's throne.

"It's the right thing to do as hosts." Acalan warned. "The paint will be less itchy when it dries all the way, but you'll have to sit through mother applying it from scratch if you keep trying to touch it so just stay still."

He had a point, but that didn't stop Metztli from sighing again, this time even more dramatically.

She never really understood why they had to host the other families. If the gods could magically make the Pyramid of Tributes appear, couldn't they also find some way of housing everyone, instead of shoving them all in the last champion's home?

"Since when did you get so bossy?" Metztli asked with a raised brow.

Acalan had been so quiet and shy when they'd been children. It was a shame that she couldn't recall the exact moment when that had changed and he'd become who he is now — still Acalan at his core, but far less timid than he used to be.

"Since you got rebellious," Acalan responded.

On any other day she would have continued to bicker with him, but just sitting in the dressing parlor without anything to do had made her tired. So much so that she simply blew off her brother's response and fought back a yawn.

Their mother had left a while ago, promising to return when it was time for the ceremony to begin. It was taking too long though, and if it took any longer, their mother would walk in to witness Metztli taking a nap.

"Do you think Atzi will be all dressed up tonight? I can't remember the last time I saw that woman without her veil," Metztli said.

She already knew the answer, but she was trying to spark up any conversation that would keep her awake. She watched her brother carefully and noted the slight wave of panic came over his face at the mention of the priestess.

Metztli had suspected that he was hiding something, but after seeing that, she knew it for sure.

"Probably not…perhaps though, she may want to look nice just in case the gods make an appearance," Acalan responded, stumbling over his words.

Metztli was careful not to change the expression on her face. It was better if he wasn't aware of how curious she was about the time he had spent with Atzi earlier. There was a skill to this sort of thing. Metztli believed she was good at interrogating someone, but she'd only really tested her tactics on her brother. Luckily he was the only person she wanted answers from at this moment.

"Do you think the gods are well preserved? Or very ugly?" she wondered aloud, changing the topic of their conversation just enough so that her brother would drop his guard enough that she could ask a more revealing question. "I feel like the portraits we've seen of them do them far too much justice. It wouldn't be fair if they were immortal *and* gorgeous."

"Well, nothing about life is really fair is it?" her brother responded quickly. "They probably are immortal and gorgeous all at once. How else would they be able to hold so much power over us?" His tone was far more bitter than she had expected it to be.

"Wow…for a moment there it sounded like you dislike the gods as much as I do. Has something changed, brother?" Metztli questioned as casually as she could.

Her tone was toeing the line between playful and interrogative. She was so close to getting answers, she just needed to play her cards perfectly and Acalan would hand them over without much thought.

They were both silent for a moment. She tried not to stare too intently. His gaze dropped to his hands. He was fidgeting with his heir ring, which could only mean he was nervous.

"Everything changes when you're this close to handing your destiny to the gods," he asserted.

The response wasn't nearly as clear as Metztli had hoped for. She knew whatever he was hiding from her was far more than just nervous jitters.

"I think you mean fate, Acalan," she said, correcting her brother. "Destiny is predetermined. We were destined to be heirs of this house. We had no choice in that but fate is ours to do whatever we wish with."

It felt strange to correct her brother like this. For someone who spent the majority of his time with a book in his hands, it was odd that he didn't know the true definitions of these words.

"You wound me. I know the difference between fate and destiny. I meant what I said," Acalan responded, turning his gaze from the ring on his finger to meet Metztli's eyes.

That couldn't be right, though. Was her brother actually implying that the tournament was predetermined in some way? That couldn't possibly be true. The tournament was a pure spectacle of entertainment for the gods — how could the outcome already be decided?

"Is there something you know that I don't know about this tournament, Acalan?" Metztli questioned.

She knew her brother well enough to know he wanted to tell her. Why else would he reveal his true thoughts about the tournament? When he didn't respond, she couldn't help but question Atzi's involvement in all of this. Was it the priestess who kept him from revealing whatever he knew?

"Whatever it is, you can tell me. I'm your sister. I've always been your secret keeper. Did I suddenly lose my title without knowing?"

Metztli added, breaking the tension between them.

The silence that followed was so tangible that Metztli thought she might be able to reach out and physically touch it. She knew, without a shadow of a doubt that there was something he wanted to say but was too scared to. But what could possibly be worse than the tournament itself?

"Acalan!! Metztli!!" Their mother's voice suddenly beamed through the dressing parlor. "The ceremony is starting! I must say, I managed to take a peak at a few of the other heirs and they all looked very handsome and beautiful, but none quite as striking as both of you."

Metztli had no choice but to stand from where she was sitting and pretend to be as excited as her mother was. Her conversation with Acalan was far from finished, but they had duties to attend to.

"I'm willing to wager it's because none of them have a mother nearly as committed as you," Metztli said, saving them both from a line of questioning from their mother.

It was easy enough to do considering that Metztli felt her words to be true. She knew that her mother viewed their family's lack of heirs as a flaw of her own, but Metztli did not, nor did her father or brother. Big families were traditional amongst the high born families, but being a small family is what had allowed them to bloom with one another.

They weren't a perfect family by any means, but Metztli would have bet anything that they were far closer than most.

"It's true, mother," Acalan chimed in. "There is no mother more dedicated and loving than you amongst the houses."

The panic and hesitation from before was gone now. It left Metztli curious, but now was not the time to press her brother again.

Tiny tears formed in their mother's eyes. She might have not given the House of Life a handful of heirs, but Xara had loved her children. Her entire life had been dedicated to caring for them, to loving them unconditionally. What more could a family ask for?

"You two flatter me far more than I deserve," she said with a bright smile. "Being your mother has been the greatest pleasure of my life, and it will continue to be when you both return home. Now, let us show the other houses the greatness of our family, yes?"

Metztli nodded in response. She imagined that her brother did quite the same, but she didn't have a moment to look back at him before they were walking through the hallways of their now lively home.

The conversation she'd been having with her brother was still heavy on her mind, but she needed to push those emotions aside from now. She'd been waiting what felt like her entire life to truly know who she would be competing against, and aside from the House of Flor and the House of Blood, there was still so much to discover about the other heirs.

Regardless of who was presented at the ceremony, it would bring her relief to simply know who she would be fighting. Knowledge was currency unlike anything else, and Metztli wanted to be rich with it, she had to be because she had every intention of returning home with her brother.

Winning was the only option for them.

Acalan was wrong, this wasn't a matter of destiny.

It was their fate.

ACALAN

Acalan had never been more grateful to see his mother. In truth, he would have revealed much more to Metztli if she hadn't returned. And then his oath of secrecy with Atzi would have been void. He would have told Metztli whatever she wanted to know, even if that meant betraying the trust Atzi had placed with him.

Even as they walked through their palace, Acalan knew there was no escaping the truth now. It was only a matter of time before his sister found another opportunity to continue her interrogation, and Acalan wasn't sure that he would be able to keep the information that he knew to himself.

The lively music being played in the great hall grew louder as they neared the entrance. There were people everywhere — not just the people of Tu'nethe, but also those who had come in celebration from the other houses, too.

Crowds of giddy people made it appear like there was a rainbow sea in front of the prince. He could only tell the royals apart from common folk by the outrageous amount of gold and silver they wore.

Then again, Acalan knew he was also wearing an abundant amount of gold jewelry as well.

There were a few familiar faces in the crowd. This should have been comforting, but Acalan didn't feel that way when he caught the eye of the oldest male heir from the House of Wind. The prince could not recall his name, but there was a distinct look of arrogance on his face that made him recognizable.

His gaze swept across the room, settling on the family from the House of Rain, all huddled up together. There were so many of them, all dressed to the hilt in the most luxurious of clothing. It was impossible for Acalan to tell which ones were bastards and which ones were true-born heirs. He supposed that didn't matter at the end of the day. Bastards or not, they were enemies through and through.

In a strange way, it was beautiful seeing them all together. Acalan thought that perhaps this is how it always should have been. He knew from his history books that before the war this is exactly how the people of Mexica had lived. There were no such things as houses before. They'd been a united front but that's exactly what had made them so dangerous in the first place, wasn't it? For the gods, it was far more strategic to keep them separated. How else would the people of Mexica become so reliant on the gods and their resources?

Whether it was the promise of a good harvest or gold, the gods provided for their houses when they felt like it. The House of Blood was proof of that contingency.

"It's beautiful isn't it?" their mother asked over the noise.

He turned to his sister and she seemed equally mesmerized by it all. He wasn't surprised though, the prophecy said she would flourish under this environment.

Acalan wasn't sure if he should be scared or relieved. The latter was better though, so he decided to settle with those emotions instead.

"I've never seen the palace so full of people!" Metztli exclaimed with a bright smile on her face.

He could feel the gazes of their guests on them, but it didn't bother Acalan as much as it would have on any other occasion. It was difficult to be bothered when his sister was busy lighting up the room.

"It is indeed," their mother said, beckoning them to follow her. "The last time it was this full was twenty-five years ago when your father entered the tournament with his brother. Now come along, your father is waiting for us."

From her eyes Acalan could tell she was reminiscing about those earlier days when she'd a young woman, hoping and praying that her beloved would return home. Now she was a mother wishing for her children to return. It was an outrageous thing to promise, but somehow he just knew they would, they had to. They couldn't leave their mother childless.

Besides, destiny had plans for Metztli.

Plans he had to ensure were fulfilled.

Acalan followed along after his mother, looking back every few moments to ensure Metztli was still following closely behind them. They'd never been in a crowd this large, and there was a sudden fear that he would somehow lose her amid the chaos of the party. Metztli was smart though, Acalan knew that.

When their father came into sight, Acalan almost didn't recognize him. Tenoch looked more regal than he'd ever had. He was dressed in a similar style of clothing to what Acalan was wearing. Something about the similarities in their clothing filled Acalan with pride. Not because of his title as the primary heir of their house, but because he was Tenoch's son and that meant something, titles or not.

Their father's heir mark on his chest was visible through the golden sash he wore. He typically hid the marking of a bright sun and its rays on his skin, but he was purposely bearing it for everyone to see now.

It served as a reminder to the other houses that he'd won twenty-five years ago. He'd killed and fought valiantly to win, and now his children would do the same. Whether it actually instilled fear in the other houses, Acalan was unsure, but he desperately needed it to.

"Just in time! The ceremony is about to begin. The houses will be present from the most distant to Tu'nethe, starting with the House of Blood and then ending with us," their father started explaining.

Acalan did his best to listen despite the distracting crowd surrounding them. It was a shame how little he actually knew about what this ceremony really entailed.

"It goes by far quicker than you think, so stay attentive and watch closely," their father continued. "When it's our turn to present, you do not have to say anything. You will simply stand by me as my heirs. I should have briefed you both on this before but the day has been a bit hectic. Do not worry, everything will be just fine. Now sit. And regardless of who is presented, do not show any fear, is it them who should fear you." He beckoned for them to sit.

Their seats were closest to the steps of the stage where his father's throne typically lived but it was gone for the celebration. The sight was slightly eerie, only because it was a sight Acalan hoped wouldn't remain for long.

Acalan knew this was a part of the entertainment factor of the tournament, but it served them strategically. Once they knew exactly who they would be competing against, they'd be able to strategize better. The first borns were a given, and they knew that Necalli's cousin Coatl and the younger sister from the House of Flor would compete. But that still left three heirs to be revealed.

"Are you nervous?" Acalan turned to ask his sister. "It looks like the gods will not be making an appearance after all."

She didn't look at him, but he knew that Metztli was good at hiding her feelings. She could be harboring so much emotion and still look stone cold.

"No, none of them can really be worse than the sisters from the House of Flor," she said. "If we're lucky they'll just all kill each other within the first few hours and then we'll just be left fending a few more off. And the gods, well, for their safety they should stay away too."

Acalan wasn't surprised by his sister's response, Metztli had always been braver than him.

"Do you think they'll be scared when they see us?" he asked.

The question was genuine. He didn't think of himself as being intimidating at all. Metztli, on the other hand, did have an intimidating aura about her. It was like she could strike at any given moment, so perhaps the other heirs would be scared of her and, in turn, be scared of him as well.

"They're at least curious about us," she mused. "They would have to be after we skipped training this morning, and then there was the courtyard incident. That might have been enough for them to truly think of us as competitors."

All of the families had been seated at random throughout the front half of the room, while the common folk sat towards the back. If the high-born families hadn't been wearing their house colors, it would have been almost impossible to spot them within the rows of chairs that were separated by an aisle.

That was, of course, meant for the chosen heirs to walk through and be displayed for everyone to see and judge them.

"They were certainly scared when you attacked Necalli," Acalan said. "He's lucky I was there to stop you, I think you could have really hurt him otherwise."

"I intend to once the tournament starts. I won't taunt him the way he taunted me, but if there's an opportunity then I will hurt him, and I won't think about it twice."

The idea of killing someone still made him want to crawl into his own skin, but he better understood now that it was simply what they had to do to survive. If it was between his sister's life or someone else's, Acalan was sure he wouldn't hesitate, but he would avoid taking a life like he avoided plague.

"I won't stop you," Acalan remarked.

Metztli's expression did not change but he could see the relief in her eyes and he knew he was to blame for that. If he hadn't been so cruel to her the day before, then she wouldn't fear his judgment. She didn't have to be scared though. They were both just doing what they could to survive.

"I have my eyes on the younger sister from the House of Flor too," Metztli continued. "The one who said your blood would taste sweet and mine bitter."

Acalan's brow furrowed. He would support his sister, but he was still taken aback at the fact that it seemed like she had a mental list of everyone she intended to get her hands on, or more accurately, stick her spear through.

Acalan was relieved when his father stood from where he'd been sitting at the end of their row, and raised the signal for the music to stop. The great hall went quiet as their father walked up the steps to where his throne was usually placed. It had been moved for the ceremony, but that didn't matter, he could still command a room without it.

The golden crown sitting on his father's head didn't falter for a single moment. He held his chest and chin high, and in that moment he was not their loving father — the man who had taught Acalan how to make his own arrows, or who had spent hours teaching Metztli how to properly grip her spear.

He was the man who ruled over all of them.

For the most part, the houses were left to their own devices, but it was their father who allowed it to be that way and it was Acalan who would keep it so when his time to reign came.

The crowd was suddenly clapping. Acalan had been so lost in his thoughts that he'd missed his father's speech entirely. Whatever Tenoch had said didn't really matter though, Acalan could tell that everyone in the room had been reminded of the reality they lived in. He could also tell that the other houses were hungry for power.

Power that Acalan was unwilling to give. Power that belonged to their house. Power that Metztli would someday need if the prophecy was true.

"Ugh…could they have worn something more gaudy?" Metztli whispered, prompting Acalan's gaze to move from their father to Necalli, his cousin Coatl, and the emperor of the House of Blood.

Metztli was right, they had certainly made an attempt to make a statement with their wardrobe. Their skirts were cut right above their knees and the fabric was so red it almost looked like it had been soaked in real blood. Maybe it had — he wouldn't put the House of Blood above doing something like that.

"I thought the House of Blood had an abundance of silver, not gold?" Acalan questioned as he watched them walk up the aisle and begin to climb the steps.

They radiated a sense of confidence that filled Acalan with rage. This wasn't an emotion that he was used to, but he welcomed it. He welcomed anything that might help him push through the tournament.

"A jab at father I'm sure. It must have cost them plenty," Metztli remarked.

With as many rituals and sacrifices as the House of Blood committed, they should have been the most plentiful amongst the houses, but they were not. Eztli, the Goddess of Blood, was known for her cruelty, so perhaps it wasn't that surprising that the House of Blood lacked wealth.

"Do you think those marks on their right arms are related to the rituals they've been a part of?" Metztli asked.

It hadn't occurred to Acalan that they were, but now that Metztli had mentioned it, they probably did correspond to just that.

"Maybe…don't let that scare you, most of their victims are willing. It'll be different when they're being attacked at the same time."

He should have been afraid, but he couldn't find it in himself to be. Whatever they were to face, they would face it together, and together they could be unstoppable.

Yaotl Cruz, the Emperor of the House of Blood stood before the crowd while Necalli and Coatl took their places behind him. The man seemed to bloom under the attention he was given but that didn't surprise Acalan, considering what his father had shared about the man with his children.

Yaotl started by thanking their father and naming him a gracious host. It seemed more sarcastic than genuine, but Acalan imagined that the House of Blood was still bitter over the House of Life maintaining their reign for the last fifty years.

"I won't bore you all with a long speech regarding why my heirs will triumph over the others within the Pyramid of Tributes," the emperor said. "Their actions will speak for themselves." Suddenly it was no surprise that Necalli radiated arrogance the way he did.

"Many of you know them already, but for the few of you that don't, I will formally introduce them. My first heir and first born son, Necalli Cruz. He is mighty and I'm sure the rest of you will agree." Yaotl stepped to the side slightly so that his son could truly bask in his ten seconds of glory.

"My second heir is my nephew, Coatl Cruz. His father was taken from us during the last Tournament of Heirs. I have raised him since he was a boy and that makes him as good as a son. Coatl seeks redemption, and redemption he will find." The emperor turned his gaze to find Metztli and Acalan in the roaring crowd.

The House of Blood seemed to be well practiced in the art of intimidation, but Acalan couldn't let their aggressions bother him. The moment he allowed their intimidation to work, was the moment that he and Metztli would lose the Tournament of Heirs, and that was not something Acalan was prepared to allow.

The crowd continued cheering for the House of Blood as they

were ushered down the steps and back down the aisle. A familiar voice rang through Acalan's ears, causing him to turn slightly in his chair. There she was.

Citlalic Cruz was the most beautiful woman Acalan had ever seen. Even now as she wore a blood red gown embellished in gold, he was certain there was no beauty like her. Every thought of the tournament drifted away swiftly. He could only think of her fine features and how desperately he wanted to see them up close.

He wanted to know everything about her, what books she enjoyed reading, if she preferred tea or xocoatl in the morning. Given the chance he would give her anything she could ever want, a tower of chocolate, a home full of gold embellishments…

"You're drooling again," Metztli remarked, interrupting his thoughts.

"She's marvelous," Acalan whispered in return.

He was sure his desires were unrequited. He'd never even spoken a word to Citlalic, and even if he returned home, how would he seek the woman out? How would he explain all of the terrible things he'd had to do to win?

"She'd be a fool not to want you," Metztli said, as if reading his thoughts.

Time after time, Metztli somehow found a way to comfort him without even knowing his worries.

"Time will tell." Acalan said.

Despite his desires, he knew better than to excite himself with such possibilities. It was far more likely that the woman would hate him after all of this, than for her to desire him as well. Life couldn't possibly be completely unfair though and maybe, just maybe she too felt pulled to him.

Destiny was inevitable.

And if it somehow pulled them towards one another, then Acalan would happily welcome that possibility with open arms.

METZTLI

Metztli knew better than to encourage her brother in his romantic endeavors but a part of her simply could not stop herself. She had never seen Acalan so mesmerized by anything or anyone.

Citlalic was beautiful, there was no doubt about it. The fabric of her dress hugged her hips tightly, exposing her figure in a way that was modest but revealing all at once. The woman would have been alluring to any man by her looks alone, but Metztli could tell it was more than that with Acalan.

Citlalic was sweet and gentle. Metztli knew this from the way she observed the princess embrace her father, Necalli, and Coatl once they were back in their seats. The action was not full of pride or arrogance, but love. A gentle heart was exactly what her brother would need in a wife someday.

That is, if they returned home.

Until then, Metztli had to pull her brother back into the ceremony. This was important. While they already knew who would be competing for the House of Blood and House of Flor, they were still in the dark about who would be fighting for the House of Serpent. This house wasn't known for their physical abilities. In fact, as they walked through the crowd, dressed in emerald green and silver, nothing about them looked very frightening.

Both men were lean but lacked strength. Metztli recognized the first born heir from being introduced to him but was surprised to find the man who followed him. The wrinkles on the man's face told her that he was far older, perhaps an uncle or older cousin. He walked up the steps behind the younger heir with his chest held high and hands bundled into fists.

It looked like he was scared, and he should be.

Age brought wisdom but he would never be nearly as quick or mentally agile as the rest of them. That was something definitely worthy of fear.

It was typical for the houses to choose two men, though in truth Metztli found that tradition to be a bit laughable. It wasn't like whatever she had in between her legs dictated her strength or her ability to kill.

In a tournament like this one, what mattered was a combination of physical and mental strength. Technique could only push you so far, but inner strength and having the ability to push oneself beyond what they believed to be their limit. That's what made a winner.

The two heirs were presented swiftly. She'd been right in assuming the companion was an uncle. The man had to have already celebrated his thirtieth name day at least. Experience like that could be difficult to defeat, but she could also tell by the way he looked at the crowd before dropping his gaze back to his feet, that the man was frightened and fear placed a limit on how much someone could do.

Regardless, if they met face to face, Metztli had no doubt that the man would underestimate her and her strength both mentally and physically. This was something that Metztli had grown accustomed to when it came to men.

That was fine. She was happy to prove them all wrong.

The House of Rain went next. Once again, two men wearing a dark shade of blue walked down the aisle behind their father. Metztli recognized them both to be bastard sons of the emperor. Even if she hadn't recognized them, the way that they walked with smiles on their faces, happily waving at the crowds would have been more than enough of an indicator that they weren't used to being displayed like this.

Being bastards made them dangerous. They had so much to prove and knowing that they already brought shame to their family was probably enough for them to want to do something to remedy that.

Besides, out of all the royal houses in Mexica, the House of Rain was most known for causing trouble. The royal family was beyond impulsive. On more than one occasion her father had stepped in to end battles between the House of Rain and many other houses, including the House of Life itself.

Impulsiveness was a good trait to compete against though. Being impulsive only meant that they were weak minded and immature. Metztli could handle that — she was sure of it.

Each time a house presented their heirs, Metztli watched as her brother turned around in his chair under the guise that he was studying the tributes chosen to compete. But Metztli knew the truth. If she asked her brother what the heirs had been wearing she was sure he wouldn't be able to recall. But if she asked him which hand the gold band that Citlalic was wearing was on, he would no doubt respond instantly.

She wanted to be angry with Acalan for not paying attention, but she couldn't find it within herself to be. So she let him admire Citlalic from afar. That is, until the House of Wind stood from their seats and made the long walk to the makeshift stage in front of them.

Unlike the others, the House of Wind was presenting a male and female heir. They were siblings — Metztli remembered that from when she'd met them the day before. They walked side by side, keeping their gazes forward, ignoring the crowd and the families that they passed. It was a bit unnatural how in sync they were with their father. Even Metztli and Acalan hadn't quite perfected that.

"Pay attention to these two," she whispered to her brother as the pair drew closer.

If she was going to be truly scared of anyone it would have to be the House of Wind. They weren't terribly strong by any means, but the House of Wind was known for their inventions and intelligence. They were amongst the more wealthy houses too, which gave them all of the resources they needed to win the tournament if they so wished.

It was never known how the House of Wind would do in these tournaments, at least that's what Metztli had gathered from her conversations with her father. One thing was certain though: they were hungry for power. A natural consequence of spending centuries under the reign of another house.

Metztli could see as much from the way the older heir caught her eyes as he settled upon the stage behind his father. The moment had been brief, but she could tell from the way he'd held her gaze that he intended to do whatever it took to win.

They were dressed far differently than the other houses. While everyone else had worn traditional Aztec clothing with matching colors as their home banners, The brother and sister from the House of Wind had donned what Metztli recognized to be pants.

She'd seen them before on occasion when merchants came into the city offering new fashions, but Metztli found them to be unnecessary, beyond that they looked funny and she had no clue how she was supposed to move fluidly in something that constricted her legs. So, she always declined the merchants when they'd offered them to her.

The tops of their outfits were funny looking, too. The fabric was so orange that Metztli felt like she might go blind if she looked at it for too long. They were both wearing practically the same thing. The fabric clung on to their necks tightly before bellowing out as it went further down their body. It was see-through enough that Metztli could tell they both had taken heir marks.

This didn't bother her, while her body remained untouched by ink and bone, they'd taken a mark that didn't really belong to them quite yet. They would regret it later when their bodies were being set into their graves.

When someone died in the tournament, they weren't really heirs anymore. They were sacred amongst the houses of course, but they were fallen heirs regardless. Just people who could have been but never had the opportunity to be.

"I have waited twenty-five years to stand before you all today," the emperor began, "and in those twenty-five years, I've had more than enough time to prepare my heirs for the tournament they will face in the coming days. I have no doubt that this generation of heirs will bring change to the House of Wind. We will know power once again." His people drank in his words as a promise.

But in Metztli's eyes that was plain stupid: anyone who was half competent knew better than to promise something like that.

"Twenty-five years has also given us the time to develop a new weapon, something never seen before, something that will surely aid my heirs within the Pyramid of Tributes," the man continued. "I'm afraid I cannot reveal it now as that would spoil all the fun, but I am honored to present my heirs before you." As he named each of them, he stepped aside.

The crowd roared once again and the heirs from the House of Wind walked back down the aisle. Metztli could not deny that she was nervous now. This weapon could be anything, and she would likely not know what it was until she was face to face with these heirs.

Metztli quickly decided it was probably best to avoid them as much as they could within the Pyramid of Tributes. Everyone would be at each other's throats anyway, so with a little bit of luck, the brother and sister from the House of Wind would be taken out before Metztli and Acalan even had the opportunity to meet them face to face.

"I bet Nenetl would have a few choice words about their garments," Acalan teased, breaking Metztli's concentration.

"If you ever see me wearing pants, shoot an arrow through one of my legs," Metztli responded, with the smallest glint of laughter, causing her mother to turn and offer her a knowing look that said, *stop fooling around or else.*

Metztli smiled in return. One burst of laughter was enough, she'd had her fun. The House of Flor would present their heirs next, and then it would be their turn to walk up the aisle and steps to be presented by their father.

"If the demon sisters turn to look at us, keep a straight face," Metztli whispered softly, the playfulness in her tone still present. "Remember they're out for blood."

But the more Metztli had thought about it throughout the day, the more she realized that neither of them were likely good fighters. Why else would they need to do something as extreme as carve their teeth into pointy peaks?

Metztli had never even considered doing so but it was because she knew she was lethal with her weapon. She'd caught plenty of boars and deer in her life all with her spear, and hunting a person couldn't really be that different right? At least, she desperately hoped so.

"Is that even allowed?" Acalan questioned. "Mutilating your body for the tournament seems like an unfair advantage."

Metztli could sense the concern in his voice. She'd question the same thing, but the rules of the tournament were simple: Two blood bound heirs could enter the tournament together and leave together if they both remained alive.

Aside from that, each heir was allowed one cotton sack, all of the same size, and whatever they could fit in there aside from their weapon of choice. If their weapons were their bodies, then Metztli was sure that fell well within the rules.

"The gods will allow anything that they think would make for an entertaining tournament," Metztli answered. "I'm sure they're not the first to do this, maybe I should have replaced my fingers with blades"

She was only slightly confused when there was no response from her brother but as she followed his gaze and found the two sisters from the House of Flor walking through the crowd, along with their father Ohtli, Metztli went silent too.

They were wearing the most beautiful lavender silk sheaths, but they were barely covering their skin. Their lips were closed tightly, an intimidating line that was meant to place fear in the other heirs.

As they passed by they turned slightly to face Metztli and Acalan. They didn't actually look at Metztli, however. Instead, they kept their eyes fixed on her brother.

Metztli loathed them entirely. She understood that they were hungry for power, and she knew that it was likely that they were under pressure to win the tournament as well, but they shouldn't have chosen Metztli and her brother as their targets. They'd made a mistake in doing so because now Metztli viewed them as targets as well.

"Don't let them scare you," Metztli whispered so softly she was unsure if her brother even heard her. "They might have sharp teeth but their minds are weak. Trust me."

She wouldn't let these sisters get to his head. She needed him to be unphased if they were going to survive the tournament.

Acalan turned to look at her. She could tell that he was at least intimidated by them, but she could also see the feeling fade away as they kept their gaze on one another.

Good. As long as the feeling never stayed for too long, then they would be okay.

It wasn't long before Ohtli was speaking. Unlike the other emperors who had just presented their heirs, the man was pacing from one side to the stage to the other. He was truly making a spectacle of himself, but then again, the House of Flor did love attention.

"My daughters are unlike any of the heirs that have been presented before you today," Ohtli began. "Not only are they beautiful but they are also intelligent and fierce. The House of Flor has come close to winning the Tournament of Heirs many times, and while some of the emperors have stood before you today, making promises for victory, I am here to tell you that those promises will not be fulfilled." He paused next to Xochitl.

Metztli found it strange that there was so much pride interlaced with his words. Almost winning was not something to brag about, and his daughters, as fearsome as they may be, could not guarantee victory for the House of Flor.

"I have chosen my two oldest daughters to compete in the Tournament of Heirs. They have trained their entire lives, killed when it was requested of them, and on their own accord have made their bodies into weapons of mass mortality. It is my honor to present Xochitl and Atlatonan Flores as my chosen heirs." Ohtli beamed with pride.

The man was well spoken. That much was clear from the crowd's response, but if the sisters were about to reveal what Metztli thought they would, the cheering from the crowd would soon halt rapidly.

Xochitl and Atlatonan bowed slightly at the applause before standing straight again.

In almost perfect unison, both sisters opened their mouths. Not in a smile but in a hiss. They looked like animals, predators ready to attack. Those who could see that their teeth were sharpened into peaks gasped and a few let out fearful screams.

Metztli turned to look at her family. Her father looked unphased. It wasn't surprising after years of ruling over Mexica. She was sure that he'd seen sights that were far worse. She was surprised that her mother looked unphased by the display, too.

She had been expecting quite the opposite, but maybe their mother had also seen horrors throughout her years as an empress. Acalan looked shocked but she couldn't see an ounce of fear within him. She was proud of him.

Both sisters followed their father back down the aisle. They kept the same awful expression on their faces, revealing what they'd done to themselves to everyone. No one spoke or moved as they walked by, the lively hall went completely silent until they were back in their seats.

"Remember what I said." Their father turned to them, whispering before he kissed their mother on her cheek. "Be proud. You've both prepared for this moment even if you don't realize it"

Metztli nodded as she rose, quickly adjusting her garments. She might not have fangs for teeth or blades for fingers, but she was a force to be reckoned with and so was Acalan.

"Ready?" Metztli asked her brother softly, waiting for him to respond before making another move.

"I'm ready," her brother affirmed.

Metztli took a deep breath, enjoying the last moments before she was officially named heir in the Tournament.

ACALAN

Goosebumps formed on Acalan's skin as he rose from his seat. He knew this would be quick. He didn't have to do anything besides follow behind his father and keep a straight face, and yet, it felt like this was the most daunting moment in his life thus far.

Acalan kissed his mother on the cheek before following behind his father. Metztli did the same which put a gentle smile on their mother's face. Xara was keeping a brave face but Acalan knew she was suffering inside. She never spoke of it, but Acalan was aware that his mother felt like she'd failed their family somehow in only being able to provide two heirs.

Women in these empires were only expected to do one thing: Provide as many heirs as humanly possible, even if it meant endangering their own well being to do so.

Their father was a good man though. The best that Acalan had ever known. He was grateful that Tenoch had not allowed his wife to further harm herself in the process of trying to produce more heirs. Losing one child had been enough for the empire of the House of Life to draw the line.

Acalan knew from what he'd read about the House of Blood that Yaotl, their emperor, had not been nearly as wise when it came to his wife's desire to produce more heirs. The similarities between their houses were almost uncanny.

Both Yaotl and Tenoch had lost brother's in the tournament. Yaotl, too, had a son and a daughter as heirs, but in the pursuit for more, Yaotl had lost his wife and two unborn children. A tragedy to say the least — one that Acalan hoped he would never know himself.

The prince tried to shake those thoughts out of his mind as he walked down the aisle and up the steps. This felt far more natural than he thought it would, but, then again, he was in his own home.

His chest naturally lifted as he turned to face the crowd. There were so many unknown faces amongst the familiar ones and that was not nearly as comforting as it should have been. It was difficult to find any comfort at all when the prince knew he was being judged by every person present for the ceremony.

He turned his gaze to his sister, just for a split second, but it was enough to see that she was in her element. There was no doubt about it. This didn't surprise Acalan. She'd been preparing her entire life for this and while Acalan had done so as well, there was no denying that Metztli had put in far more effort than he had.

His father started by thanking everyone in attendance. He couldn't see his father's face but he knew that he was likely baring a welcoming smile. Acalan kept his expressions straight, there was no smile, no sneer, or anything else. In truth, he was unsure how he should feel about the people in front of them.

They'd come here in support of the tournament and the other houses, so naturally Acalan should view them as enemies. This was all these people had ever known, though. They'd never even considered what their lives could be like if they were united under one house, one people. Acalan didn't blame them for it. He doubted that anyone other than the royal families spent time thinking about the Tournament of Heirs.

"Twenty-five years ago, I stood in the very spot where my son and daughter stand today," their father began, his tone somewhat mournful. "I was accompanied by my brother Chimalli who gave his life in exchange for mine. It was because of his sacrifice that I won the Tournament of Heirs."

Acalan had been taught to believe that loyalty to one's family often came with sacrifices that must be made and while he was elated to have his father alive and well, the prince could not stop himself from hoping that he and Metztli would never be put in the same position.

"The journey that our children will embark on is not an easy one," their father continued. "I can tell you all from experience that the Tournament of Heirs was one of the most difficult experiences of my life, but all good things come from sacrifice. It is because of this that I have been blessed with a gift from the gods, and why I reign over you all. It is my deepest desire that my children will uphold my legacy and follow in my footsteps."

Many people in the crowd nodded in agreement. The emperors' might not like the fact that they hadn't had control over Mexica in centuries, but there was no doubting that Tenoch had made their realm peaceful. He would be remembered for that, even when his time to cross over to the afterlife came.

"I will not stand before you all and make promises that cannot be kept. The reality of the tournament is much different than what is often told in stories and myth. All I can promise is that my son, Acalan, and my daughter, Metztli, have prepared their entire lives for this moment. This was not a choice for my children, but they have taken their duties and embraced them. Their fates may be unknown, but I will always remain undeniably proud of both of them."

Tenoch stepped aside then, allowing for Metztli and Acalan to take a slight step forward. The people screamed and clapped for Metztli and himself, but they had done so for all of the heirs that had been presented. Acalan couldn't help but wonder with whom their alliances truly lay.

It was brutal not knowing. He knew that none of their opinions would help them during the tournament, but under the gazes of everyone, he felt like he was drowning.

There was a sudden burning sensation in his chest. As a boy Acalan had nearly drowned in a lake once, and it had felt just like this. His breath hitched despite his efforts to calm himself. The feeling only worsened when he found Citlalic in the crowd. They locked eyes and there was something familiar in the way that she looked at him.

It felt like she could see right through him, just as Metztli often did.

He panicked until a soft hand grasped his. He knew it was Metztli. She always knew when he needed her the most. A deep sigh escaped him the moment she did this. It was audible, but he hoped that it hadn't been too obvious to everyone in the crowd. She pulled their arms above their heads, which only made the crowd cheer even louder for them. He would need to thank her later for keeping him afloat.

Their father thanked the crowd once more before they were escorted off the steps. Instead of returning to their chairs their father led them down the long aisle and out of the great hall. Acalan leaned against one of the walls as soon as he could, frightened that if he didn't he would risk falling over.

"Hey, you did fine in there. Don't worry it was harder than I thought it would be as well. Just standing there while everyone's beady little eyes are examining you — but really you did fine, right father?" Metztli asked as she rubbed his arm in a comforting motion.

He hadn't felt like he'd done well at all, but his sister wouldn't lie to him, of that he was certain.

"The crowd loved both of you, there is no need to worry. Besides, this is only a formality. Their opinions of you do not reflect what your performance will be like in the tournament." Their father explained.

Acalan knew that already but it was still comforting to hear. These ceremonies used to matter a great deal but it was because the gods used to make appearances. There had been no gods in appearance today, nor did he think that the gods would choose to make one for the rest of the evening.

The reminder of this made him feel momentarily safe. He was still in his home and he didn't have to worry about staying alive, not until they entered the Pyramid of Tributes.

Acalan had to repeat this to himself a few times before he believed it, but eventually he did. His posture straightened slightly then. The timing was nearly perfect because people were starting to flood out of the great hall. He nodded curtly at anyone who he made eye contact with. It was the least he could do without making a fool out of himself again.

"What now, father?" he asked.

He was eager to get away from everyone but he also knew that there were duties he needed to attend to with his family.

"Once we find your mother, then it will be time to join the others

for the celebration. You know this, Acalan. Try to calm yourself —
remember that the tournament hasn't begun," Tenoch responded
quietly as he, too, nodded and waved to their guests.

His father had never been more wrong. Metztli had been right
earlier. The tournament had begun the moment the heirs arrived in
their home. They might not have entered the Pyramid of Tributes
yet, but beneath this celebration — the false smiles and bright music
— Acalan knew the tournament had already begun. And there was
no stopping it now.

Acalan did his best to regain his composure as he caught sight
of his mother. Aside from a few dried tears on her face, it didn't look
like she was under too much strain. Acalan knew that couldn't be
entirely true. If he was feeling like he was drowning, he could only
imagine that his mother was feeling much worse. It was just that she
knew better than to let everyone know how she was feeling.

"You two did wonderful," Xara said, pulling her children into a
soft embrace. "I am so proud of you both. So, so proud."

"Thank you mother, you prepared us well," Acalan responded,
leaning his forehead gently on his mother's.

They still had a day before they would be forced to enter the
Pyramid of Tributes, but the prince couldn't help but wonder if this
would be the last time he would feel his mother's embrace.

"We should get going, we wouldn't want to miss our own
celebration right?" their father asked.

"I'm starving...please tell me there will be food!" Metztli
questioned in a tone half full of concern and half full of much
needed mischief.

Acalan couldn't help but smile as he pulled away from his
mother. His sister had been complaining about being hungry for
hours now. He hadn't had much of an appetite for days, but a meal
with his family would be nice, even if it was under the watchful
gazes of their guests.

"Only the finest for my children." Their father ruffled Metztli's
hair playfully. "There may or may not be a spread of tamales waiting
for you, daughter"

A bright smile appeared on his sister's face. Tamales were

only made on very special occasions and they were amongst her favorite foods.

"And there may also be an abundance of chocolate cookies for you, Acalan,"Tenoch added,"but of course I don't want either of you to over indulge. Be mindful of how close the tournament is."

"I make no promises father, you know how I feel about chocolate." Acalan responded playfully.

He was happy to see that his difference in tone put a smile on his family's face. No one could ensure that they would return, so there was no use in wasting his last hours with his family sulking instead of enjoying their company.

"Then I will turn a blind eye and pretend I see nothing." His father gave a playful wink."Now let's go. Keep your heads high. Remember, they are in your home. They are only guests here and you two are heirs to this empire."

Acalan nodded confidently and he raised his chest again. As much as he wanted to, he couldn't just be a son and brother right now. He had to be an heir, a prince, and nothing else.

Metztli took his arm as they walked behind their parents, making sure not to lose them in the crowd. It was an awfully lady-like thing to do and not like Metztli at all. But perhaps she understood that for the rest of the evening and until they were in the privacy of their rooms, they had roles to play and duties to fulfill.

They would be okay, Acalan was sure of it. It would just be a few hours and then they could go back to just being Acalan and Metztli, and while they slept they wouldn't need to worry about prophecies or the tournament. They could just rest.

Until then Acalan would put on a brave face. It was all he could do for now.

Besides, he was still hopeful for a dance with the Princess of Blood.

12

METZTLI

Metztli gripped her brother's arm as they walked out of the palace to where the celebration was being held outside of their home. The field outside of the palace had been beautifully arranged with long wooden tables where their guests could sit and enjoy the feast. Lively music was playing even louder than it had been within, and by the looks of it, their guests were truly enjoying themselves. Somehow there were even more people waiting to receive the heirs out here.

"Where did all of these people come from?" Metztli questioned.

Both of their parents laughed at the question. But Metztli was being genuine, she couldn't imagine traveling anywhere for a tournament like this. If anything she was very willing to travel very far away from it.

"They've all traveled for the occasion of course," their mother explained before turning to wave at a guest. "More will arrive in the coming days. It may seem strange, but many people look forward to the Tournament of Heirs. We may not agree, but it is our duty to be gracious hosts regardless."

Metztli raised an eyebrow in confusion. She couldn't believe that the people of Mexica were truly so brainwashed. She'd met many of the people in Tu'nethe and they all seemed intelligent, but following the gods so blindly was just plain stupid.

"It's your turn to calm down," Acalan said as he offered Metztli a smile.

The princess rolled her eyes but forced herself to smile back. Acalan was right, she could not insult their guests, nor could she walk around all night with a sullen expression on her face.

"Why don't the both of you stand in line for the feast while your mother and I greet some of our guests?" their father suggested. "We'll meet you back at our table." He pointed towards the table nearest to the entrance of the palace that held a small sign with their family name.

"Sure, make sure to greet them for me as well," Metztli responded with a false bright smile that made her mother raise a brow.

The princess would likely do anything to get out of greeting their guests and it was for the best. She wasn't exactly known for her patience and that hadn't magically changed overnight.

"Keep an eye on your sister for us," their father instructed Acalan, making her brother chuckle as they walked away to attend to their duties as hosts.

Metztli elbowed her brother slightly to make him stop laughing before they made their way to the line for the feast. Despite being highborn, Metztli and Acalan were used to doing things like this. During celebrations and holidays that were spent with their people, they were never served first simply because of who they were.

It was obvious by the way that some of their highborn guests wore irritated faces that they were not used to this treatment. That alone was almost enough to make the princess laugh.

"Look over there, near the front of the line. It looks like the Empress from the House of Flor is about to burst a blood vessel," Metztli whispered to her brother, only allowing the slightest giggle to follow her words.

She watched intently as her brother's gaze found the angry woman. It truly looked like she was about to throw a fit, similar to the one's Metztli used to throw as a child when she was only allowed one slice of chocolate cake.

"That woman is mental!" Acalan whispered back.

Metztli couldn't agree more. The line itself was moving rather quickly, so it wasn't long before they were nearing the front. Luckily, the empress was given a plate of her choosing before a tantrum ensued, though Metztli thought that would have been rather entertaining to watch.

While the princess waited, she looked around the party. It was obvious that the younger bastard from the House of Rain was trying to woo the sister from the House of Wind, and, by all accounts, it seemed like he was winning that battle. He wasn't the only one of the male heirs making an attempt to be bed either.

Necalli and his family sat quietly together. That was a bit strange. Metztli had imagined that they would love a good party, but despite the music playing and dancers that had been hired to entertain, the Cruz family simply ate, chatting with one another and no one else.

"You're drooling," Acalan spoke, interrupting Metztli's thoughts.

The princess couldn't help but laugh in response. His taunt was rich considering he had been caught staring at the princess from the House of Blood on more than one occasion. Besides, Metztli was hardly drooling, regardless of how handsome Necalli looked.

"Shut up," Metztli responded simply as she beckoned for her brother to take a step forward in line.

The princess found it astounding how much a big meal could improve her mood. She'd eaten enough for at least two people if not three, but who could blame her? There had been an array of the most delicious dishes Tu'ncthe had to offer. From tamales, pozole, and tlacoyos, Metztli had eaten so much that she didn't even get a chance to look at the dessert table.

She truly didn't mind if their guests found it unladylike when she filled her plate not once, not twice but three times. Quite frankly she only stopped eating when her mother warned her that she'd had more than enough for one evening unless she had imminent plans to be sick, which she did not.

"You're awfully quiet," Acalan said as she was finishing her last plate.

She was being quiet — mostly because she felt like she could hardly breathe in her gown after eating so much, but also because she couldn't stop thinking. No matter how much she tried, the tournament found its way back into her mind. It intertwined itself in her very being, making her wonder if this is all there was to life: the tournament and nothing else.

"I fear I ate too much, and If I pop a stitch mother will surely scold me," Metztli said with a forced smile.

"I told you to stop after your second serving, but you never listen do you?" Acalan teased, his smile bright.

The sight of it was enough to put a smile on Metztli's face, too. In the grand scheme of things she would rather die in the tournament than return home without her brother at her side. Living without him would be cruel. It would never feel right, a wound that time would never be able to heal.

"Anyway… I couldn't have gotten more than a couple hours of sleep last night so I think I'll turn in early," Acalan announced, stretching his arms above his head and presenting what could possibly be the most false yawn she'd ever seen, and she'd seen plenty. "Do tell mother I apologize but I have to rest before the tournament, I'm sure you—"

"Absolutely not, you are not leaving me here to suffer alone! Besides, you said you'd ask Citlalic for a dance tonight. Don't be a chicken! Go ask her! She looks like she's suffering, go rescue her from her misery."

She might have not understood this newfound affection her brother felt for the princess from the House of Blood, but she wouldn't let him enter the Pyramid of Tributes without at least exploring his feelings. Plus, Citlalic did indeed look like she was in need of rescuing.

Necalli and his father had disappeared so the princess was seated at their assigned table with her cousin. She had a book in her hands, but surely she wanted to enjoy the party as well. If she was anything like Acalan then Metztli knew that Citlalic was probably just waiting for an invitation of sorts.

"Is that really wise though? I mean look at her, she's clearly enjoying her book. As someone who enjoys literature I think it would be better to just leave her to her own devices, don't you think?" Acalan questioned as he slowly stood from his seat, preparing his escape.

Metztli was standing before him only a second later, blocking his exit. Had Acalan truly thought she would just let him go without at least trying to speak to the princess?

"Nope! If you don't go ask her this very second, I will go find mother and I'll…I'll tell her…I'll tell her about the time you pushed me into the river!" Metztli announced.

Acalan had never pushed her into a river, but how would their mother know? Acalan's eyebrow raised at the sudden threat from his sister.

"I never pushed you into the river!" Acalan snapped.

He took a step forward, but Metztli didn't move. She had already made up her mind. She would not let her brother go until he'd at least talked to the princess. After all, this could be his one opportunity to make an impression on her, the only opportunity for Citlalic to know him for who he truly was.

"Mother doesn't know that!" Metztli said, lowering her voice conspiratorially. "She'll only see you fleeing and she'll have no reason but to believe me because of it!"

Despite what Acalan might think of himself, she knew him to be a good man. He'd be a good husband when the time came, and he deserved to indulge in a bit of fun, even if it was just a dance with a princess who had caught his interest.

"This is truly unfair of you! If she hates me for this then it's… it's your fault!" Acalan pouted in return.

Metztli chuckled at his display. That was a sort of guilt she was more than willing to live with. Their days were too numbered to leave this matter to destiny. She would much rather the princess tell him she was not interested than have her brother wonder for the rest of his life about what could have been.

"That is quite alright. Now go speak to her, she seems kind,

Acalan. Besides, how interesting could her book really be?" Metztli said as she fixed her brother's golden sash.

As a woman she recognized that it was quite likely that the princess found her brother interesting as well. She would be a fool not to, while all the other suitors their age were cold-hearted her brother's heart remained warm. Any half competent woman would be able to see that.

"Fine…Just…Stay here, in case this goes wrong," Acalan ordered.

Metztli nodded in return. If that's what it would take for her brother to make a move, then she would stand there all evening. It was the right thing to do for someone who loved her as unconditionally as her brother did.

Metztli watched as he walked away, chest and chin held high. She nearly chased after him to remind her brother to just be himself. The man who he truly was more than enough, he didn't have to pretend to be anyone else.

It wasn't until he was slightly out of view that Metztli moved. She didn't stop until she found a convenient place near the dessert table where she could watch, and she was happy to find that she could now see her parents too.

They'd been dancing for what felt like hours now, Metztli didn't mind though, they were both smiling brightly and looking far younger than they ever had. The princess had to practically force her gaze away from her parents to find her brother again.

From what she could tell he'd found his way to the table where Citlalic was seated with her cousin. Her brother and father were absent but perhaps that was better for Acalan. It was sweet the way the princess immediately brightened at the sight of Acalan, even more so when she put her book down and took his hand. Metztli hadn't had a doubt that this would go well for her brother, but she hadn't expected the happiness that it would bring her.

She certainly didn't regret threatening him now.

"Young love is charming isn't it?" Atzi spoke, causing Metztli to jump back, recoiling from the sudden company she'd acquired.

"Gods, Atzi! Warn me next time before you scare the living lights out of me," Metztli said as she took a step away from the woman.

Despite being a priestess, it seemed the woman knew no sense of personal space.

"Watch your tongue Metztli, the gods are always listening and it would be unwise to use their name in vain," Atzi responded.

Despite knowing her words to be true, Metztli could not find it in herself to actually care. Did Atzi want her on her hands and knees worshiping the gods for punishing her over a war she hadn't even been alive to see?

"While I do appreciate the suggestion, I will take my chances," Metztli replied sarcastically.

She'd never known peace with Atzi. Even when she was a baby, Metztli's mother claimed that Atzi had refused to hold her. Why that was, Metztli was unsure, but she did not care. It's not like she enjoyed the old woman's presence anymore than Atzi enjoyed hers.

"Even if your actions endanger your brother?" Atzi questioned.

Her words caused Metztli to pause. She'd had this thought before. The idea that her actions could somehow harm her brother was a sickening one, enough that all the food she'd indulged in was threatening to come right back up just at the thought of her brother being punished for her beliefs.

"Have you come just to pester me?" Metztli fumed, squeezing her fists tight enough that she was sure her knuckles had gone white. "I mean no disrespect, Atzi, but I'd like to watch my brother in peace. Can you not just grant me this one thing? The tournament will start the day after tomorrow and then if you have any luck at all, I'll be out of your hair forever!"

It might have been cruel but she knew she was her brother's only chance of getting out of the tournament alive. Atzi had always seemed so dearly attached to him, so couldn't she just leave Metztli alone for what remained of her freedom?

"It pains me that you believe I would be happy to see you die Metztli, that is far from the truth. Regardless, even if that thought brought me joy, you will not die, I'm sure of it. You're too stubborn to not survive."

Metztli whined. She'd had enough of this woman for a lifetime. She did not wish to die. She wanted to return home more than anything but perhaps there was some comfort in knowing she would no longer have to deal with this priestess if she did meet her end.

"Well I may be stubborn, but there will be nothing I can do to survive if one of the sisters from the House of Flor sinks their teeth into me," Metztli argued, She hardly believed either of them would get close enough to do so, but there was always a chance, she was very well aware of that.

"Do stay away from those two at all costs. I'd be willing to wager that they're possessed," Atzi warned.

Her words were slightly shocking. Metztli could only recall the woman ever criticizing her and no one else. In fact, Metztli was always at the center of her scolding, even if she hadn't done anything wrong to begin with.

"More evil than me? I doubt it. You've been trying to beat the evil out of me since I was born."

She waited for Atzi to agree with her, but the old woman did not. Her expression remained the same: tight lipped, stern, and cold.

"Despite what you might think I believe of you, I know you are nothing like them, Metztli. You are kind-hearted and selfless. A stubborn child, yes. Disobedient? Always. Disrespectful? Without a doubt but… you are good. You must remember that when you enter the Pyramid of Tributes."

Metztli turned to really look at the woman. Her expression remained the same as it had before, but there was something different about her. There was a sadness in her eyes that Metztli didn't quite understand.

She was unsure how to accept the woman's compliments. They had been followed by numerous insults, but she had complimented Metztli which was…strange, to say the least.

"I highly doubt my behavior will matter if I return home," Metztli retorted. "Shouldn't you be telling Acalan this? Need I remind you that he is this empire's prized heir? I think not, you've treated him as such for as long as I can remember, and I do remember quite a lot Atzi."

"Everything I did was with good reason, Metztli." Atzi folded her arms across her chest. "You would have not known how to accept my love even if I offered it. You may not believe me and that is fine. I know I have never been kind to you, but the time will come when you will need me, and you must know that when that time comes, I will be utterly devoted to you. Just as I have been with your brother."

Her voice shook slightly as she spoke. It was so unlike her that it confused Metztli. She had no doubt that this had something to do with whatever the woman and Acalan had discussed earlier.

Metztli did not respond, she couldn't find it in herself to do so. She just looked at the woman angrily, hoping that would be enough to drive the priestess away.

"You are special Metztli, as is your brother. I simply do not want you to forget that amidst the chaos you will see and experience. You must remain true to yourself, the tournament is just…it is just the beginning of what destiny has for you," Atzi said in a warning tone.

Metztli wanted to respond. She wanted to cause a scene and tell the woman to leave her alone, but instead she stayed silent and watched as the woman turned and walked away.

She'd had enough of this. She was not special. She was just like every other heir present at this godforsaken celebration. If she heard another word about destiny she would simply diminish. The only thing she cared about was her fate. It would be her actions that would bring them victory — not some predetermined destiny. Of that, Metztli could not be more certain.

ACALAN

"I must warn you, I'm terribly uncoordinated," Acalan said nervously as he led the princess to join the other couples dancing.

As he spoke, he looked over his shoulder and found Citlalic smiling brightly and giggling. The princess's smile was easily the most beautiful sight his eyes had ever been blessed with.

"I'll watch my toes then," the princess responded playfully as they finally reached the dance floor.

They were surrounded by a sea of people, but as Acalan turned to fully face Citlalic and take in her beauty, she was the only person who held his attention. She grasped his hand and placed his other on her waist. The prince had to take a deep breath to keep himself calm, but that didn't stop his heart from racing as they started swaying to the music.

"Are you nervous?" Citlalic questioned gently with a curious tilt to her head.

Acalan shook his head quickly in response. It was a lie, of course. He was far more nervous than he had been before being presented earlier. This wasn't his first time dancing with a woman but this was the first time he'd ever felt pulled to anyone before. The princess before him was mesmerizing, like an art piece that deserved to be cherished with love and care.

"It's okay if you are. I find myself a bit nervous too," Citlalic continued, offering a comforting smile.

The prince chuckled at that. Citlalic had absolutely no reason to be nervous — he was just a prince after all. Aside from that, Acalan didn't believe there was anything terribly special about him that could warrant her being nervous.

"You have no reason to be, I promise," Acalan assured the princess before raising his arm to spin her.

For the first moment in what felt like years, Acalan did not think about the tournament. Every thought of it drifted away swiftly as the princess spun out of his grasp and back into his arms.

As he danced with Citlalic and held her fragile figure against his own, he couldn't help but feel like this was the closest he'd ever come to having the love his novels spoke about.

"I thought you said you were a bad dancer," Citlalic teased while her eyes sparkled.

The prince laughed once more. In the presence of the princess he was all smiles, laughter, and nothing else.

"I'm trying very hard not to mess up," Acalan confessed with a soft smile.

Perhaps that was why he couldn't find it in himself to think about the tournament at all. In between admiring her beauty, keeping up with the conversation, and desperately trying not to step on her toes, there was very little room left in his mind for anything else.

"Are you this gracious with all the women you dance with?" Citlalic questioned playfully.

Acalan shook his head quickly again. For starters, it wasn't very often that he felt inclined to dance with anyone but even when he did, he'd never really been this careful or eager to impress.

"No. Only the ones that are as beautiful as you," Acalan pulled the princess in closer. "None of them are as beautiful as you though," he whispered softly.

Of that he was completely and utterly confident.

As Acalan pulled away, he noted the slight blush that had settled on Citlalic's cheeks. It had taken courage to compliment her so openly, but she deserved to know how he felt.

They danced for what felt like a very long time, conversing about all sorts of things from books to their favorite foods. Before Acalan couldn't understand why he felt so pulled to the princess, but now he did. She was a dream, one that he hoped to never wake from.

The prince was in the middle of speaking of his family's garden when he noticed the sudden spark in her eyes. He couldn't imagine that much grew in the House of Blood, not with what he knew of their home and the circumstances that they lived under.

"Would you…would you like to see them?" he asked timidly. "The gardens, I mean."

He knew this was wrong. He had no right to form an attachment to someone knowing he could die in the matter of days, and he also knew that it was cruel to offer these things to her when he had no way of assuring that they could actually be, but he also couldn't stop himself.

Citlalic had to know that there were better ways of living, that she did not need to remain in the House of Blood if she did not want to. "Yes! I would love that!" she said excitedly. "I'll just tell my cousin where I'll be so he doesn't worry."

She didn't let him respond before she pulled away and made way for the table where her cousin was still seated. Acalan followed closely behind, only stopping to give the princess space to speak to Coatl.

He couldn't help but note the slight look of confusion and concern on Coatl's face. That was to be expected. It wasn't necessarily improper for a princess to be alone with a prince but it could be looked down upon. Acalan didn't harbor any ill intentions though. He really just wanted to show her the gardens of his home and see her light up at the sight of the roses and tulips that grew there.

Acalan offered her cousin a gentle smile, a sort of peace offering that promised he would return the princess unharmed and untouched. Coatl must have sensed that Acalan was sincere because he gave Citlalic a soft nod, and then she was making her way back to him.

Acalan had never been more happy to see a woman walk

towards him.

"Let's go!" Citlalic beamed as she grasped his hand in her own. "I've tried to grow gardens many times back home but they never take! I bet yours is beautiful!"

Acalan's gaze lowered to see their hands intertwined with one another. Her touch made him feel warm with delight. He wanted to promise her the world and more, but he couldn't, not yet anyway, not until he secured his return home and his empire with it. "My father and mother grew it together," Acalan said as he pulled her along and back into the palace. "It's a bit romantic, isn't it?"

The palace itself was quite empty as all of its occupants were outside celebrating with the rest of Tu'nethe as well as the other houses and their guests. Acalan and Citlalic raced through the torch lit passages, giggling like children until they finally reached the garden he'd spoken so fondly about. They were beautiful during the day but even more so under the moonlight.

However, they did not compare to how beautiful Citlalic looked as she took it all in. Her eyes went wide at all of the different varieties of plants and flowers they had growing in their home.

"Your words did not do it justice…this is…it's stunning Acalan, truly." Citlalic took a few steps forward to take it all in.

He'd always known he was fortunate. Tournament or not, he'd been raised with riches and beauties, such as this very garden. Admittedly, it was something he'd taken for granted until now. He understood that as he watched the princess admire it all.

"You're free to explore," he encouraged. "My mother's collection is quite vast. I'm sure she would be more than happy to gift you plants to take back to your home, if you so wished."

He followed behind her, never too close but never too far. He was well aware of what this could look like, of what she might believe his intentions to be, but he just wanted to spend time with her.

"That is a very kind offer, but they would not survive the passage home I'm afraid. And even if they did, I would not know how to care for them," Citlalic responded, turning to look at him.

He knew his emotions were irrational, but he couldn't help but look at her under the moonlight and think of everything he could offer her and everything she could give him in return.

"Surely I could lend you a book on agriculture," he suggested playfully. "You'd have to promise to return it though. I'm very particular on who I lend my books to."

He knew he was entering dangerous territory. He was, by all accounts, a man of his word, and although he wanted to promise her his very being, he could not, not until he had possession of his own life. Citlalic seemed to know that too, because her smile diminished slightly at the proposition.

"I would have accepted that offer in another life," she said, her voice reaching barely above a whisper. "I cannot in this one, but you should know that in another I would have."

Acalan took a step forward, grasping her hand in his own, just as she had earlier. He wasn't sure what to say, but he didn't want to leave it at this. It would be a shame for the night to end this way. "I understand…but you should know that in another life I would have promised you much more than just some flowers and books on how to nurture them."

He'd managed to ignore the tournament for a little while, but the thought of it had crawled its way back into his mind. It was relentless, unwilling to let him enjoy even a few moments of peace. "My loyalty must stand with my own house, with my brother and my cousin but in another life, I would have enjoyed hearing these promises, and I would have accepted them." Citlalic moved her gaze from Acalan to roses next to her.

"My brother and cousin will not return home," she continued. "I've come to terms with that, but that will leave me as the sole heir of my house and I have duties, just as you do. It's not a matter of want, I hope you know that."

He'd never considered that she could be left to be the sole heir of the House of Blood if neither Necalli or Coatl found themselves victorious at the end of the tournament. He was slightly confused on why she was so confident that they wouldn't survive. Both men were quite strong, and he could tell from the markings on their bodies that they'd already killed before. That put them one step ahead of Metztli and Acalan already.

"You sound so certain of their deaths, " Acalan said curiously.

He waited patiently for a response, but she did not give him one. He knew nothing aside from the familiar look in her eye that reminded him of the way Atzi had looked at him when he'd first entered her sanctuary that morning.

Atzi had assured him no one else knew. She'd made him swear to secrecy.

"You know, don't you?" Acalan questioned.

The words had escaped him without permission. He immediately knew he'd said too much. If the princess hadn't known anything and was merely beginning to mourn her brother and cousin, then he'd just revealed something, not everything but something.

"I know a great deal of things, but I know most about your sister," Citlalic responded quietly.

"Whatever you think you know, you're wrong," Acalan said, a bit more harshly than he intended to. But he'd already failed his sister enough in mentioning it at all.

It was his duty to protect Metztli just as much as it was her duty to protect him. He wouldn't let false narratives be spread about her, even if it was by the tongue of the most beautiful woman he'd ever had the pleasure of knowing.

"I mean no harm, revealing what I know would only endanger me as well," Citlalic muttered in response.

He appreciated that she was being gentle despite his harshness, but just the thought of it causing her any pain made him rage from within.

"How so?" Acalan inquired, taking another step forward.

They were now as close as they had been when they were dancing. He expected the princess to take a step back, but she did not.

"I cannot say Acalan, just as you cannot say what you know about your sister. It is complicated, but I will tell you someday, when the time is right. And when you and your sister find yourselves in need of allyship with the House of Blood, just know that I will be more than willing. That is all I can say." Citlalic said as she looked deep into his eyes.

He knew she could see right through him, but it wasn't an

intrusion, not like when Metztli did it.

Citlalic was gentle. She was everything good left in their world. Even if he could have her, Acalan wasn't sure that he deserved her. That thought was both comforting and ruinous all at once. He hated that he knew exactly what she was speaking about and he had to put an end to this conversation, even if he was enjoying her company much more than he should.

"In another life I would have liked to kiss you right now, instead of speaking of these things," Acalan whispered breathlessly.

Once again the words had slipped right out of him. It was just a little alarming how little control he had of his tongue at the moment.

"You can kiss me, if you'd like," she said, drawing a little closer. "In this life, I wouldn't deny you that."

That confirmation was all that Acalan needed to bridge the gap between them. It was all too natural the way he pulled her in by her waist while his other hand cradled her cheek. This wasn't his first kiss by any means, but it was the first time that it had truly meant something. He could tell that from the way his lips moved against hers in a gentle rhythm.

They were perfectly in sync.

She'd already been intoxicating to him before, but how could he ever stop chasing her now? It was impossible now knowing that she tasted so sweet, like chocolate but without the bitter aftertaste. She was perfect, and, duties aside, Acalan desired her more than he'd ever desired anyone before.

They remained that way for a little while, bodies pressed against one another, her gentle hands tangled in his curls while their lips danced to a rhythm only they knew. Acalan only pulled away in search of air, but he regretted it the moment that he did. Almost as much as he regretted kissing her in the first place.

No other woman would ever compare to her. On top of all of his other responsibilities he now had to find a way to keep her, too. That, however, was a responsibility he was more than willing to bare.

"We should return, before my family becomes suspicious," Citlalic suggested, her tone still soft and gentle. "I hardly doubt they'd like to find me wrapped in your arms."

Acalan wanted quite the opposite of what she was suggesting but it was the wise thing to do.

"Of course," he agreed, his voice trembling slightly. "Before we go, though…you should know that I'm willing to fight for you in this life, if that's what you want. If what is said about my sister is true, then…there would be a way."

He might not have been promising anything directly but it certainly felt like he was.

METZTLI

Metztli was angry. The only thing keeping her at the celebration instead of leaving in search of the comfort of her room was the fact that she'd somehow lost sight of Acalan in the midst of her conversation with the priestess.

Citlalic had disappeared, too. Though to be frank this did not alarm her one bit. She knew her brother to be a gentleman, so wherever they were, she was quite certain that the princess was in good hands.

She'd gone back to the table where they'd been seated before, and it wasn't long before her mother had joined her in search of some respite after having spent hours dancing with her husband. Meanwhile, Tenoch mingled with their guests, like a true emperor.

It was a relief when her mother did not ask of her brother's whereabouts. Faking a smile was already more than Metztli felt like she could give. Meanwhile, the other heirs were mingling with one another, and she'd already watched as a few of them drifted away hand in hand.

That was simply something she could not understand. She didn't really want to die without knowing the touch of a man, but she was also not jumping at the idea of sleeping with anyone she was about to do battle with. Given the options, she would gladly die a virgin instead of giving her virtue away to any of the other heirs.

"Why don't you go find your father and share a dance with him?" Xara suggested. "You look terribly bored just sitting here darling."

While she would have gladly danced with her father on any other occasion, it felt unwise to do so under the thousands of gazes that followed them today. It was unfortunate, the last time she remembered dancing with her father must have been years ago when they'd celebrated her parents' twentieth year of marriage. This was just another reason why she couldn't bare the idea of dying, there were still too many memories to be made.

"While that is a lovely idea, I'm a terrible dancer, I think it best I do not embarrass myself more than I need to this evening." Despite her sour mood she was still saddened to see her mother's bright smile falter just a little bit.

"For someone who trains as much as you do Metztli, you really are quite clumsy when it comes to dancing. We'll have to work on that when you return home. How else will we find you a handsome suitor?" Xara questioned, her bright smile appearing again.

Metztli could not think of marriage right now. She knew the natural order of things. Marriage would bring children, and under the circumstances she lived in, children could only bring more death.

"Mother, if I return home, I assure you I will have my pick of the litter. They will not care if I am a clumsy dancer, they'll all just want the opportunity to be wed to me. But believe me, I am planning on being as picky as I can be. He must be handsome, of course, kind hearted, if possible, and he must find me funny. It would be terrible to marry someone who—"

Metztli stopped speaking when her mother's gaze moved from her to someone behind them. From the look on her mother's face she could tell it was someone unwelcome. That should have been enough to tell her it was Necalli, but her curiosity peaked, and she found herself turning to take the sight of him in herself.

"Perhaps he's come to apologize?" her mother wondered.

He might have, but there was absolutely no way she would be accepting his apologies. Regardless of how regal he looked in his red and gold garb.

Their incident from before was still fresh in Metztli's memory, and while it was one thing to tease her publically, it was another to taunt her with the mention of trying to bed her. The moment Necalli had even thought of the suggestion, he'd earned himself a very high spot on Metztli's kill list.

"Am I interrupting something?" Necalli broke in. "I was just hoping to steal the princess for a dance. That is, of course, if she'd be willing to take my hand."

She hadn't been expecting this proposition. It was ironic, really, considering she'd just told Acalan about how unladylike it was to deny someone a dance.

Those rules didn't apply to Metztli, though, and even if they did, she would make an exception in order to decline Necalli.

"You'd have to get on your hands and knees and apologize first before I would ever consider doing that," Metztli responded coldly. "Move along, find someone else to pester."

Her mother nearly choked on her glass of pulque, but Metztli did not turn to face her. Instead, she kept her gaze fixed on Necalli. Fury raged in her chest as a devious smirk settled on his lips.

"I didn't peg you for a sadist but I suppose, if that's what it will take then I am under your mercy," Necalli replied.

Metztli was sure that he was just taunting her. He wouldn't actually do as she'd asked, right?

At least that's what she believed until Necalli started crouching down until he was on one knee. She watched carefully, waiting for his other to touch the floor. She was far from a sadist, but she could not deny that she was quite enjoying this sight.

"Metztli stop this nonsense! Necalli stand!" Xara commanded. "I will not allow a prince to kneel in my home, and you must not taunt my daughter this way. It only feeds her dislike of you."

Metztli was disappointed when Necalli stood back up. Seeing him on his knees begging for forgiveness would have at least made coming to this celebration worthwhile.

"I'm afraid I cannot ignore orders from the empress, but I would still like that dance if you'd join me," Necalli said.

Metztli had to stop herself from laughing, only because her mother was already angry.

"She would love to," her mother responded before she could.

Naturally the princess turned as quickly as she could to face her mother. She was more than old enough to speak for herself, and she did not, in fact, want to dance with the Prince of Blood. She didn't even want to look at him for longer than needed.

"*I would not love that,*" Metztli said through her teeth.

She didn't want to upset her mother more than she already had, but this was entirely unfair. She wasn't bothering anyone. In fact, she'd stayed out of everyone's way for the majority of the evening. She should be rewarded for doing so, not punished.

"Lovely, to the dance floor then?" Necalli asked as he reached his hand out for her.

Metztli looked back at Necalli with a glare. She'd met plenty of intolerable people during her life, but none of them compared to Necalli Cruz.

"It's just one dance and then you can be excused to your room. Remember you represent our empire, not only yourself," her mother whispered as she leaned in close so only Metztli could hear.

She knew her mother was right, and the thought of being able to escape back to her room was a tempting one, but that didn't stop Metztli from rolling her eyes as she stood from her seat. She took Necalli's hand aggressively and faked a smile.

"It seems I cannot disobey the empress's orders either," Metztli said, making her opinion of this whole ordeal quite clear.

She'd rather have another conversation with Atzi than spend even one minute dancing with Necalli, and yet here she was, obeying her mother's orders in order to appease her.

Necalli laughed gently, which only angered Metztli even more, but she still followed behind him as he led the both of them to where the others were dancing. She was more than vaguely aware of the eyes following them. A few whispers and gasps crept through the crowd, and she could only begin to imagine what the other heirs were saying about her right about now.

They probably believed there was some truth to what Necalli had implied before.

"One dance," Metztli sneered. "That is all, do you understand?"

He rolled his eyes before settling one of his hands on her waist. His other hand grasped her own. She wasn't enjoying any bit of this, but Necalli seemed quite amused by it all. At least he was enjoying himself, because she certainly was not.

"Two dances," Necalli countered.

The prince was not asking, he was just making Metztli aware of the decision he'd made. This might have worked on another woman but it didn't with Metztli. She was only standing there with him to appease her mother, not because she desired to dance with him.

"I hate to break this to you, but your charm does not work with me. One dance. That is all. Now start moving your feet before I leave," Metztli commanded.

He'd called her a sadist, but there was no doubt that he was the one who was enjoying playing this game for dominance. Necalli did as she asked and started guiding her to the slow tune of a flute playing. Metztli wasn't nearly as uncomfortable as she thought she would be but that didn't mean she was enjoying this.

"I was not aware that you found me to be charming," he mused, "that's quite the compliment, Metztli. But I hate to break this to you —you promised your mother one dance. And I'd like to call in the favor you owe me for a second dance. Two dances. Not one."

"Are you sure you want to call in the favor now? If I were you I would save it for the tournament. Or were you hoping that two dances would be enough to convince me to allow you to bed me?" Metztli taunted, her tone full of daggers and poison.

If a second dance would liberate her from whatever favor he believed she owed him then that was fine. But Necalli was incompetent if he believed a few dances between them would lead to anything else.

"If I was truly trying to convince you to join me in bed, then you'd already be convinced, trust me," Necalli assured Metztli as he swayed her back and forth.

She could feel his hand slowly moving to fill the dip at the bottom of her spine. She flinched at the sudden intrusion before taking the hand that had been resting on Necalli's shoulder and moving his hand further up her back.

"But you do want to bed me, don't you? You'd love the opportunity. You don't have to confess that for me to know it to be true," Metztli responded teasingly.

He could argue otherwise but it would do nothing to convince her.. She'd been alive long enough to be able to recognize desire in a man. Necalli was far from the first to ever seek her out. Quite frankly, she did not understand why. She found herself to be beautiful but there were plenty of beautiful women present, so why her?

"Sure, I would love to bed you but so does everyone else here," Necalli teased as he effortlessly pulled her closer to his body. "The women and the men, they would all love the opportunity to know you intimately. It wouldn't be any fun though, not unless you wanted me as much as I want you…You must be curious at least? Aren't you?"

He was a good bit taller than her, but that didn't stop Metztli from tilting her head slightly to look Necalli right in the eyes.

"You disgust me," Metztli spat.

She did not deny the accusations brought against her though. Necalli seemed to see right through her anyway, so there was no point in denying that she'd imagined what it would be like to be touched by him. Just thinking of it now brought goosebumps to her skin that she was unable to shake.

"Perhaps I do, but lust and disgust can coincide can't they?" Necalli questioned, spinning her so the fabric of her skirt bellowed. Metztli was grateful for the slight relief.

Suddenly, she was facing the prince again, his arm wrapped around her waist, leaving no space between them. Necalli leaned down slightly then until his lips were almost grazing her ear. Metztli wanted to pull away, but she couldn't find the strength in her to do so.

"It's perfectly natural for you to want me," he whispered, "even if you are a princess…I'm afraid you've waited too long to indulge in these feelings. It would be completely wrong to play out your desires on the holy day of mourning."

That was quite enough for the princess. She wanted to appease her mother and she wanted to rid herself of the favor she owed him, but she couldn't take any more of this taunting. Necalli was relentless and deep down she was afraid that she wouldn't be able to resist him if this continued for any longer.

She pushed him away as quickly as she could manage before taking a deep breath. Her mother had been right, even seduction could be used as a weapon in the Tournament of Heirs, but it would not work on her. She would much rather be eaten alive by the demon sisters from the House of Flor than to go down over desires she could not control.

"I hope I haunt you in your dreams tonight because that is as close as you will ever get to knowing me intimately. Now go get your fill of women before you die in the tournament," Metztli scoffed before turning to walk away.

It hadn't been a full dance per say, but it had been enough of a dance that she felt like she'd earned the reward of retreating to her room.

"Metztli!" Necalli called out for her.

She should have just kept walking and ignored his beckoning, but she found herself turning slightly to look at him. His expression was softer than it had been before, and he looked breathless. He'd been fine just moments ago. Surely her words hadn't been so harsh that they caused this reaction from him.

"Like calls to like," he said. "You and I aren't so different. Remember that when we find each other inside the pyramid."

She was sure she misheard him. Aside from both being heirs they were nothing alike. I mean sure, they were both stubborn and strong willed. They both had empires to protect, and they both desired each other more than they should, but she could never be like him. While her heart was warm, his was cold, she was sure of it.

"Goodnight Necalli," Metztli simply said before turning and making way to her room.

She didn't stop to say goodnight to her mother or father, nor did she look for her brother. The last thing she wanted right now was an interrogation from any of them. She just wanted to lay in her bed and forget she even knew what it was like to feel Necalli's touch on her body.

Yes, that would certainly bring some relief.

Metzti had only just entered the palace when she spotted Xochitl, the oldest sister from the House of Flor. She'd had enough for one evening, and she certainly didn't want to have another interaction with this heir. Metztli made every attempt to simply walk by. She was starting to believe she was in the clear when the woman's voice rang through the hall.

"Don't let his charms fool you," Xochitl warned. "We all have secrets, it just so happens that his are larger than most."

It was strange seeing Xochitl outside of her vicious state.

"Right…I hope you enjoyed your evening, Xochitl. Rest well, we're all going to need it," Metztli responded before swiftly making her escape.

She did not look back at the woman as she walked away.

The warning had come out of nowhere but Metztli couldn't deny that it had been needed. Necalli was charming. And she had no doubts that he was hiding secrets, but as Xochitl said, they all were. Whatever those secrets were, Metztli didn't care to know, they would be of no use to her if either of them found themselves dead. After all it would come down to that, wouldn't it? Only two blood bound heirs could win, and if it was between Necalli and Coatl, or Acalan and herself, she would find no problem with striking the final blow.

Acalan

Acalan was practically grinning ear from ear by the time he walked Citlalic back to the celebration. He'd returned her safe and sound, just as he had promised and had even gone as far as to press a soft kiss on the back of her hand before bidding the princess a good night.

He would have liked to spend the entire evening with her even if it meant missing sleep in order to do so but there was still so much to be done. His conversation with the princess had only made him more curious about the prophecy. If Citlalic knew about it, then there was no way of assuring that others didn't as well.

Acalan made quick work of finding his father and mother, thanking them for the evening and wishing the both of them a goodnight before he started to search for Metztli. He'd learned from his mother that one of the guards had seen her retreat back into the palace a bit earlier in the evening.

It seemed a little bit unfair that she hadn't let him do the same, though admittedly, he was quite delighted with how the evening had gone. Even if the Tournament of Heirs ended terribly, he would always have the memory of what it felt like to feel Citlalic's lips on his own.

Acalan soon found himself outside Metztli's door. He knocked softly. It was late, but he highly doubted his sister was asleep. After getting no response, he knocked again, this time stating that it was him so she would know it was not some unwanted guest. That seemed to work because he could hear her footsteps approaching, then the door knob twisted and…

She looked disheveled.

Acalan couldn't quite tell if it was rage or something else though. He'd never really seen the emotion that was painted on her face.

"Are you alright?" he questioned. "Mother said you left early."

He was still battling with the guilt that he felt from the realization that he'd been a terrible older brother, and while they only had a day and some hours now before they would enter the tournament, there was still some time for redemption, starting with this.

"Did she say anything else?" Metztli asked frantically, pulling on Acalan's arm and dragging him into her bedroom before shutting the door behind them.

He could tell by the look on her face that whatever had happened, she was embarrassed by it. That didn't make any sense though. The last time he'd seen his sister embarrassed had been when they were much younger. Even earlier in the day when she'd attacked Necalli, she had only looked rageful, not embarrassed at all.

"No…nothing else…" Acalan responded as he leaned against the wall.

"In that case, yes, I am fine. You look very delighted though, have you come to tell me good news? Just don't tell me you felt compelled to propose because I will not hesitate to hurt you."

He knew then that something had definitely happened, even more so when she took a seat on the edge of her bed, crossed her legs and wrapped her cotton blanket around her body like she was trying to shield herself from the rest of the world.

There was a strategy in speaking to Metztli, Acalan was very much aware of that. If he wanted her to open up about her feelings then he would need to do the same, and he would need to do it well. Otherwise she would send him away to his room without ever mentioning a word about what had happened that made her so upset.

The notion that he'd proposed was a bit funny. He was very fond of Citlalic but he would never make a commitment to anyone like that before at least having control over his own life. He needed to figure out a way to survive the tournament, rule his empire, and somehow have Citlalic too.

"Well it just happened so quickly…" Acalan started, teasing his sister.

He felt awful when rage did not settle in her eyes, instead he was met with sadness and worry. He'd never been much of a comedian but it hadn't been his intention to worry his sister more than she already was.

There was an immense amount of pressure on Acalan's shoulders, but he knew that Metztli was carrying even more. After all, it couldn't be easy knowing your life's purpose was to keep your older brother alive. Acalan knew that wasn't truly her destiny though, there was more out there for her, the prophecy said so.

"Sorry, I was just trying to be funny. I didn't propose, I know right from wrong, believe it or not. I would have though, as crazy as that sounds. If the tournament didn't exist, I truly think I would have. Citlalic is nothing short of a dream come true" He took a seat beside his sister.

It had been far too long since they'd both sat on her bed and just spoke. Still, she had always been his confidant and he knew that she would understand what he was going through.

Actually, she was quite literally the only person who could truly understand because she was living under the same circumstances as him.

"I'm sorry, Acalan…maybe there's still hope though? You know I'll do everything in my power to get you back home. There will be more time once our lives are truly our own." Her hand reached from under her blanket to rub his shoulder comfortingly.

Acalan hadn't realized how much he'd needed it until it was happening, so he was grateful for the gesture, even if it was something as small as this. For a moment he considered telling his sister that Citlalic knew something about the tournament, but after a couple seconds of debating it in his mind, he opted not to. His sister was already worried beyond belief, and he didn't want to be the reason she became even more worried.

"I think that's the issue though, she seems to like me just as much as I like her, but you're right. As long as we return home there'll be much more time. Besides, I did kiss her at the end of it all so I can't complain too much," Acalan confessed with a sheepish grin.

He laughed slightly when his sister gasped at his revelation.

He couldn't blame her for being surprised, even now he was quite impressed with himself for having the courage to kiss the princess.

"I didn't know you had it in you!" She pulled back, a look of pride breaking through her furrowed brow for a moment before she frowned again.

"As your friend I am very happy for you, but as your sister I must warn you that is as far as it should go for now, and you must agree or I'll escort you back to your bedroom and sleep on the floor to ensure you don't plan on having any visitors," his sister warned in a serious tone, though there was a smile on her face that completely contradicted it.

That was just another reminder of how hard it must be to be in his sister's position. She couldn't enjoy just being happy for him, there were always duties getting in the way.

"I wouldn't think of it, trust me. Besides, I think this might be the last evening we're able to really sleep, so I'd much rather you rest well in the comfort of your bed than on a hard floor."

He continued, "Alright, I've told you about my evening, so it's your turn. No excuses, I don't make the rules."

His smile disappeared as he watched his sister lay down, concealing her face with a pillow. It was obvious she did not want to speak, but he knew very well it wasn't healthy to hold one's emotions in, so he waited patiently until she peaked out from behind the pillow and sighed.

"I'm alright I just…well first, Atzi had the audacity to ruin my peace, and you know how much I hate when she speaks in half truths. Tonight it felt like all of her words had different meanings but I do not have the time, or the energy to try to decipher them all."

Acalan was happy to see that his sister was opening up but her words hit him harshly. She was on to them, and while he did believe that she deserved to know about the prophecy and her involvement in it, Atzi had told him he needed to wait for the right time to tell her. Right now did not feel like the right time.

"And then, I'm sitting there with mother," Metztli continued, "bored out of my mind and Necalli decided to ask for a dance. As if what he did this afternoon wasn't bad enough, he needed to torture me further."

Acalan was quite grateful that the conversation had gone from Atzi to Necalli. It was strange but Acalan couldn't help but admire Necalli's bravery. Metztli had literally attacked him just that afternoon and there he was, trying to gain favor with her only a few hours later.

"And to make matters worse, mother forced me to dance with him. Don't worry though, I hardly argued. I figured that if it would please mother and get Necalli out of my hair, then I could suffer through a dance with him. I managed to stop myself from attacking him this time, but he's a real pain in the ass. He is charming though, so be careful, I wouldn't put it past Necalli to try his chances on you too."

Acalan raised a brow at her last comment. Even if Necalli tried something like that, it would do very little for him. Besides, he couldn't actually believe that Necalli would actually try to seduce his way into winning the tournament. Acalan had watched Necalli that afternoon and knew he was a skilled fighter.

"Well your evening sounds a lot more eventful than mine was. I'm afraid I left you in the panther's den all by yourself," Acalan said with an apologetic smile. It wasn't much but it did seem to work to some extent because Metztli sat back up and nodded in response.

"Necalli, he's brave I'll say that," Acalan continued, "but you should ignore him too. This is all a part of the tournament. Everyone is just trying to get into each other's heads. Perhaps, under different circumstances you would have found yourself flattered. The tournament just ruins everything."

He wasn't necessarily defending Necalli by any means, and he certainly wasn't happy to hear that the prince had pestered his sister once again. But if what Citlalic had said was true about there being no chance that Necalli and Coatl would return home, then Acalan didn't want to make their short lives any more miserable than they already were.

He did wish that he knew why Citlalic was so certain of this though. He supposed he should be okay knowing he wouldn't get the answers to that question, at least not until the time was right, as

Citlalic had said.

"It really does ruin everything," Metztli replied curtly as she stood from her bed. "Without the tournament I think some of these people could have been our friends, but there's no point in sulking on it for too long. Like you said, we both need to rest. Please try to sleep tonight. I'm going to try and convince our mother to let us train for a little while tomorrow. It would be perfect, all the other heirs will be with their families mourning, so we would be free to train as we please. But no reading at your desk all night. Okay?"

Acalan hardly believed that their mother would even come close to allowing them to train on the holy day of mourning, but if Metztli thought it to be necessary then he wouldn't argue. He gently ruffled her hair as passed her and opened the door. Their conversation hadn't been long by any means but it had felt good just to sit down and speak to her as siblings.

"Make sure to get some rest too, okay?" Acalan said, a genuine smile following his words.

He was about to close the door behind him when he heard his sister call for him. Acalan turned around and peaked his head into her bedroom.

"I love you, I know we don't say it very often but we should," Metztli stated, offering her brother a genuine smile too.

It was true that they didn't say it nearly as much as they should. They should have started saying it more frequently a long time ago, but there was nothing that Acalan could do to change the past.

"I love you, too. Sleep well, okay?" Acalan responded, waiting until his sister nodded softly to close the door behind him.

He might have previously failed in his brotherly duties but tonight felt like a success. It also felt like a failure to some degree. Much had been left unsaid between them and while he'd sworn an oath to secrecy with Atzi, with every minute that passed the prince couldn't help but feel like he was betraying his sister somehow by not telling her the truth.

Acalan tried desperately to shake that feeling as he walked towards his own bedroom down the hall, hoping that rest would clear his mind and consciousness.

METZTLI

great yawn escaped Metztli's lips as she was greeted by the sun. She'd slept like a log. Not one that was tossing and turning with the river's current but one that rested peacefully but the river bank.

Admittedly, she was quite grateful for this. The night before she'd hardly slept due to the taunting from the other heirs, and she was unsure if she would be able to sleep peacefully when night came again. How could she after all? It would be impossible when she knew she had to wake at the crack of dawn to make way for the Pyramid of Tributes.

As she blinked harshly and rubbed the sleep from her eyes, Metztli became vaguely aware of the fact that she didn't have years, months, or even days before the tournament began. All she had was hours, minutes, and seconds. Everything she'd ever trained for came down to this moment.

It was strange. Half of her wished the tournament would just begin now so that she could stop dreading it, and the other half hoped that she would somehow wake up and find that the tournament was just a bad dream, a manifestation of her deepest, darkest fears and nothing else.

Metztli pinched herself but, alas, no luck. She wasn't dreaming, the tournament was real and it would begin the very next day. It was obvious to Metztli that she had two options at hand. She could either try to enjoy her last day of freedom, or she could spend the entire day sulking.

The latter would be the easier option but for the sake of her family she opted for the first.

Metztli dragged her sleepy body out of bed, stretched her limbs until she no longer felt stiff and made her bed as neatly as she could. She knew her handmaidens would have been more than happy to make it for her but there was no guarantee that she would ever be able to do it herself again. Even small things like that were being taken away from her. Metztli stopped her thoughts the moment she recognized them. She'd decided not to sulk, so she would not.

She'd never lived through a day of mourning but her mother and father had explained it well enough over the years for her to know that not much would occur today. They were meant to fast until the sun set and the moon rose, in honor of the past tributes and heirs who had died in the tournament. As she began warming the water for her bath, Metztli couldn't help but think that it was a strange way to commemorate the fallen. Fasting was a traditional way of worshiping in Mexica but, would the fallen tributes really want their family members to go without food for even a day in their remembrance?

If she died, she would much rather her family throw a feast in her honor, or never speak of her again — either option would be better than having them suffer through a fast.

Aside from being unable to eat for the day, Metztli also knew that Atzi would be holding a service. It was special, not only because she would be honoring the dead, but also because it would be the last opportunity for the heirs to pray for their survival.

This felt silly to Metztli, too. She could agree that mortals had been idiots for starting a war with the gods in the first place, but if the gods were the ones who had given life to the tournament in the first place, she had no reason to believe they would be listening to the prayers sent to them.

As Metztli bathed in the warm water, she tried to think of everything that she had to do during her remaining hours of freedom. It was difficult to do so without sulking, but she kept true to the promise she'd made with herself.

Attending Atzi's service was a given, even if she begged her parents they would never allow her to skip it. She also wanted to train, but she wouldn't push far enough that it caused an argument within her family, so who knew if that desire would even come to fruition.

Most importantly, she needed to pack her bag with as many necessities as she could fit into it, without making it too heavy. It would be a challenge but it was necessary. They'd have to live off whatever they packed for days in the best case scenario. In the worst, it would be weeks.

She also needed to sharpen all of the blades she intended to take with her, including her spear, and make sure that Acalan packed accordingly, too. She thought her brother was more than capable of packing by himself but that wouldn't stop her from packing extra arrow heads just in case.

No one knew how long the tournament would last. Some lasted a few hours, while others lasted nearly a month, so she wanted to at least try to pack as well as she could. It was difficult to do though, without knowing what sort of resources would be provided.

After all of that, she just wanted to spend some time with her family, enjoy their last meal together and just be with them. Metztli had never been away from them for more than a few days, and even when her father would take her hunting, she was always with another member of her family. Even that would pose a challenge, or maybe she'd be so caught up in the tournament that she wouldn't feel homesick at all.

Metztli didn't leave her bath until the water was cold and her skin was wrinkly. She hated the feeling but it was better than having to go on with her day. She brushed her teeth vigorously with a fresh piece of tlatlauh root. She would pack more with her for the actual tournament but she doubted that brushing her teeth would even be a priority once the killing began.

Metztli oiled her skin, brushed her hair, and braided it down her back neatly. Her mother had warned her that during the day of mourning she needed to remain veiled at all times, so there was no point in trying to make it look nice.

Then, for the first time in Metztli's life, she donned a black dress. It was terribly modest and hid the figure she'd trained so hard for, but then again, she was supposed to be mourning, not focusing on how she looked. Still, she couldn't deny that her veil was beautiful. The lace was intricate and the fabric was short so she tucked a couple of pins here and there to ensure it would hold in place for the remainder of the day.

Metztli didn't exactly love what she saw in the mirror but she looked presentable. Besides, she had no one to impress.

The princess left her room in search of her brother. He was much better at getting ready for these sorts of things than she was so she really had no need to check on him, but she knew he was likely feeling as distraught as she was.

The tournament was relentless. If she died at least there would be some peace in knowing that it was finally over. The only thing really motivating her to continue her efforts to survive was the fact that she needed to stay strong for Acalan. His survival mattered more than hers, she was more than aware of that even if no one dared to say it to her directly.

Metztli knocked a few times on her brother's door before he finally opened it. He looked regal even in his mourning clothes. His skirt was long and the shirt he wore was fitted. Men had no need to veil so his curls bounced as they always had. The only adornment either of them wore were the golden heir rings on their fingers.

They would need to take those off before the tournament began. It was just another strategy designed by the gods to strip them of everything they cared about. It was cruel, but intelligent, Metztli couldn't deny that.

"Are you ready to mourn?" Her brother asked in a playful tone.

She'd promised herself not sulk today, but she didn't really have it in her to pretend to find anything amusing. She would try though, for Acalan she would do anything.

"Seems a bit strange that we have to mourn people we never even knew, don't you think?" Metztli asked as she stepped into her brother's bedroom.

She was happy to find that it was much neater than it had been the day before. There was no evidence of any visitors nor was there evidence that he'd spent the entire night reading, so she supposed that was good.

"I don't think the day of mourning is really for us though. It's for the families of the heirs. I know it's difficult to try and imagine father as anything but our father, but remember he lost a brother in the tournament, and the other families lost more than one heir," Acalan explained with a soft smile.

Metztli nodded in agreement. She felt a bit selfish for never having thought of it that way but it was difficult to think about anything other than keeping Acalan alive.

"I guess all we can do is be there for father today. We're more than capable of that, right?"

She realized that they did have something to mourn as well. It was a cruel realization, but they had to mourn who they'd been prior to the tournament because no one left it unchanged, no one at all.

"I'll be on my best behavior I promise…I mean look! I even wore my veil!" Metztli argued as she dramatically pointed to the lace fabric covering her hair.

She truly did intend on being on her best behavior, even when it came to Atzi's service. She wouldn't pray like the rest of them, but she would pretend to. That was all she could give them, and really they ought to be used to it by now.

"I did take note of that, it looks very lovely. If something happens to me in the tournament, please don't feel the need to wear it at my funeral though. Celebrate my life, don't mourn me," Acalan said. His tone never faltered, nor did his eyes ever meet hers.

Metztli had thought about them dying far more times than she would like to admit, but she'd never heard her brother openly speak of it. It tore her heart into two.

He would not die because she would not allow it.

"Don't speak of such things," Metztli half argued and half pleaded with him. "Today is hard enough and the last thing I need is the thought of you dying. Besides, you die, I die. Simple as that, I'm not returning without you."

Those were her exact plans. In the unfortunate case that her brother did meet his end, she would willingly give herself over to one of the heirs. That seemed like a much better option than returning home without him and having to face their parents alone.

"Nonsense, If I die in there and I find you in the afterlife, I'll…I'll make it miserable for you. Besides, think of this logically. If I die, our father will still need an heir. You will not get yourself killed, you'll survive and you'll let destiny do what it is intended to. Do you understand?" His tone was no longer playful nor was it sympathetic, he was giving Metztli an order like the true heir to their father's throne.

Metztli rolled her eyes in response, as much as she admired her older brother, all this talk about destiny was starting to get old. It had never come up so often before so she couldn't help but find it odd. Though, admittedly, everything about their lives felt strange.

"Father needs you, I would be useless to Tu'nethe, and I would never be the same without you." Metztli tried to explain, though she knew her words were falling on deaf ears.

She hadn't realized her brother had spent so much time thinking about this. To her it had always been clear: he died, she died. As long as he returned, she didn't matter in the grand scheme of things.

"You're right we shouldn't be speaking of this but I need to make this clear before we leave this conversation. The people of Tu'nethe would be lucky to be ruled by you. You are every bit worthy of inheriting our father's throne, even more worthy than I am. If something happens to me, don't throw away your life Metztli. And if something happens to you then I won't either. Promise?"

She didn't exactly agree with everything that he'd said. Especially not the parts about her being a worthy enough heir to rule, but she nodded in response. She didn't want the conversation to go any further than it already had.

"Fine, I promise," Metztli muttered before taking a deep breath.

She reminded herself not to sulk as she stood there for a moment, just calming herself from what they'd just discussed. At least it was over.

"C'mon. Let's go find mother and father so we can attend this service and be done with it," Metztli said, offering her brother a half smile. It was quite forced but she knew that he would appreciate it anyway. He always did.

With that, the two heirs from the House of Life made way for the great hall where Atzi's service of mourning would be held. Atzi's sanctuary was far too intimate to hold as many guests as were expected to attend, and they figured that their parents, being the gracious hosts that they'd shown to be, were likely already there.

They'd been right in assuming so, because the moment that they entered the great hall, Metztli spotted her mother and father through the crowd, near the front, sitting on benches that must have been pulled from the sanctuary of their home.

They both looked calm but Metztli knew this couldn't be easy for them. They only had two children and another who rested peacefully in the family cemetery. If the thought of losing Acalan made her skin crawl, she was sure that her parent's thoughts of losing the both of them surely made them sick.

She couldn't blame them. The thought of dying made her sick too.

ACALAN

Acalan used to feel peace when walking into Atzi's sermons, but not today.

He was sure Atzi's service would be beautiful, she always managed to make them so, but his faith had started to falter, a natural reaction to what he now knew about lies the gods told and the prophecy that had been kept from mortals for centuries.

Acalan would still try his best to enjoy it though, or at least pretend that he did, if not for his sake, then for his family's. They needed him. He recognized that in the way that Metztli had spoken to him earlier, and he saw it again in the expression painted on his mother's face.

Acalan couldn't let them down, it wasn't an option for him.

"You both look lovely," his mother said, greeting them.

"As do you mother," Acalan replied, earning a warm smile from both his mother and his father.

Now that Acalan was almost face to face with Xara, he could see that her eyes were swollen and slightly bloodshot, a clear indication that she'd been crying. She could try to hide it with a smile, but it was obvious, at least to her son.

There was no indication that his father had been crying, but Acalan didn't question it. Acalan knew that everyone dealt with grief in their own way. While Acalan and his mother would much rather cry and let it out, Metztli and their father dealt with their emotions in ways that Acalan found to be much less healthy. But now wasn't necessarily an opportune moment to lecture his family.

"Your mother has always been a sight to behold," his father said warmly, reaching over slightly to place a soft kiss on his wife's temple.

Seeing her family together seemed to lift his mother's spirits. It didn't solve all of their problems, but Acalan was at least happy knowing his mother was a little brighter.

They didn't say much once they were finally seated. Instead they remained quiet, waiting for the great hall to fill so Atzi could start her service. Acalan had never necessarily been in love with training, at least not like his sister, but today, a part of him hoped their mother would allow it. If only so he could get some of his frustrations out on a target.

Acalan turned to mention it to his sister when he noticed her gaze was fixed on Atzi. He'd known that they had had a bit of an altercation the day before, and of course he knew how much his sister disliked the priestess, but this was different. He didn't feel any rage radiating off Metztli. If anything, the look on her face seemed quite sad, perhaps a little confused as well.

"What is it?" Acalan questioned.

He must have interrupted a deep thought because Metztli turned quickly to face him, the same expression was still painted on her face.

"Nothing it's just…well Atzi is standing there, alone, and the other priestesses are all back there, talking amongst themselves, it's a bit strange don't you think?" Metztli asked. "Atzi loves the gods more than anyone we've ever known. I'm sure the other priestesses do too, but I haven't seen any of them interact with Atzi for the entirety of their stay here."

Admittedly, Acalan was a bit ashamed that he hadn't noticed what his sister did. Whether Atzi had ostracized herself from them or they'd pushed her away, he wasn't sure, but it made sense considering the secret she'd been carrying for so long. Friendship was a temptation that Atzi could not afford.

"I suppose even priestesses can be cruel," he mused. "Atzi inherited power when father won the tournament, I can only assume that's why they are staying away. I wouldn't worry too much though. Atzi is strong, and she's always enjoyed her privacy. If she wanted company, I think she would be here with us. Don't you think so?"

"Yeah, you're right, she's probably just contemplating all of the ways she can make a fool of me today," Metztli replied, her tone playful again, but Acalan could hear a bit of fear in it too.

He'd always thought it was a shame that Atzi and Metztli had never been close the way he was with her. But after having the prophecy revealed to him, he understood why it had to be that way.

Just then, Atzi started moving to the center of the stage. When the service finally started, Acalan was surprised to find that Atzi didn't speak of the gods. She didn't even really mention the tournament either aside from a short phrase about how unfortunate it was that every twenty-five years, ten or eleven young lives were lost.

Acalan couldn't deny that this at least made the service a bit more digestible, and as he turned to look at Metztli, curious to see how she felt about it, he found that she looked quite engaged.

For the first time in Acalan's life, his sister actually seemed enthralled by Atzi's teachings. It felt like some sort of miracle and yet, he was happy to have seen it at least once. He hoped to see it again if they returned home.

"While it is tragic to lose a loved one, whether that be a child, parent or friend, death is a natural part of life," Atzi explained as she walked across the stage, holding both her hands across her abdomen. "Sometimes one's destiny ends before we believe it should. What we must understand is that often, there is nothing that could have been done to prevent such events, all we can do is allow ourselves to grieve and hope that time heals the wound."

Acalan nodded softly in agreement with the priestess. If the prophecy was true as he believed it to be, then the only heir present whose destiny guaranteed anything was Metztli. That was what Acalan enjoyed most about the idea of destiny, it was almost comforting to believe everything was already predetermined, even if those promises only regarded his sister.

"Grief can be consuming," Atzi continued, her tone growing somber. "I think everyone in attendance will agree with that sentiment, but it is through grief that we learn to live in the absence of our loved ones who have passed. Sometimes we must travel through terrible storms in order to find light and peace…and what could be possibly worse than losing someone you love?"

Acalan turned to look at his father then, noting the way he squeezed his wife's hand. Atzi's words were especially true for Tenoch, it was in losing his brother that he found himself with an empire to rule and power beyond what any other emperor in Mexica knew.

The prince just hoped the same would not apply to Metztli and himself. If he lost his sister, then he would be losing all hope. And he would never be able to forgive himself for failing her in such a way.

"You may be asking yourselves, *How can we possibly honor our loved one's when we find ourselves overcome with grief?* I'm afraid the answer is not simple. That will depend entirely on who you are. What I can tell you is that the best we can do is live beyond the grief in order to honor our fallen children, loved ones, and friends. They would not want us to crumble in their absence, they would want us to bloom, to continue living and fulfilling our destinies. That is how we honor them and make them proud to have been a part of our journey." Atzi offered a comforting smile.

Everything she was saying made sense in theory, but Acalan knew that it would be rather difficult to remember all of this if he found himself in a similar situation. That much was obvious from the quiet sobs and soft sniffles that echoed throughout the great hall. Then again, if everything went accordingly, as the prophecy had predicted it would, then Acalan had no reason at all to worry. He just had to get his sister through the tournament and find a way to survive it too.

Atzi continued for a little while longer before bringing the service to a close. No one clapped, but in the silence of the hall Acalan could feel that everyone had been impacted by Atzi's words, Metztli included. After the service, his family waited to thank Atzi personally. The priestess had certainly earned it. After all, it was a great achievement to keep Metztli engaged, and she'd done it. In her very last service with them, she'd finally achieved it.

Acalan turned in his chair to look upon the crowd as he waited silently. There were plenty of crying mothers and grandmothers amongst them, all holding pieces of cotton fabric to their eyes to catch the tears coming from them. He looked for Citlalic in the crowd, and it wasn't long before he found her.

The sight filled him with dread. He was grateful that he hadn't made eye contact with the princess because she, too, was crying as she clung to onto her brother and cousin.

Without knowing exactly what Citlalic knew about the prophecy or how she'd come by her knowledge, he couldn't be too sure how accurate her revelation was. He did, however, know that she didn't believe that Necalli or Coatl would make it through the tournament – that much was certain from the way she held on to them tightly as if they would simply drift away if she did not.

Acalan wanted to comfort her, too, but he was sure that he would only make matters worse. If possible, he would find the time to check in on her, just one last time before the tournament began, just so he could remind her that if he returned home, he would fight for her, just as he had silently promised the night before.

"I do hope that my service was adequate for today, I couldn't tell when I looked out into the crowd," Atzi said, returning Acalan's focus from Citlalic and her family back to the woman who had practically been a second mother to him.

He still loved her despite the information that she'd held from her for so long. Nothing could change that, not even the prophecy.

"It was really beautiful…I liked the part about how our fallen loved ones aren't really gone if we keep the memory of them alive. It was…comforting," Metztli responded before anyone else could.

Almost in perfect unison, Acalan, his mother, and father all turned to look at Metztli with wide eyes. Acalan had been impressed by Atzi's ability to keep his sister interested, but he had never expected his sister to openly compliment Atzi's service. It was so unlike her, but he knew she was not fibbing.

"It's true Metztli," their father said. "Not a day goes by that I don't think about my brother. He may not be here with us, but he is alive in our hearts. He visits me in my dreams and in the memories I have of us as children." He wiped away a single tear that he'd let drift down his face.

It was the first real sign of emotion that he'd seen from his father in such a long time, so little and yet, big enough that Acalan knew that Atzi's words must have hit him in a wound that could never truly be healed.

"How could you possibly forget him when your daughter resembles him in character so much?" Atzi questioned.

Sometimes, it was easy to forget how old Atzi truly was. She'd watched their father grow, and Metztli and Acalan, too, but she still remained so full of life. A true child of Nemiliztli, even if the god was cruel.

"And that is also true," their mother added. "Your uncle was full of mischief and he loved adventure. He may not be here with us today, but I have no doubt that he is looking down upon us now, and that he will continue looking down on the both of you when you enter the pyramid. We may not be there physically either, but you must never feel alone. You will have each other, and we will be waiting for you two when the tournament ends." She brushed a gentle hand through Acalan's hair.

This felt too much like a final goodbye and while Acalan enjoyed his mother's comforting touch, he didn't want this conversation to continue for much longer. The tournament just brought talk of death and sorrow. They were young, they should be talking about their futures, about everything they wanted to do before they grew to Atzi's age.

"You two should listen to your mother, she has always been wise, even from a young age…" Atzi started. "I do believe this is enough talk of the tournament for one day though, and Metztli, I must also thank you for your praise. As I was writing my service for today, I thought that perhaps I have never tried hard enough to create a bridge between our differences. It was never your job to do so, you were only a child. And while I cannot remedy the past, I am glad my service was satisfactory for all of you today. Now, if you'll excuse me, I would much like to spend the day alone in my sanctuary. May you all have a blessed day." The old woman bowed slightly and started walking away.

For the second time today, Acalan's eyes went wide, and his jaw fell slightly. He never thought he would see the day where Atzi and Metztli put their differences aside. This all felt like a dream. Not a bad one by any means – it just felt too good to be true. He could tell that his sister had been touched by Atzi's words because she was desperately trying to wipe the tears away from her eyes.

The fact was that both of them had stopped being children a long time ago. The moment they knew of their responsibilities to each other and their empire, any thoughts of their childhood had drifted away. It was meaningful for Atzi to acknowledge that, despite their duties, they had only been children.

"It's okay to cry," Acalan whispered as he leaned over to wrap his arm around Metztli's shoulders.

He pressed a soft kiss into her temple and was surprised when she leaned into him, much like she had done anytime she'd been frightened or angry when they were still children. They might be adults in age, but had they ever truly developed into grown emotions? Acalan was unsure.

"Mother, if it's okay with you, I would like to train with Metztli today. I think we could both use the respite. I promise we won't take very long."

His mother didn't think twice before nodding yes in response.

"I think I would like to train with you two as well," their father interjected. "That is, if you both do not mind…It has been too long since we have all trained together."

Tenoch was no longer crying but Acalan could tell he was still emotional. It was understandable. Acalan wouldn't dare judge his father for that.

"Of course, we'd both like that," Acalan responded with a warm smile.

"Eat an orange before you train with your father," their mother half suggested and half ordered. "It warms the stomach and the heart too."

They were supposed to be fasting, it was practically a sin not to, but their mother cared more about their well-being than old traditions, that much was clear.

Acalan nodded softly as he stood, helping his sister stand as well. They would be okay. They had to be.

METZTLI

Metztli was unsure what had happened. One moment she was fine and the next she was a sobbing mess. So much so that her brother had needed to help her get back to her room. He only left her after she assured him she was okay a million times over.

She'd promised herself she would not sulk today, but she hadn't been anticipating for Atzi to apologize for her cruelty over the years, nor had she expected for anyone to acknowledge that she'd only been a helpless child when a blade had been forced in her hand.

Admittedly, Metztli had never allowed herself to admit this either.

Metztli appreciated the apology more than she could describe but at the same time it somehow made her even more worried for what was to come. Atzi had mentioned destiny far too many times for it to be a coincidence. Especially after Acalan had done the same over the course of the last few days.

The princess knew that her brother had spoken about something other than Citlalic with the priestess, even if he denied it. Something within him had changed when he returned from running that so-called errand with Atzi and whether Acalan realized it or not, his sister could recognize that whatever he was hiding from her was starting to eat him alive.

Metztli was already beginning to stretch out her shoulders by the time that Acalan came knocking at her door.

He had changed for training and managed to find two oranges while she had been collecting herself in the privacy of her room. She appreciated her brother's efforts, of course, but being kind wouldn't save him from the line of questioning he was about to endure.

"What did you think about Atzi's sermon today?" Metztli questioned, trying to seem as oblivious as she could. "I didn't get the chance to ask you before."

Acalan smiled brightly as he tossed an orange her way. That was a good sign, if she caught him off guard, he would be more likely to respond honestly.

"I thought she did wonderfully, it can't be easy to speak of grief in front of a large crowd. Plus, she impressed you. That speaks for itself."

Metztli nodded. Acalan had never lied to her about anything, at least not that she was aware of, and she hoped that he wouldn't start lying today.

"Is she that wise when you speak privately with her too?" Metztli questioned as she searched for a blade so she could slice her orange into quarters.

"Always. I'm glad you see it now, as I always have." Acalan replied quickly.

She could never deny that the priestess was wise but that didn't mean that she and Acalan were necessarily seeing eye to eye on this subject. For all she knew this was all a part of some scheme that Atzi had cooked up, and she would be damned if she allowed Acalan to fall for it.

"I'm going to ask you a question and I would appreciate it if you answered honestly," Metztli questioned as she turned around. She wanted to make sure she was really looking at her brother when she pursued the truth.

Acalan nodded hesitantly. It wasn't a verbal response, but it was more than enough confirmation for Metztli to continue.

"What have you and Atzi been hiding from me? I'm not angry, I just need to know. There's no point in denying it now. I know there's something and if I find out later that I was right and you lied to me, I'll see it as a betrayal of our trust."

Acalan's breath hitched as he absorbed her words. Panic ran through his eyes, but he said nothing as he turned his gaze to the orange that he held in his hands. There was no running away from the truth now, Metztli had made that clear.

"I had a terrible dream a few nights ago," he began. Metztli took a seat at the edge of her bed, patting the spot next to her. "I was alone in a forest that I did not recognize, and there was a panther present that spoke to me.

"The panther spoke to me about the Tournament of Heirs and what it meant for you and me. She mentioned our destinies and what they could mean for Tu'nethe. I was frightened when I woke up, hence why I sought out Atzi…I was afraid that it could be true, but Atzi reassured me that it was just a dream and nothing else."

The story was making sense for the most part, but Metztli felt like there had to be something else that needed to be said.

"What did it say? Regarding our destiny I mean," Metztli responded softly. Now that she had her brother talking, she didn't want to risk him pulling away.

"Just that we were capable of winning. I guess that's not the part that really frightened me, it was more so the knowledge of everything we would have to do to return home," Acalan replied, finally turning to meet Metztli's gaze.

The princess didn't see anything within his eyes that would lead her to believe that he was lying, and Acalan had always been a terrible liar. If all he was saying was true, however, then it would mean that Metztli was simply growing paranoid. Maybe she was, sometimes it certainly felt like it.

"And that's all? Nothing else was discussed?" Metztli questioned gently.

This was her brother's last opportunity to fess up and if he told her there was nothing else then she would need to believe him. What else was she supposed to do?

"Nothing else. We just spoke a lot about destiny and fate, it got me thinking about a lot of things. That's all it was, I promise," Acalan assured her.

His gaze never left hers and that was enough for Metztli to drop her guard for now. Acalan hadn't given her a reason not to believe him.

The princess found herself inching closer to her brother before she took a bite of her quartered orange.

"I think I'm a little more upset about the way you're choosing to eat your orange than I was about the dream to begin with." Her brother teased as he chuckled softly.

Metztli laughed, too, despite the feelings she was harboring within.

They both tried to be as careful as they could while they walked through the winding passages of their home. The last thing they needed was to get caught by anyone from the other families. Training on the day of mourning wasn't necessarily against the rules, it was just heavily frowned upon. Though, she doubted that the other heirs weren't doing a little bit of training in the comfort of their rooms on the upper floor of the palace.

Luckily the first floor was empty, making it easy for Metztli and Acalan to go unnoticed.

The sight of her father's face when they reached the training grounds was a welcoming one. He wore a warm smile as he stood outside of the entrance to their family's training arena, with two guards standing at his side. That was a smart idea. At least if they had guards standing outside, they wouldn't be taken back if anyone else tried to use the arena.

Metztli couldn't imagine that this was easy for her father. Not only was he sending his two beloved children into the hands of the gods, he was also sending his only heirs. Historically, this had never happened before, so no one really knew what would happen if her father was suddenly without any heirs at all.

"Have you both eaten?" their father asked, his voice full of worry.

"An orange just like mother asked. Have you?" Metztli asked in return.

She knew her father had been a very skillful warrior in his youth, but nowadays his duties as the emperor of the House of Life were a little more important than keeping up with training on a daily basis. He was still strong, but whether he would be able to keep up with them physically was a bit of a mystery. She supposed they were about to find out.

"Of course. I might have had two oranges, but don't tell your mother, she only saw me grab one," her father said, earning a soft chain of laughter from both Metztli and Acalan.

"You should lead today, father, just like you used to when we were children," Acalan said brightly as he rested his bow and arrows in a safe spot against the wall.

Metztli did the same with her spear. She loved that thing more than any of her other possessions, so she intended to keep it safe and in one piece for as long as she could.

"Well, I'm a bit out of practice but I'm sure I can manage…Why don't we start with a bit of running? I might still be quicker than the both of you," their father teased them before getting a head start on the both of them.

Initially Tenoch was able to keep up with them. They ran in circles around the arena. It was easy for Metztli and Acalan – they'd been doing this since they were children, always preparing for their imminent destiny. At some point though their father started gasping in search of air and they did not.

Metztli and Acalan continued running, never getting tired, simply more and more sweaty. Their father stopped when it was too much for him, grabbing a quick drink of water from the small natural fountain in the center of the arena.

"I am severely out of shape," he announced as he watched his children recover with ease.

Metztli giggled but in her mind, she was trying to remember when their father had gone from this larger than life figure to who he was today. He was still the best father she could have asked for. It was just that time had gone by quickly and he wasn't quite as nimble as he used to be.

"Don't worry father…it hurts me too," Acalan said in between jagged breaths.

This only caused Metztli to giggle again. While her brother was capable of keeping up with her and her stamina, she was definitely still the fitter one between the two of them. Then again, that was to be expected considering that Acalan spent all his free time with his nose in a book while she spent her time here, training and pushing her body to new limits.

"Well while you two catch your breath, why don't I set up some targets? Would that be okay?" Metztli asked, taking one last drink from the fountain.

She truly did feel just fine, a little winded at most but this was usually when she pushed herself to do even more. From the moment she'd been handed a blade she knew she had no room to be weak.

Her father nodded in agreement, so Metztli started setting a target board up for Acalan and one for herself.

Handling a spear the way that Metztli did required full body strength. Most of it came from her legs, hips, and arms. But truthfully, there wasn't a part of her body that wasn't being used when she swung it into the air, letting it fly directly towards her target.

She had the muscles to prove it too. Strong arms, an equally defined abdomen, and her thighs were muscular enough that she was grateful Tu'nethe hadn't acquired a taste for pants quite yet.

"Shall we get started?" Metztli said as she grabbed her spear.

Acalan groaned softly but he ran to grab his bow too. Their father had once been skilled in using a Macuahuitl, a paddle of sorts with sharp blades lining the outside. Very useful for close combat, but it couldn't really be slung at a target, so he wouldn't be joining them for this portion.

Metztli found it slightly curious that neither of them had chosen a Macuahuitl as their weapon of choice. Maybe they should have, to honor their father, but the weapons that they had chosen were perfectly suited for them. There was no doubt about that.

"Let's start with a round of ten, but of course, it only counts if you actually hit the center of the target," their father ordered.

This training session was beginning to resemble their childhood sessions more and more. Even more so when Acalan stepped forward to go first. Being that he was the older of the two he had always gone first. Even when Metztli had outgrown him in skill.

Acalan had two years of training on top of Metztli, but she'd caught up and surpassed them by the time that he turned thirteen and she was eleven. Metztli didn't brag about this, at least not outwardly.

Acalan did great, it had only taken him twelve shots to get to ten perfect rounds. Their father adjusted his stance slightly halfway through. Metztli was aware that they both knew his stance wouldn't really matter when someone inevitably came running towards Acalan in hopes of attacking him, but they let their father correct his form anyway, if only to appease him.

Metztli went next, her father let her swing her spear a few times, and every time she hit the center of the target with ease. A spear could do real damage. Arrows could too but, if you were stabbed with a spear, it was unlikely that you would recover. The wound was always too messy to treat before its victim bled out.

"Stop," their father commanded sternly when Metztli had tried to set up for another swing. She didn't think that she was doing anything wrong. If she had been, she wouldn't have hit her targets dead center each time. But she did as she was told, and waited for her father's critique.

"I didn't teach you to throw your spear that way," Tenoch said harshly. "Your hips are misaligned, and if you want your spear to stab through someone and not just into them, you're going to need to throw much harder than that."

Metztli turned slightly to look at her brother, who seemed equally shocked by their father's words. She'd been throwing spears since she was strong enough to hold one in her hands. She knew how to do this like she knew how to breathe, and their father had never critiqued her otherwise.

"Oh…I-I didn't realize…I'll try again…"

She was unsure how to take the criticism, it was difficult to process when she'd never really received any to begin with, and when she had, their father had always delivered it with a warm smile, so this was different.

She tried not to take it to heart as she retrieved her spear, positioned herself as perfectly as she could and launched it through the air. She'd used all of her strength this time, and her spear landed in the center again, so she was sure that her father would be happy with it when she turned. But as she did, she was only met with a disappointed look and a heavy sigh.

ACALAN

Acalan was thoroughly confused at the scene unfolding before him. While he'd always been perfect in the eyes of his mother and Atzi, Metztli had been much the same in the eyes of their father. Every one of Metztli's achievements had been celebrated by him, so this was bizarre.

The way the prince saw it, Metztli had been doing perfectly fine, she'd always been fiercely spirited, and she was a much better fighter than him so he couldn't understand where all of this sudden criticism was coming from.

"I'm sorry, I'm just not really understanding what I'm doing wrong," his sister countered before their father could lob another heated critique her way.

Acalan didn't understand what she was doing wrong either. In fact, he leaned slightly to his right so he could barely see the back of the target and found that the spear had gone through it cleanly. Not at an angle but straight through it. It had been a perfect throw and it would have certainly killed someone if the target had been made of flesh and not wood.

"It looks good to me, father… it went straight through the target," Acalan announced. He could tell from the expression on his father's face that he was frustrated but the prince did not understand why.

Their father had been fine a few moments ago. He'd even complimented Acalan despite the fact that he'd made a few mistakes. This wasn't fair. There was no reason why their father should be upset with Metztli.

"Do not defend your sister!" Their father responded in a shout, pointing his finger at Acalan harshly.

Acalan flinched at the sudden aggression. He couldn't remember the last time their father had yelled at either of them. Though he vaguely remembered a time when they'd both snuck out of the palace to roam through the forest. That occasion had warranted screaming though, and this one did not.

"Do either of you understand that it will only take one mistake within the pyramid for you to meet death? One mistake. Not many. JUST ONE!" their father fumed.

Acalan was taken aback. Of course, they understood. That fact had practically been beaten into each of them from the moment they'd begun training for this godforsaken tournament. It was all that they knew, all that they'd ever been allowed to know. Nothing had ever been more important than the tournament, not to Acalan, and certainly not to Metztli.

"Of course, we do…I'll just try again, better this time," his sister responded calmly.

It wasn't like her to not lash out in moments like this, but he could see that she was trying her best to obey the orders given to her. Their father had been quite pleased with Acalan's performance, but in truth, it should have been him receiving the scolding, not his sister. She'd given up her life to train for this. While Acalan went off and did other things to amuse himself, his sister had stayed, training for more hours than what was expected of her. She never stopped. Winning the tournament often seemed like her only purpose in life.

Their father did not respond, he simply watched as Metztli retrieved her spear once again, stretched out her neck and shoulders and adjusted her grip. She took a deep breath before raising it over her head, using every bit of strength in her body to swing it forward.

Time seemed to still as the spear cut through the air and dug itself deep into the board. Acalan hadn't realized that he'd been holding his own breath during this, but he had, and the moment the spear hit the target, he released it with relief when it hit dead center again.

Acalan watched closely as Metztli turned to look over her shoulder, practically pleading for any bit of praise that either of them could offer. But she didn't get a word, instead their father walked straight past her and to the board. He methodically analyzed it as if it had not been perfect, but it was.

"Better, now do that again," their father ordered sternly.

Even though his tone was still harsher than what Metztli deserved, she seemed to light up slightly at the brief praise. It wasn't really praise though, was it? His father had always been so kind with her, so gentle despite what they were training for, but none of that remained today.

Acalan stood by patiently, holding his bow behind him while Metztli went through the motion far too many times for him to keep track of. They'd switched boards numerous times now, but their father wasn't satisfied quite yet.

Metztli was strong, and she had will like no other person that Acalan had ever known, but there was only so much her body could do before beginning to fail her. This was ridiculous in Acalan's mind, and it made no strategic sense. In the tournament she wouldn't have to throw her spear over and over again. Just once, just one blow of the blade would be enough to kill anyone who tried to test them.

"She…She's growing tired father, perhaps that's enough for today," Acalan suggested in a whisper. "There is still more to do."

Metztli might have thought that she was hiding the pain well, but Acalan could see it clearly in the way her arms shook slightly right before throwing her spear. He couldn't stand by and watch as she pushed herself to ruin. Even if it was to appease their father. She'd done enough for one day, and her throws were only getting worse because of how many times she'd forced the spear back into her hands.

Acalan was aware of this, and he knew his father was too.

"It's fine, I can do more," Metztli argued as she brushed off the lingering sweat from her forehead.

Their father didn't move an inch, he simply watched as his daughter pushed herself to new limits. Acalan respected their father, he'd been exactly what they needed him to be as they'd grown, but this…this was cruel, and he knew his sister wouldn't stop herself. She was far too proud and driven to push away a challenge.

The only person she'd ever been truly worried about impressing had been their father and it seemed that he was using that to his advantage right now. Before, Acalan wouldn't have said a word, he would have allowed this to go on for as long as it needed to, but if he were to do that now, it would only make him cruel, too. And he already felt guilty about lying to her before.

Acalan looked at his father once more, gritting his teeth before he approached his sister and took the spear she held so desperately, out of her hands. He hated that he was being forced to be the only sensible one between the three of them, but if that was the role that he needed to fulfill to ensure she would be okay, then that was fine. He would proudly suffer through it for her sake.

"Give. Me. My. Spear," Metztli commanded with jagged words.

Acalan welcomed her anger. Appeasing their father wasn't worth hurting herself. She would thank him later for doing this, he was sure of it.

"Enough is enough," Acalan argued in return, holding her spear as far away from her as he possibly could. "You've proven yourself plenty Metztli, there's no need to overwork *yourself for useless praise.*"

"Is that what you believe my critique to be, son? Useless praise?" their father questioned, his chest held high in the air.

"Yes – that is exactly what I believe it to be today," Acalan fumed. "She's overworking herself, risking injury to win your praise. She's done enough. Her entire life she's done more than what was expected of her, the least you could do as our father is acknowledge that instead of watching her work like a dog for your approval."

Going against his father was something he'd never done before, but it certainly felt like this moment called for it. In truth, he should have defended his sister long ago. Maybe not by screaming at their father, but by dragging her out of the training arena when they were younger; by forcing her to discover hobbies she truly enjoyed instead of standing by and just watching her work herself into the shell of a person that she was today.

"Acalan, it's fine. You do not need to defend me, I'm fine," Metztli pleaded with him as she fought to grasp the handle to her spear.

When he turned to look at his sister though, he could tell that she was everything but fine.

"Do you wish to die Acalan?" Tenoch cut in angrily. "Is it your dream to never return home? To never see me or your mother again?"

The question seemed rather ignorant. Of course, Acalan wanted to live. He wanted them both to survive the tournament so that they could return home and see the prophecy come to fruition.

"Are you suggesting that I could ever want anything else? That I could possibly wish for my own death or for the death of my sister?" Acalan questioned fiercely, letting his words linger.

"Of course not…" he continued. "There is nothing more that I want than for Metztli and I to return home. There is nothing that I will not do to ensure it. That is why I've put a stop to this, how do you expect her to enter the Pyramid of Tributes tomorrow with the last memory of our father being this one?"

He had always looked away from his fear of killing and taking someone's life in exchange for his own, but today as he spoke, confronting their father, he embraced this fear. It was what made him human, what made his heart good to the core. But he was ready to fold up his heart and store it away somewhere out of reach in his mind.

Acalan would kill if needed. He would do it for his parents and their empire, but most of all he would do it for his sister, because in no world, did she deserve to have to face the brunt of the tournament alone.

"While I'm proud to see that you've finally found your bravery, it's you two who do not understand me," Tencoh said, his tone just slightly less harsh than it had been before. "Tomorrow you will enter the Pyramid of Tributes. You will sign your name away to the gods in blood, and neither of you will survive if your sister makes a single mistake when you are in that pyramid. I have seen the terror of what happens within those walls. All humanity and compassion will be gone, there will be nothing that I or your mother can do to save you.

"We always speak of how Metztli resembles your uncle. He was an honorable man, and even more so, an honorable brother. He was my best friend, and he is dead. One mistake took him away from this family. I will not allow for one mistake to take either of you from me. There are only so many battles a man can survive before he is left with nothing. Despite all the good that my brother was, he was impulsive, uncontrollable during his fits of anger, as are you, Metztli."

Their father turned to look at Metztli, and Acalan immediately knew that his father's words had been a mistake. It would take a miracle for them to not break his sister.

"I do not wish for you to die, their father continued. "I do not wish for you to make a mistake and be taken from this family forever."

Acalan could sense his father's fear and sorrow, it was practically radiating off him. Their father was no longer standing tall. If anything, he looked rather small as his shoulders hunched forward in defeat.

None of them spoke for what felt like a long time. They simply looked at one another until Acalan handed Metztli her spear.

"If that is what you believe Father, then perhaps it is best that you become comfortable with the idea of my death," Metztli muttered softly before turning to leave.

Their father shouted for her to return, Acalan couldn't blame him. When he'd been cruel to his sister, he'd wanted to do the same the moment he'd realized his mistake.

"Have you realized what you've done? We will not survive the tournament if she thinks you do not believe in her," Acalan simply said before he chased after his sister.

If anyone was capable of winning this tournament, it was Metztli. Not him, or any of the other heirs.

Winning this tournament was Metztli's destiny. Acalan just had to ensure she believed it despite their father's words. It was the only way they'd survive.

Metztli

etztli had never felt so useless. Her father's words had reopened a wound she'd been able to ignore before but now it was impossible. Guilt riddled her bones at the thought of being responsible for deaths that hadn't even occurred yet.

It wasn't like the princess had never been given criticism before. She'd actually been given plenty throughout her years of training, but her father had never been so callous with his words.

The logical part of her mind told her that her father's emotions were simply high. Everyone's were. It was impossible for them not to be with the stakes at hand. But how else was she to react to this? How could her father not acknowledge the sacrifices she'd made in preparing for the tournament and the immense strain on her heart caused by this responsibility that had been handed to her?

It had all been a waste of time. That was much clear from the way her father had spoken to her just now. Her father must have been seeing something she could not because this entire time she'd believed herself more than capable of winning.

What did he see in her that made him so sure she would make a lethal mistake and risk the future of their empire?

Metztli searched for the answer, thinking back to every time she had been uncontrollable. There were plenty of memories to go through, the latest one only being from the day before, but she only lashed out when there was a good reason to. It was that very rage that she had hoped would help her bring victory home. That she would be so rageful at the idea of someone wanting to hurt her brother, that she would have no problem in taking lives.

Metztli couldn't find it in herself to stop when she heard her brother chasing after her while she ran to her room. He begged her to stop and wait for him but there was no use. If their father didn't believe in her, then perhaps all hope was lost. Maybe Acalan also saw that impulsiveness, the inability to control her rage when it hit her with the force of a hundred stones.

"I just want to be alone!" Metztli shouted as she frantically fumbled with her doorknob.

Everything was difficult today. On top of that her muscles ached. She would regret it in the morning but then what? Would it even matter? Sore or not, her father believed she was incapable of getting through the tournament without making a lethal mistake.

"No! You've been alone long enough," Acalan pleaded. "I won't let you be alone through this or the tournament and I'm not leaving. I'm here, you have to know that I'm here for you now, and I'll be here for you when the tournament begins and ends."

Metztli wanted to believe him. Acalan was her brother, so honorable, kind and brave. He was her best friend just as her father and his brother had been, but the thought of failing in her duties was too much. She'd met her breaking point.

"You can't promise that!" Metztli argued bitterly. "You know you can't promise me anything. Tomorrow we enter the pyramid and for all we know we'll die the moment it begins, so don't promise me a single thing!"

They'd made so many promises to each other before, but she knew now how unwise that had been. Neither of them could promise each other anything. All they could do was try to survive

until it was over, but Metztli was tired of trying. She'd been trying to be perfect her entire life.

Enough was enough.

There was a moment of silence before Acalan grasped her shoulders, turning her around so she was forced to look at him. In his eyes she could see hesitancy, like he was debating what to say.

In his eyes she also saw sadness, and that broke her heart. It always seemed to when it came to her brother because he was too good for this world. He was too kind and warm to be going through any of this. He should have been able to inherit their father's throne without facing the tournament first.

"There is no one that I believe more capable of winning this tournament," he said. "None of those other heirs have the heart or compassion that you do...I believe in you, I always have and I always will."

After so many years of knowing someone, it was easy to tell lies from the truth, but this...this was genuine, straight from the heart.

Metztli fell apart for the second time that day, wrapping her arms around her brother and sobbing into his chest. If he believed her capable, then maybe she was. But what if she wasn't? What if she did commit a lethal mistake that ended in both of their deaths? The stakes were infinitely too high. And this wasn't just about their lives, but the lives of their people too. What would become of Tu'nethe and the House of Life if they did not succeed in this?

"I'm sorry," Acalan whispered as his head rested on hers. "I've left you to carry this burden for too long on your own. I should have been there with you, training every day, making sure you were taken care of too... this burden, it is not only yours Metztli. You're my sister, my best friend. I know I shouldn't promise you anything, but I am, I'm promising to take care of you until the very last moment that I can...you just have to believe me."

She couldn't remember the last time he'd held her like this, but it must have been when they were children, when she still depended on him for comfort instead of bottling up all her feelings and hoping she wouldn't overflow with emotion. She didn't want to be taken care of, it just wasn't in her nature, but she had to accept this, if not for herself then for her brother.

"Do you really believe we can win?" she asked, pulling away slightly to dry her tears with her sleeve.

Acalan didn't need to respond, his answer was clearly written on his expression. He believed in her and in them. And at that moment, it didn't matter if the rest of the world did not believe in her, her father included. As long as Acalan believed in her, that was enough, because it was he who would be competing alongside her, not anyone else. His opinion was the only one that mattered now.

"And father believes this too, you have to know that in your heart," Acalan replied. "He just spent all morning thinking of his brother. I'm sure the memory of his death is still vivid in his mind, but you aren't our uncle. You're better, father knows that too. He's just scared, we all are, aren't we?"

"We can't afford to be scared, Acalan," Metztli reminded her brother.

It wasn't exactly the sort of thing that either of them could control, but it was the truth. Being scared would only harm them in the end. And if there was any moment to be brave it was now.

Acalan smiled, before grasping the door handle behind her.

"Then we will just pretend that we are not, and hope that we believe it to be true by tomorrow. There's still much to do today. Why don't we occupy ourselves with more important matters, yes?"

Metztli agreed with a silent nod before she entered her room. She didn't want to think about death, or the fact that these very well could be the last moments she ever spent in the comfort of her room, but she did, only for a moment before her brother's words replayed in her mind.

"Shall we pack our bags then?" Metztli asked, leaning her spear against the wall. "I need to sharpen my blades." Acalan picked his bow off the ground in response. There was no avoiding the tournament now, but they could prepare for it, and they could pretend that everything would be okay.

"Do you not think six blades is enough?" Acalan questioned as Metztli reached to sharpen her seventh.

She couldn't help but roll her eyes in response. Of course six was not enough. In truth, she wouldn't be satisfied even if she managed to cram in all of the blades she owned in her bag, but she'd decided on eight just in case. Some she would carry on her body and the rest would be safely stored in her pack, just in case she needed them.

"I'm bringing eight, and I expect you to do the same. How many arrowheads are you planning on bringing?" Metztli asked. "We can make some if we need to."

She thought packing would be much easier but with everything laid out on her floor, she was struggling to comprehend how she would be able to fit everything in one sack.

Then again, it was a courtesy that the gods allowed them to bring anything at all. In the past, hundreds of years ago, the heirs would go in with nothing but the clothing on their backs. She was glad that rule had changed, at least now they could bring some essentials that would help them through.

"Eight...alright, duly noted," Acalan replied confidently. "I think I have sixty made, that should be enough. I can reuse the same arrowhead a few times. Besides, these tournaments never last more than a week."

Metztli was honestly impressed. Sixty was a good number, but she would still pack a few more just in case. Historically, her brother was correct. The tournament often ended quickly but they needed to prepare in case it didn't. Some of their competitors were fierce, and she doubted that any of them would go down without a fight. Ideally most of them would kill each other off before Metztli and Acalan had to be a part of it.

"That's an adequate amount, just don't get too overconfident. Each tournament is different, and the gods just get more and more creative with time."

Aside from the killing and inhumanity they would see within the walls of the pyramid, not knowing any other specifics was perhaps the scariest part. They truly had no idea what they would be walking into. Her father's tournament had been held in a desert with no fresh water or prey to hunt other than the other heirs. For all they knew they'd be walking into a maze with no end in sight.

"I'm not," Acalan retorted, "but logistically, there's only twelve heirs. Some will die of natural causes and others will be killed as soon as the trumpets sing…We could be stuck in there for weeks. But realistically we probably won't be. I guess that's sort of comforting, isn't it? If we think we just have to survive a few days, it will make it easier."

She neatly folded a thin blanket and shoved it into the bottom of her sack. She doubted that she would be able to sleep while the tournament was happening, but a blanket would at least keep her warm if it was cold.

"If that makes you feel better then let's go with that, but to make me feel better we should prepare well," she said. "I think this is everything I will need, though. Now I just need to run down to the kitchens for more dried meat…maybe some fresh fruit if I have the space to spare. You can wait here if you want, I'll be quick." She stood from where she'd planted herself on the floor.

She was quick to reach for her veil. While she'd taken it off to train, the last thing she wanted was to be caught without it now.

"Actually," Acalan started, the slight guilt in his tone made her turn quickly to face him.

She doubted her brother had a bad bone in his body but the way he spoke made her nervous. Everything was putting her on edge today. She only relaxed slightly when he laughed softly at the expression on her face.

"I was just going to say that I wanted to go find Citlalic, she seemed pretty upset this morning after Atzi's service…so I just thought I might check on her. Do you think that's too much? Too forward maybe?" Acalan questioned nervously.

If anything, Metztli was relieved that this was what her brother had to say, and not something completely out of pocket. She found it sweet that he was still wondering whether the princess actually liked him.

"Too forward? You kissed the girl last night, Acalan," Metztli teased as she wiggled her eyebrows and laughed. "Go check on her if you feel the need, I'm sure she would be happy to see you…especially since you two are you know…in love!"

That alone was enough for Acalan to quickly stand as if he were to defend himself, but he didn't, because nothing that Metztli said was untrue.

"I'll meet you back here before supper, okay? If you see father before then, just try to be calm. And if you see Necalli…just don't kill him, let him enjoy his last living hours, got it?" Acalan ordered kindly.

It was strange how he was growing into an emperor right before her. Years ago, an order like the one he'd just given wouldn't have come easily to Acalan, but it did now. Seeing her brother in this new light was the perfect motivation to win, because she wanted to see him crowned someday. She wanted to see what would become of their empire under his care.

"Of course, your grace…now go! Don't keep your lover waiting too long." Metztli teased.

She was happy to see that her words made Acalan smile and laugh to himself. He walked away with a little pep in his step, and this didn't go unnoticed by Metztli. If anything it put a smile on her face, too.

ACALAN

Acalan made his way across the second floor to the guest quarters of his home in search of the princess. He'd been thinking about doing so all day despite everything that had happened. He was sure it was not just his family suffering through these final moments. As cruel as the other heirs seemed to be, they were all here for the same thing.

To win for their families.

Admittedly, Acalan found it a little unfortunate that Citlalic was from one of the opposing houses. The odds were stacked against them in every regard. They were supposed to hate one another because of the unfortunate divide that had been placed between their families, but Acalan did not hate her. It was quite the opposite, actually. His sister had claimed it was love and though that seemed a bit irrational to confess, he couldn't really think of another word to describe what he was feeling deep in his chest.

That's all that Acalan could think of as he approached the hall where he knew the Cruz family had been given rooms. Upon entering the narrow corridor, he was met with a series of identical wooden doors that bore no markings signaling which family member resided in which room. He wasn't necessarily afraid of Necalli, his father, or their cousin Coatl, but he knew what this would look like to them.

A prince seeking out a marriageable princess could only really mean one thing. While this thought did make Acalan nervous, he realized that those were his intentions. If he won, he would return and find a way to win her hand at any cost. He supposed that it was better for her family to know that sooner rather than later.

Acalan knocked softly on the first door. He desperately hoped that he'd somehow guessed correctly, but being that there were three other options, he knew the odds were stacked against him at this moment. Still, he waited patiently until he heard footsteps approaching. The doorknob shook, and he was met face to face with none other than Necalli Cruz.

"Acalan Amos…you know, I was hoping I would see you today," Necalli taunted at the sight of him.

If anyone had asked the prince what he thought he would do in a moment like this, he would have guessed that he would freeze completely, but he did not. If his sister was not afraid of Necalli then he had no reason to be afraid of him either.

"Were you?" Acalan questioned confidently. "I don't mean to disappoint, but I'm actually looking for your sister. Do you know which room is hers?"

He found it bizarre how Necalli leaned so passively against the doorframe. His arms were crossed against his chest, but he didn't seem upset by the mention of his sister.

"Citlalic? Well of course I know which room is hers. But I'll only tell you if you tell me where your sister is," Necalli said, bargaining with Acalan.

Unfortunately, Acalan knew how intolerable Metztli found Necalli, so there was no possible way he was about to give that information away, even if he did want to see Citlalic. He could, after all, just keep knocking on the doors until he found her.

"Sadly, I don't think my sister wants to see you."

He didn't want to openly say that Metztli was looking forward to Necalli's death, though a part of him was sure the Prince of Blood already knew that to be true. If Acalan returned home Citlalic would be there, but if Metztli returned, that meant Necalli had been lost to the pyramid. Necalli had to understand that, right?

"Well, it was worth a shot, don't you think? My sister is in the gardens. I would be cautious though, Necalli responded casually. "She's mourning our mother today, so I'm not sure if she'll want company."

Acalan was slightly taken aback, he hadn't expected for Necalli to give up the information as quickly as he did, nor had he considered that the Cruz family would be mourning the loss of their empress. Acalan felt stupid for not having considered that earlier. He'd never lost anyone dear to his heart, but he still wanted to see Citlalic, if anything he could try to make her smile. He nodded before turning to leave in search of the princess.

"Wait!" Necalli shouted, causing Acalan to turn back on his heel to face him. He wasn't sure what would come next, but he could sense that it wasn't aggression.

"Whatever my sister told you last night…If you truly care about her like it seems that you do, take care of her when all of this is over. She's strong but I would feel better knowing that someone is going to take care of her," Necalli confessed.

Acalan couldn't help but sigh deeply. Quite frankly he was getting very tired of these last minute confessions. He would much rather everyone keep what they knew to themselves. Only because it made him question everything that he knew.

He was seeing a different side to Necalli though. This wasn't the man who had pestered his sister over the last few days. He was just a brother who wanted to care for his sister, and Acalan understood him at that level.

"Of course," Acalan responded before turning again to leave.

This time Necalli did not move to stop him, and he was grateful for it, because he wanted nothing more than to see Citlalic.

Acalan rushed as quickly as he could to the gardens of his home. It was a beautiful day outside. He didn't find Citlalic immediately, but the gardens were vast, so he walked around, passing through an arch wrapped with roses before spotting his princess.

Acalan was saddened to find that Citlalic looked even more disturbed than she had when he'd seen her that morning. Her eyes were puffy, an obvious indicator that she had been crying for quite some time. He didn't say anything as he sat on the bench with her. Even if he did want to speak, Acalan was unsure that he'd really have the appropriate words to say.

"How did you know where to find me?" she peered at him with curious eyes.

Acalan knew that this wasn't pain that he could fix, but he

wanted to. It wasn't fair that someone with such a beautiful heart should ever be upset like this.

"Your brother – he told me you'd be here." Acalan explained as he wrapped his arm around her shoulders. "It was kind of him to tell me where you were."

He was happy when she leaned into his embrace, practically melting into him. That was fine, if this is what she needed to feel better then Acalan was happy to oblige.

"He is kind at heart, I know it may not seem like it, but he is," Citlalic said.

A soft sniffle escaped her. Acalan was unsure if he should mention her mother, it didn't seem like the right thing to do when his mother was well and alive. And Xara was probably sobbing too right now.

For a half a second Acalan debated if he should be with his mother instead, but he knew his mother would just send him away if he tried to comfort her, so he stayed.

"My sister would disagree but, I see the good in him," he said. "If we weren't in these circumstances, I think I would have enjoyed his friendship."

He wasn't lying. Honestly, his feelings about Necalli were conflicting. He admired Necalli's need to ensure his sister would be taken care of, if Acalan were in his shoes he would have asked the same of Necalli. At the same time though, he knew how much of a pain in the ass Necalli had been to Metztli, and she came first, always.

"He likes your sister I think…he won't confess it of course but I can see it in him. I should apologize for his behavior. I know he comes off as arrogant, but our lives have been difficult, we don't have a family like yours, he's just never been taught how to process his feelings, and I think…he's scared because he knows what's to come." Citlalic buried herself deeper in his chest.

Acalan allowed her to do this, as he brushed a hand through her hair. It was comforting to him too because a part of him understood how Necalli must feel. Acalan's family was caring and warm. They'd always loved Acalan and Metztli for who they were, but he knew that the other houses had different expectations for their male heirs.

Acalan was unsure of who he would be if he hadn't been allowed to cry as a young boy. If he'd been met with an open hand instead of open arms when he showed any ounce of emotion. As a man, he also knew for a fact that Necalli was infatuated with Metztli. There was no question about it, and he couldn't blame Necalli. His sister was one of a kind, unlike any other woman in Mexica. She'd already had her fair share of suitors even before Necalli came around.

He also thought that in an ideal world they might have been good for one another. Metztli had been crafted from pure fire and Necalli seemed to have been crafted from the same torch. Vicious fire was most often only controlled when fought with fire, so in an ideal world, he could have seen his sister being quite happy with the Prince of Blood.

"I think she likes him too. If she didn't, I don't believe she would be so infuriated by his taunting," Acalan confessed, noting the slight smile that appeared on Citlalic's lips. "He's not the first man who's taunted her like this, but he is the first to elicit such a strong reaction from her.

"Unfortunately, this is a matter of destiny," he continued. "As much as I find myself curious to know what could come of those two. Only two blood bound heirs can win. I suppose it just wasn't destined to be between them. It's a shame. I hate the thought of Metztli having to sacrifice love to fulfill her destiny."

"Your sister is our only hope. Whatever happens during the tournament…it has to for the good of our people," Citlalic responded, her tone was calmer now that she'd stopped crying.

"Your brother knows too, doesn't he?" Acalan questioned.

He didn't want Citlalic to think he was accusing her of anything, he was just curious as to what exactly the Cruz heirs believed they knew. Right now, it felt like they were speaking in half-truths, and that just felt wrong, so utterly wrong.

"He does, and so does Coatl. I'm afraid that's all I can say though," Citlalic answered.

Acalan hadn't really expected her to explain everything to him, but he had gained a little more information, so he was grateful for that. The latter half of her words did spark a thought within him though. Maybe Citlalic couldn't say anything, but perhaps she could confirm what she did and didn't know if he simply presented information before her. They wouldn't have to speak a word. She would just have to nod yes or no.

"Can I take you to my room? I have an idea, but I can't say it out loud if the gods are really listening. It will make sense there though, I promise."

It wasn't until the words really left him that he realized what he was asking for. The evening before he'd stolen her away to these very gardens but that had been different. It was a public space, and his room was…well it had complete privacy.

As Citlalic looked at him with wide eyes, he could see the moment that the thought flashed through her. For a second, he expected a firm slap across his face, but it never came.

"Okay," Citlalic replied before pulling away from him to stand. She gripped his hand in her own while her other wiped away the tears still present on her skin.

Acalan didn't say anything else. Mostly because he wanted to remain quiet as they tiptoed through the palace, hoping to remain unseen. They managed quite fine, and soon found themselves in front of his bedroom door. Acalan opened the door for her, holding it until she walked through it. He just hoped his plan would work, the risk they were taking was too big for it not to.

ACALAN

At first, Citlalic had been amused by the number of books the shelves of Acalan's bedroom held. He let the princess roam as much as she liked. He was grateful he had left it as neat as it was. It wasn't like he'd necessarily been expecting a guest, he just liked it this way. She took a book from the shelf. Had it been anyone else, Acalan would have cringed at the sight. His books were his most prized possessions, but he knew that they would be safe in the gentle hands of the princess.

"I thought you didn't indulge in romance?" Citlalic asked as she held the book up.

Acalan smiled and chuckled nervously in return. He had hundreds of books in his room, and she had to pick *that* one to examine out of all of them? She didn't seem to judge him for it though, so that was good, much better than he imagined a moment like this one might be.

"There are a few more on the shelf below if you're curious," Acalan responded as he brushed a hand through his hair.

His collection of romance novels was not vast, but he did have a few of them. He supposed it was a little embarrassing but he couldn't find it in himself to be. He wanted to be honest with her in every way…She looked even more beautiful here in his library as the sun shined through his windows.

"Would you mind if I borrowed this one?" Citlalic asked, holding up a novel he didn't immediately recognize. "Just while the tournament goes on. It'll help distract me."

To be quite honest she could have held up his most prized possession and he would have still nodded yes. Anything that she wanted, he was willing to give to her.

He watched as she slowly walked back to him, smiling softly before she took a seat at the edge of his neatly made bed. He'd never had a woman in his room before, but this felt natural. That had to be a sign of something.

He collected a few of the books that had been piled on his desk, along with a pencil and a piece of parchment. In theory this would be rather simple, it was just a matter of whether the princess wanted to participate or not. He saw no reason why she wouldn't want to though. If she really did know about the prophecy, then combining what they knew could only help Metztli in the end.

Acalan took a seat right next to her, placing the books on the other side of him so they were as close as they could be.

Before explaining anything, Acalan pulled Atzi's book of the tournament's history on his lap. He swiped through the pages until he found the first paragraph that had confounded him and when he found it, he brought up the piece of parchment and scribbled a few words down.

Nod – yes or no.

Acalan gave Citlalic a few moments to read it and make her decision. He watched her for a moment. As she brought her gentle hand to brush her hair behind her ear, he thought that the princess might decline, but instead she nodded softly and inched even closer to him. His heart was racing, but he continued anyway. It was better if he tried to ignore these newfound feelings.

Acalan dragged his finger to the sentence that had first puzzled him. The one that stated that it hadn't been the Goddess of Blood who had suggested the tournament in the first place but, rather, the God of Life. Once he was sure that Citlalic had read the sentence, he quickly jotted down his question.

Is this true?

He didn't have to wait very long for Citlalic to respond with a confident yes. That didn't surprise him. Atzi had confirmed that much through various historical books and documents, but Acalan was excited about the fact that this was working.

His careful line of questioning continued. He didn't believe that Citlalic had any bad intentions, and she had already revealed some information to him that perhaps she shouldn't have, but he was still cautious, building up his trust with her in every question that he asked.

Some questions were directly about the tournament while others were about the House of Blood. A few hinted at the prophecy. Each time she looked at him with a stare that said she already knew. Somehow, he didn't doubt that. She'd said enough even if she wasn't willing to tell him exactly how she knew what she did. He understood Citlalic in that respect. When it came to his family, he was willing to do anything to protect them, starting with winning the tournament.

Acalan thought he'd asked everything that he could until Citlalic took the parchment and pencil from his hands, jotting down her own question. She kept the piece of parchment close enough to her body that he couldn't see what she was writing. A little part of him was nervous as he waited patiently. But in all fairness, he'd just spent the last hour questioning her, so it only seemed right that she got to ask him a few questions too.

It was only a few moments later when she placed the piece of parchment back in front of him.

Prophecy?

Acalan froze. The question was clearly written on the parchment filled with scribbles. He'd been thinking about the prophecy so much over the last few days that he thought he might be used to it by now, but the mention of it even in written form still startled him, making his heart stop and mouth run dry. He knew he shouldn't be speaking of this with anyone, not even Citlalic.

Acalan's entire body had gone tense. Citlalic must have noticed this because the next thing he knew, a soft hand was rubbing his back. Acalan melted in her touch. But still, he couldn't find the strength to respond, not physically or verbally.

"You don't have to respond if you don't want to…it won't make me think any less of you," Citlalic whispered softly. She was so close, too close even.

Goosebumps raised on his skin at the sound of her voice. The princess was beyond intoxicating. This should have made her dangerous, but it did not. She should have pushed for an answer, but she didn't. Then again, hadn't his silence been an answer on its own?

"Maybe this is enough for one day," Acalan replied. "There's nothing either of us can do now except wait."

He stood half frantically, collecting all of the books laid out on his bed as well as the parchment and pencil. He lit the piece of parchment with a torch that always stayed ablaze in his room. That's how serious this information was. He couldn't risk it leaving this room. He was avoiding looking back at Citlalic even though he wanted to, even when she rose from the bed as well and wrapped her arms around him from behind.

"Can I ask you one last question?" Citlalic said softly.

Without even knowing the question, Acalan knew he should deny her this. They'd said enough, risked enough for one day. Still, he couldn't stop himself from turning to her. Both of his hands rose to cradle her gentle face in his hands. Everyone involved in this tournament was too good, too kind to be corrupted with the information they had, that was perhaps the most tragic part of this.

"Ask away," Acalan responded softly, holding the princess as close to him as he possibly could.

"Kiss me. Please," Citlalic asked in a tone that resembled pleading more than anything else.

His brow furrowed slightly at the opportunity before him. He tried to find a reason in his mind to say no, to push her away gently and never think about kissing her again. But he couldn't. There was no reason in his mind that was viable enough for him to do anything but lean in slowly and capture her lips with his own.

Their lives were too complicated for him to deny her this. The connection that they shared seemed to be the only thing that wasn't complicated, it was simple and real, so tangible that he felt he could reach out and grasp it. Instead, he reached to grasp her waist while Citlalic's hand found its way to his hair, pulling enough that a whimper left his lips.

Acalan pulled away only a moment later, breathless and filled with desire for something he'd never had before, something he'd never given himself the opportunity to even want. Citlalic was staring right back at him, doe eyed and breathtakingly gorgeous.

By all accounts it seemed she desired the same thing. This was reckless. They shouldn't even indulge the idea. Acalan was aware of this enough that he took a step back, making himself lean against his desk, his hands gripping the edge of it until his knuckles turned white.

Putting distance between them could only help for so long though because the princess took a step forward, closing the gap Acalan had put between them. He didn't stop her from touching him, cradling his jaw with her delicate hands and brushing her thumb over his cheek.

"Let me give you this, please," Citlalic pleaded with him. "It is all I have to offer, and you are the only man who could ever come close to deserving it." Her lips brushed over his softly, making Acalan squeeze his eyes shut in response.

He didn't want to deny her this. That's the last thing he wanted to do but, the stakes were already so high. If they did this, if he allowed her to give him this moment, then there would be no going back. He would ruin her for any other man who ever desired her, and in turn it would ruin him too, because what woman could ever compare to her?

None, absolutely no one.

"You don't need to give me anything Citlalic, it will not change the way I feel for you if you do…this is not a matter of want, it is a matter of responsibility. I cannot ruin you in good conscience." Acalan allowed his eyes to flutter back open.

Big mistake. It was even more difficult to deny her this desire when he was looking at her. She was like an angel, too good for this world and far too good for him. "You could never ruin me…and no one would have to know. My entire life has already been decided for me, as it has been for you. Let us do this for us, even if it is the only thing we ever get to decide for ourselves."

He could not recall the last time he'd done something for himself. Every decision he made was for the good of his people and his family. In a way, he felt like he'd earned this, hadn't he? Perhaps so, but he could not go forward with this unless she knew the consequences and what it meant for the both of them. There would be no going back from this.

"I would ruin you…because if I had you once Citlalic I would never stop wanting you. Morning and night my mind would be filled with the thoughts of you. My heart would always burn for you and no one else. I would never stop fighting to have you. Is that what you truly want?" Acalan questioned, wide eyed, half hoping she would simply say no so that they could move forward from this.

"What else could I ever possibly ask for?" Citlalic affirmed as confidently as he'd ever heard anyone speak before.

Acalan didn't give himself a second to breathe before he was pulling the princess back into his arms, devouring her lips with his while still trying to remain gentle. That's what she deserved. He knew that.

He kissed her passionately until he was sure he'd committed the feeling to memory, and only then did he allow his lips to drift further down until he was kissing the soft skin of her neck. Citlalic moaned softly in his arms, encouraging him to go further. That wasn't a problem. Acalan had a detailed list in his mind of everything he wanted to do with her, starting with this.

He let his hands roam her body until they found purchase below her hips. All of the years of training his father had put him through, finally came in handy because he lifted the princess with ease, earning a slight yelp from her, which he happily met with a smile.

He didn't stop until he had her splayed out on his bed, hovering over her. He took her in with nothing but the utmost respect and admiration for her and everything that she was.

"Are you sure?" Acalan then asked, a warm smile painted on his lips. "We can stop right now. It will not hurt me if you've changed your mind."

"I've never wanted anything more than this," the princess

muttered, reaching up to caress him.

Acalan nodded softly in response before enveloping his lips with hers again. It was short but filled with desire for more, so much more.

He continued kissing down her jaw and over the curve of her breasts. There was not a single part of her body that he did not want to touch and know completely, but before anything else he wanted to please her. He had learned enough from his romance novels to know he should put her pleasure before his, so he continued, inching down her body slowly until he was met with the hem of her gown. It was beautiful but he wanted to rip it off her and promise her another dress.

Acalan kissed up her legs then, alternating from side to side as he slowly moved the fabric away to gain access to more skin…

"Can I?" Acalan questioned softly, waiting for approval before he hooked his fingers through her undergarments and pulled the piece of fabric off her.

He'd meant for it to go smoothly but the fabric had gotten stuck on her ankle, earring a giggle from her which only made him smile even more.

"What exactly are you planning to do? Do you not know how this works? It's okay if you don't I-"

"I know exactly how this works…just trust me, you can do that right?" Acalan interrupted before the princess could finish her sentiment.

"Of course…always," Citlalic affirmed.

That was all that Acalan needed to know before he began pressing soft kisses into her legs and inner thighs. Her soft whimpers and the sound of her breath hitching only motivated him more as he spread her legs wider with ease, positioning them over his shoulders.

There was no going back now.

After all was said and done, Acalan and Citlalic laid next to one another underneath his blankets. They hadn't bothered to get dressed, though it was probably the smarter thing to do. Instead Acalan happily laid there with Citlalic in his arms. He was brushing a gentle hand through her hair while she traced her fingers along the scars on his chest. None of them had grand stories, at least nothing above the mischief he and Metztli had gotten into as children. He imagined he would have more by the time the tournament ended, only those would carry much more meaning than the ones he had now.

"Thank you…It was perfect," Citlalic said as she adjusted slightly, leaning up on her forearm so that they could look at each other.

This was certainly a view Acalan wanted more of.

"I particularly liked that thing you did with your tongue, where did you learn that? Actually…no! Don't tell me, I'd find her and rip her to pieces," Citlalic continued playfully.

It was the most violent thing he'd ever heard her say but he knew there was no real malice behind her words.

"There's never been anyone else, just you…I read about it once, thought I might give it a try," Acalan said, reaching to brush a strand of her hair out of her face.

Citlalic looked surprised by his confession, but it was true, there had never been anyone else. Had he kissed other women? Sure, but he'd never allowed it go this far.

"Oh…well then this is all the more special, we're blood bound forever then," Citlalic responded so passively that Acalan almost didn't catch the revelation sewn between her words.

"What do you mean?" Acalan questioned with a curious tilt to his head.

"Oh…is this not common knowledge in Tu'nethe? When two pure souls come together, they become blood bound as one. It's Eztli's first law," the princess explained simply.

Acalan was a bit taken aback by the confession. This was certainly not something he'd been aware of before. There were now a million questions in his mind that he was sure his princess would be more than happy to answer.

That is, until there was a knock at the door.

METZTLI

Metztli Amos did not know the meaning of patience. It just wasn't in her blood to sit around waiting for something to happen. She'd tried to keep herself occupied over the last few hours that she'd spent waiting for her brother but there was only so much she could do. She'd snuck to the kitchen to grab more dried meat, as many handfuls of nuts as she could manage being that she only had a small cotton bag to conceal them in, and a couple pieces of fresh fruit.

It was likely they would have prey to hunt for fresh meat in the pyramid, but if their tournament was anything like their father's then they would not be able to, and the last thing they needed to worry about was starving before they could win.

After she'd successfully done that, she'd managed to return to her room completely unseen, which was good. She wasn't exactly in the mood to reconcile with her father, nor was she in the mood to see any of the other heirs, Necalli especially.

Their conversation from the night before was still bothering her. He'd seemed so desperate when he'd called out for her.

Like calls to Like

Metztli was still wondering what he'd meant by that. It's not like they really knew each other. Because of the tournament, they knew a good bit about each other's families, but they didn't know each other intimately. It was better that way, ultimately. The last thing she needed was to grow a friendship with anyone who wasn't guaranteed to return home.

Admittedly, it wasn't like Metztli had very many friendships apart from her brother. She'd been ostracized from the other young women at a very young age, and the boys they used to play with stopped talking to her when she grew into a more womanly figure.

Well, they didn't really stop speaking to her – it was just that they'd started speaking to her differently and she hated that. Hated that she'd somehow grown more interesting when she'd become more beautiful.

All of these thoughts plagued Metztli's mind as she finished packing her bag. She thought it would be too heavy with all of the things she was carrying but it turned out to be perfect.

After she'd done everything that she could, Metztli found herself growing more and more irritated. She truly had tried to be patient with her brother, knowing that he was with Citlalic, but her patience ran rather thin when she didn't find a way to occupy herself. She had tried everything. She'd even picked up one of the books Acalan had gifted her on her birthday, but alas, it was quite unentertaining.

Suppertime was quickly approaching, and she wouldn't let Acalan skip out on that. Metztli remained upset with her father, but she wouldn't allow herself to miss these final moments with her family. There was still a chance that these memories were all she would have to take into the afterlife. It would be a shame if that was the case, but it could happen, she was very aware of that as she walked across the hallway to knock on her brother's door.

In the best case scenario, he'd just fallen asleep, and in the worst he wouldn't be there at all. There was only one way of finding out, so she knocked softly on the door before calling his name.

Metztli was relieved when she heard footsteps walking around his room. That is until a couple seconds later when she heard hushed whispering and the footsteps of another.

A number of possibilities ran through her mind. Acalan was a gentleman so perhaps he was just showing Citlalic his library. That was the possibility that made most sense in her mind, but it didn't correlate with hurried footsteps and the amount of time it was taking for Acalan to actually open the door.

"ACALAN!" Metztli shouted through the door. "OPEN THE DOOR RIGHT NOW OR I'M COMING IN!"

Her hands had balled up into tiny fists as she stood there waiting for him to appear. She didn't want to believe that her brother had committed the act she was already accusing him of in her mind, but if not, why was it taking him so long to respond?

"DO NOT COME IN!" Acalan shouted back.

Honestly, if it had been anyone other than the princess she would have just turned away and allowed her brother this privacy, but this felt wrong. Time and time again they had been warned about the House of Blood, how devious they were and how they would stop at nothing to get what they desired most.

Power.

Metztli had not sensed any ill intent from the Princess of Blood but how could anyone ever be sure? Even her mother had warned her that seduction could be a weapon in the Tournament of Heirs.

Citlalic was not competing but if she believed it would make Acalan weaker, Metztli did not put it past the princess to use her body as a tool.

The doorknob was already in her hand when the door finally flew open, making her jerk back and nearly fall for what would have been the hundredth time this week. She looked at her brother with ferocious eyes that told him there would be a scolding soon, whether he liked it or not.

"It's lovely to see you again Metztli…I um…I should be going, I'm sure my family will be looking for me. I hope the both of you enjoy the rest of your evening," Citlalic said, turning to Metztli to curtsey slightly before she slipped out of the doorway.

The Princess of Blood made a mistake though because she turned back before leaving and locked eyes with Acalan. Metztli might have never truly experienced love, but she'd seen that same look in the way her parents often exchanged words silently. This was much worse than she'd been expecting.

Metztli examined the room before saying anything to her brother. His bed was made but looked as if it had been undone seconds before. Anyone who knew Acalan knew he liked to keep his room tidy, yet everything in it now resembled that of a frantic rendezvous. Her brother didn't have to confess to the act for her to know what had happened. And as his teammate, she was quite disappointed with his actions. As his sister and best friend, however, there was a tiny piece of her that was oddly proud. She didn't think her brother had it in him to seduce the Princess of Blood.

"Should I start calling her sister now or when we return from the tournament?" Metztli questioned.

She didn't want to be angry with her brother, not with the tournament drawing ever closer, but she also wouldn't applaud him for this behavior.

"I uh…I have no idea what you're talking about," Acalan said, defending himself as if what he'd done wasn't clearly painted in his room and written across his face.

"Hmm…so what you mean to say is that you did not just in fact bed, Citlalic Cruz?" Metztli crossed her arms against her chest.

He'd already committed the act, the least he could do was not lie to her. After so many years of knowing one another, Metztli believed that he knew she could tell when he was lying. Her brother did not respond though, instead he just stood there like a little boy who'd been caught stealing sweets from the kitchen.

"Admit to it now or I'll chase after Citlalic and have her confirm it for me. Your choice," Metztli said.

She knew which option her brother would choose, and she really had no desire to scare Citlalic anymore than she probably already did.

"Will you forgive me if I do confess?" Acalan responded with an awkward smile on his face.

For someone as intelligent as Acalan, he really could be an idiot when it came to these things. Did Metztli agree with his actions? Absolutely not. Would she have done the same in his shoes?

No, actually. She had been offered the same thing plenty of times now from Necalli and she'd found the strength to say no. Acalan was her brother though, and there wasn't a single thing that he could do that would warrant never being forgiven by her.

"How can you possibly be so bright and dull at the same time?" Metztli questioned, playfully throwing a jab at his arm.

Usually, he masterfully moved away but this time he did not. He simply whined when her fist made contact with his arm.

"Am I supposed to take that response as a yes?" Acalan questioned as he rubbed the spot on his arm where she'd hit him.

His response made Metztli roll her eyes. Love was really making him dull, and she did not approve of that one bit.

"Yes. I'll forgive you and your primal urges. I am not proud of what you've done though, I must make that clear, and if she tells anyone about what just occurred then Necalli and Coatl will surely come looking for us the moment the tournament begins…

"And you know that if something happens to you during the tournament, she will not be able to marry, if they somehow figure out you've tainted her purity."

It wasn't necessarily the scolding she thought he deserved but it was better than screaming at him or not saying anything at all. What was done was done. He couldn't take back an action like the one he'd just committed, and he would have to suffer the consequences.

Though she hardly believed that marrying the princess was a consequence in his eyes.

"I know," he replied, "and I plan to use that as motivation to win, along with everything else we both carry on our shoulders. I know this does not make sense to you but someday it will. When you meet the right person, you won't be able to resist either."

She doubted there was a living man out there who would really make her feel that way.

"Can you fix yourself so we can go have supper?" she snapped. "I'm starving."

Talking about his love affairs was fine but speaking of her own was crossing a line she did not intend to anytime soon. Even if they returned, she would only take a husband because that's what was expected of her, not because she desired it. And she would be happy simply knowing her brother was happy, that would be enough for her.

"Fix what? I'm dressed aren't I?" Acalan questioned as he took a peek in his mirror.

He was indeed clothed, but he looked disheveled. There was no other word to describe it. For starters his hair was a mess.. He reeked of the princess as well. No one knew them better than their mother did, and if he didn't fix this now, Xara would know exactly what her son was guilty of.

"Comb your hair and cover yourself in incense or something

because mother will be able to smell your sin from a mile away if you do not," Metztli ordered. "And do it quickly, you've already made my patience run thin." She was happy when Acalan stepped away to grab another change of clothing, slipping into the bathing chambers.

At least he was listening to her orders, otherwise they would have another entirely different problem to deal with. Metztli had to step out of the room as well, seeing it in its state only made her slightly nauseous with worry. She desperately hoped that the Princess of Blood was as good as she seemed to be, because otherwise this could spell complete ruin for them.

A few minutes later Acalan returned with damp hair, different clothing, and a new scent. He still looked guilty, but this was better and with any luck their mother wouldn't suspect anything at all. At least she hoped so.

After the debacle that was training with their father that morning, she didn't want anything else to go wrong today, she just wanted to enjoy the remaining moments she had with them, try to sleep as much as she could, and then wake up to accept her fate.

"Better," Metztli announced, looking him over. "Now c'mon lover boy, our parents are probably waiting for us, and I don't exactly want to explain why we were late."

Metztli hoped that dinner would be a pleasant affair, she wasn't sure she could take anymore drama. It was comforting to know the rest of her family likely couldn't either, she just had to survive dinner and a night's sleep. Or at least, that's what she was pretending she had to survive in order for everything to be well.

ACALAN

etztli stumbling in on them had been Acalan's mistake. He was very aware of this as they walked across the palace to where their parent's quarters were. He was grateful at least that it had been his sister who had come looking for him and not someone else. If that had been the case it could have been ruinous. It still was in a way, even if Metztli had agreed to forgive him for what he'd done with the Princess of Blood.

Acalan tried desperately not to think about what had just occurred, that was probably the better thing to do considering they were about to meet with their parents. It was difficult though. The memories of Citilac crying out his name were still vivid in his mind, haunting and comforting him all at once.

He didn't regret what they'd done. It had been liberating and he was now carrying new information about blood bonding that could be useful. Truly it was a miracle that the tournament had been alive for as long as it had without anyone discovering this truth.

He pondered if perhaps it had been common knowledge all along and he and Metztli had simply been too isolated to know these traditions existed. He'd read extensively about the House of Blood and their ways of living though, and never once had found anything that spoke of Eztli's law of blood bonding two pure souls to one another. Then again, the history books at his disposal had been written by priestesses and priests in Tu'nethe, loyal members of the House of Life who would have likely not wanted to speak more of the House of Blood than they needed to.

If what the princess had claimed was true, then that opened a world of possibilities for the tournament's outcome. It was strange that no one had used it as a way to win. But then again, why would they? The goal of the tournament was and had always been to return with your own kin.

In doing so the tributes would not only bring victory and power to their house, but they'd be granted a wish between the two winners if both heirs from the same house managed to survive the bloodshed. If the winning heirs were from different houses, Acalan could only assume the chaos that would ensue.

Admittedly, he and his sister had never actually discussed what they'd ask for in the case that they won. In the rare case that two blood bound heirs did survive the entirety of the tournament, the wish was usually given to the rightful heir of the throne. It could be shared amongst the two, but he'd only read of a few occasions when that had actually occurred.

More often than not, there was only one winner to enjoy the glory and benefits of winning. If he and his sister managed to make it out alive though, he'd share the triumph with his sister, whether she wanted to ask for a magical gift or riches, Acalan didn't really care. He just wanted to see his sister happy and alive.

Acalan's thoughts were cut short as they arrived at their parents' chambers. As much as his mind wanted to drift off into thoughts of the tournament, he needed to focus on his family now. Or more so, he needed to focus on getting Metztli through this family dinner without anyone sparking an argument.

If he could ask for anything right now, Acalan would just wish for one more happy day with his family. That, combined with everything else would be enough to get him through the Tournament of Heirs, it had to.

"Wait a second…before we go in there just remember that father does believe in you. I'm sure he feels terrible over what he said, I'm not saying you should let it go forever but just try to enjoy tonight.

Okay?" Acalan said, pulling his sister away from the door so that they could have this moment alone before anything else.

Metztli's eyes responded before she could, telling him that she wanted to enjoy this last moment with their parents too. He could still see the wound caused by their father's words behind her gaze, but there was love there too.

Love was enough for now.

"I know," Metztli responded before pulling away to open the door. "C'mon, I don't want to keep them waiting any longer."

Instantly Acalan was met with the scent of what he believed to be Mole – chocolate mixed with spices and dried peppers. They'd both had an orange earlier but that wasn't nearly enough to sate his appetite. Aside from that he also found himself exhausted from his activities with the princess.

Stop thinking of her, Acalan pleaded with himself.

That was a battle he knew he was unlikely to win. It was impossible to not think of the way she'd touched him, or the way her back had arched slightly when he touched her with an expertise he didn't know he possessed. Still, Acalan pushed the thoughts of Citlalic away for now. He could think of her later when supper was done and he was back in the privacy of his room, but until then he had to exile her from his mind, or at least try to.

"The children are here!" their mother exclaimed with bright eyes as they passed the doorway and entered their parents private dining quarters.

Throughout the years, they'd shared many meals there as a family. It was easier than having a table set for four in the great hall. Within the walls of this room, they could just be themselves. They didn't have to be a prince and princess, or an empress and emperor, they just had to be a family.

Neither Acalan nor Metztli could respond before their mother pulled them into a tight embrace. Acalan was easily a head or two taller than his mother, but that didn't stop Xara from using all of the strength in her petite figure to squeeze them as tightly as she could. It wasn't until Acalan looked up from his mother's embrace that he saw his father behind her.

He looked broken. Selfishly Acalan thought that it served him right, but as his son, he wanted to tell his father that everything would be okay. That Metztli was just fine and that they could make it through these last moments together without hurting each other anymore than they already had.

"Mother, I am happy to see you, too, but I cannot breathe!" Metztli complained, causing their mother's embrace to loosen just enough that she could pull away and really take a look at each of them.

Xara admired her children like they were her most prized possessions, rare gems that could never be replaced or remade.

Their mother let go of them then before placing two comforting hands on each of their shoulders, pushing them forward gently and towards the table that had already been set.

"Your mother wanted to do something special for the both of you, being that this will be our last meal together until you return, if the gods allow it," their father said, pulling their mother into his arms while she curled into him.

Acalan knew love because he'd been surrounded by it his entire life. He wouldn't settle for less than what his father and mother had, nor would he allow Metztli to, if the time ever came.

When he thought of everything that could be, he thought of Citlalic, and how easily she would fit in with them. She wouldn't have to face the cruelty that was the House of Blood if he brought her here where he could take care of her, just as his father cared for their mother.

"Mother! You didn't have to go through all this trouble. We have cooks for a reason…This must have taken you hours!" Metztli exclaimed.

Acalan knew her words to be genuine but, he could also see how eager she was to dig into the meal before them. It had been so long since their mother had cooked a meal for her family.

"It was no trouble at all. I just wanted to do something special for you two." Their mother beckoned them to sit with a wave of her hand. "I'm afraid there is not much guidance I can offer on the tournament, but I can offer the both of you a home cooked meal and all the love in my heart. So, sit. We've been fasting for too long."

Everyone took their seats then. Traditionally, the emperor of a house took the head of the table, but for as long as Acalan could remember there had been no chair there. Instead, their mother sat right next to Tenoch, a simple gesture that said they were equals, and Metztli took the seat across from their father like she always had.

When they were really little Metztli wouldn't even sit in a chair. Instead, she would sit in their father's lap and wait until he spoon fed her. He knew his sister had chosen the seat out of second nature, but the look on her face told him she regretted it already.

"What are you two waiting for? Dig in!" their mother commanded.

"No prayer?" Acalan questioned, knowing that his sister would happily skip the portion of supper if the choice was up to her.

Acalan didn't really care for prayer at the moment either. Not when he knew what he did about the prophecy and what the gods had done to hide it from the masses for centuries.

"No," Their father responded sternly.

The tone of his voice made Metztli and Acalan look towards him. He sounded vexed.

"After speaking with Atzi and asking for guidance, we've decided to not pray until the both of you return. The gods do not deserve our worship until they return you to us," their father explained.

"Isn't that dangerous?" Metztli then asked.

She wasn't being argumentative. In fact, her tone was calm and her head was turned slightly in a curious tilt. She was looking at their father directly now instead of avoiding his gaze as she'd done before.

"Atzi doesn't believe so…it's become clear to your mother and I that prayers will not save either of you, neither will hope." Their father paused before continuing his speech. "What will save you is everything that you know and everything that we've taught the both of you. I do not wish to speak of the tournament any longer, but I will say one more thing, something I should have said long ago…"

Acalan could see tears welling in his father's eyes – everyone could. Tenoch was a loving father in all regards, but he didn't cry, not in front of them anyway. Acalan watched as their mother leaned into their father, holding him much like he'd held her before. Metztli had gone slightly pale as tears came to her eyes, too.

"You two are no longer children in the eyes of the gods and our people, but in the eyes of your mother and I, you always will be," their father confessed. "Many must think that my greatest achievement in life has been winning the Tournament of Heirs, but it is not. My greatest achievement has, and always will be, raising the both of you.

"I would enter the tournament myself if I could, I would do it all again if it meant saving either of you, but alas, the gods, for as good as they are, they are also as equally cruel…Now, if we could enjoy a supper as a family, your mother and I would appreciate it. That is all that we ask of you."

With every word his father had spoken, a deep wound within the prince healed more and more. One that he hadn't even known was there to begin with. Acalan only imagined that their father's sentiment did quite the same for Metztli.

His sister broke the silence. "Well, you cannot enter the tournament father. I'm afraid you are far too slow now…Really mother, he used to be able to keep up with Acalan and I a few years ago but you should have seen him today, huffing and puffing like he'd run the entire length of Tu'nethe."

She was the first to dig into the Mole their mother had prepared, placing not one but two turkey legs on her plate along with a heaping spoonful of rice.

All was well for now.

Metztli

The rest of dinner was anything but quiet as the Amos family took turns sharing their favorite memories of each other. There was no further mention of the tournament either, which momentarily allowed Metztli to forget about the entire thing. Instead, she chuckled at the endless amount of stories they had as a family, some of them all together, others of just Metztli and Acalan. None of them involved grand excursions or fancy gifts. Their stories were just of days that they'd spent together, disregarding their royal duties regardless of the consequences involved, much like they were doing now.

Dinner was followed by an everlasting game of cards between all of them as the moon rose. They'd been playing for sweets which made the stakes just high enough that everyone became far too competitive. Their mother was the best at playing though, she always had been, even when Metztli and Acalan were little.

By the end of the evening there was a tiny mountain of sweets by Xara's side, all of which she divided equally for her children. She'd ordered them to pack the sweets in their bags, just in case they needed a reminder of home when the tournament became too difficult. Metztli had no doubt that moment would indeed come.

After that, they all huddled together in a warm embrace, tears falling freely down each face. They were all just pretending that they would wake up tomorrow and everything would be okay, that Metztli and Acalan wouldn't have to wake at the break of dawn to get dressed to the hilt with weaponry and make the walk to the Pyramid of Tributes just outside the city they called home.

Their parents would be right there with them of course, but it would be different, there would be too many eyes on them for them to share a moment like this. The knowledge of that was tortuous enough.

Their mother and father both placed soft kisses on both of their temples before leaving them to make way back to their rooms. In some ways Metztli felt that it was like a silent prayer between them all. Not to the gods, just a prayer amongst themselves. She'd never been able to believe in the gods, but she could believe in her family.

In truth, she didn't need anything else to be motivated to win, just knowing that they'd be together again when all was said and done was motivation enough to slice through anyone who came their way.

"Try to get some sleep okay," Metztli said as they arrived back at her brother's door. "And do not, by any means, seek out the princess tonight. We both need to rest as much as we can before tomorrow, understood?"

She tried to be as gentle as she could be with him. And the suggestion was every bit for herself as much as it was for Acalan. She'd been waiting for this moment practically all day, but now that it was here, she was dreading it. They'd already stayed up later than they should have to spend more time with their parents, but she could see herself, tossing and turning all night long, too filled with worry and despair to sleep.

"I won't, I promise…I just need to finish packing my bag and I'll go right to bed. I promise," Acalan responded right as they stepped foot in front of the door to his room.

Metztli's first instinct was to scold him for not having packed his bag already. They'd quite literally had all day to do so, and he'd waited for the absolute last moment. But she couldn't find it in her to do it. Instead, Metztli wrapped her arms around her brother, resting her head gently on his chest. She would see him in the morning, but it wouldn't be the same.

"Goodnight," she said before pulling away, offering a genuine smile to hide the pain.

"I'm just across the hall if you need me, okay?" Acalan reminded her.

It had been many years since she'd last sought refuge in her brother's room during the night. She knew he must have only offered because he sensed the turmoil she was going through, because of this Metztli simply nodded before heading across the hall and into her room.

The princess wasted no time in changing into more comfortable clothes to sleep in. She debated unpacking her bag so she could pack it once more just to make sure she had everything she needed but she knew that would just be a waste of time and she was in desperate need of sleep.

Defeated, Metztli dragged herself underneath her covers and blankets. She picked up the book she'd left on her nightstand. Earlier it had nearly caused her to drift into sleep, with any luck it would do much the same now when she needed it most.

Six chapters later, the book had done nothing but bore her near to death. Sleep wasn't coming no matter how hard she begged for it.

There was a single thought that was plaguing her mind and inhibiting her from finding peace.

She was scared of death.

Why this fear had waited until now to rise into her consciousness she was not sure, but she couldn't stop thinking of it. If she died during the tournament, she would be remembered as Atzi had said in her service that morning. But Metztli did not want to be remembered. She wanted to live and breathe. She wanted to wake every morning and fall asleep every night. Most of all, she wanted to see her brother live too. He deserved it more than she did, and their empire needed him.

Earlier, Acalan had said that she was every bit as capable of ruling as he was, but her brother was wrong. She was not fit to rule, she'd never bothered to learn how. She knew close to nothing about the other houses, not the way that her brother did. She did not want to die, and she did not want Acalan to die either.

Perhaps that is why Metztli found herself slipping out of bed and into a robe. She grasped the torch that kept her bedroom lit at night, tightly in her hands. Apparently, she'd suddenly grown scared of the dark too.

Metztli didn't think twice before closing her door behind her, walking across the hall and knocking softly on her brother's door. Earlier she'd waited so long for Acalan to respond, but now he was right there.

"Everything okay?" Acalan asked as he ushered Metztli into his room.

She placed her torch in one of the empty holders on the wall before responding.

"No," Metztli said quite plainly before taking a seat at the edge of his bed.

She was happy when her brother joined her. If she was going to sulk she would rather do it with him than alone.

"I don't want to die," Metztli confessed, turning to look at her brother.

She was met with his comforting gaze, just as she had been every time she had sought him out when they were children, when she had been frightened by a night terror, or had managed to convince herself there was a creature living in her room.

"We won't," Acalan responded more confidently than she had expected him to.

Acalan by nature was a very practical person, there was never a maybe, he either knew or did not, and right now he was speaking as if he knew. This confused her to no end.

"How can you be so sure?" Metztli questioned as she fiddled with the heir ring on her finger.

It was such a beautiful piece of jewelry, made of gold and embossed with their family's banner, a man wearing a feathered crown. Still, it was because of their bloodline that they had to compete and while she loved her father and mother, sometimes she wished they'd never had her or Acalan. After all, that was the only way they could have truly escaped the Tournament of Heirs.

"I just do, I have a sixth sense about these things…" he tried to explain. "If it makes you feel any better, I'm scared of dying too, but we won't. We'll be back home in a few days and we'll put the tournament behind us forever. We have too much to do to die."

The more he talked the more she believed him. She supposed that was a good thing, it was probably why she'd come here in the first place, seeking comfort she knew she would only be able to find in his words.

"Absolutely no dying then, promise?" Metztli asked, reaching out her pinky to interlock it with his.

She knew better than to promise these sorts of things, but it would make her feel better. If they swore an oath they couldn't break it, and if they pinky swore, well, that had been even more legitimate in their eyes when they were children.

"Promise," Acalan responded confidently. He wrapped his pinky around hers and it was done.

They'd made a promise they could not break. They would enter the tournament, kill anyone who got in their way, and return home to put it all behind them. She would be there to help pick up the pieces of Acalan that no longer were complete, and he would do the same for her, just as they'd always done.

"Alright, well, I guess I will leave you to sleep then…See you at dawn okay?" Metztli said as she stood. A yawn escaped her mouth which was a good indication that she felt better. Hopefully she could manage to sleep a few hours before the sun rose to meet them.

"Just sleep here," her brother suggested.

She raised an eyebrow at the thought. She hadn't slept in her brother's bed since they were children. Or more so since her father had handed her a blade along with the responsibility of keeping Acalan alive long enough to see his reign come to fruition.

"We're not children anymore," she said.

They hadn't been children for a very long time, but how could anyone possibly have a childhood when they had the responsibilities that Metztli and Acalan did? From the moment the tournament had been explained to her, she'd left her childhood in the past, never to be seen again.

"C'mon, it will make me feel better. Besides, I think our mother will enjoy the sight when she comes to wake me in the morning," Acalan said.

He was right. Their mother would enjoy the sight, and she would sleep better knowing her brother was near.

"Fine, scooch over then and you better not snore or I'll hit you,"

Metztli responded, waiting for her brother to find his place on the other side of his bed.

She slid underneath the covers and let out a sigh. She was finally tired, exhausted from everything that had happened that day and eager to get at least a little bit of rest before they entered the Pyramid of Tributes.

"For the record, you're the one who snores, not me. When you think I'm snoring it's only because you can hear yourself snoring in your sleep," Acalan asserted playfully.

Metztli laughed, knowing it was true.

Silence filled Acalan's room for a few moments as they both stared up at the ceiling. Acalan had been obsessed with astrology when they were younger. The interest had worn off with the years and had been replaced with history, but there were still carvings of stars and constellations that their father had made in order to please him.

Whether they died during the tournament or afterwards of old age, those carvings would remain there for centuries to come. The thought of that was oddly comforting.

"Metztli?" Acalan whispered, causing Metztli to move her gaze from the ceiling to her brother.

Once again, she was met with his warm expression.

"Yeah?"

"If we could do this all over again. I would try to be a better brother to you," he confessed. "I'm sorry that I failed in this lifetime but, given the opportunity, I would be better."

Metztli just shook her head silently. She hated that he believed he'd been anything but the brother she needed. Neither of them was perfect, Metztli had her flaws as did Acalan, but if she had been given the opportunity she wouldn't have gone back to change anything. They'd done the best that they could with the circumstances that had been handed to them.

"You were the perfect brother in this lifetime, Acalan," she said confidently. "Given the chance I would keep things as they are. Regardless of what happens in the tournament, I don't want you to ever think otherwise."

Acalan did not argue in return, and she was grateful for that.

It wasn't long before both of them closed their eyes and drifted into a peaceful slumber filled with dreams of the short childhood they'd had and all of the memories they'd collected over the years.

295

ACALAN

Acalan could not recall the last time he'd slept this well. But it couldn't have been more than a few hours before there was a loud knock at his door, followed by his mother's voice filling the room. That hadn't happened in a long time either.

For the most part, Acalan had been left to his own devices over the years. He woke whenever it seemed most appropriate, and as long as he trained every day with his sister, nothing else was really expected from him.

Today was different.

The prince squeezed his eyes shut for a moment before blinking away the sleep. It was still dark outside. When he turned, he found his sister curled into a ball, still sleeping. Had it been up to him he would have allowed her to sleep for however long suited her, but it wasn't up to Acalan. Nothing was anymore, because today they would enter the Pyramid of Tributes, sign their names away in blood, and hope to return home.

Silently, Acalan slipped out of bed and stretched his limbs, being careful not to disturb Metztli. Even if it would only earn her a couple more minutes of sleep, he wanted her to have them. The door creaked open and with it came his mother dressed in the finest of her clothing. She looked beautiful – young and vibrant. But Acalan knew it was all a show. He couldn't help but wonder how long she'd been up for.

A gentle smile formed over her lips when she spotted Metztli. When they were younger, their mother would slip into Acalan's room and often find Metztli there. It was a frequent occurrence that suddenly stopped one day. At the time it had seemed like the natural order of things but if Acalan could go back he would have cherished those moments more, just as he had done the night before when she'd come to his room, frightened at the idea of death.

"She looks so peaceful, just like when you two were children," Xara said, taking a seat at the edge of Acalan's bed and brushing her fingers gently through Metztli's hair.

"She's been like that all night…do we have to wake her? " Acalan question. He already knew the answer but there was no harm in asking.

Last night, Metztli had said that he'd been the perfect brother to her, which was good to hear of course, but it didn't help quell the creeping feeling that he'd failed her somehow. He wouldn't fail her again though. She had a prophecy to fulfill, and they had an empire to return to, so he would not, by any circumstances, fail his sister again.

Their mother had a sorrowful look on her face. "I'm afraid so…I had breakfast prepared for the both of you. Something light to keep your bellies full for a little while. All will be fine, let's just get the both of you ready to go."

Acalan watched as his mother gently shook Metztli awake. He supposed their mother was right, there was no more avoiding the tournament, so it was better if they just got ready now.

Metztli whined as she woke, stretching her arms and yawning. It looked like she'd slept well, too, so Acalan supposed that was at least something to be grateful for.

"Is it time?" Metztli asked, looking to her mother as if she'd somehow found a way out of this mess.

Their mother had not though. The only way to get out of the tournament was by winning it.

"It is darling…Let's get the both of you dressed, shall we?" their mother ordered in the most gentle of voices.

Metztli pushed herself up, so she was sitting. She looked at Acalan, took a deep breath and sighed. They'd had so many years to prepare for the tournament and it had still come too fast.

"Let's do this," Metztli said as confidently as Acalan had ever heard her say anything. He would never wish this responsibility on anyone, but with Metztli as his companion, and the need to return home and save Citlalic from the misery that was the House of Blood, he felt more motivated than ever to win.

The next hour was spent getting dressed. Acalan thought the clothing he'd picked out was just fine, but Metztli had disagreed. Admittedly, Acalan understood her concerns. Every little detail mattered now, even the clothing that they wore had to be a strategic choice that could either aid them within the pyramid or lead them to death.

Acalan decided on a skirt that could be adjusted to either fall right below his knee or above his ankles, along with a tight fitted tunic and that would dry quickly underneath the sun. He had more than enough blades strapped to his body and while it was slightly uncomfortable, the prince did not argue. Instead, he found it much wiser to just obey Metztli's requests. He figured he'd be doing a lot of that in the coming days.

It wasn't long before they had said farewell to their home, hopefully not forever but at least for the next couple days. They joined their father and the other heirs, their families and the people who had come from foreign places in support of the great houses of Mexica, outside of the palace gates. Why anyone would choose to travel for something like this was a complete mystery to Acalan. They would just be waiting and waiting until they killed each other off and a champion remained. That thought made Acalan's breakfast threaten to come right back up, but he held it in.

"What's taking so long?" Metztli questioned, clearly irritated.

Acalan couldn't blame his sister for feeling that way. The more they sat around like ducks, the more that dread built up in them. The House of Blood was still missing, Acalan had noticed that because he'd looked for his princess the moment they'd stepped outside.

"The members of the House of Blood and their heirs will be meeting us shortly and then we will be on our way," their father responded. "Atzi is finalizing her last ritual. All in good time, Metztli. Enjoy these last moments."

"This better have nothing to do with your lover," Metztli whispered to Acalan, digging her elbow into his side.

Acalan rolled his eyes in response. He understood his sister's need to be cautious, but Citlalic wouldn't have said anything to anyone. She'd been just as frightened as he had been when Metztli came knocking at his door.

"She is not my lover, stop calling her that," Acalan said equally as quiet.

The word lover made Citlalic sound like she was passing form of entertainment in his life, and she was not. She was everything but that.

"Oh right, sorry, what I meant to say is that this better have nothing to do with my sister-in-law,"

Metztli responded playfully.

Before Acalan could respond, his sister was speaking again.

"It's almost like we summoned her," Metztli said, causing Acalan to turn to face the entrance of their home. There Citlalic was – not walking behind her father, brother, or cousin, but in front of them. His memories did not do the princess justice. She was far more alluring than he remembered.

"And there's Atzi… Hmm, that's strange. You don't think they were talking, do you?" Metztli mused as she pointed towards the priestess who was trailing behind the House of Blood.

The sight was curious. The House of Blood had their own priestess so there was really no reason for any of them to consult with Atzi…that is of course unless it was talk of the prophecy.

This sudden realization brought chills to Acalan's skin. He wasn't worried about Citlalic or Necalli's intentions. If they knew about the prophecy, then they would know it was better to stay out of Metztli's way and just let her fulfill it. He was just worried that he'd said too much and now Atzi knew he'd broken his oath to secrecy.

"They probably just walked out at the same time," Acalan assured, though, honestly, it was more for him than it was for his sister.

The members of the House of Blood joined the rest of them near the back of their crowd. It was a shame that they were so far away. He'd been hoping to speak to Citlalic at least one more time before he entered the pyramid. They were forming a line of sorts, and since the House of Life currently held reign over the other houses, they were up front. They'd be the first to enter the pyramid. It was partially advantageous, but just as equally frightening.

"Keep your heads held up high," their father said. "It is time to go."

Acalan swallowed, he didn't feel ready to go. He tightened the grip on his bow and adjusted the arrows strapped to his chest. The bag he was carrying wasn't necessarily heavy. It was just the weight of responsibility that made him feel like he was drowning mid-air.

They were walking straight towards their destiny and there was nothing they could do to stop.

Moving his legs was agonizing but Acalan managed to do so. It would be an embarrassment if his body caused a scene now in front of all the other heirs and their families, right before they walked into bloodshed. He only found peace in the promise he and his sister had made the night before. Acalan was in all regards a man of his word, they would leave the Tournament of Heirs as champions, even if that meant having to put his morals aside to do so.

Acalan found it curious how silent everyone was. The only thing that could be heard was their footsteps as they walked into the city. There were people lining the streets, but no one said a thing. They just looked at them with admiration.

Tu'nethe was relatively small in comparison to the other houses and the cities they ruled over, but it was their home. Acalan recognized the people gawking at them. He'd frequented the vendors and shops lining the streets. He wanted to be angry with these people, but he couldn't be. They didn't know what he did, and even if they did, it was practically engraved into their society to worship the gods. If anything good happened, it was because of the gods; and if anything bad happened, it was because they hadn't worshiped enough. But Metztli would change things, the prophecy said so. Acalan just hoped he would be alive long enough to see it.

"Is it just me or is that blind man looking right at us?" Metztli whispered.

When Acalan turned his gaze, there was no doubt in his mind that the blind man sitting on the ground was indeed looking straight at them. From where they stood, Acalan could see that the man's eyes were hues of gray and blue mixed together, but if he was blind, there was no possible way he could be following their every step…Right?

"Just try to ignore his gaze," Acalan suggested before turning away from the man.

Acalan continued walking, keeping pace with his father and mother who walked in front of them. He'd noted before that they hadn't stopped to wave and smile at anyone, they'd simply looked forward with their chins held high. If they could keep their composure, then Acalan could as well.

"Mesi! Mesi!" a man's voice suddenly cut through the silence.

It took no less than a second for Acalan to recognize that it was coming from the blind man, and it took even less time for him to realize that the man was speaking to Metztli. To make matters worse, the man was reaching out his arms as if to touch her.

Metztli looked back at her brother, obviously confused as she took a few steps towards Acalan and away from the man. She looked frightened of the word itself, not the man.

Mesi was an ancient word, but Acalan knew what it meant. *Messiah.*

"Messiah? Do you think the gods have shown themselves yet?" Metztli questioned as they continued moving forward.

She had a tight grip on his arm, and he couldn't blame her. If he was in her shoes, he would be doing the same thing. Acalan tried to not make it too obvious that he was relieved she hadn't connected any dots in her mind.

"They must have," Acalan lied. "You know how the gods are. They love attention."

Atzi had warned him that the time would come where he would be the one who needed to tell Metztli the truth of who she was. The priestess had also told him he would know without a doubt when that time finally came. She was right because while Acalan wanted to confess everything he knew to his sister, he knew it wasn't the right time.

For now, all that Acalan could do was survive and wait for the right moment to come.

Metztli

For the rest of their journey to the Pyramid of Tributes, Metztli could not shake the blind man from her mind. Blind or not he had a look of absolute admiration on his face. Messiah could mean plenty of things though. She supposed that she and Acalan were messiahs of sorts in their own right. They weren't necessarily going to bring liberation to their people, but if they won, their father would continue ruling over the other houses of Mexica, and the throne would someday be passed to Acalan who had every attribute that a great ruler should.

Besides, her brother was right, the gods did love when the masses doted on them.

"Holy…Shit," Metztli whispered under her breath the moment that the Pyramid of Tributes came into view.

She'd never seen it before with her own eyes. This field outside of their city was usually empty, but every twenty-five years the gods would use their magic to make the pyramid appear out of thin air. It was massive and looked like it was completely made out of gold. The god's faces had been carved into the front of the pyramid as well and while it was an impressive sight, it also made Metztli wildly uncomfortable.

Beside the Pyramid of Tributes, there was a colosseum large enough to seat everyone in the entirety of Mexica. The two structures were interconnected by an underground tunnel, Metztli knew that from listening to her father's stories over the years.

"Holy shit, indeed," her brother responded, prompting Metztli to turn and look at him.

He looked even more astounded than she did, which had already been obvious by the un-prince-like language coming from him.

"It will feel far more vast once you're inside," their father interjected as he placed his hands on each of their shoulders. "That might not seem comforting, but it will be. The more spread out you can be, the longer it is possible to survive."

Metztli hadn't planned on entering the tournament to hide the entire time, but she supposed her father was right.

"How will we know it is time to enter?" Metztli questioned as they continued their march.

In truth, she was hoping it would begin right away. That would be better than just standing around, waiting for the gods to decide if they were worthy of entering or not.

"The gates will rise, and the god's acolytes will come out. You two, along with the other heirs will join them. I can't say much else. What they choose to do after you're in their possession is up to them."

Metztli could sense her father's misery in his voice, and she thought back to what he'd said the day before, about entering the tournament himself if given the opportunity.

Love was violent. He'd taught her that. If she had to kill and maim in order to save her brother she would. Without question.

"We'll be fine, let's get there before we start worrying okay?" Acalan suggested, prompting Metztli to respond with a shake of her head.

Even if she didn't want to wait too long, she knew the gods were greedy. They'd been waiting twenty-five years for this and they'd want to see bloodshed as quickly as they could.

Metztli allowed herself to look up at the god's golden faces. Given the opportunity, she wouldn't hesitate to give them a piece of her mind. She would scold them for allowing the Tournament of Heirs to continue as long as it had and most of all the princess would make sure that they knew of the blood that stained their hands.

Every life lost within the Pyramid of Tributes was because of the gods.

The moment they arrived at the field that held the Pyramid of Tributes, Metztli dropped her spear and the bag that laid heavy on her shoulders. She'd thought she had packed the perfect amount, but a few hours of walking had proved her wrong. She could suffer through some physical pain though, especially if it meant they would have all the supplies they needed to survive the tournament.

"Now we wait," their mother announced with a heavy sigh.

Waiting was the worst part for Metztli, and she couldn't imagine that it was any better for her parents or brother. If anything, she and Acalan would have it easy. The tournament would keep them busy until they either died or won, but their parents would wait here patiently, with little to no knowledge of what was occurring within the pyramid.

Tents were already being raised by the various houses and their servants. She hated the idea of her parents sleeping in a tent – albeit it was a grand tent, with sleeping cots and much more.

"There is no need to worry mother. I may not have sharpened my teeth, but I do plan on keeping Acalan and I alive for as long as I can…Have a little faith in me." Metztli said as she rolled out her shoulders.

She shot her mother a wink. She could have said that she was devastatingly terrified but that wouldn't do any of them any good. Xara shook her head playfully as she moved to stand behind her daughter. Her gentle hands rolled out the stiff knots that had already formed, and they were gone almost instantly. There was very little that a mother's touch could not fix.

"I have an abundance of faith in you and your brother. I am just terribly inpatient," her mother responded.

That was a lie if Metztli had ever heard one. Her mother had always been the most patient person she'd ever known. However, things were different now as Metztli stood still, allowing her mother to braid her hair. This time she was not doing it just to please her mother, she was allowing it for herself, too.

"Why is no one braiding my hair? I'm feeling a bit left out over here," Acalan interjected.

Metztli couldn't help but laugh, regardless of the circumstances that they were in, even more so when their father walked up to Acalan and stood behind him.

"Would you like one or two braids, son?" their father asked as he ruffled Acalan's hair.

Everyone laughed and for a moment, once again, they were just a family and nothing else. Their outward expression did cause a few heads to turn, and they certainly earned a few disapproving stares but Metztli could not find it in herself to care.

They waited for hours.

It seemed ridiculous that they'd been woken up at the crack of dawn to just sit and wait for the gaudy pyramid gates to finally open. In the meantime, they'd eaten just a little bit, played card games for a little while, and then there was silence. Acalan was splayed out, laying in the grass with a book in his hands while Metztli sharpened her blades for a third time.

The sharper the better.

She was unsure if Acalan believed he was fooling anyone, but he was not. If she had noticed his gaze wander to Citlalic on more than a handful of occasions now, she was sure that their parents had too. She wanted to tell him to just get up and go speak to the princess instead of staring, but that was unwise.

Atzi was also missing once again which worried Metztli for some reason. It was strange. For years she wished the priestess would just disappear, but now that she seemingly had, Metztli wanted her to return. It almost felt like there was a missing piece of her family, even if that piece was the old woman who had been cruel to Metztli her entire life.

"Where's Atzi?" Metztli asked, cutting through the silence that had settled over their temporary campsite.

Acalan shrugged in response. That seemed like a strange thing to do when he'd basically been obsessed with the priestess and her teachings, from the moment he'd been born.

"Atzi is…struggling at the moment," their father replied. "She loves the both of you as if you were her grandchildren. It is not easy for her, seeing this day finally come."

It was a rehearsed response, and it didn't really satisfy Metztli's curiosity. Atzi should be there with them, whispering senseless prayers that wouldn't be heard by the gods, but she was not.

Metztli hadn't realized she could actually miss the woman.

The princess had just opened her mouth to respond when a loud noise interrupted her. She turned to look, already knowing what she'd find. The gates were rising. There was no time left.

The tournament was about to begin.

Metztli inhaled and squeezed her eyes shut as tightly as she could, accepting every fear she had in her body. She didn't want to die, and she didn't want Acalan to die either. As she exhaled she let all of her fears wash away. She needed to be strong for her family, and little strength was found in fear.

"Will you walk with us?" Metztli asked as she gathered her things and strapped her bag back onto her body.

When she turned to look at Acalan he was pale and almost looked like he was going to be sick.

The feeling was mutual.

"I'm afraid we must stay here…Let us not say goodbye. We will all see each other again in a matter of days, maybe even hours," said their father.

He beckoned them into an embrace, holding their mother with his other arm. Xara looked just far more fragile than she ever had before.

Nothing else was said for a few moments, they simply embraced, as did the other families with their respective heirs. There were no final prayers, no goodbyes, just the mutual understanding that this was it. Everything they'd ever trained for had led them to this.

"Fight hard. Until you can no longer fight," their mother whispered as she gripped onto their bodies, using all the strength left in her. "Do what you must. Your father and I will be here to help pick up the pieces when you return."

A few tears escaped Metztli but she didn't dare open her eyes. She knew she would find her brother in the same state if she did.

This didn't even feel real, like someone would suddenly come out of the pyramid and tell them this was just a cruel joke. Metztli wished desperately for this to happen, but it never did.

"Xara, you must let them go," their father said finally after a few minutes.

Metztli could hear the ache in his voice. He had been holding onto them just as tightly, but now his grip loosened. Xara obeyed, loosening her grip too. When Metztli finally opened her eyes and pulled away, she wished she hadn't.

There was no worse sight than seeing your own mother mourn you before you're even gone.

"We'll make you proud," Metztli said plainly as she wiped away the remaining tears on her face with her sleeve.

The last thing that she did was slip her heir ring off her finger. Acalan did the same, at least their parents would still have those in the case that they didn't return.

"Keep these safe for us until we return," Acalan said.

Metztli could hear him straining to keep his voice from trembling. Their father accepted the rings and held them close to his heart.

It was time to go. Metztli couldn't stand it any longer, so she started walking, pulling her brother along with her. Her grip on her spear was tight enough that she could feel it tearing into her skin.

They hadn't outright said the words "I love you" but they didn't need to. Some things were better left unsaid, and Metztli didn't need to hear it for her to know the sentiment to be true.

"Don't look back," Metztli whispered to her brother. "It'll make this more difficult."

Their mother's sobs had only gotten louder as they walked further and further away, seeing Xara in that state would only make matters worse. Metztli was sure of it.

"Are you ready?" her brother whispered back.

Metztli was grateful for that. She wasn't sure how much more of this she could take.

"Yes. Are you?" Metztli responded.

No smile painted her features. Her body was filled with rage and that's exactly what she needed right now. Rage would win them this tournament.

"Yes." Acalan responded and Metztli believed him. She had no choice but to do so.

As the two heirs of the House of Life approached the Pyramid of Tributes, they were met with a line of acolytes, some women, some men, all dressed head to toe in white. Most of the heirs were waiting at the mouth of the pyramid already. They looked irritated by the fact that Metztli and Acalan had taken so long to arrive. But if they had to go first then Metztli was going to take her sweet time.

The princess kept her head held high as they passed the other heirs, and she dug her spear in the ground when they reached the front of the line. She didn't dare look at the sisters from the House of Flor, far too afraid of what she would find if she did.

"Acalan and Metztli Amos…the gods await you," a male acolyte said as he stepped before them. "Come with me."

Just the sight of the man brought goosebumps to Metztli's skin. She turned to look at her brother, pushing away the eerie feeling. Acalan nodded softly.

There was no one else in the world she would rather do this with.

They were going to win this tournament, and they were going to do so together.

DAY ONE OF

The Tournament of Heirs

ACALAN

Amid the chaos and confusion, Acalan had forgotten to say goodbye to Citlalic. He knew it was wrong but that's all he could think about as he and Metztli followed the acolyte into the Pyramid of Tributes.

The hallway was dimly lit by torches hung along the wall, but they did little to hide the darkness within the pyramid. When his sister had asked him if he was ready, he hadn't lied. He did feel ready and far more prepared than he'd ever had. Acalan just wished it hadn't taken him so long to get his priorities straight, but he was completely present now and ready to fight.

The acolyte said nothing as he showed them into a small room at the end of the hallway. He simply handed them a knife, expecting them to know what to do. It was Acalan's duty to go first, so he grasped the blade and dug a thin line into his skin. The pain was uncomfortable, but he knew it could be worse. As the blood began to drip down his palm, the acolyte placed a wooden bowl beneath his hand to collect some of it before taking the knife back from Acalan.

He cleaned the knife off on his white robes, staining the fabric bright red before handing the knife to Metztli. His sister showed no hesitation in cutting into her own palm and letting the blood trickle into the bowl. Acalan's eyes widened just a bit when his sister squeezed her palm tightly and looked right into the acolyte's eyes.

More beast than woman, Acalan thought to himself, recalling the way Atzi had described his sister only a few days ago.

The acolyte smiled in return, prompting Acalan's blood to boil but he kept his calm, saving the rage building up in his body for when the right moment came. They were both handed a strip of cotton fabric for their hands and given a moment to wrap their wounds while the acolyte prepared the quill and parchment. It was time to sign their lives away in blood.

Acalan went first once again, leaning over slightly to read over the contract. Nothing was written that he didn't already know. The rules were simple.

Six houses.

Twelve heirs.

Only two blood bound tributes could win.

Without any hesitation, Acalan signed his life away before passing the quill for Metztli to do the same. He watched his sister's eyes browse the parchment before signing. The acolyte nodded curtly then, rolled the parchment up and slipped it into his robes before turning to grasp the bowl again, offering it to Acalan first.

For the first time in this process Acalan was confused, but he took the bowl anyway and held it in his hands for a few moments…

"Drink," the acolyte commanded as if he could hear Acalan's thoughts.

Acalan's eyes widened at the instruction. He knew they were to be put to sleep before the tournament started, but he'd expected for it to be done in a much different way. But there was no point in arguing, so Acalan tipped the bowl and quickly sipped from it before handing it to Metztli.

Knowing the truth of who had started the tournament, he found it interesting how much effort Nemiliztli had put into making this seem like it was Eztli's doing. Contracts signed in blood. Blood magic used to put them to sleep. No wonder no other heir had questioned what they'd been told.

Metztli didn't seem fazed by the fact that they were drinking blood. She simply filled her mouth with it, swallowed, and wiped her chin with her sleeve, causing the blood lingering on her lips to smear slightly on her skin. She looked terrifying, if Acalan didn't know his sister well, he would have been afraid of her.

Once the acolyte was satisfied, he took the bowl back from Metztli's hands.

"Follow me," the man said simply before they left the room and entered the hallway once again.

When they'd first entered the room, Acalan had thought it was the last room at the very end of the hallway. But now he realized the hallway was much longer and there were other rooms too. It was strange, but the gods were strange and no mortal truly understood their magic. They were led into another room. This one held two beds. Acalan was happy to see them because the blood magic used on them was starting to work. His eyes were growing heavier by the second.

"Sleep. When you wake, you will be within the arena," the acolyte informed them. "When you hear the trumpets of death sing, the bloodshed will begin. Understood?"

Acalan didn't even realize he'd put his things down on the ground and had taken a seat at the edge of one of the tiny beds until he found himself shaking his head. It was cruel for the gods to deliver vital information about the tournament when they were in this state.

Acalan's vision went blurry as he laid his body down. He could vaguely hear his sister calling his name but couldn't find the strength to respond, and before he knew it, he was sinking into a deep, dreamless slumber.

Acalan's body lunged forward violently.

He was gasping for air and his body ached. It took the prince multiple seconds to realize he was awake. As soon as he regained a semblance of consciousness, Acalan's gaze moved rapidly. He was in a forest, but it wasn't just any forest. It was the forest he'd been in the night he'd had that strange dream, the one that had sent him searching for more information.

He'd been so distracted by the scene in front of him that it took far longer than it should have for him to realize his sister was nowhere near him. Frantically he got on his feet, looking everywhere around him. Her spear was there, as was his bow and bag, but Metztli and the rest of her belongings were gone.

Think, Acalan, think! the prince pleaded with himself as he found the strength to stand through the dense greenery surrounding him.

This was wrong, no one had told them they could be separated. He needed to find his sister and he needed to do so quickly. The acolyte had been clear, the tournament begins when the trumpets sing their song of death and Acalan needed to find Metztli before the trumpets sang.

A deep breath escaped Acalan as he tried to think of this logically. He wasn't quick with change the way his sister was, but he was good at thinking of things step by step. He made a mental map of all he knew.

He hadn't heard the trumpets sing so the tournament hadn't started yet, and he had no idea which heirs were awake, or whether they had been separated from their companions as well. Acalan knew far less than he wished he did.

"METZTLI!" Acalan screamed. He knew very well that he could be attracting other heirs right to him, but they couldn't hurt each other yet, not without being punished for it with a quick and sudden death.

He waited patiently to hear something, anything that could lead him to his sister but there was nothing aside from the wind crashing into the trees above him.

Acalan had a difficult decision to make. If he moved and Metztli was close, then he would only be increasing the distance between them...but if Metztli was far and he didn't move the distance between them would remain.

A desperate scream escaped Acalan as he circled frantically, taking in the sight of the forest and its trees, so tall that they seemed to almost touch the sky.

What was he supposed to do?

He couldn't just stand there and wait for something to happen. He had to take a risk and move.

Acalan strapped everything to his body tightly and gripped his bow in one hand while the other gripped Metztli's spear. He started pacing through the arena, calling his sister's name, and waiting for a few seconds each time, hoping for a response. In doing this, the prince realized that the pyramid really did seem more vast now that he was in it. It was terrifying, realizing how much distance could have been between his sister and himself.

He didn't stop moving until he could hear his heartbeat starting to race. Another desperate yell escaped him as he bent over, gripping a tree in an attempt to catch his breath. He was beginning to worry that he would have to search from one end of the forest to the other in order to find her…was there even an end and a beginning to this place? Acalan's heart dropped to his stomach at the thought.

It was then, right in that moment when he'd begun to lose hope, that he heard something. It wasn't a scream, but it was much more than Acalan had heard thus far. The noise had been so faint that he had to guess which direction it was coming from, but as he moved, he realized it was the sound of pounding, similar to the way his sister would often pound on his door when she wanted to wake him.

"METZTLI?!" Acalan yelled again, in a last-ditch effort to find her.

He had a good feeling about this, like there was an invisible string slowly pulling them together.

BANG!

Acalan immediately turned at the noise, it was much closer than he assumed but it was coming from the most unexpected of places…Surely it couldn't actually be coming from within the walls of the pyramid.

BANG! BANG!

Acalan took a step back, slightly frightened…It could be his sister, but it could also be something else. Logically, he knew the gods wouldn't release beasts until the tournament truly began but the possibility still remained.

The prince took a few steps forward, looking side to side as he pressed a hand against the cold tan stone. He was lucky that he'd managed to go unnoticed thus far, that much was obvious from the lack of heirs in sight.

It was only a few seconds later when Acalan felt the pounding continue against his palm. It was so faint that for a moment he considered if he was imaging it out of pure desperation to find some clue that could lead him to Metztli.

When the faint pounding continued Acalan did the sensible thing and pressed an ear against the rugged stone before him, hoping that he hadn't gone entirely mad already.

"GET ME OUT OF HERE!" Metztli screamed, the sound of her voice startled Acalan so much that he nearly fell backwards.

Even with his ear against the wall, her voice had been faint. A part of him understood now. Assuming there were other heirs stuck in the walls as well, it was a perfect tactic to kill off half of them. If they couldn't be found, they couldn't be saved and hence, they would die and just like that, half of heirs would be left without their companions.

"METZTLI! I'M GOING TO GET YOU OUT!" Acalan screamed as loud as he could.

His eyes frantically searched for something to break the stone but all he found were sticks that had fallen from the branches above, his bow and arrows, and Metztli's spear. None of these would help him break through the solid rock.

Of course, the gods wouldn't have just let them break their companions out, the more complicated the challenge, the more entertaining it would be.

But the gods weren't really that bright in the grand scheme of things. If they had been, they would have stuck Acalan in the wall and left Metztli to get him out of there. This was perhaps the only trial that Acalan was best suited for. If he couldn't physically break Metztli out of there, then he had to get her out some other way. But what could possibly be more challenging than a physical trial?

A mental one.

Acalan started pushing the stones, hoping that by doing so, one of them would release his sister from her confinement. He was starting to lose faith in this method until one of them gave way. He waited for a few seconds to see if anything else would happen, but nothing did.

Acalan continued pushing on more and more stones and slowly they started turning. It wasn't in a uniform pattern, but it was enough that it made him realize this was a puzzle. And Acalan had solved hundreds of puzzles in his life. He just had to figure out exactly what he was solving for.

"IT'S A PUZZLE!" Acalan yelled once again before holding his ear to the stone. "ARE THERE ANY CLUES IN THERE?"

"IT'S DARK, ACALAN, I CAN'T SEE ANYTHING!" Metztli responded frantically.

No luck there he supposed, he would just have to keep turning stones until something clicked, so he frantically did just that. Every few seconds he'd take a step backward, trying to make sense of the figure forming before him. The image seemed familiar, but he couldn't quite grasp it.

The prince knew they were running out of time, so he took a deep breath and looked at the wall again. At first it was fuzzy, but then slowly, as his mind began moving things around, the image started to cohere.

It was their house's banner symbol, the drawing of a man and his tall, feathered crown.

The prince could have kicked himself for not realizing it sooner. He'd already started moving the stones around again when the ground rumbled underneath him. Metztli's scream was so loud that he heard it without being pressed against the wall. He didn't have the time to ask his sister what was happening, he just had to move and do so quickly.

The image was now clear to him but there had to be a missing piece because nothing was happening.

The ground rumbled beneath his feet again and he heard Metztli screech once more before he realized he needed to reposition them all so the image was made of the darker stones instead of the lighter ones. Or at least that's what Acalan hoped was the issue. Sweat dripped down the crown of his head.

Suddenly, the stones began to move on their own, revealing an opening in the wall through which Metztli lunged forward, practically falling into his arms. She was covered in debris and gasping for air. She could recover from all of that though, what mattered was that she wasn't dead.

"T-The W-Walls W-Were closing in," Metztli explained breathlessly as she regained her composure.

"You're okay now," Acalan said softly, brushing the dirt off her face as he tried to calm her. "Don't worry. You're out"

That's what mattered right now. He hadn't failed his sister, he'd saved her.

"H-Has it s-started?" Metztli questioned as she frantically moved her head and took in the sight of the forest they'd been placed in.

"No…not yet. Is your bag in there?" Acalan questioned as he peeked into the crevice where she'd been stuffed but he didn't see anything. That could not be good.

"No…you don't have my stuff!?" Metztli asked almost angrily as she looked around him to take inventory, but Acalan had nothing but his bag, his bow and arrow, and her spear.

"FUCK! They took my stuff, didn't they?" Metztli asked, completely enraged.

Acalan knew she wasn't angry with him, more so just angry with the world.

"It appears so," Acalan said in a gentle tone. "It's okay, we'll make do with what we have. That's all we can do now."

He watched as she brushed the fallen strands of her hair out of her face and nodded.

"It's fine, let's just get moving before the tournament starts."

Acalan could practically see the frustration fuming off of her, but he let her be. If he were in her position, he would have done the same.

Metztli grabbed her spear from where it laid on the ground and looked back at him. They didn't have all the supplies they'd hoped for, but they had each other. That was more than enough for now.

Metztli

Metztli was trying to remain calm, but it was difficult after what had just happened. Aside from the walls slowly closing in on her, what had been truly terrifying was the idea that she might die alone and that in doing so, she would be leaving her brother to fend for himself.

Even in the afterlife she would have never forgiven herself for failing to protect her brother.

There was no point in dwelling on what could have happened though. Nothing was happening the way it should have. Her bag was gone and with it all those hours she'd spent diligently planning what she would bring, were gone too. All she could do as they silently walked through the forest was be grateful that the gods had left her spear and that she and Acalan were still together.

"How many of them do you think figured out the puzzle?" Metztli asked quietly.

They hadn't even come close to encountering another heir yet which was a relief.

"I don't know. When the ground started shaking I thought that meant the tournament was about to begin, but I haven't heard the trumpets yet. Nor have I seen any other heirs," Acalan explained.

Metztli nodded. The less noise they made in these early moments the better. They'd been taught that most of the bloodshed occurred at the very beginning when the heirs were ravenous for blood, but something about this tournament felt different. Like it wouldn't be like any of the other tournaments that had ever been held. It had started uniquely enough that she knew the gods had gotten tired of the norm.

While they were trying to remain quiet, there was no doubt that the silence within the pyramid was almost eerie. Metztli had imagined that there wouldn't be a moment of silence between the screams of agony from the bloodshed but the tournament hadn't started yet so maybe that was still to come.

"How long do you think they kept us unconscious?" Acalan wondered.

She didn't feel too stiff which made her think they hadn't been sleeping for too long, a few hours at most. Otherwise, she would have felt the need to stretch her limbs. If she had to guess, it was around supper time.

"A few hours is my guess…but who knows. I suppose if they kept us comfortable it could have been more. It doesn't matter, what matters is when the tournament begins," Metztli responded as she halted her pace.

It was important that they kept moving but she also didn't want them to tire before the tournament actually started.

"Let's stop for now. No point in using our energy yet…this seems wrong, doesn't it? It's too calm, too quiet," Metztli added as she planted herself by the trunk of a tree.

The shock from waking up in a dark crevice unable to move hadn't worn off completely, but she felt better being able to breathe without the worry of being crushed in between the walls of the pyramid.

"They're just trying to make us nervous," Acalan said quietly as he put down his things and sat next to her.

Metztli felt that her brother was at least partially right. She was nervous as she sat there, knowing that the trumpets could sing at any moment. If she'd learned anything about the tournament from her father, it was that everything within the tournament was intentional.

"Right…well, can I look through your bag? I just want to see what we're working with." Metztli asked with a half-smile.

It was just a little bit lighter than she remembered her own being which made her nervous. She'd trusted Acalan to pack the way she'd asked, but who knew what her brother had thought was necessary to bring.

A tiny sting of disappointment rang through Metztli as she pulled out his blanket. Hers was gone but they would never fall asleep at the same time anyway, so they could make due with just

Acalan's for now. She was in slightly better spirits when she found he'd packed eight blades just as she'd asked, and more than enough arrow heads to last him. Metztli also found the sweets their mother had given him the night before, along with some food that wouldn't be enough for the both of them if the tournament ended up being longer than a few days. They could always hunt, provided if the gods had supplied them with prey that wasn't just the other heirs.

Metztli was fine with everything until she pulled out a few books and Acalan's journal from the bottom of the bag. A heavy sigh left her as she held up one of the books with an expression that said, *Did you really have to?*

Acalan smiled softly before grabbing one of them. Well, that was one way of answering. Entertainment wasn't necessarily a necessity in this situation but if it helped her brother get through this then she couldn't be angry, just slightly disappointed that he'd added more weight than he should have.

"Why do you like books so much?" Metztli questioned as she flipped through one. It was a historical one she'd never read before and didn't care to. What else did she need to know besides the fact that the gods hated mortals, and she hated the gods in return?

"I don't know…I just do," Acalan mumbled. "When I read it feels like I'm somewhere else, like I'm not really here in Tu'nethe. I guess it's a distraction, you know?"

She'd never seen books that way. She'd liked bedtime stories when they were little, but the moment the books thrown in her hands had gone from adventures to academics, she'd despised them with all her might. She knew of course that there were novels with adventures in them meant to entertain mortals her age, but she'd never picked one that was convincing enough for her to finish.

"Distractions are nice, I guess," Metztli responded, beginning to throw everything back into the bag. She let Acalan keep the book in his hands. Between the two of them, he was more in need of a distraction than she was.

Metztli had been so distracted in the chaos of the tournament that she'd hardly realized they were in a forest. This was good tactically, much better than being thrown into a desert without any natural resources.

It didn't help that the landscape was beautiful, everything from the tall trees to the colorful flowers that bloomed amidst the dirt, made it feel like they were back home.

"In the forest... soft winds sigh...Trees reach high towards the sky...Streams flow gently, wild and free...Nature's song, a symphony," Metztli recited.

It had come naturally to her, but she was very aware of the fact that one, it rhymed, and two, it read like someone half her age had written it.

"That was...beautiful," Acalan said, prompting her gaze to move from the forest to him.

She was expecting to be met with another smirk or a look of disappointment, but her brother's expression was far from it. He looked impressed, like she'd actually recited something worth repeating.

"Shut up," Metztli responded.

Being a poet wasn't a terrible thing by any means, it was just that it was too gentle. Poets spoke about the beauty in the world, they recited hymns about love and prosperity, but it was difficult for Metztli to find beauty in such things. The only thing beautiful in her life was the love her family shared for one another, that was it.

"I'm not joking. That was really good! A little vague but every poet just needs to find their muse. You must have one somewhere in you, you just have to look for it."

She now wished she hadn't recited her poem at all. Metztli could see it now: her brother would pester her about this for as long as he could. But the fact remained, Metztli was not soft and gentle, she was a warrior, a huntress, violence encapsulated in a person.

She was not and would never be a poet.

The princess shivered slightly as she watched a flock of birds fly right above them. That couldn't be good. Before she could say anything or even turn to her brother. She heard it, or more so heard them.

The trumpets of death were singing their tragic song.

The tournament had officially begun.

Metztli turned to say something to her brother when she felt the most horrendous burning sensation on her left arm, like something was being seared straight into her skin. Her brother screamed as she moved to apply pressure to the pain in hopes that it would help, it did not.

Metztli wanted to scream too, but the tournament had begun, and they needed to remain quiet. She bit her tongue and turned to look at her brother with pleading eyes, and in return he bit back the pain too.

Tears had welled in Metztli's eyes by the time the burning stopped, and she was able to remove her hand. Her eyes widened at what was revealed underneath.

There were suddenly twelve marks on her left arm, made up of the six colors that represented each house in Mexica. Being that there were two of each color, it didn't take much consideration for her to know what this meant. This is how they would know how many heirs remained. The pain was suddenly worth it. They wouldn't exactly know which of the pairs were gone, but they would know when they were close to returning home.

"Do you think this means what I think it does?" Acalan questioned.

Metztli nodded in response. There was no other logical explanation. It was a gift if nothing else. She thought they quite deserved it after what they'd already been through already.

"I guess we'll see, if the lines start disappearing. Then we'll know for sure," Metztli responded.

It felt wrong to want to see the lines dissipate, but if it was between them and the others, Metztli did not feel guilty for wanting the others dead.

"We should start moving, father said we can't stay in one spot for too long," Metztli said as she stood, brushing off the dirt that had accumulated on her clothes and skin.

She'd expected to feel more frantic upon knowing the tournament had started, but the panic never came.

They started moving gracefully through the forest, being as quiet as they could be, but every time they took a step, the branches and leaves underneath them made too much noise.

They were playing a game of predator and prey, and Metztli was not willing to become prey.

"Take your sandals off," Metztli commanded as she stopped walking.

It wasn't a suggestion, but an order. They were lucky in a way. While Metztli and Acalan had grown up near forests, she knew some of the heirs had been surrounded by stone and deserts. They wouldn't know how to move around a forest while remaining unnoticed.

It also helped that Metztli already had an aversion to wearing sandals anyway. Her brother? Not so much, but he would manage just as she did.

Without the sandals they were nearly silent. The only thing Metztli could hear was her own heartbeat racing and her accelerated breathing. Her spear was gripped as tightly as it could be, and she was prepared to launch it straight into someone's chest if she needed to.

The thought of killing someone had never sat easy on her mind, but she could do it, she would do anything for her brother.

Every few moments or so she would turn her gaze to Acalan, only to find that he was gripping his bow just as tightly as she was holding her spear. He had an arrow threaded through, ready to fire if the moment arose. There were so many moments in their lives where Metztli had found herself proud of her brother, but never to this extent. He looked powerful. They both were in their own way.

This was it.

It was time to hunt.

ACALAN

calan and Metztli had been lurking through the thick forest for what felt like hours. The sky had begun to grow dark and aside from a horrific scream that had split the silence a few hours ago, they had yet to actually encounter any of the other heirs.

Everything about this felt wrong. They'd been told this would go differently. Most of the bloodshed always occurred right at the beginning when the heirs and their companions were still strong and well nourished. But so far there was nothing.

In the Tournament of Heirs, everything was intentional. Acalan didn't necessarily find himself excited about the bloodshed. In fact, he hoped that he and Metztli could somehow stay very far away from it for as long as they could. They would have to fight at some point, Acalan knew that. No one in the history of the tournament had been able to get out of it without at least killing one other heir.

In the highly unlikely event that Acalan and Metztli somehow got through this without causing harm to their competitors, Acalan knew the gods wouldn't like it. They found entertainment in seeing them frantic and filled with bloodlust, so how dull would it be if they did not behave the way they were supposed to?

Regardless, Acalan had already accepted his destiny. He knew he would need to do terrible things for the both of them to survive, and he was ready for it. At least that's what he kept repeating to himself in hopes that he would eventually believe this to be true.

"We should find somewhere to sleep for the night," Acalan whispered.

They'd done far from anything extraneous for the day, but his bare feet ached against the wet soil beneath them. They needed to eat as well, even if their food rations had been cut in half. Not eating would just cause them to grow weak before they encountered their first fight. He knew his sister would argue but this was one thing he was unwilling to compromise on.

"Just a little longer and we'll settle in for the evening, okay?" Metztli replied in an equally quiet whisper.

Knowing he'd likely have to argue with her later on about how much they should eat, Acalan simply nodded in response and kept pace with her. His hand had gone stiff as well from holding his bow and arrow so tightly, but he had to. If someone appeared out of nowhere, he would have to be ready to shoot. And not just to hurt them, but to kill. Given the opportunity he would make it a quick death and an arrow straight to the heart guaranteed it.

Acalan stopped walking when his sister did, it was quite abrupt and the grass field they were standing in was far too open for Metztli to consider it safe enough for the evening. The knowledge of this and the way she looked around cautiously told him there had to be something else going through her mind.

"Do you smell that?" Metztli asked.

Acalan's brow raised slightly, and he sniffed the air but found nothing strange. It smelled like any other rainforest would. It was lovely and quite frankly the scent reminded him of the Copalli incense he would light every evening in his room back home. It should have been comforting but it was just another reminder of everything they could lose if they didn't see this through.

"The forest?" Acalan questioned.

He wasn't surprised when his sister shook her head and took a deep breath. He couldn't quite understand exactly what she was smelling. Then again, Metztli had always been far better at hunting than he was. That's why when they hunted with their father she would always return with a boar while he returned with a few birds he'd managed to shoot.

"No…It's…It's fresh blood. You really can't smell it?" Metztli responded, the last bit of her words slightly harsher than the first.

She wasn't trying to be rude. Acalan could tell from the look on her face that she was simply shocked by the fact that Acalan couldn't smell it too. He tried again, just for his sister's sake, but there was nothing but the scent of the Copalli and Ahuehuete trees that surrounded them.

"Should we perhaps move away from the scent of blood?" Acalan asked.

That seemed like the right thing to do. He checked his arm quickly, but all twelve marks remained. It was a miracle in its own that somehow all of the heirs had managed to figure out how to get their companions out, assuming everyone had been given the same challenge. That was something that Acalan hardly believed he would ever get the answer to. By the end of this, most of them would be dead.

"We could…or we could, walk towards it," Metztli suggested.

Acalan immediately shook his head in a firm way that said, *absolutely NOT.* Why would they risk their lives so early on in the tournament? Besides, Acalan couldn't smell anything, for all he knew Metztli just *believed* that she could sense fresh blood.

"Why not?" Metztli inquired as if the answer wasn't as obvious as it could possibly be.

"Because the sun is going down, I'm hungry, and I do not want to go chasing a fight when we don't need to," Acalan explained frantically, barely taking breaths in between his words. "We might find a dead heir, or we could find a trap. Do you want to walk straight into a trap Metztli?"

Metztli sighed, rolled her eyes, and started walking away. She looked defeated but Acalan knew she was good at these sorts of things. Lying was something she'd gotten rather good at over the years, and while he thought highly of her, he would not put it past his sister to lie if she believed what she was doing was right.

"Where are you going?!" Acalan questioned as he followed closely behind her, grasping her arm, and pulling her back.

"Away from the scent of blood, though, honestly, I don't really understand why we wouldn't go. If we managed to find an heir then that would be one less person in the tournament, a step closer to returning home," Metztli said as she pulled away and continued stomping through the forest.

It's not that Acalan didn't understand her, he did. But once the bloodshed really started it would never end. He found Metztli more than capable of fighting and winning whichever battles they had before them, but he didn't want to risk their safety, not yet, not until they absolutely had to.

"Are you sure?" he questioned as he grasped her once again.

He knew this would upset her, but it was a question that had to be asked. He knew that even if his sister lied it wouldn't be with bad intentions. Metztli had always done what she believed was the best for him. It was just that in this case they happened to disagree.

Metztli was prepared to slay all of them, all ten heirs they were competing against, but Acalan...well, even one life taken by his hands would leave a permanent mark on his soul. He was willing to do it if the circumstances called for him to, but until they did, he would much prefer to keep his soul unmarked.

"Yes. Now let's keep moving, you want to find a place to rest for the evening, don't you?" Metztli said, like he'd somehow hurt her by insinuating that she was lying.

That was fine, Acalan was more than prepared to mend any wounds they made in the arena when they returned home, but they needed to return home for him to do so.

They walked in silence for a long while. Every spot that Acalan thought Metztli might approve of didn't seem to be good enough. They'd already argued enough for one day, so he just followed her quietly. She probably knew better than he did anyway.

It was moments like this one that made him feel guilty. It wasn't that he hadn't prepared for the Tournament of Heirs. He'd trained diligently. He was more than a good shot with his bow, but he'd never gone the extra mile, not like his sister had.

Acalan was about to start apologizing when he heard a gasp escape Metztli. Not a soft one but one that told him that if he looked in the same direction as she did, he would likely find something he didn't want to. He looked away as quickly as he could, too panicked to do anything else as his sister took a step backward and gripped his arm with her hand. She was protecting him, as she always had.

It was with that realization that Acalan forced himself to look. He'd wanted to be a better brother to her and now was his chance, so he pried his eyes open, and forced himself to take in the sight before him.

"Who would do that?" Metztli questioned in a frightened whisper. Acalan swallowed harshly as he tried to find the words to respond to her.

Before them was an heir, the older man from the House of Serpent. He'd been attacked viciously, there was no doubt about it, stabbed so many times that it made Acalan believe it was a violent and vengeful death. Not the sort that he was prepared to deliver if he needed to. Violence itself was common for the tournament, that was true, but this was far more brutal than any death that had ever been described to them.

"I don't know…" Acalan finally responded.

He was so caught up in the sight of a dead man in front of him that he hadn't considered the fact that while it was possible they'd run into the body by accident, it was also possible that Metztli had led them here, ignoring his wishes. Even if he had thought about this it wouldn't have mattered, death was all consuming, and seeing a death like this one made Acalan forget about everything else.

"I didn't hear the trumpets, they're supposed to sing every time an heir dies, aren't they?" Metztli questioned as she continued holding on to him.

In theory she was correct. At least that's how things had been done traditionally, but nothing about their tournament was turning out to be very traditional at all. They'd been marked at the beginning, so perhaps the trumpets didn't even matter anymore.

"They're supposed to. Should we check? If he's alive?." Acalan suggested even as he made an attempt to pull her away.

The tournament was dangerous enough on its own. The last thing they needed was to be putting themselves in even more dangerous situations. Metztli stayed still though, grounding herself like a tree that was unable to be moved.

"No…this is the only way we'll find out if the marks mean anything at all or if we've just been mutilated for the god's delight. If this was a trap someone would have attacked us by now, don't you think?" Metztli responded, calmly.

Admittedly, when her reasoning was sound it was difficult to deny her. If the other heirs who had brutally attacked him were still around, they wouldn't have waited to attack Acalan and Metztli.

"Okay. Fine, but we have to be careful, we'll do it quickly and then we'll leave, got it?"

Metztli nodded before she grasped her spear with both hands and started walking forward to get a closer look at the man. Acalan followed closely behind with an arrow notched in his bow. They hovered over the man. His wounds were even worse now than Acalan could see them up close. He hadn't just been stabbed. It looked like a blade had been dug into chest and twisted to create a gaping hole there.

Whoever did this was a maniac, they were killing for sport, not for duty. It was wrong, so utterly wrong.

"He looks dead to me," Metztli responded quietly.

She didn't seem as affected by the sight as Acalan was but from the gasp that had escaped her before, Acalan knew she was bluffing, and if that made her feel better then he wouldn't complain about it, not now that they stood over a dead man's body.

They stared at him, examining the man for a few more moments before a sharp and quick gasp left the older man's mouth. Both Metztli and Acalan immediately stepped backwards. The prince was ready to shoot, he was expecting for this to have been a ploy all along to reel them in, but nothing happened.

The man remained unconscious from the wounds he'd suffered. But he wasn't dead. He was suffering, he would die there alone, and in a strange way that broke Acalan's heart too.

"He's barely alive. That explains the lack of trumpets," Acalan whispered as he placed himself in front of his sister.

He was playing mind games with himself, contemplating if it

was the right thing to do to leave the man to suffer or offer him a peaceful quick death. Every avenue his mind took led to one thing. If he were the man, he would want someone to end his suffering.

"We should…we should kill him, make it quick so he doesn't suffer anymore," Acalan suggested, his voice cracking slightly as he spoke.

Quite frankly, Acalan couldn't even believe that he'd managed to get the words out, but they would be just as cruel as the people who hurt the man to begin with if they just let him lay there and suffer until his body gave out.

Metztli seemed shocked by the suggestion, but after a few seconds her gaze softened, and she nodded. They would be doing the right thing in ending the man's pain.

Acalan watched as she took the initiative and took a few steps forward, raising her spear. But she hesitated. His thoughts were racing. Every bone in his body was telling him to stop her and do it himself. He'd been the one to suggest it, so it only seemed fair that he do this. But he didn't move an inch, he didn't speak up or stop her as she lowered her blade straight into the man's chest.

Metztli's first kill.

Acalan supposed it was better that it had happened this way instead of it being during a fight. This had been a merciful death, it was a blessing for the man, but that didn't stop guilt from spreading through the prince as Metztli pulled her spear out of the man.

It was done. Not even a second later did the trumpets sing, signaling the first death of the tournament. Acalan turned to look at his left arm. He caught the mark dissipating, leaving an empty spot. There were still eleven heirs left.

This was only the beginning.

"Let's go find somewhere to sleep," Metztli suggested, stone faced as she walked away from the man.

Again, Acalan knew he should have been the one to do it, but he had stood there and done nothing to stop his sister as she ended the man's pain. There was nothing Acalan could do now aside from follow his sister and lay a comforting hand on her shoulder as they walked.

This didn't make her a killer.

If anything, she was a savior in his eyes. Just as the prophecy had described her to be.

Metztli

Metztli had just killed a man.

That's all she could think about as she sat against a tree, nibbling on a piece of dried meat that had been seasoned far too heavily for her liking. She said nothing as she recalled how easy it had been to puncture the man's body and plunge her spear straight into his heart. It shouldn't have been so easy. Her whole life she'd trained and trained so that when this day came she would be physically strong enough to do it. But killing the man really hadn't taken any physical strength at all. It was all mental.

She appreciated that her brother hadn't said a word about it, not yet anyway. These were emotions she was finding difficult to comprehend, even if it had been a merciful death, as her brother had described it. That didn't take away from the fact that she'd stabbed someone through the chest and watched as life left their body. The only good thing that had come from it was that they now knew that the trumpets did sing their song of death when someone died, and the marks disappeared along with them too.

The mark that had been placed on her heart would never leave though, of that she was certain.

Metztli ate as much as she could manage. It was difficult when she felt like she was going to be sick at any minute. That wasn't the sort of thing a warrior did though. She knew that a true warrior would have embraced their first kill instead of trying to run from it. That was the only thing motivating her to keep the little food she'd eaten that day in her belly. Well, that and the fact that she knew that at any moment they could be attacked. She needed any strength she could get, even if it was from over salted, dry meat.

She was feeling homesick already despite having only been away from home for a day. Or at least she assumed they'd only been gone for a day. It was difficult to tell when they had no true way of telling time. At home they used the sun and moon to tell hours and minutes. Their home had been built with an intricate design so that with every passing hour a shadow in the shape of their house banner would slowly appear and then disappear when a new day started. They could depend on nothing like that here though. If the gods wished, they could simply make it day until the tournament ended or remove the moon so they would be in pitch darkness.

Metztli did eventually grow tired of the silence that had fallen over them. She was sulking which seemed to be one of things she'd become very good at doing over the past few days. If she had the opportunity to speak to her past self, she was sure that the woman looking back at her would be disgusted with the amount of weakness she was showing.

Ultimately, Metztli had to remember one thing and one thing only. It was perhaps the most important thing her father had ever taught her.

Love is violent.

Only in turmoil could souls truly be bound. Metztli knew her father had always loved their mother, but she suspected that their love had only grown when they'd lost a newborn child. It was a terrible thought, she knew that. But it was love that left marks deep and wide, open wounds just waiting to be made deeper.

If violence was what was required of her then that's what she would be, violence could envelope her if it meant proving that she loved her brother and the empire they might someday inherit.

"You should get some sleep," Metztli said a bit more plainly than she intended to. "I'll take the first watch."

She tried to mend her words with a broken smile. Metztli already knew how likely it was that her brother was beating himself up about this, but she'd made a promise to take care of all the killing they had to do, and she intended on keeping it.

"You sure? I can take the first watch if you're tired, it's really okay," Acalan responded. His voice was comforting, which just so happened to be exactly what Metztli was needing right about now.

"I'm okay," she said. "You sleep and I'll wake you up in a couple hours when it's my turn. We don't know what tomorrow will bring so we might as well rest while we can."

Acalan nodded before retrieving the blanket from his bag. The gods had decided to make the night chilly, but a fire would just tell everyone where they were. So while Metztli would have loved to sit guard, wrapped around a blanket with a warm fire to comfort her, she knew it was a luxury they could not afford.

Acalan laid down, using the blanket to cover himself and his bag as a makeshift pillow. It was the best that they could do until they found more supplies, even if they used to belong to dead heirs.

"The stars are gone," Acalan said, prompting Metztli to look up and follow his gaze.

He was right, there were no stars in the sky despite the fact that the sky back at home was littered with them. She suspected that was the gods' doing too. They were removing everything that the heirs could find comfort in.

"In love with the stars again, are we?" Metztli teased softly, a gentle jab at her brother and how enthused he'd been with astrology when they were younger.

It was a fairly interesting topic of course. According to some stories, the stars could help you tell a lot about the type of person someone would be. Metztli highly doubted that, even if it was something interesting to believe in. It was also said that that's how the original houses were formed. If you were born during a specific time of the year, you were placed in a house that correlated with it.

"I never fell out of love with them, I just found more interesting topics," Acalan explained, a long sigh escaping him as he turned on his back to view the sky completely.

Metztli wished she understood him but she did not. Her only passion was training. On occasion she allowed herself respite in walks through the garden and sunbathing for so long that her skin turned red. That was it, she'd never allowed herself anything beyond that.

"I know, I was just teasing. I wish I could bring back the stars for you, but I can't, you'll have to sleep without them I'm afraid."

Acalan seemingly understood because he grew quiet. She watched as he fought back the urge to fall asleep.

"Hey, Metztli?" Acalan said.

"Yeah?" she responded quietly.

She already knew exactly what he was about to say. His expression said it all. She didn't want to admit it, but she knew that his next words would partially heal her. That is, until it was time to kill someone else.

"What you did today was a good thing. Father would be proud of you for bringing someone's misery to an end,"

"Yeah, I think he would have done the same thing," Metztli confessed.

Even if that was true, it didn't fix the ache in her heart for having done it. It was just something she couldn't explain no matter how much she wanted to. She knew she had to shake the feeling though. Metztli would need to kill more than just one man for this to end well for the both of them.

"I just…I thought it would be harder to do it, you know?" she then said, turning her gaze from the trees illuminated by the moonlight to face her brother. "But it was so easy, too easy. I guess it reminded me of how fragile we really are. That's not exactly what I want to be reminded of right now."

"But isn't that the very thing that makes us so special?" Acalan questioned.

Confusion flooded Metztli. She simply couldn't wrap her mind around how being fragile could be a good thing, at least not in the circumstances that they found themselves in.

"Life is important to us because it can be so easily taken away," he continued. "If we were immortal like the gods, there would be very little consequence. You can do as much harm as you want when you know you won't be punished for it."

It took a few moments for Metztli to really absorb his words and the meaning behind them. She supposed that he was right, having a conscience and knowing right from wrong, did inherently make them different from the gods. Still, they were in a tournament that was forcing them to act otherwise. They had to lean into the darkness within them instead of running from it. That was much harder than Metztli had imagined it would be.

Before Metztli could respond, she sensed movement in the bushes surrounding them. It only took a second for the princess to rise from where she was sitting and grasp her spear, ready to strike. Her brother was just a few seconds slower, but he got to his feet too, gripping his bow tightly, ready to aim and shoot. Neither of them said a word as they watched, waiting for whatever was rustling the leaves to appear.

Another sound came from behind them, Metztli turned as quickly as she could. It was difficult to see without the sun shining from above them, but she knew that she'd heard something or someone. Quite frankly she didn't know which option would be best.

In the Tournament of Heirs, it was known that this was a battle to the death and not just among the heirs themselves. Terrible beasts with hungry eyes and sharp teeth could be released, too, if that's what the gods found most entertaining, and no one would ever know what they were until it was too late.

Movement in the bushes continued, getting louder as their unknown visitor drew closer and closer. The bush in front of them parted slowly, prompting Metztli to raise her spear higher as she prepared to attack whoever or whatever it may be…

But it was just that it wasn't a beast or a human.

It was a dog.

"Are you seeing what I'm seeing?" Acalan questioned, a little bit of fear still present in his tone.

By the looks of it, the dog was a stray. He sat back on his hind legs, with its tongue stuck out like he was tired and hoping for a respite.

Metztli reached out toward the dog, as if to let him catch her scent, still very aware that for all she knew this could still be a trap. The gods had magic that was unknown to them. If they so wished, this dog could turn into a beast and slaughter them both without warning.

"How did a dog get in here?" Acalan wondered.

"I don't know…do you think it's harmless? Maybe it's a stray and just managed to sneak in."

She was still waiting to be attacked but the hairless dog in front of her did nothing. He just stared at her with wide eyes. Admittedly the pup was adorable, she'd always wanted a dog as a child, but her father had said she had no room to fit the responsibility of it.

"Only one way to find out…Come here, you hungry?" Acalan said, giving his sister no time to protest before he was leaning down to place his bow on the ground and beckoning for the dog to come closer.

Metztli watched, waiting for something terrible to happen but nothing did. The dog simply trotted over and licked Acalan's face with delight.

"Just a stray…must have snuck in like you said," Acalan said, petting him with a gentle hand. "You'd think the gods would have set better security…or maybe it's just really smart…is that it, puppy? Are you just really really smart?"

The dog couldn't really be that smart though. If one of the other heirs found him, they'd kill and eat him. He should have stayed far, far away from the Pyramid of Tributes.

"Can we keep him?" Acalan questioned with bright eyes.

It was a stupid question in all regards. Taking care of themselves and each other was responsibility enough, how would a dog do them any good? What if it barked and gave their location away?

Still, as Metztli looked at the poor puppy, she also couldn't find it in her to say no. She knew what destiny it would have if they abandoned it now. If he was truly helpless then they had to do what was right, even if that meant bringing a dog home when this whole ordeal was said and done.

"I guess…but if he barks even once, he's turning into dinner, understand?"

Her brother didn't respond with words, but he nodded enthusiastically before reaching into their bag for some dried meat. Well, there went all hopes of rationing appropriately.

As soon as she was sure that all was well, Metztli sat back down against the tree and watched as her brother played with the pup until he fell asleep. Maybe it had been stupid to decide to care for him, but it had brought a smile to Acalan's face and that was worth a lot. Even more so when the pup trotted over and planted himself in Metztli's lap.

"You're a stupid dog, you know that?"

The puppy just looked at her with wide eyes as he settled into her lap. He was a stupid dog, but he was their stupid dog for now.

Day Two of

The Tournament of Heirs

ACALAN

calan had woken up sometime before dawn. His slumber wasn't restful, but it was enough to get through another day. For whatever reason the heirs had decided to remain silent thus far but that couldn't last forever, especially not after Metztli had taken the man from the House of Serpent out of his misery the day before.

The heirs would be hungry for blood, and it was only really a matter of time before the bloodshed truly started.

It was for this very reason that Acalan had argued with his sister to get a couple hours of sleep before they moved for the day. When he'd woken, she was still sitting against the tree with their new puppy drooling all over her. Acalan had made sure to commit the sight to memory. Aside from returning home, nothing good ever happened in the Tournament of Heirs, but this moment felt worth remembering.

What wasn't good was the way that Metztli's head bobbed slightly as she fought off being tired, so while it took some convincing, Acalan managed to persuade her to sleep underneath a blanket for just a little while. He had no way of telling time within the Pyramid of Tributes, but from where the sun sat low in the sky, he knew it was still early. Early enough that the other heirs were likely still sleeping or staying hidden.

In the meantime, Acalan ate a piece of fresh fruit, and shared a little bit with their new dog who hadn't transformed into a beast overnight. A miracle really, but from the looks of it, this puppy had really just managed to find a way in and now he was stuck, just as they were. Metztli had assumed it was a stray, but he looked far too well taken care of to be one.

Then again, stray dogs in Tu'nethe were often taken care of by their people. The Xoloitzcuintle pups that roamed the streets of their city were loved by all, not only because they were adorable, but also because they were said to be a gift from the God of Lightning, made from his very bones to protect mortals and be their companions. The God of Lightning had disappeared many years ago, long before the Tournament of Heirs had started, but his presence remained in the pups that filled Mexica's streets.

Acalan played with the dog for a little while before sitting back down and pulling out his journal. He still remembered the look on Metztli's face when she found it hidden at the bottom of his bag. He knew it wasn't a necessity and it would only add extra weight, but journaling would keep him sane. He wanted to document everything that occurred to them so it could be added to the histories back home.

Well, that and he still had questions about the prophecy that he was trying to find answers to. It was difficult puzzling through the prophecy on his own and he wished that Atzi would have given him more information long before. But there was no point in dwelling, all he could do now was take the peaceful hours of their morning and put them to good use.

The prince started by recording the events from the day before. Acalan made a note that while the puppy remained nameless for now, he would not be forever.

He then flipped through his journal until he found the pages he'd already filled with information about the tournament and the prophecy. Atzi believed that Metztli was the prophesied heir for a few reasons.

The prophesied heir was someone who the god's will seemingly did not work on, and it quite clearly had never worked on Metztli. Even as a baby she'd cried and cried at the mention of the gods and Acalan did not have a single memory where Metztli had actually enjoyed partaking in worship. Her father's gift to tell the truth from lies didn't seem to work on Metztli either, which only proved this to be even more true.

The prophecy also spoke of a female heir and Metztli was just that. Admittedly, this did confuse Acalan. When he'd first been visited by the panther in his dream, she'd been seeking him out, but perhaps Atzi knew more of the prophecy than she did. After all, sometimes it felt like the woman was just as ancient as the gods themselves.

Lastly, Metztli was by far the most selfless person that Atzi had ever known and Acalan couldn't agree more with this. His sister often spoke of the sacrifices she was willing to commit for him and their people like they were nothing but simple tasks, but Acalan knew otherwise. Just the day before she'd shown both the dying heir and Acalan mercy by taking the initiative to end the man's suffering. Even now Acalan was unsure if he would have been able to do it himself.

Acalan thought about Atzi's reasoning for believing Metztli was the prophesied heir for a long time. It wasn't that he believed otherwise, the proof was all there. Even if there had been no proof at all, he'd always known that his sister was special, he just wasn't aware of the extent of how special she truly was. Still, it felt like there was something missing, he was just unsure of what it could be.

The prince moved quickly when his sister started rousing from her slumber. He had just enough time to sneak everything back into his bag before she stretched her arms above her head, opened her dark eyes and yawned loudly.

"Feeling better?" Acalan questioned kindly as he noted that she looked grumpy, but Metztli always looked slightly grumpy.

"The floor is hard. I miss my bed," Metztli replied, as she rubbed her eyes awake.

Acalan had felt that too, but hopefully the tournament would only last for a few more days at most.

"You should have something to eat before we head out," Acalan responded, digging in their bag for a piece of fruit. "We haven't heard or seen anyone so take your time. There's no point in moving if we don't have to."

A little bit of sugar and having something in her stomach would do her well, Acalan had no doubt about that.

"We? Please don't tell me you're referring to you and the dog," Metztli said as she caught the orange Acalan gently threw her way.

Even if she'd just woken up, she was still incredibly agile.

"I definitely am," Acalan replied, a quiet chain of laughter following his words. "I think having him is more beneficial than you think. Every time a bird flies by, he turns his little head way before I do. I was thinking we should give him a name though. It feels weird to just refer to him as a *dog*, you know?"

He was met with a look of disapproval but he'd already known to expect that, so it didn't bother him.

"You name him, he's your dog, not mine," Metztli said.

Her words were accompanied by an eyeroll as she pulled out a blade that had been strapped to her leg and cut into the orange. Acalan hated when she did that. It was far messier than just peeling the first layer of it.

"Xolo – that suits him I think," Acalan announced as he threw a small stick for the dog to chase after and return to him.

"You can't name the dog after its breed," Metztli said with a quarter of her orange still in her mouth. "Really, you shouldn't be naming him at all, but if you're going to, at least pick something original."

He did suppose that there was some truth behind her words though, even if Xolo sounded very bad ass in Acalan's mind.

"Any suggestions then?"

Sometimes when dealing with his sister he just had to prod at her enough until she finally gave in. There were quirks to Metztli that no one quite knew besides Acalan, but he hoped that wouldn't remain so forever. Not because he didn't love being Metztli's brother, he absolutely did, but because she deserved to find love outside of their family as well.

"Nope, not my dog. Just don't name him Xolo or I'll chase him away," Metztli responded sternly as she finished her orange, wiped her mouth with the sleeve of her shirt and stood, stretching out her legs and rolling out her shoulders.

Sleeping on the ground was really hard on their bodies, and if it was hard for them then Acalan couldn't imagine it would be any better for the other heirs, especially for the two sisters from the House of Flor who'd grown up practically being bathed in every form of comfort that existed.

"Have you stretched?" Metztli asked as rolled out her back.

Acalan hadn't, nor did he want to, but he found himself standing to stretch with her anyway.

"What do you think today might be like?" he asked as he pulled his arm across his body, using the other to stretch the muscles in his arm until he found that strange combination of pleasure and pain.

"No clue…It's strange, I know I should be hoping that it's peaceful but a part of me just wishes the bloodshed would start so we can end this and return home. I don't want to spend any more days than I have to here, you know?" Metztli explained.

"That makes sense…It's bad either way I guess. We either stay here longer and avoid as many confrontations as we can, or we seek confrontation and risk dying in the process but return home sooner if everything goes our way," Acalan reflected.

He knew that his sister had done a lot of strategizing on her own, but he'd done some, too. Acalan also knew that they would likely not have the same opinions on this, but the least he could do is try to convince his sister that he was right on this one.

"I say we play it safe," he continued. "Confrontations will come whether we like it or not. It's impossible to make it through this tournament without them, but if spending a few more days in here is what it takes to remain relatively safe for as long as we can, then why not do that? Mother and father won't be judging us on who we killed or did not kill in here, nor will the other houses, they'll be too busy mourning to even consider it."

His reasoning was sound, and he tried to present it in a way that he knew would resonate with Metztli. They might have had different strategies in mind, but their goal still remained the same.

Win the tournament and return home.

"If we do that then you'll have to shoot some birds or something because we'll run out of food if we're here for too long," Metztli shot back.

Quite frankly if that's what he had to do for her to agree to remain hidden for as long as possible, then he would not argue. If anything, it would help him feel more useful too, so he nodded enthusiastically before saluting his sister playfully.

"Alright, let's pack up then," Metztli said, seemingly agreeing to terms she'd set for their deal. "We should try to find a natural water source today. Your flask is almost empty, and we won't survive very long if we're hungry and dehydrated on top of it."

Acalan thought of arguing, it was likely that everyone would be looking for a source of water right about now, but if they did so quietly, which they had proven to be more than capable of, then everything would be just fine. Besides, he knew she was right, they could survive longer with empty stomachs than they could without water. If that was the one task they had for the day besides staying alive, Acalan could agree to that.

The prince helped pack up their belongings to make it look like they'd never been there to begin with. It didn't take very long considering that they only had Acalan's bag to live out of.

In no time they were beginning their journey again, this time with their unnamed pup following closely behind them. The dog was lucky he'd encountered them before anyone else because otherwise his destiny could have been a lot worse.

Metztli

It felt strange to feel grateful for anything considering the predicament that they were in, but Metztli couldn't help but feel that way as they walked through the forest, barefoot and in near complete silence.

It also felt wrong to want to thank the gods who had chosen this scenery for them, Metztli would never dare to actually do so, not to their faces anyway. Instead, she simply walked, searching for water, hoping not to encounter another heir, and to at least be able to find a small pond before the end of the day while keeping her brother and herself alive.

This forest was god made, but it resembled the forests from back home much more than she liked. Knowing that only brought an eerie feeling that made her want to crawl out of her own skin. She couldn't deny that it was helpful though. And the wetter the soil was beneath their feet, the closer they might be to a water source. Finding a river would be a blessing, because though Metztli would never choose to eat fish on her own accord it was still food. A pond would do though, all of them could use a little bit of water right about now, the dog included.

As they walked, going unnoticed by anyone or anything, Metztli found herself quite impressed that the dog hadn't barked or really made any noise at all. He was nearly as silent as they were, and he kept pace with them despite his short legs. Metztli had absolutely no idea what they would do with him if they managed to return home.

Would the gods even allow for them to take him home as part of the reward?

That was only partially why Metztli refused to name him. The idea of losing Acalan alone was too much for her soul to bare, but to add another life to it, even if it was the life of a dog… Metztli was sure that if she lost them both she would simply cease to exist. She would never be herself again.

Even if all three of them somehow managed to survive, there was still a chance that she would find herself a shell and nothing else.

Luck seemed to be favoring them though, because they had still not encountered anyone, and in the distance, Metztli could hear water moving swiftly. She turned to look at her brother who seemed to have noticed the noise too. Even the unnamed dog seemed to be turning his ear slightly to try and identify where it was coming from.

It occurred to Metztli that if they were going to be protecting and taking care of this dog then he needed to pull his weight. There was doubt that his ears were far more sensitive to noise than Metztli and Acalan's were, so if he could help them find water, he would have earned his dinner for that day.

Metztli crouched and placed her spear on the ground momentarily to pet him behind his ears.

"Good boy, now go find the water, okay?" Metztli whispered in a playful tone.

Regardless of how ridiculous she might have looked in the moment, it worked because the pup wagged his tail and began to lead them forward. Maybe he wasn't as stupid as she thought.

"I'm never forgetting that," Acalan teased quietly as they walked a little bit faster to follow the dog.

She rolled her eyes and pushed him off course a little bit. If they managed to win the Tournament of Heirs, he could tease her about what she'd done within the pyramid to keep them alive as much as he wanted but until then Acalan was better off keeping his mouth shut.

Highly unlikely of course, but Metztli could still dream.

From the sound of the rushing water, it had to be a river ahead and not a still pond or lake. If that was the case, they wouldn't be able to fish without risking being taken by the current, but they could still collect some water at least.

Assuming that any of the other heirs hadn't found it first.

As they came into a clearing, the river unfurled before them. It was vast and broad, and the water was rushing through it at a rapid pace. Luckily there were no other heirs in sight, prompting a sigh to escape Metztli as she took it all in. Not only was it a relief to have found water at all, but it was also breathtakingly beautiful.

"Do you think we could try to catch some fish?" Metztli asked with a bright smile.

She was speaking louder than she had since the tournament had started. Admittedly it felt good to do so after spending almost an entire day whispering. They could afford to be a little louder now that their voices were hidden from the sound of the rushing river.

She watched as Acalan considered her proposal. Spearing fish would be a little difficult without risking being pulled by the current, but if they found the perfect angle for Acalan to catch them with his bow and arrow, then they might be headed towards an early lunch.

"It's worth the try…Would be a little easier if we had a net though," Acalan replied, and from the look on his face, Metztli could tell he was already trying to find the vantage point to try and shoot from.

"I packed a net, but said net is with the gods," Metztli responded sarcastically.

She'd packed so many things that would be useful to them. Her list of belongings had been perfectly crafted and it had taken her years to get it that way but there was nothing she could do to get her bag back. All she could do was try to make the best out of the little that they did have for now.

"You think they'll give me my bag back if we win?" Metztli asked.

Aside from her blades, nothing in the bag had any real value, but the least they could do was return it, right? That was only assuming that the gods played fair, which they had already proven incapable of.

"Uh…I don't know," replied Acalan, moving closer to the river. "I'll make sure to ask them if we have the opportunity to talk to them though."

Metztli had only been vaguely aware of how out in the open they were. Now that she was watching her brother venture closer to the river, the sight made her uncomfortable, but she scanned the area again and found no one, so they were safe for now.

The dog was already drinking water by the edge of the river by the time that Acalan gracefully climbed up a tall rock. She watched as he mapped it out in his head, trying to figure out if he could properly aim without this being a complete waste of time. Metztli didn't offer any advice while he did this. Quite frankly she just didn't have any advice to give, the only way she knew how to spear was to stab the fish. Much easier in her eyes but she also didn't want to risk drowning.

"So, what do you think?" she asked.

They could either try or not try at all but spending too much time out in the open was a risk she was unwilling to take. Acalan began pulling out a bit of rope from his bag. Why he had assumed rope would be more useful than a net, Metztli was not sure, but if he was thinking what she was thinking, then he just might be right.

"The water is moving too fast for me to aim properly, but if we tie a rope to the end of the arrows I can shoot, hope to hit something and then we can try to reel the fish in."

Okay, so maybe her brother had just so happened to have packed something useful after all, but Metztli wouldn't thank him for it until they had bellies full of cooked fish.

"You shoot, I'll reel," she said. "And pass me your flask, I don't want to forget to fill it up before we go."

It came naturally to the princess to give orders. While this was a useful trait, she was unsure what she would do with it once the Tournament of Heirs was just a bad memory. Her brother had said he would need her to help him rule over the House of Life and its people, but to what extent? Metztli had never thought to ask, maybe she could once this was all over.

Acalan took a last sip from the flask before throwing it to Metztli. She caught it with ease and filled it partially so she could have a sip of her own. The princess hadn't realized how thirsty she was until the water hit her parched throat. She drank all the water she collected before filling it once more and passing it to her brother.

"Ready when you are," Metztli said, offering her brother a real smile before getting into position.

She was happy to find that the dog remained silent. He seemed content to just be around them. If the gods were as simple as the dog, then there would have never been war and the Tournament of Heirs would have never been started.

Perhaps, they needed to be more like him and less like themselves.

"Bark if you sense anyone okay?" Metztli ordered the pup.

She was unsure whether he actually understood her, but she was satisfied with the curious tilt he gave her. Metztli was thinking less and less about making him dinner and more and more of giving him a proper name when he earned it.

Acalan tied the piece of rope to the arrow, positioned his bow and shot it towards the sky. Metztli had tried training with a bow and arrow a long time ago, but she'd never enjoyed it. It felt like she was just guessing where the arrow would go instead of having control of her aim. Her spear on the other hand went exactly where she asked it to.

As the princess tugged on the piece of rope, hoping there was a fish at the end of it; she figured that Acalan would probably say quite the same if he was asked about spears. It had never really felt like she'd picked the weapon, more so that the weapon had picked her and there was something uniquely empowering about that feeling.

It took a few tries for Acalan to get the hang of shooting ahead of the current, so while they didn't catch anything during the first few attempts, they did eventually reel in two fish, and they'd only used up one arrow while doing so. Metztli had thought that was quite enough, a fish for him and a fish for her was far more than they were planning to eat anyways. But of course, her brother insisted that he had to try to catch one more for their dog. Metztli wanted to argue but it had been because of the pup that they'd gotten to the river in the first place, so she let her brother try for one more.

This last shot was proving to be slightly more difficult than the others. They must have just gotten lucky before because Acalan had now used two more arrows and they'd caught nothing else. A shame really because the dog deserved a fish of his own.

Metztli let Acalan try one more time and watched carefully as he prepared to shoot, angling his bow a little differently before letting the arrow shoot through the sky. It landed a little bit farther than the rest of the arrows had, which prompted Metztli to pull on the rope a bit harder than she had before. Upon reeling it in, she was happy to find a third fish at the end of it.

"You got it!" Metztli exclaimed, holding the fish over her head like it was some trophy and not the dead carcass of an animal.

She expected her brother to respond just as brightly as she had, but instead she found that his gaze was somewhere else. He was squinting like he was trying to find something in the distance. Before she could turn to look, the dog began to growl. Her brother was already making his way off the rock when she turned to examine the sight herself.

It took a few seconds for Metztli to recognize the sisters from the House of Flor, and even when the sight of them finally cohered, it took even longer to realize who they were with. An unexpected alliance had formed.

Metztli had already believed the sisters from the House of Flor to be dangerous purely due to their bloodlust but pairing them with the heirs from the House of Wind and their unknown newly invented weapon, could be catastrophic. And Metztli Amos was not prepared to be a part of a catastrophe.

The princess fell to her knees as quickly as she could, gathering their things. The heirs had clearly seen them too, that much was obvious from the way they scattered, trying to find a way around the river in search of their prey.

"Run!" Metztli shouted to her brother as she held the fish in her hands, still trying to keep a tight grasp on her spear. No good could come from this, Metztli was more than aware of this as she sprinted back into the forest behind her brother.

23
ACALAN

Acalan's ears filled with the sound of their feet rushing through the fallen leaves and branches of the forest. It all happened so quickly. One moment they were peacefully catching fish and the next they were nearly face to face with the heirs from the House of Flor and Wind. Even with a river between them, Acalan knew better than to stop running.

As Metztli had described it before, Acalan and his sister were conciliation prizes for the other houses and their inability to win the Tournament of Heirs for so many years. A river wasn't nearly enough to stop them from collecting what they believed they were owed. At the same time, Metztli and Acalan had too much to lose to risk a confrontation between all of them. In their own way, they were hungry for power too.

So, they ran, taking wild turns and sliding down dirt slopes until their chests began to burn and their bodies began to give out. Even then the prince continued running, making sure to look to his side every few seconds to ensure his sister was close behind. The last thing he needed was to lose track of her. He'd entered the Tournament of Heirs with one goal: to protect his sister at any cost and that was exactly what he was prepared to do.

It wasn't until their dog tripped over a branch that they took a moment to pause. The pup seemed to be fine. He was just a little frazzled and couldn't stop panting, none of them could. Even Metztli, who had the best stamina out of anyone that Acalan had ever known, seemed to be winded as she dropped their fish and stood guard. She held her spear as if she were ready to attack at any moment while Acalan bent over and nearly collapsed to the ground. This encounter had been too close, and they weren't exactly in the clear just yet.

"*They couldn't have caught up*," Acalan assured his sister through jagged breaths.

Honestly, he wasn't sure if that was true at all but he wanted to believe it was. The idea of having to start running again made the prince go lightheaded. For all the training they'd done, nothing could have really prepared them to exhaust their skills and deal with heightened emotions all at the same time.

His sister shushed him with the wave of her hand before tilting her head towards where they'd come from. She was waiting for a sign that the others were near, but it never came. Acalan would have tried to do the same, but it was difficult to hear anything over the sound of his heart threatening to beat out of his chest.

"We need to keep moving," Metztli finally said with a stern look on her face.

Acalan whined softly as his body collapsed onto the floor dramatically. He'd managed to catch his breath, but his chest still burned. If the others were near, they would have caught up already, but they hadn't and while a confrontation wasn't in their best interest, pushing their bodies to the breaking point wasn't wise either.

"I think we lost them. Can't we rest for a second? I can hardly breathe."

The prince wasn't surprised when his sister shot him a disappointed glare, but he did find himself startled when she rotated her spear and softly jabbed him in the ribs with the wooden end of it.

"What was that for?!" Acalan questioned as he bolted forward, rubbing the pain away from the spot where she'd hit him.

"For being lazy! Now get up, if we stop moving, we risk them finding us, and I really don't feel like dying today," she said.

While her tone was slightly callous, Acalan knew his sister didn't really mean any harm. Plus, he wasn't really keen on the idea of either of them dying, so while his legs trembled and ached, he managed to get up from the ground to look for their flask. Once it was in his hands, he drank just a little bit before handing it to his sister so she could replenish too. After all, they could just as easily die from dehydration. Having a bowl for their pup would have been nice because after he was finished drinking out of Acalan's hands, the prince was desperately missing having soap readily available to him.

"Do we have to run?" Acalan questioned as he wiped his hands off on a small towel he'd packed.

"Do you want to live?" Metztli quipped with a raised eyebrow before jabbing him once more with the wooden side of her spear.

Honestly her line of questioning hurt more than her physical taunt. Of course, Acalan wanted to live, he wanted nothing more than to see them both leave the Pyramid of Tributes, and he was willing to give anything to see that come true. He just wished that his sister could stop doubting that he felt that way.

"We're both here for the same reason, Metztli. Don't forget that."

The prince started trotting forward before his sister could respond. These were stressful times for everyone, but it wouldn't kill her to be nice or to at least consider that they both were sharing the responsibilities they'd been given. Even with that thought, Acalan knew it was likely that he would regret responding the way he had later. Not because what he said was malicious, just because he knew he could never really understand the amount of pressure his sister had on her shoulders.

It was one thing to be told you'd be competing in a tournament to the death, and it was an entirely different situation to be told you'd be competing with the sole responsibility of making sure your older brother made it through the tournament. Acalan could only begin to imagine what that knowledge must have done to his sister's morale.

They carefully jogged through the forest for a few hours almost in complete silence, only taking breaks here and there to rest their feet or nibble on dried meat and a handful of nuts that Acalan had packed. It wasn't much, but it kept them going.

Every so often Acalan would check his arm for the remaining heirs alive, but the colorful marks still remained. The marks themselves resembled brush strokes and aside from the meaning behind them they were still beautiful to the eye.

It felt surreal that they were halfway through the second day of the tournament and eleven heirs still remained. It should have been a relief to know only one life had been lost thus far, but it was not. The longer they refrained from killing one another, the longer it would take for this tournament to end.

"Should we stop to eat?" Acalan questioned when they came upon a secluded spot in the forest.

It was surrounded by trees but had a plain spot in the center where they could sit without being seen. Honestly, it was probably a good spot to just settle down for the evening, but the more they kept moving, the less likely they were to be found.

"Might as well," Metztli responded as quietly as she could.

Acalan found himself pleased when neither of them mentioned the conversation from earlier. If anything, he knew that his sister's lack of comment on it was a profession of guilt in itself. They didn't need to apologize though. The prince knew that the love they shared for one another, their house, and their people, was more than enough to get over a slight scuffle.

"Want me to clean the fish?" Metztli offered kindly.

Being that she was much better with butchering than he was, Acalan handed her the fish they'd stuffed in their bag without the slightest argument. They'd always worked better as a team, so he started digging out a small hole with his hands.

"Are you planning on baking them in the ground?" Metztli questioned.

Acalan nodded. It would take longer than if they were to just start a fire and let the fish cook through, but this way they could cover the hole with rocks and whatever smoke was made would dissipate before ever reaching the sky.

"Good. I wasn't keen on eating mine raw," she said with a slight chuckle.

Acalan agreed with that too. If they were going to eat anything they might as well do it safely, otherwise they'd be signing up for trouble they were not prepared for. Every tournament, an heir or two died from natural causes, drowning or severe dehydration most often, but dying from food-borne illness was almost laughable.

"There's a little sack of salt in my bag in case you want to season the fish," Acalan said, turning.

He only caught half of her expression of disbelief. It might have seemed silly at the moment, but she'd thank him later when she was eating salted fish.

"I didn't pack it for our food, it's good for wounds," Acalan confessed. "If you place a little bit of salt into them it will burn, but it will also dry it enough to avoid infection. I just didn't want us dying out here over something like that."

"Hmm, smart. I'm not complaining just so you know. I just think it's funny how we packed so differently," Metztli said.

With that Acalan could also agree. Being that he himself had helped her pack, he knew that she'd focused more on weapons and food so when it came to packing his things, he focused on the necessities she hadn't thought about. In truth they should have packed a little more evenly. But Then again, how could they have known that Metztli's bag would be taken from her before the tournament even started?

"Well, if you end up tripping and need some of my salt let me know," Acalan teased as he started on the fire.

He'd never actually made one on his own, but it couldn't be that difficult. He'd found some dried leaves and twigs for the base of it and used a thin branch he'd found on the ground to make the actual fire. It took a few attempts, but after a few times shifting his hands back and forth at a ferocious pace, he'd managed to make a spark which spread through the hole. Acalan only added a piece of parchment from his journal as extra precaution so that the fire would burn long enough for the fish to actually cook.

"Ready for the fish?" Metztli asked.

This was far from a delicious meal, but it would do them good to eat fresh meat instead of the over-spiced dry strips that Acalan had packed. Their bodies would surely thank them for it too.

"Yup, bring it over," Acalan said.

He waited until Metztli brought over the three fish. They weren't perfectly clean, but she'd done a good enough job. She'd also managed to weave a little bed for them from the leaves that had fallen from the Copalli trees above them. Acalan wasn't all that surprised from the sight. His sister had always been quite resourceful.

He lowered the fish into the hole and covered it with as many rocks as he could find.

They did a good job at hiding the smoke that was coming up from the hole but that didn't stop him from watching it closely just in case anything changed. They'd already been spotted once today, and Acalan didn't want to risk being spotted again.

"Now we wait," he said as he took a seat against the tree his sister was leaning on.

This wasn't paradise by any means, but he was happy to be there with her. Had anyone else been chosen as his companion, he would have likely already found himself dead. Metztli had always been his saving grace, and that hadn't changed, if anything his appreciation for her had only grown.

Metztli

Metztli felt uneasy.

There was no other way to describe how she was feeling besides using that word. They'd only been in the tournament for two days but for a moment there she'd forgotten that other heirs were present, and that, regardless of how calm everything seemed to be around them, they were still in near constant danger.

"Do you think we can stay here for the night?" Acalan asked, his voice was soft, but he'd still managed to interrupt her thoughts.

While Metztli's first instinct was to say no, she took a moment to consider the options before them. It was a good spot to settle in for the evening, particularly because of how well hidden it was. But staying in one place for long made her anxious.

"What if we have supper, walk around until it starts getting darker and then come back here?" Metztli offered as a compromise.

She wasn't exactly comfortable with coming back once they left, but as long as they moved around for a little while it was unlikely that any trouble would come from it. At least, that's what she hoped.

"What do you think, boy? Sounds like a good plan?" Acalan asked the dog that still had no name.

It was strange though, instead of agreeing, the pup whined softly before climbing out of her brother's lap. Metztli knew better than to disregard whatever the canine was trying to tell them. She watched carefully as he trotted over to the edge of their temporary campsite, his ears perked up high, prompting Metztli to believe he could hear something they could not.

"Get up," Metztli whispered as she quickly stood, grasping her spear tightly.

If there was something or someone in the forest that they

couldn't see, running from it wouldn't do them any good now.

"You see or sense anything and you shoot. Understood?" Metztli commanded quietly, whether it was a human or an animal, both of them had to be prepared to fight if they wanted to live.

From deep in the thicket of bushes that surrounded them came a low growl. From the sound of it Metztli knew it was much larger than a dog. Neither of them moved or breathed as the beast stepped out of the greenery, stalking towards the fire pit where Metztli and Acalan stood like statues.

It was a jaguar with paws large enough to stomp their heads in if it wanted to. Its eyes shone in the dark of the underbrush, and it seemed to disregard their dog as it took a step closer. It must have smelled the blood from the fish. That or the gods were in need of some form of entertainment. They were probably bored out of their minds as none of the heirs had tried to kill each other yet.

"I take it back, don't move," Metztli whispered.

She'd learned from her father that it was best to stay still when it came to these sorts of beasts. The jaguar would either rummage through their things and leave, or decide to take their pack as a consolation prize for his time. Either way Metztli was prepared. Jaguars weren't impossible to kill, just difficult.

Very, very difficult.

She continued watching as the jaguar circled them, sniffing in search of something to eat. The princess wanted to scream for it to just use its big paws to take their fish and leave but the animal would likely not understand her. Besides, the sound of her shouting would no doubt startle the beast into attacking them both.

Metztli found some comfort in the fact that the animal simply looked bored. It could have attacked the moment it saw them, but it did not, so perhaps they were safer than they thought. The princess was truly beginning to believe that as it began venturing back into the forest.

That is, until their dog chased after the jaguar, barking at the beast, warning it to never return. The jaguar turned, snapping its sharp teeth towards the pup. Metztli was frozen but she knew had to do something. She couldn't let their dog die because it was trying to protect them.

The princess released the deep breath she was holding in, raised her arm, and sent her spear hurtling through the air with a scream that was almost unrecognizable. She'd aimed for the jaguar's side, and her blade did strike him. Not deep enough to kill but deep enough to annoy the living daylights out of him.

Great.

Now the jaguar was angry and had a new victim on its mind.

Metztli pushed her brother out of the way before grabbing for the blade strapped to her thigh. The beast roared as it reached her, biting into the air as if to take a piece straight out of her, but the princess managed to move out of the way and stab the beast in its side at the same time.

"Acalan run!" Metztli pleaded with her brother as she paced a couple steps back, preparing for the jaguar to pounce towards her again.

"NO!" Metztli argued as her brother attempted to shoot the beast with his bow.

His aim was impeccable, but the beast was too large and now he had a spear dangling from one side and an arrow sticking out of the other. Not only that, but the jaguar paid no attention to Metztli, its attention was now on her brother.

Metztli was close enough to the pile of hot rocks that they'd stacked to grasp one and hurl it towards the beast, knocking it on the other side of its head. She'd made the decision so quickly that she hadn't considered that in doing so she would burn her hand in the process. That was, however, a simple price to pay in exchange for her brother's life. Her left hand ached, but she was too busy taking a few steps back and yelling at the beast to attack her instead.

She ran towards the beast before purposefully sliding against the dirt, landing her underneath the belly of the great beast that wanted to make a meal out of her. She slid her blade against its stomach until she wasn't underneath it anymore. The beast howled out in pain, but it wasn't dead, not yet.

Metztli had no time to stand before the jaguar was rushing towards her again. She was sure this was how she would die, eaten by a beast instead of being killed by an heir from one of the opposing houses. The princess figured that was a much better way of dying as she braced herself and shut her eyes, hoping the beast would make her death quick.

She only opened her eyes when she felt the weight of the beast on her body. For a moment she'd thought she'd already gone numb from the violence of being eaten alive, until she heard them.

"Perfect aim, every time," Necalli's voice rang out.

He wasn't lying because he had managed to aim his Macuahuitl straight for the jaguar's head. Not only that, but he'd done so with enough strength that he'd killed the beast, causing it to collapse on top of Metztli.

"ACALAN, RUN!" Metztli screamed.

It was one thing to fight a beast and it was another thing to fight off the two heirs from the House of Blood.

"Acalan, stay," Necalli ordered with an aggressive finger before turning back to Metztli. "Princess, calm down, we come in peace."

She didn't believe a word that he said. She bared her teeth at him and hissed as she tried to push the jaguar's massive body off herself to no avail.

For a moment she turned to look at her brother who held his bow at the ready. The odds were still stacked against him if it came down to a fight, Metztli knew that, and she was sure that her brother did as well. It was in moments like this one that she wished he was less noble. He should have just run and taken the dog with him instead of staying and trying to protect her.

"Touch him and I'll slit your throat with my bare hands," Metztli warned, locking eyes with Necalli.

She only wanted to strangle the man even more when he laughed, pulled her spear out of the jaguar's side, and threw it onto the ground beside her.

"I just saved your life, princess. You should be kinder to me. You owe me two favors now, just so we're clear," Necalli teased as he knelt down to get closer to her face.

The Prince of Blood was insufferable, and he seemed to pride himself on being so which only frustrated her more.

"Get away from her! I'll shoot you if you don't! I really will!" Acalan warned them, but Metztli could see the way his bow was trembling in his hands.

"No, you won't. Unless you want to explain to my sister how you killed me? Yeah, I didn't think so," Necalli responded.

Metztli continued trying to maneuver the beast off her, if only so she could have the opportunity to claw at Necalli's perfectly stupid face.

"Coatl, give me a hand. It looks like the princess is having a hard time over here," Necalli said.

Metztli had no choice but to watch as Necalli and his cousin ground themselves on one side of the beast and used all their strength to push on the animal's carcass until it rolled off her body. She took a deep breath before abandoning her spear, crawling out from beneath the jaguar's body, and running to stand in front of her brother as quickly as she could. The princess was expecting a fight, but instead she was met with a raised brow from Necalli. Coatl seemed to be equally amused.

"What do you want?" Metztli questioned, still angry about the fact that Necalli had come to her rescue.

It could have been anyone else, literally anyone else, but it had been the Prince of Blood who had saved her from becoming a meal.

"I want a lot of things princess. A thank you would be great for starters," Necalli said with a devious smirk on his face that she wanted to slap away.

Metztli spit towards him instead, that was as much gratitude as she was willing to show.

"Hmm, they must have different customs in the House of Life. That's not how we say thank you, now is it, Coatl?" Necalli turned to ask his cousin who shook his head in response.

"I'm only going to ask one more time. What. Do. You. Want?" Metztli interrupted. After almost being eaten by a jaguar she wasn't exactly in the mood for their games.

"Why must you do everything the hard way?" Necalli asked but Metztli did not respond.

He was the one making things difficult, not her. She was simply protecting her family, just as she was sure Necalli would if it was Citlalic in here with him instead of his cousin.

"Fine. We want an alliance," Necalli said clearly.

It took a few seconds for Metztli to really grasp his words before she laughed. He couldn't be serious. The House of Life was notorious for never allying with anyone, much less the House of Blood.

"No. Now can we go?" Metztli questioned.

Necalli and Coatl had plenty of opportunities to attack them and they did not. Metztli could only assume this meant they wouldn't, at least not right now.

"Oh…sorry, I wasn't asking you. I was asking Acalan, the heir to your house," Necalli said. "Companions have little say within the Pyramid of Tributes I'm afraid."

He was right. She wasn't the direct heir to her father's empire. Coming from Necalli she knew this had less to do with her being a woman and more to do with the fact that he just enjoyed annoying her to no end. Luckily, Metztli knew what her brother would say. Or at least she thought she did. She was growing more and more suspicious as seconds passed without a proper response from Acalan.

"Tell him, the answer is no," Metztli ordered in a whisper, nudging her brother's ribs with her elbow.

When she turned to look at him, she was thoroughly disappointed that he actually seemed conflicted.

"I-I….I need to speak to Necalli alone," Acalan said, pushing past his sister.

She gripped his arm before he could get very far. Metztli would be completely damned if she allowed her brother to walk away with Necalli. That was asking for death, and she would not under any circumstances allow him to die.

"If this is about Citlalic, drop it right now," she warned. "She doesn't matter as much as our survival does."

She knew immediately after she'd said it that she'd chosen the wrong words because whether she liked it or not Citlalic was important to her brother. He was blinded and made stupid by love.

"I know what I'm doing," Acalan hissed as he pulled his arm out of her grasp.

Necalli had reminded her that there was nothing she could do. She was just his companion, her rank was below his whether she liked it or not, so all she could do was sit there and hope that he really did know what he was doing.

"Necalli, you lay a finger on my brother, and I'll win this tournament out of spite and slaughter your sister in cold blood, the moment I return home," Metztli warned.

Necalli's devious smirk returned as she had expected. But she had not expected to see the sight of her brother fuming at her words. It was just a threat. Something to try and bargain for Acalan's life. Surely he knew she would never actually do such a thing…right?

"That is enough! I don't want to hear another word from you while I speak to Necalli, privately, do you understand?" Acalan questioned in a near growl.

Metztli flinched at the tone of his voice. He'd never spoken to her like that. Even when they'd fought a few days before, his voice had been full of sorrow and this was pure anger. She could only find the strength to nod and hold back tears as she watched her brother and Necalli walk into the forest alone.

ACALAN

calan was still fuming by the time he walked into the forest with Necalli following closely behind. He knew his sister well, and he knew that she would never harm another being without there being a good reason for it but knowing that didn't make it any easier to hear her speaking of Citlalic in such a vicious manner.

Necalli, on the other hand, seemed untouched by her words. Acalan assumed it was because the Prince of Blood knew it was an empty threat, but he couldn't be certain. The topic that was of more importance was this newfound offer for an alliance.

A week ago, Acalan would have never entertained the idea of entering an alliance with any of the houses, most certainly not the House of Blood. But things had changed since then. If Necalli could help him carry the burden of keeping Metztli alive long enough for her to win, then that was something Acalan would consider. He would do it wisely of course, but it wasn't an opportunity that he was about to pass up without at least discussing it with the prince. Even if that upset his sister.

"What exactly is there to discuss? My offer was clear," Necalli said sternly when they were finally far enough that they could discuss matters privately.

Acalan scoffed at Necalli. An alliance of this nature could change the entire course of the tournament, and while his instincts told him to trust Necalli, the prince needed to be careful.

"If I agree to an alliance, what's in it for you?" Acalan pressed.

Even if Necalli knew who Metztli was, his life still had to have some sort of value to him, right?

Metztli and Acalan only had one goal. They were going to return home, and they were going to do so together. Acalan needed Necalli to understand that they were serious about that before agreeing to anything.

"If she gets out of here alive, things will change," Necalli began. "I need them to change for my people and my family."

Acalan knew that the House of Blood was not nearly as fortunate as the others so that reasoning was sound, but was Necalli really willing to give up his life for it? It was one thing to believe he was willing to make that sacrifice and another to face death and still follow through.

"And you're willing to give your life for that?" Acalan asked. "You know how this ends. Either Metztli and I leave this tournament together or we don't leave at all."

"I know. We came prepared for that," Necalli said, holding up his necklace.

At first glance it was nothing more than that: a simple locket on a chain. That was, until Necalli opened the locket and revealed something that resembled a medicinal tablet. It only took a few seconds for Acalan to understand.

"It's nightshade, ground up, highly concentrated. I pop this into my mouth, and I'm gone seconds later. Coatl has one too. Like I said, I need Metztli to survive this thing so the prophecy can come true."

Acalan flinched at the mention of the prophecy. No one other than Atzi had spoken about it so freely, but then again, if Necalli was ready to die, he didn't have much to hide from the gods or anyone else.

"Don't...Just don't speak of it out loud," Acalan said sternly though his eyes told another story.

His gaze was pleading. He didn't want to risk anyone else finding out, much less his sister.

"Why haven't you told her? She deserves to know who she is,"

Necalli questioned with a raised brow.

That was a question that Acalan had been asking himself over and over again from the moment he'd found out about the prophecy. Atzi's words had been clear though. Acalan had to be the one to tell her, and he would know when the moment was right. So far, nothing had led him to believe that she needed to know, not yet.

"That's none of your concern. If I agree to this alliance, you and Coatl have to agree to keep your mouths' shut. Understood?" Acalan demanded.

He knew what the consequences were if Metztli found out before destiny had intended her to. She couldn't know, not until Acalan was certain that she wouldn't lose control of the power the prophecy gave her. As much as he loved his sister, he did recognize that she could be reckless at times, and she could not, under any circumstances, be reckless with the prophecy.

"Sounds like we have a deal. That is what you're saying, right?" Necalli asked, prompting Acalan to pause for a moment.

His instincts were telling him that this was the right decision. It couldn't have been by coincidence alone that he'd fallen in love so quickly with Citlalic, nor could it be that they'd known about Metztli and what she was for longer than he had.

Acalan and Metztli were strong and there was still a chance that they could survive on their own, but it would be stupid to not take this opportunity for guaranteed protection. Besides, he hardly believed that Necalli and Coatl would be able to betray them without Metztli sensing their intentions first.

"Don't even think about screwing us over," Acalan warned before extending his arm.

Necalli smirked as he grasped it and shook.

It was done, the two heirs had come to an agreement.

An alliance had been made.

Metztli

Metztli wasn't angry. She was more so disappointed in herself for having gone as far as she had. The mention of the princess from the House of Blood should have never left her mouth, even if she believed that was the only way to get through to Necalli. That plan had obviously failed because instead of being angry, Necalli only seemed entertained by her open show of violence, and Acalan was clearly upset with his sister for stooping so low.

Unfortunately, Necalli was like a scab, itchy and near infection. The sort that you wanted to pull at but know you shouldn't. Metztli had never been patient though, and she'd always pulled them, making herself bleed only to regret touching the wound in the first place. Necalli was the worst of scabs, and she could only hope that Acalan would be smart enough to realize that before it was too late.

Knowing this made Metztli want to rush after her brother. It wasn't safe for him to be alone with Necalli, nor was it safe for her to be alone with Coatl.

As they sat together, the beastly man kept offering her smiles, but she didn't trust him. It was difficult to do when they had such visible marks on their bodies. Metztli knew what they were for, she could count the numbers of lives they'd sacrificed in the name of their goddess and anyone willing to commit such atrocities was a walking red flag, begging to be noticed.

The princess kept a close eye on Coatl from where he sat while she stood and beckoned for their dog to follow her as she checked on the fish. Her sigh was audible when she realized it had been charred, far too burned to be edible now.

Well, that's what she got for picking a fight with a beast.

"Where did the dog come from?" Coatl asked in a kind voice.

Metztli turned to snarl at him. Acalan might be okay with entertaining small talk, but she was not. The princess was just waiting for her brother to return so they could all go their separate ways. That is, unless Necalli somehow managed to talk her brother into an alliance. If matters had been settled before the tournament, Metztli would have not argued, but approaching them two days into the tournament seemed far too suspicious for Metztli to simply look past it.

"Is he friendly or will he bite if I try to pet him?" Coatl questioned as he made funny faces at the pup, trying to catch his attention.

"He might not bite, but I will," Metztli retorted, fed up with the fact that she was even waiting for her brother to return.

The more time Acalan spent with Necalli, the more likely the Prince of Blood was to convince her brother of something they did not need. Sure, she had almost been eaten by a jaguar, but she'd done her duty and protected her brother in the process. They didn't need an alliance to survive this. Metztli was sure of that.

The Princess was startled when the most genuine laughter filled the air. She turned to look at Coatl. The man was laying on his side and holding onto his stomach. What exactly he thought was so amusing, Metztli did not know.

"Good one!" Coatl said, prompting Metztli's eyebrow to raise in confusion.

Nothing that she had said had been intended to be taken as a joke. She was being serious. Had her tone made Coatl believe anything else?

Before the princess could respond, she heard rustling in the forest and footsteps approaching. Her face broke into a smile at the sight of her brother. He seemed to be unharmed. That didn't last for very long though. He didn't have to say a word for Metztli to know what he'd done. It was written across his face in the way his gaze ignored hers while Necalli looked straight at the princess, almost taunting her now that he'd fooled her brother.

"No," Metztli growled as she paced towards her brother.

Acalan threw his hands up in surrender, a quiet way of saying, *what's done is done, there's nothing we can do now.*

She'd never truly been disappointed in her brother. Even when she'd found Citlalic in his bedroom, the feeling of disappointment had washed away quickly, but this was something entirely different. Their father had always insisted on one rule for the both of them when it came to the Tournament of Heirs.

Absolutely no alliances.

"Don't worry. We'll separate when it's down to five heirs," Acalan assured her but it did nothing to calm how Metztli felt about being forced into an alliance with the House of Blood.

Necalli could have promised to separate, but what if he chose not to at the last minute? They didn't have room to make mistakes, and this one would end in death. Metztli was more sure of that than she had ever been sure of anything in her life.

"What's going to stop them from killing us in our sleep!" Metztli argued in return.

"If I wanted to kill you, wouldn't I have just let that Jaguar eat you?" Necalli wondered idly.

Metztli turned to him. The way he spoke reminded her of the evening when they'd shared a dance. *Like calls to like.*

It was at that moment that she realized Necalli had planned this all along. And her brother had fallen right into his trap.

Without second thought, Metztli lunged forward in hopes of strangling Necalli to death. She'd had enough of him. Even if he was mesmerizing when he wanted to be, she didn't want to hear another word come out of his stupid mouth.

Acalan managed to get a grip on her before she could cause any real injury. Metztli fought her brother's grip, pleading with him to let her end this once and for all, but he didn't. Instead, he shushed her softly and promised her that everything would be okay. As if that was something he could guarantee. It was even less true now that he'd chosen to ally with the House of Blood.

"You trust me. Don't you?" Acalan questioned as he turned her around to face him.

Yes, no, maybe? All these were applicable answers but only one of them held any truth.

Yes. She did trust her brother. She trusted him with her life but that didn't mean that Acalan couldn't be blinded by Necalli's charm. No one seemed to be immune to that.

"Of course I do…but this will not end well, you have to believe me," Metztli whispered, a few tears streaming down her face as she spoke.

She knew her words were falling on deaf ears because Acalan simply shook his head and pulled her close to his chest.

"Just trust me," Acalan whispered over and over again.

Metztli knew there was no point in arguing any further. What was done was done. The only thing she could do now was keep her brother safe from the House of Blood and its heirs.

DAY THREE OF

THE TOURNAMENT OF HEIRS

ACALAN

calan hadn't allowed himself a single moment of rest the night prior. He already felt like he was being tortured by the way his sister looked at him every time they found each other's eyes. Even when the trumpets went off sometime in the middle of the night and the mark for the last heir of the House of Serpent disappeared, Acalan couldn't seem to make his sister say a word to him.

She was making him feel guilty for the decision that he'd made, but if this decision ensured that they'd both return home, then that would make his guilt feel worthy of baring at least. Besides, Metztli couldn't stay angry with him forever.

The sun eventually rose, just as it had the morning before, but things were different now. They were no longer alone. Now they had a blanket of protection. Between Necalli, Coatl, Metztli, and himself, Acalan found it hard to imagine that they could encounter an opponent they couldn't overcome with ease, regardless of whether it was human or not.

He did, of course, wish that his sister would speak to him. Even if it was just a series of cruel words, Acalan believed that it would be much better than simply trailing in front of her in complete silence.

The prince was grateful that Necalli had ended his pestering. That didn't exactly earn the Prince of Blood any favors with Metztli though. Acalan could see that she still despised him regardless.

"We found a waterfall on our first day here. I wouldn't mind a quick dip in the water if that's okay with the both of you?" Coatl suggested, looking over his shoulder.

Acalan turned as if to ask his sister what she thought of the proposition. Neither of them had showered or bathed since the first day of the tournament. Acalan wasn't all that dirty per say, but Metztli was still covered in the jaguar's blood from the day before and she was starting to smell, so bathing would be for the best.

Instead of responding, his sister quickly moved her gaze away from him. Acalan didn't want to make all the decisions for them, but he would if he had to.

"That would be great," Acalan replied, offering a kind smile in return.

Coatl was much different than Acalan had expected the man to be. Despite resembling a beast, he was genuine, and Necalli had a way of making his cousin laugh even with the most simple of gestures. Acalan wondered if perhaps it was easier to enjoy life knowing that it would all end soon.

If they went through with their plans then Necalli and Coatl would have simple, quick deaths. They would feel no pain. They would just cease to exist the moment the nightshade tablets touched their tongue.

Acalan did remember thinking that Coatl seemed to be very noble during their first meeting, especially when he spoke of his father and his intention to honor the man. How could one honor their fallen loved ones more than by dying for a prophecy that would fix everything? That was far more noble than dying at the hands of an heir filled with bloodlust.

"I'm not bathing with them around," Metztli whispered as she tugged on Acalan's arm, making him halt in his steps.

Those weren't exactly the words he wanted to hear but it was much better than walking around in complete silence.

Before Acalan could respond Necalli and Coatl stopped in their tracks too, waiting for them to continue. An alliance was an alliance. From now until four more heirs found themselves dead, there would be no separating them.

The Prince of Blood looked like he had a sharp remark on the tip of his tongue but before he could say anything Acalan warned him with his eyes, right now was not the moment to try and get under Metztli's skin anymore than he already had.

"We'll catch up with the both of you in a second," Acalan said, and that seemed to be enough for both Necalli and Coatl to understand that Acalan needed a moment alone with his sister.

"You should bathe, you're covered in blood," Acalan tried to reason with his sister as best he could. "The scent can attract other predators, you know that."

"No, I know that it's just…I can't bathe around Necalli," Metztli countered. "You don't see me that way because I'm your sister, but Necalli has made it obvious that he *does* see me that way."

The realization made Acalan's eyes grow wide. In the midst of the chaos that had been the last few days he'd nearly forgotten of the passes that Necalli had made towards Metztli. They had to find a way to make this work though because he hadn't been lying. The scent of blood would eventually attract something or someone.

"I should have thought of that…What if you bathe after us? I'll make sure Necalli doesn't try anything," Acalan said.

"I don't want you alone with them."

"Metztli…they won't hurt me. Citlalic told me something, I can't tell you what it is, not yet, but I promise you it guarantees that they won't do anything. They want to help, that's all," Acalan tried to explain. It was difficult to do so when all he had to offer were half-truths but at the same time it was better than nothing at all.

He watched as Metztli's eyebrow rose in confusion, he wanted to tell her the truth about everything, but it wasn't the time, not yet. Last night she'd said she trusted him, so she would have to continue doing so for this to work.

"No. You lied to me before, I can tell you're hiding something from me and that's not like you. You're terrible at keeping secrets so just tell me," Metztli argued but not out of anger.

Acalan could see in her eyes that she was filled with frustration and sorrow. Telling her could fix that in the best-case scenario but in the worst…it would only make things more complicated and Acalan couldn't risk the latter. Not yet.

He gripped her shoulders with one hand and cupped her cheek with the other, forcing Metztli to look at him.

"I want to," he assured her, "and I will, I promise that the moment that I can, I'll tell you everything that I know. We just need to get through the tournament first, and Necalli and Coatl are going to help us do that. Yesterday you said you trusted me, so trust me. I would never do anything that could harm our chances of returning home." It was all he could say without revealing too much.

"Fine, but if they try anything, I'm not kidding, Acalan. I will not hesitate to kill them. Do you understand?" Metztli questioned in return.

Everything else in his mind was a mess but this he understood loud and clear. He hoped that Necalli and Coatl did too because they were putting their lives more at risk than anyone else.

"I won't stop you if it comes to that," Acalan responded. That was enough for Metztli to agree with a firm nod of her head.

She wiggled out of his grip and took a few steps forward before turning back.

"We should name the dog, like you said. Maybe tonight when we've settled in for the evening."

Now those words were like music to Acalan's ears, and apparently to the dog's too because his tail wagged furiously, prompting Acalan to laugh as quietly as he could. He took a few steps to meet his sister and wrap an arm around her shoulders.

"What if we named him *Emperor of Doom*, that has a nice ring to it, don't you think?" Acalan teased, earning an eye roll from his sister as they walked to meet Necalli and Coatl.

"God, just don't let Coatl hear you. He thinks everything is funny even when it's not," Metztli replied as she tried to hide her own laughter.

Things weren't perfect between them. Nor was Acalan sure that they ever would be, but they were okay for now and they could win the tournament while just being okay.

The walk to the waterfall was long and there had been a few moments when Acalan was sure that Necalli and Coatl were lost. He couldn't blame them. A forest was difficult to navigate if you didn't know how to do so. The House of Blood was surrounded by stone, so he hardly believed that either of them had the amount of experience that he and Metztli did in such an environment.

"Wow..." Acalan whispered at first sight of the cascading water.

The waterfall was massive, far too large to fit within the Pyramid of Tributes. That was just another testimony to how powerful the gods were. In hindsight, Acalan understood why his sister had always felt a certain distaste for the gods. It wasn't fair that they could hold so much power over their children and yet hardly interfered with their everyday life.

No, they waited for twenty-five years to pass between each generation, just so they could come back and torture their mortal children again.

"The water's freezing so be careful when you get in," Necalli warned as he tugged the hem of his shirt up and over his head. He was shirtless before Acalan could interject. When Acalan turned to look at Metztli, she was already turned away, pretending to look at something else. This was by all regards, far more awkward then Acalan had intended it to be.

Instead of saying anything and making matters worse, Acalan put his belongings down and undressed too. The quicker they bathed, the quicker Metztli would be able to and the quicker they could be out of this situation. Out of all the things his father had prepared him for, this had certainly not been on that list.

He understood why Metztli was uncomfortable with the entire situation though. It made perfect sense, but fixing it was an entirely different battle. He couldn't just force Necalli to never look at her again.

The prince dipped his feet into the water. It was indeed freezing, but that was fine. Necalli and Coatl followed suit behind Acalan while Metztli stayed back, opting to sharpen her spear while they bathed.

"Is she not joining us?" Necalli questioned. This time his tone wasn't full of the typical arrogance that typically consumed the Prince of Blood.

If anything, it seemed like he was actually worried about Metztli. That was different but Acalan supposed it made sense, considering who Metztli was and everything that she was destined to do.

"It's um…not proper for a princess to bathe with three men present," Acalan tried to explain with a firm nod.

That was a whole load of bullshit though because Metztli wasn't the sort of princess that cared about what was proper and what was not. On top of that Acalan knew his words were hypocritical. He had done a number of things with Citlalic that were also very improper for a prince to do with a princess.

"She likes me doesn't she?" Necalli exclaimed, prompting Acalan to quickly turn his gaze towards his sister.

She seemed not to have heard, which was a blessing. The last thing Acalan needed was for her to hear Necalli. Not because it was untrue, but because Acalan knew it was far too close to the truth. Regardless, Necalli and Coatl would be dead in a matter of days. No good could come from whatever Necalli was thinking.

"She does not, and don't say anything else like that because she's looking for any reason to kill either of you," Acalan warned.

"That just sounds like a challenge to me," Necalli responded with that devious smirk on his face he loved to show.

Acalan was starting to understand why his sister hated it so much.

"I'm not kidding. Drop it," Acalan said sternly, raising his chest in the water so he was at least a head taller than Necalli. Unwise? Maybe, but at the end of the day he was the heir of the House of Life. Most importantly he was Metztli's brother and her protector, the prophecy said so. And while Acalan had failed in a lot of things. He would not fail in this.

"Fine but, in another life, I would have had every intention of properly courting her. You should know that," Necalli said.

His words struck Acalan harder than they should have. He'd said the same thing to Citlalic just a few days before. In some ways Acalan knew it was unfair that he had Citlalic, and Metztli had no one. Necalli would have been good for her, but life wasn't fair.

Acalan didn't respond. He couldn't find the words. Instead, he just dipped his head under the water and washed the dirt off his body. The quicker this was over, the better.

Metztli

Sitting by the edge of the shore, unable to turn and look was a sort of torture that Metztli had never experienced, nor did she intend to for any longer than what was necessary. The tournament itself was far more difficult than anyone could have prepared her for, and on top of that she was now dealing with a flood of incomprehensible emotions.

Over the last few days, she'd already begun to suspect that Acalan was hiding something from her, but having her brother confirm those suspicions was confusing to say the least. At the same time though, she did trust him, and she couldn't find it in herself to argue or barter for more information. The tournament was already taking so much from her, and she couldn't afford to give it any more.

A heavy sigh escaped Metztli's lips as she finally allowed herself to look, just for a single moment and no longer. She reasoned with herself that it was just so that she could estimate how long it would be before she could wash away the blood that had seeped into her skin. This was, of course, only half the truth. The other half was that she was curious.

Metztli was a princess first and foremost, and her brother's companion for the Tournament of Heirs. But that didn't make her immune to human temptation.

Necalli's body seemed to shimmer in the water, his muscles contracting and stiffening when he stood or moved a certain way. She wondered if it would have been better to give in to her attraction from the moment it had come about, if she had, she wouldn't be sitting here like a bitch in heat. Even after staring for a moment too long, Metztli simply couldn't make herself look away.

She knew there was no use in entertaining such thoughts. What she wanted could never occur because of who they were: two heirs from opposing houses that somehow ended up in an alliance that would surely kill one of them, if not both. Had a sadder reality ever existed? Metztli wasn't sure, nor did she believe she would ever find out.

Metztli had to stop herself from gasping aloud when Necalli's gaze met her own. She was mortified and slightly ashamed of the fact that he'd even caught her looking. Necalli already took every opportunity to tease her about anything and everything. This would only make it worse.

But he wasn't looking at her like he usually did. There was no arrogant smile on his face. Instead, his lips stayed in a calm, thin line. And before Metztli could truly grasp the meaning of his gaze, Necalli looked away, forcing her to do the same.

The princess stood hurriedly and stretched her legs. Her heart was racing much faster than it did even after a long run. She hated feeling this way; completely unsure of what to call this emotion. It was just that when Necalli looked at her, she could somehow sense that he was really looking at her and not through her like everyone else did. It was like he really saw her for what she was. And being seen like that – well, that was much more dangerous than their alliance.

The princess tried to keep herself distracted for as long as she could. Anything was better than contemplating Necalli and his intentions. They didn't really matter at the end of the day. If Necalli stayed true to his word, then they could be separated before the day ended. Only four more heirs had to die, and then she could be rid of him.

Death was inevitable. Not only in the Pyramid of Tributes, but everywhere. It was just a matter of time before they all met their ends.

"It's your turn," Acalan said, placing a hand on her shoulder.

Metztli had been so lost in her own thoughts that a yelp escaped her as she jumped back from her brother. That was partially because of how cold her brother's hand felt on her skin, but also because of what she'd been thinking about. She'd had plenty of sinful thoughts throughout her life, but they'd never been accompanied with the guilt that she felt when she thought of Necalli.

"I'll be quick," Metztli said, desperately trying to hide the shame that she felt.

Necalli's gaze was burning a hole through her. It was uncomfortable and yet delightful all at once.

"No, take your time, we'll hold the fort down. The water is freezing though, just so you know." Her brother warned. He seemed not to have noticed the change in her demeanor.

A dip in freezing water would do her some good, and perhaps with her bath, these conflicting thoughts that had raised within her would disappear as well.

Metztli waited until she found the most secluded area to undress, opting to leave her undergarments on just in case Necalli did have a wandering eye. She washed her clothes as quickly as she could. It was either that or continue smelling of fresh blood and the latter was far too dangerous.

Once she had rung as much blood as she could from her clothing, Metztli laid her clothing out in the sun, hoping they would dry quickly as she dipped her feet into the water. She felt like perhaps her pain tolerance was slightly higher than that of Acalan, Necalli or Coatl because the water was cold, but it certainly wasn't freezing. If anything, it felt good against her warm skin, and worked wonders in washing away all the blood that remained on her. At home she enjoyed scalding hot baths, but this wasn't too bad either.

Being that her brother had told her to take as much time as she liked, Metztli swam a short distance until she was on the other side of the waterfall. It was easier to really wash herself off completely, behind the privacy of the falling water. She didn't like that she couldn't see through the other way either, but she would be quick.

Necalli and Coatl had yet to do anything that would make her believe they wouldn't keep to the alliance, but it was confusing why they wanted an alliance in the first place. Coatl alone could have won the Tournament of Heirs if he wanted to, so it wasn't like this alliance would benefit him or Necalli in any way.

Once she was as clean as she could be, Metztli swam back to the hidden area she'd found. The princess had nothing to dry herself off with, so she simply stood in the sun for a little while. Doing so only did half the trick but it was better than slipping back into her clothing while entirely wet. She quickly braided her hair and while it wasn't nearly as neat or beautiful as when her mother did it, it still got the job done. The princess knew better than to keep her hair down when they could be attacked at any moment. Giving their enemy any advantage was not something she was willing to do.

When she returned to the group, she found them all still undressed and eating while seemingly deep in conversation. The sight was quite strange honestly. Acalan had friends when they were younger, but he was naturally a rather solitary person. He somehow seemed to fit right in with Necalli and Coatl though, which was something that Metztli could have never predicted.

"I think I prefer you drenched in blood," Necalli said when he caught sight of her.

It was almost a relief to see he was back to his natural state because it made it easier to look at him without feeling shame. When he wanted to be intolerable, he truly could be. It was one of his special talents.

"Maybe that's why I washed it off," Metztli responded sternly.

"Alright, that's enough of that...we should get going," Acalan announced as he stood up and started dressing himself. "The last time Metztli and I stayed somewhere for too long it didn't end well."

Metztli had yet to forget the way the sisters from the House of Flor had looked at both of them when they'd been spotted across the river the day before...

"What happened? If you don't mind me asking," Coatl questioned as he stood and began to dress.

Metztli didn't mind looking at him. He was far too muscular for her liking and while she had told her mother that she someday hoped for a husband who would laugh at her jokes, she didn't mean that she wanted a husband who would laugh at everything she said, even when she didn't mean to be funny.

"We encountered the sisters from the House of Flor and the brother and sister from the House of Wind yesterday. There was a river between us so nothing happened, but it seemed like they were in an alliance. I can't think of why else they would have been together," Metztli explained.

"Well, the heirs from the House of Wind are weak. They're fully dependent on their new weapon to get them through the tournament," Necalli stated confidently enough that it was hard not to believe him.

"What about the sisters from the House of Flor? You know them well, don't you?" Metztli asked.

She hadn't meant for it to sound as accusatory as it did, but she had reason to be weary. Necalli had said he'd known the sisters for a long time, not only that, but Xochitl herself had warned Metztli not to fall for Necalli's charm. The princess still couldn't help but wonder if that meant that at some point, Xochitl had fallen for it herself.

"Both of them are good fighters but they're depending on close combat, hence the teeth."

Necalli seemed to collapse in on himself, as if he was hiding something.

"What do you think about them, Coatl?" she turned. "Surely you know them as well as Necalli, right?"

She watched him closely as he considered how to respond. If they were in a true alliance then Necalli and Coatl had a responsibility to not withhold information, and yet they were. Metztli quickly turned to look at her brother. She didn't have to say anything to get her point across.

"This alliance means nothing if you two are unwilling to tell us the truth," Metztli said with her chest held high.

"No," Necalli countered, "this alliance means nothing if you are unwilling to trust us. We're not hiding anything. They aren't particularly skilled in anything. Their family is expecting them to win. That's the only thing that makes them dangerous."

"Everyone wants to win," she retorted. But every other house had spare heirs and the House of Life did not.

"Well, isn't that what makes this so entertaining for the gods?" Necalli said, holding Metztli's gaze. "Everyone wants to win but only two heirs can return home. If the stakes were low then the gods wouldn't care. They already care so little for us."

For the first time in all the conversations that they'd shared,

Metztli actually agreed with Necalli. He'd said that *like calls to like*. Did that mean that he hated the gods and everything they did, too?

"I hate to be the bearer of bad news, but the gods we speak so lowly of are watching us," Acalan interjected. "So unless either of you want to be punished, I suggest we move along."

Metztli forced her gaze away from Necalli, picking up her spear and waiting for them to dress completely so that they could go.

For a long time, Metztli had considered what she'd do if given the opportunity to stand before the gods. It was said that some of the victorious heirs kissed their feet, thanking the gods for allowing them to win. Metztli would do no such thing. If she and Acalan won, the gods would have had no part in it, they would win because of the sacrifices she and her brother were prepared to make. Not because the gods allowed it, but because of the bloodshed caused by their own hands.

The thought was reckless, Metztli knew that, but when she found herself before the gods, she would not thank them for anything. No, she would thank everyone who ever helped her train. She would thank her father for showing her the way, and she would thank her brother for powering through by her side. Hell, she would even thank the heirs she'd killed in the process. But never, not once, would she ever bend her knee and thank the gods for her success.

26

ACALAN

They were only three days in and Acalan already missed the comfort of his home. To be fair, he'd started missing Tu'nethe the moment they'd walked out of the city and made way for the Pyramid of Tributes. But each passing second was just making matters worse. All Acalan wanted to do was win this thing so that he and Metztli could be presented in front of the gods and be done with the tournament forever.

The prince was also vaguely aware of how selfish his thought was as he walked behind the group. While he still had the option of returning home, it seemed that Coatl and Necalli had already made peace with their destinies. They would not leave the Pyramid of Tributes, they would never see or embrace their families again. All because of a revelation a priestess had thousands of years ago.

The day of reckoning would come and when it did, Metztli would be ready for it. Until then all Acalan could do was carry this secret with him. It was difficult to not think back to what Necalli had said the day before. Metztli did deserve to know that she had more purpose than what she believed, but it wasn't worth telling her if it meant risking the prophecy. He had to make sure she was ready for the power the prophecy would give her and that she wouldn't lose control when she found out. It felt like an impossible duty, but Acalan had no option but to follow along, it was all he could do for now.

"You okay?" Necalli asked quietly.

Coatl and Metztli seemed too involved in their own conversation to hear the Prince of Blood. From what Acalan had gathered, Coatl was explaining some sort of ceremony to her. From the expression on Metztli's face, he could tell that whatever it was that Coatl was explaining, it was not pleasant.

Every one of his instincts was telling Acalan to trust Necalli as if he had a bigger role to play in all of this. That thought was quickly shot down by the reminder that the options for winning were slim. Metztli or Acalan could win separately. They could both die, and with them the prophecy would die too…or in the most ideal of situations, they would both find a way to win and return home. Necalli's destiny was death, but it seemed like the prince viewed dying for someone like Metztli as an honorable way to go.

"I have a lot on my mind, but yeah…she's alive so I'm okay," Acalan responded.

That seemed like an okay response, not perfect by any means but at least he wasn't lying or pouring out his feelings either. He could have told Necalli that he was starting to miss Citlalic and was looking forward to seeing and holding her in his arms again, but that seemed like an unfair thought to confess.

Acalan was slightly taken aback when he felt Necalli place a comforting hand on his shoulder.

"You two are going to make it out of here. It's already been written in our history," Necalli said.

The Prince of Blood often spoke with a sense of confidence that confused Acalan. The prophecy would only live as long as Metztli did, and even with the added protection from the House of Blood, nothing could truly guarantee that the both of them would return home.

"Did Citlalic say so?" Acalan inquired, careful to keep his voice low.

"Obviously…Citlalic knows things. She always has," Necalli replied with a laugh.

It wasn't much of a response, but slowly the pieces were beginning to line up in Acalan's mind. If Citlalic had always known *things* then perhaps no one had told her about the prophecy. There were other ways, ancient gifts that by all accounts had been long gone… Then again, it wasn't like Acalan was prepared to trust histories when he'd caught lies woven into them already.

"She's special, too, isn't she?" Acalan asked.

It felt dangerous to speak those words out loud, but they weren't necessarily incriminating. Besides, Acalan imagined that the gods were currently feasting as they fumed with irritation over the lack of bloodshed. He just hoped they would be too entertained by their own sorrow to listen too closely to the conversations that were being had.

"Of course she is. And you must treat her as such. She deserves no less," Necalli said, offering Acalan a genuine smile that only seemed to appear when he spoke of his sister.

Acalan knew the feeling. Siblinghood was unlike anything else. One could marry and build bonds with complete strangers, but marriages could fail. Siblings were forever, magically tied by blood bonds forged through love.

"I have every intention of doing so," Acalan assured him, offering Necalli a smile in return.

If he was in Necalli's shoes, he would have asked Necalli for the same. A part of him wished he could, if only so his sister could experience true love just as he had.

They walked for a couple more hours, being careful to stay out of sight and avoid the other heirs until supper time neared. Now that they were in an alliance, they could afford to find somewhere to stay for the evening much earlier instead of moving around frantically until their bodies gave up on them.

Acalan was tired after having not slept for a single minute the day before, so he imagined that Metztli was tired as well. The prince was looking forward to a bit of respite until Metztli stopped them abruptly.

"There's something wrong," Metztli claimed as she circled in place, obviously searching for something they could not sense or see.

Necalli looked towards the prince with a curious stare. Acalan understood the Prince of Blood's curiosity. This was now the second time that his sister seemed to sense something before anyone else did.

"Why don't we check the perimeter?" Necalli offered as he turned to look at Coatl who nodded in agreement.

"Be careful," Acalan warned, knowing that the last time his sister had sensed something, it had ended in death.

"Of course. Wish me luck princess," Necalli teased before he and Coatl ventured into the depths of the forest around them.

Everything was quiet. There was no movement in the trees around them and even their dog fell silent.

"What is it? Beyond just feeling like something's wrong," Acalan whispered.

He couldn't help his sister unless he knew what was happening in her mind and what she was feeling. Intuition was a strange thing to be sure. There was no explanation for why ones' body could somehow sense danger before it came. Acalan had felt it many times before on his own adventures with his sister, especially right before they often got caught.

"It's…It's just a feeling, like someone is watching us," Metztli confessed.

Acalan wanted to remind his sister that they were actively being watched by the gods but that felt useless considering that he'd already reminded her of that just hours before.

"I wouldn't blame you for being slightly paranoid considering our circumstances," Acalan assured her before placing a soft kiss on her temple.

His gesture seemed to put her slightly at ease – not all the way but to some extent. They stood there and waited for Necalli and Coatl's return.

It was only a few minutes later that a vicious scream torched through the air. Acalan's body went stiff, and his breath stilled. It sounded like Necalli.

His sister pulled on his arm. She was saying something, but her voice was failing to reach his ears. He just watched as she looked towards the direction from where the scream had come and back to him. Neither of them could afford to panic in a moment like this and yet Acalan was doing just that. Once again, he was frozen with fear.

"We either run towards them or away from them. Make a decision now!" Metztli demanded, wrenching Acalan from his trance. "No one has to know if we break the alliance, I wouldn't dare tell a soul, but you need to tell me what to do, I can't leave you here alone. We either help them together or we don't help them at all."

With every word, Acalan became more and more conscious. The idea of running away was a comforting one, and he had no doubt that Metztli was telling the truth. She wouldn't say a word to anyone if he chose to be a coward, but Acalan would know. He would remember having not tried to save them when it was late at night, and he held Citlalic in his arms. If he was to be an emperor one day, then he needed to learn how to make difficult decisions.

Acalan took a deep breath before grasping his bow tightly in his hands and threading an arrow through the string. They would not run because they were not cowards.

"How do we do this?" he asked.

He couldn't tell if his sister was relieved or felt betrayed by his response. Quite frankly there was a mixture of both emotions on her face. The truth remained though. Acalan felt that he needed Coatl and Necalli to win this tournament. He had agreed to an alliance and Acalan, the heir to the House of Life, would not let them die alone.

"Quietly, it's better if they don't see us coming...If...If something goes wrong I need you to promise that you'll run, do you understand? You run until you get to the waterfall, and I'll meet you back there, with or without Necalli and Coatl, understood?" Metztli commanded in a tone that made it clear her words were not suggestions.

Metztli raised a finger to her lips, reminding Acalan that they needed to be completely silent before she leaned down to whisper to their dog. Acalan could only assume she was asking him to find Necalli and Coatl because a few seconds later his little feet were pacing into the forest. Acalan and Metztli followed as closely as they could while still remaining silent until the dog stopped before a row of tall bushes that kept them hidden. Just beyond, they caught sight of Necalli and Coatl.

Necalli was hanging upside down from a tree. He must have fallen into a trap set carefully by who Acalan now recognized to be the heirs from the House of Rain. They watched as the prince repeatedly tried to untie himself only to be laughed at by the heirs while they held a knife to Coatl's throat.

Killing was part of the tournament, but the heirs from the House of Rain seemed to be enjoying it far more than they should – or at least far more than Acalan could imagine himself doing.

That thought was conflicted by a new set of emotions Acalan didn't recognize. It was almost like he wanted to punish the heirs for being so heartless. He did not want to kill them, but he certainly wouldn't mind digging his knuckles into their faces.

"Should I shoot them?" Acalan whispered.

It was perhaps not the brightest of ideas, but it was something, and much better than just standing there and waiting for one of the heirs to decide to dig their blade into Coatl.

"No, you could only shoot one of them before the other would panic," Metztli explained as she squeezed her eyes shut, trying desperately to formulate a plan. "We need a distraction.

"I'm going to circle to the other side and make noise," she continued. "With any luck one of them will leave to investigate… then you can shoot the other and free Coatl. I'll take care of the other one while you two free Necalli. But if something goes wrong you run and don't look back. Take the dog with you."

Acalan felt uncomfortable with the idea of leaving his sister to fight one of the heirs on her own, but he knew that she was more than capable. He couldn't think of a better plan so this is what it would have to be. If he heard her scream, then he would send Coatl after her and take care of Necalli on his own.

He just had to shoot straight. That's all he had to do.

"Are you sure about this?" Acalan asked, his tone full of worry.

"Yes – I can do this," Metztli said confidently.

Acalan had never doubted his sister, and he wouldn't start doubting her today.

METZTLI

Metztli was not scared. Not in the way that she supposed she should be. The princess knew this would come at some point. Getting through the Tournament of Heirs without killing was impossible, though, to be quite honest, she never imagined that she would be putting herself in this position to save an ally, much less for the heirs from the House of Blood.

Her brother was far too noble of a person to let them die. Metztli should have felt the same way but had her brother agreed to run, she would have never looked back. She would have forced herself to never think of Necalli and Coatl ever again.

Selfish?

Maybe. But being selfish was better than being dead.

Still, she willed herself to quietly circle the campsite without making a sound or being seen. One heir she could handle without a doubt. She was just worried about doing so quickly enough that she could return to Acalan and the others.

Coatl and Necalli were her sworn enemies according to the contract that she and Acalan had signed in blood, but they didn't deserve to be tortured to death either. When the time came an honorable death would suite them just fine. But they did not need to die now, not when the bastards from the House of Rain were killing for sport.

Once she could clearly see them through the bushes on the other side, the princess stilled almost completely. Seeing Necalli in such a vulnerable position should have brought her joy but it did not. Nor did she find it pleasant to see Coatl on his knees with a knife pressed to his throat. Realistically, Coatl was big enough to take on both of the bastards, but he was too noble to risk Necalli's life, just as her brother was.

Like calls to like.

Metztli hated that Necalli had spoken those words to her. She couldn't seem to get them out of her mind, no matter how hard she tried. With every moment spent with Necalli she was beginning to notice the resemblance between them, more and more. Destiny was cruel, setting them in each other's path only to push them into the tournament. Whatever friendship they could have had, had been spoiled from the beginning, even if they could understand one another better than most.

"Focus," Metztli pleaded with herself in a whisper while she spun her spear into position.

She had to make haste. There was no time to think of anything else right now. Her blade was hungry for blood, and she would feed it until it was satisfied.

Love is violent. She knew that to be the truth. She saw it in herself and her need to protect her brother at all costs. She saw it in the way Coatl spoke of his house's ceremonies and sacrifices and how they shook him to his core. As violent as these sacrifices were, they had to be done, she had to save them, if only to make herself redeemable to Citlalic when they returned home.

The princess allowed herself one deep breath before getting into position, hiding beneath the greenery that surrounded her.

"Think, Metztli, think," the princess spoke to herself quietly.

The clock in her mind was quickly ticking down. Her mind was frantic, searching for some kind of distraction that didn't completely reveal who she was while still revealing exactly where to find her. Fortunately, the only plausible option was something she was quite talented in. All those years of chasing behind her father during hunts were coming to good use.

The princess inhaled deeply. As she released her breath, she allowed for sound to release too. The song was low pitched and quick, echoing through the forest and floating through the air. She was mimicking the Chachalaca birds that were native to the forests back home. The sounds were anything but melodic, but they were accurate, and she watched as they sparked curiosity within the heirs who held her allies captive. They looked in her direction but did not move so she tried again and again.

It wasn't working. Not in the way that she had intended for it to. The strategy had been sound but it had been chosen with the assumption that these heirs were stupid enough to come looking for birds to catch as a meal. Apparently, they were not.

The ticking of the imaginary clock in her mind would not stop. She had to do something to lure at least one of them away and she had to do it quickly.

Without second thought, Metztli inhaled deeply once more. This time she screamed a war cry that could not be mistaken for anything but an heir hungry for blood. In a way she was just that. The second heir to an empire, ready to spill blood in exchange for life.

This time the heirs looked at one another in a panic. She could not hear them but from the way they moved and pointed at one another, she knew they were deciding who should investigate. When the younger of the two moved towards her direction with a blade in his hand she felt relief. They weren't stupid enough to fall for the sound of birds, but they were stupid enough to believe that they could somehow take her down with just a blade.

Had they not been taught better? Underestimating a woman was already amongst one of the most ridiculous things a man could do. But underestimating a woman with a purpose was a fatal mistake. Metztli knew this as she placed her spear into position, gripping it tightly as she prepared to aim. This heir did not deserve a noble death, but she would give him that. One strike through the heart, that's all it would take. That's all that stood between her and returning to Acalan.

She waited behind the greenery until the man came pacing into the area where she was hidden. Metztli should have swung her spear the very moment she'd seen him, but she faltered when she recognized the fear in his eyes as he searched for any evidence of life.

He might have been cruel but in many ways, Metztli was quite the same. They were barely of age, fighting for their lives and for their houses. That was a responsibility far too large for anyone.

All hesitation left her body the moment the man turned and

found her. It was him or her, one of them had to die and as cruel as it was, Metztli had every intention of returning to her brother. Even if that meant gouging into the wound that had been created the first time she'd taken someone's life.

In an instant, Metztli swung her spear, aiming straight for the man's chest. She'd given him just enough time to raise his blade and throw it in her direction, but it was far too late for her to move out of the way.

The sharp blade grazed her cheek making the princess howl from the sudden swipe. It landed in the tree right next to her. She quickly pressed into the wound with her hand to confirm that she wasn't dead yet. She was still breathing. Metztli reminded herself of this when she finally lifted her gaze to find the man on the ground, gripping the spear as blood poured out of his mouth.

She hadn't hit his heart, rather the center of his chest. She stood there and watched in disbelief and panic. He was suffering and it was because of her. The princess fell to her knees and crawled to his side. There was no comforting the man as he bled to death. All she could think to do was end the misery that was his life.

"I'm sorry," Metztli whispered softly before grasping one of her blades and plunging it into his chest.

This time her aim was fatal. The princess kept her eyes tightly shut until she could no longer hear him gasping for air. It was done. Another mercy kill. Except, she'd been the one to torture this time around. Even if it was unintentional, he had suffered. Enemy or not, no one deserved to experience such a thing.

She only opened her eyes briefly to take out her blade and close his eyes shut. A second later the trumpets went off and another mark disappeared from her arm. It was then that she realized she hadn't heard one go off earlier which could only mean one of two things.

Her brother's aim had not been lethal.

Or else, he hadn't shot at all.

That was enough to move Metztli from where she knelt. She pulled her spear out of the man and ran back through the forest until she found Acalan and their allies. A deep sigh of relief passed through her as she spotted Acalan high in the tree, cutting through the rope that held Necalli upside down while Coatl prepared to catch him.

"There she is! My hero!" Necalli exclaimed.

Metztli raised a brow in annoyance. After what she'd just done, she couldn't think of herself as a hero, but she imagined that Necalli had been upside down long enough for it to disrupt his usual train of thought.

The sight before her didn't explain why another trumpet hadn't gone off though so her gaze quickly searched the ground only to find the other heir lying on the ground, unconscious with an arrow sticking through his shoulder.

"He's not dead," Metztli stated, her tone was a mixture of assertion and confusion. Why hadn't they killed him?

Acalan was a good shot, he only missed when he wanted to.

"Coatl knocked him out clean with a headbutt before he ripped through the ropes himself. You should have seen it! He's practically a beast," Acalan explained. From his tone Metztli could tell that her brother had been quite entertained by the sight, but it still didn't explain why they hadn't killed the man instead of ignoring his unconscious body while they untied Necalli.

"But why isn't he dead?" Metztli questioned, taking a few steps forward before she felt blood dripping down her cheek.

As Necalli caught sight of this, his body staggered in a panic. It almost looked like he was trying to reach out for her.

Metztli's eyes widened at Necalli's reaction to seeing her injured, and suddenly she understood why they had chosen to save him. The blood had certainly rushed to his brain. Perhaps another woman would have found it sweet, but Metztli just found it strange.

"Necalli doesn't do well upside down," Coatl clarified.

Metztli didn't even think to question the man and it was only a few seconds later that Acalan managed to cut through the thick rope and Necalli came falling down, straight into his cousin's arms. The sight was quite comedic, so much so that Metztli couldn't stop herself from laughing.

As he tried to regain his footing, his eyes rolled back into his head, and he fell to the forest floor. The slightest bit of worry rose within Metztli, but Coatl just laid him down gently before wiping his hands clean.

"He'll be fine, just needs a moment," Coatl explained.

Coatl moved right past her and straight towards the other unconscious heir while Acalan climbed down the tree. She didn't dare move, too afraid that if she did she would have to watch another man die. One was plenty for a day.

The princess did flinch slightly at the sound of a neck cracking behind her, and then again when another trumpet went off. Coatl had made it quick. At least, there was no suffering in how the remaining heir's life had ended.

"You okay? What happened to your cheek?" Acalan asked when he finally reached her, pulling her into a tight embrace.

Okay was an overestimation of how she felt but this guilt would wear off with time. At least, she hoped it would.

"Yeah, he threw his blade, just barely caught my cheek. I'm fine. It will leave a scar though."

It was unfortunate, the scar would just act as a reminder of what she'd done to survive. Every day she would look in the mirror and see it, only to be brought back to the moment when she'd speared through someone's chest.

"I think it will suit you," Acalan responded as he let her go to reach for their bag which was being guarded by their dog.

The sight made Metztli giggle once again. Maybe the scar would suit her, she thought. She was far too beautiful for one scar, or even many to take away from her beauty.

Acalan handed her a clean rag to press into her cheek. He let her know that as soon as the wound stopped bleeding, he intended to press salt into it. Metztli did not argue. The healing properties would do her good, and aside from that, she did feel like she deserved just a little bit of pain for what she'd done. So, she just nodded in response before kneeling and beckoning for their dog. She found comfort in the way his tail swung at the sight of her. She'd done what she'd needed to. Regardless of how awful her actions made her feel, the fact remained that they were safe now and that was all the princess could ask for.

The next few hours weren't nearly as grueling as the start of the day had been. They moved from where they were as soon as Necalli regained consciousness and was able to walk without stumbling. Metztli had hesitated but she offered him an orange to help. It's what her mother would have done and right now she wanted to resemble anyone but herself. Thankfully the sugar in the fresh piece of fruit seemed to be exactly what Necalli needed. Soon, they were searching for another, less tainted place to settle in for the evening.

Metztli was grateful for this, she hadn't slept at all the night before and while she was growing more comfortable with their allies, she still wasn't fond of the idea of sleeping around them. Not if it meant leaving Acalan to fend for himself. Resting would help though, which is exactly why Metztli was sitting against a tree with Acalan by her side, their dog between them while Necalli and Coatl looked for something to eat. They'd insisted it was the least they could do after being rescued. Metztli didn't even consider arguing with them. In fact, she agreed.

"What about Bear?" Acalan suggested.

They'd been trying to come up with a name for the dog for at least an hour, but nothing seemed to suit the small yet fearless pup. Metztli rolled her eyes at the suggestion. She always hated when people named their pets after other animals.

"If he was a bear then I think the name would suit him," Metztli responded.

She knew she was being difficult. Her brother must have already suggested a hundred names and she'd said no to all of them. To be fair though, their dog didn't seem to like any of them either.

"Fine, then you come up with something. I've run out of ideas."

He leaned back against the tree, closing his eyes momentarily. She knew that he must be rather spent after having not slept for almost two full days. Metztli would make sure that he slept first that evening. It seemed like the right thing to do, but she also couldn't imagine that she would be getting much sleep either considering the thoughts of the blood that stained her soul.

Metztli took a good look at their furry friend, searching for a name that suited him. Given that he'd helped them so much already, the princess felt that he deserved a name that was royal in nature. Then he would fit right in with their family. She thought long and hard, and, in the end, only one name came to mind. Metztli desperately hoped that her brother would agree.

"Xuki," Metztli said softly. The dog's ears perked up immediately and his tail began to wag.

"Xuki? Hmm…I like it. It's fitting. Xuki it is," Acalan responded with a bright smile on his face.

With one less task on their shoulders, Metztli felt like she could breathe a little more. This feeling only grew when Necalli and Coatl returned, holding dead birds in each of their hands. They certainly were very resourceful.

"I'll dig a hole!" Acalan exclaimed, obviously impressed by the sight.

Metztli found it rather sweet that her brother wanted to help. She, on the other hand, was perfectly content to just sit by and watch. That's all she had the energy to do at the moment.

"Be careful," Metztli warned in a gentle tone.

Her brother rolled his eyes in return before standing to help.

She continued playing with Xuki for a little while, feeding him small bits of dried meat whenever he did something particularly adorable or wise. How the dog came to be in the pyramid was still a bit of a mystery, but now knowing how the other heirs behaved, Metztli felt quite grateful that the pup had run into them first.

"You took care of the other heir by yourself?" Necalli questioned, interrupting her peace as he replaced Acalan and sat next to her.

Truly he was incredibly lucky that she wasn't in the mood to argue with him.

"Well he's dead, so…" Metztli responded plainly in hopes that if she spoke of what had happened in such a way, it would start feeling like it really did mean nothing. But she'd killed someone. Really killed someone, not just ended their life out of mercy.

"First kill?" Necalli asked sincerely, as he reached out to pet Xuki.

She would have told him to keep his hands to himself, but the dog seemed to like his touch. Maybe she would have enjoyed Necalli's touch too but there was no way of knowing now. It was simply too late.

"No. I killed one of the heirs on the first day. Well, not really killed, I just ended it," Metztli explained while she handed him the dried strip of meat.

From the corner of her eye, she could see that while Acalan was working diligently on digging the hole to cook in, Coatl had taken to cleaning the birds. In a strange way, she couldn't deny that they all worked well together. If it were possible for all four of them to win, she would have gladly shared the victory with them.

"The first is always the hardest," Necalli said.

Metztli wished that was true but even speaking of what she'd done was making the wound on her soul expand. She just hoped it wouldn't be irreparable by the time she returned home.

"How many have you killed? In general, I mean," Metztli asked.

The question was quite forward. She wasn't sure if she would have asked such a thing if she wasn't so sleep deprived. But there was no taking it back now. She watched as Necalli sighed and ran a hand through his thick curls, which was far more alluring that it should have been.

"Too many. You don't want to know," he said.

Metztli supposed that he was right. Regardless of the number, even one was too many. Then again, she'd killed two people in the matter of three days, so she really wasn't all that different than he was.

"It's not like how they say," Necalli continued. "I know how it looks from an outside perspective but the people we sacrifice are almost always willing participants. They're bathed in riches and eat better than we do for months before they're sacrificed. I don't like it, but they live better than my family does. My father has always fought to keep it that way."

This was all new information to Metztli. For as long as she could remember, she thought that they just took people out of their homes and forced them under a blade. She couldn't imagine why anyone would volunteer to be sacrificed out of their own will. She herself could never do something like that, but then again, she did have a certain aversion to the gods that not many shared.

"Will you fight to keep it that way if you win the tournament?" Metztli questioned curiously, Necalli was after all, the first-born heir of his house.

The stakes were perhaps not as great as they were for Metztli and Acalan, considering his sister could take their father's throne. But he still had much to lose.

"I will not win, but my sister hopes to change things if she can, when it is her time," Necalli responded without a second thought.

It was like his words were more fact than opinion. It only took Metztli a few seconds to remember that they were all keeping something from her.

"You could win," she ventured. "I'm tired. If you wanted, you could kill me right now. I'd put up a fight, but you'd win."

"No. It's not written in my destiny I'm afraid. Besides, I could never dream of killing you. I think your beauty would haunt me for lifetimes if I tried," Necalli declared.

His words made Metztli's cheeks grow warm. She was awfully embarrassed by it, but in the times before, when he'd spoken of her beauty, he'd spoken of it differently. This was the first time that it felt like he truly meant it with absolutely no intention of luring her into bed.

"I hate destiny. Bit more of a fate person myself," Metztli explained with a half-smile. "So much of our lives is already decided for us. Only seems fair that we get a say in something too. Besides, if you did kill me, I would haunt you in this lifetime and in every other."

Necalli laughed at her words but for the first time it did not upset her. If anything her smile grew with the sound of it.

"I'll keep that in mind…Your destiny is good though. I only wish that I could live long enough to see it myself. Don't worry about me or Coatl, we know what roles we play in this," Necalli quipped.

From the tone of his voice, it really did sound like he was content with the path chosen for him. But his words still felt wrong.

"Hmm…well I don't know what role I play in this, enlighten

me, please," Metztli mused.

She was careful to keep her gaze locked with his. If Necalli was as truly mesmerized by her as he claimed, then this little test of hers could work. The princess watched as he battled with himself, going back and forth between telling her and keeping the truth a secret. In a moment of bravery, Metztli reached towards him, brushing her hand over his and keeping it there.

"Please," Metztli whispered.

Her mother had told her seduction was a tool to use against men, and she watched as it began to work. It had to work because this was her only chance of finding out the truth.

"Anyone want to play cards?" Acalan interrupted as he approached them.

Of course, Acalan had to interrupt and blow her chances. She nearly growled at him. It would have been a fair response to what he'd done.

"Yes! That's exactly what we need!" Necalli said. He moved his hand from underneath Metztli's, seemingly relieved to have been saved.

Metztli nodded too, not nearly as excited to play cards as everyone else seemed to be. But with the slight flood of adrenaline finally draining from her, she would rather play than cause any more trouble for one evening. So, they would play cards for a little while, eat, and then rest. Tomorrow would be a new day and the princess had a feeling that this tournament would end soon, so she would just do what was expected of her. It was all that she could do for now.

DAY FOUR OF

The Tournament of Heirs

27
ACALAN

Acalan woke to find his sister sleeping peacefully against a tree with Xuki in her lap. She and Necalli were supposed to be keeping guard for the night, but she must have given in to the need to close her eyes at some point in the evening. From what Acalan could tell Necalli seemed more than happy to stand guard on his own while Metztli slept peacefully. He was just grateful that the two of them had managed to get some sleep before entering the fourth day of the tournament.

A new day brought the opportunity to change everything.

The prince stretched his limbs and yawned loudly as he shook off any remaining effects of slumber before checking the marks on his arm. Eight heirs still remained, but yesterday was proof of how quickly that could change. It really was only a matter of hours before two more lives were taken, and then Necalli and Coatl would leave in hopes of hunting the remaining two heirs. Assuming they would keep to their word, that meant that Acalan and his sister could be presented to the gods by nightfall.

The thought should have been comforting because from the moment that they'd stepped foot within the Pyramid of Tributes, Acalan was ready to go home. But now he felt conflicted by the notion that good men like Necalli and his cousin would need to die in order for them to return to Tu'nethe. It wasn't fair, but nothing in their lives had ever truly been.

"Do you know how long she's been sleeping for?" Acalan quietly asked Necalli.

Coatl and Metztli were still unconscious, and he had no intention to wake them.

"She fell asleep a little bit after you did. I didn't want to wake her though. I know how draining it can be to take someone's life," Necalli replied in a whisper.

It was easy for Acalan to forget that Necalli and Coatl were killers in their own right, too. Not just because of the Tournament of Heirs, but because of the traditions that the House of Blood kept alive. Perhaps the prince should have been quicker to judge Necalli and Coatl for it but he couldn't find it in himself to do so. Their goddess was demanding, and what else could they do besides obey? The prophecy was clear. Only Metztli could produce change.

"She'll be fine, my sister is stronger than most," Acalan said as he rummaged through his bag to find the remaining pieces of fruit he'd packed.

There was just enough for everyone to have one of their own, and with any luck the tournament would end before their lack of food actually became a problem.

"If you think so highly of your sister, why not tell her the truth?" Necalli asked, swiftly catching the orange and taking a knife to it when Acalan tossed it his way.

Acalan was entertained by watching the way Necalli ate his orange, splitting it into quarters before devouring its sweet flesh. He only knew one other person who ate it in such a messy way and that was his sister.

"My sister hates peeling oranges too. She says it leaves her hands smelling like citrus for the rest of the day," Acalan started explaining before realizing he'd gone completely off topic for a moment.

Who could blame him though? It was rather curious how similar Necalli and Metztli were. A perfect match. One that Acalan would have happily sat by and watched flourish into something else if it wasn't for this wretched tournament. Still, Necalli seemed confused by the confession, so Acalan shook the thought from his mind before speaking again.

"Sorry, what was your question again?" Acalan asked, this time ready to listen.

Necalli repeated himself quietly. Metztli was still snoring softly and there was a trail of drool running down her chin, indicating that she really must have been exhausted.

"I'm worried she'll lose control when she finds out," Acalan explained. "What if it's too much for her to handle?"

His dreams had warned him of that much, and it was a concern that Atzi shared with Acalan as well.

"This is about Metztli gaining control, not losing it," Necalli said in an assured tone.

"How so?" Acalan asked.

It was an interesting sentiment, Acalan couldn't deny that, but from what he'd gathered his sister was already in control, wasn't she? How else could Metztli do everything she did, train every day, rain or shine, and commit to her responsibilities if she was not completely in control?

He watched as Necalli threw his head back softly and sighed. This was obviously something he'd been thinking about a lot.

"It's like...when you start a painting. At first everything is blurry. There's splotches of color here and there but it's not until you gain control of your creation that you can see the beauty within the painting. She needs to gain control of her destiny for it to be fulfilled, for beauty and peace to come to fruition," Necalli clarified.

Acalan nodded softly as he tried to grasp the meaning behind Necalli's words. He supposed his point of view was just as sound as Acalan's was, but that didn't change anything, at least not for now. As far as Acalan was concerned he was still prepared to wait until the perfect moment to tell his sister the truth behind the prophecy.

"Are you a painter then?" Acalan questioned, turning the topic of conversation into something else before it was too difficult for either of them to continue.

Necalli laughed quietly before pointing to the other orange, beckoning for Acalan to pass it along, which he did despite his better judgment.

"Is that what you gathered from my words?" he asked.

"Well, I had no idea you were a lover of the arts," Acalan said, smiling to himself.

He must have spoken louder than he had intended because Metztli's eyes flickered open while her arms stretched above her. She looked peaceful for a moment before panic ensued.

"How long have I been asleep?" she questioned.

Acalan laughed. Maybe this would be enough to prove to his sister that Necalli and Coatl meant no harm. Their alliance was far stronger than any other alliance made for the Tournament of Heirs.

"Just a little while," Necalli responded in an obvious lie.

Acalan didn't correct him. He recognized what Necalli was doing. Acalan would have done the same if their places were switched and Citlalic was here instead of Metztli. Lying in general was sinful, but if it's done to protect those you love, is it truly a bad thing?

"Oh…well thank you for letting me sleep," Metztli responded, far friendlier than Acalan would have expected her to be.

It was a bit strange watching Metztli and Necalli interact without either of them trying to kill the other, but at the same time it was sweet. Far sweeter of an interaction than Acalan had ever watched his sister have with another man.

"Yeah of course…I'm gonna go wake Coatl but you should eat, princess," Necalli said, handing Metztli the peeled orange. "I have a feeling today is going to be a big day."

It wasn't until that very second that Acalan realized that Necalli had been listening very closely, particularly to the part when he'd confessed that Metztli hated peeling her oranges. It was the most simple of gestures but to Acalan it meant the world. It just added to his growing list of reasons why Necalli was too good of a man to die.

"Do you think this is poisoned?" Metztli whispered after Necalli stood and walked away to wake Coatl.

Today would be a big day for all of them and for Necalli and Coatl it very may be their last. The prince did his best to push that thought away and instead laughed at Metztli for asking something so absurd.

"No, I watched him peel it, he was just being kind," Acalan replied.

That morning Acalan had been quite convinced that it was only a matter of minutes, maybe hours before another heir died, but eight marks still remained on everyone's arms. The next few hours were spent doing a whole lot of nothing. Well, except for packing up their things, walking around and then settling down in a new area for a little while.

"Shouldn't we just start hunting the other heirs?" Metztli questioned as she paced back and forth.

His sister was beginning to go stir crazy, but he couldn't blame her. Acalan was also starting to grow rather anxious for this tournament to end. Their options were slim though. Chasing after the other heirs would mean running into the other alliance. Four against four was an even fight, but why not wait for them to kill each other off? Perhaps if they did, Necalli and Coatl wouldn't have to kill anyone.

"No. They're waiting for us to do that," Necalli intervened faster than Acalan could.

"So, we're supposed to just sit here and what? Wait for them to come to us?" Metztli argued in return.

"Necalli and Coatl know the sisters from the House of Flor best. If they think it's better to wait, we will," Acalan said, butting into the middle of what was about to become an argument if he didn't intervene.

"Those two have been pampered their entire lives. Any minute now they'll lose their patience and make every attempt to kill the heirs from the House of Wind. We just have to remain patient," Coatl added, trying to reason with a very frustrated Metztli.

Acalan watched closely as his sister tried to find an argument, she'd always been oddly good at doing so.

"What about the weapon? Wouldn't that be enough for the siblings from the House of Wind to overpower them?" Metztli argued, prompting Acalan to throw his head back in defeat.

"Perhaps, but it's not like we know anything about the weapon. For all we know there's no weapon at all," Necalli quipped in return.

Admittedly, the Prince of Blood did make a good point, none of them had actually seen the weapon, so for all they knew it wasn't nearly as dangerous as they thought it to be. Necalli's response obviously frustrated Metztli though. That much was obvious from the way she stood with her arms crossed against her chest and her eyebrows furrowed in irritation.

"You can't be serious," she snapped. "That kind of wishful thinking will lead to all of our deaths. Besides, the emperor was clear, it's been in the works for twenty-five years, that's more than enough time to come up with something deadly."

Acalan felt conflicted as he listened to his sister. She had a good point too. Aside from fear mongering, it didn't make much sense for the emperor from the House of Wind to taunt them with a new weapon unless it was as serious as he claimed it to be.

"She has a point…" Coatl said as his gaze shifted from his hands to his cousin.

Necalli rolled his eyes while Metztli's chest filled with pride. It was an interesting sight to be sure, and if Acalan had to pick a side he would always pick his sister.

"Maybe she does but that doesn't change the fact that we know nothing about it! It could be anything. If Cuauhtémoc was just using his bow, then I would go after them right now, but he isn't, which means we should stay as far away as we can," Necalli responded in defeat.

Acalan watched as a spark lit within his sister's eyes. He felt much the same. Necalli had perhaps not realized it, but he'd just given them a key piece of information that could help them.

"He uses a bow? Well then it must be something like a bow, right?" Acalan said. "It would be stupid to train with a weapon for so long and then throw your heir into a tournament to the death with something completely unfamiliar."

A bow was pretty dangerous on its own though, so the prince found it difficult to think about how it could be made even more dangerous.

"It doesn't matter what it is! I'm not risking any of you to find it or them. You two want to survive until the very end, right? Then we wait. Unless either of you have a death wish I'm not aware of," Necalli argued with a tone full of anger.

Seconds passed and no one responded. Acalan could see that Metztli was itching to say something, but she was holding back. Acalan didn't want to go after the other heirs, but he wondered if Necalli was simply trying to hold onto the little bit of life he had left. He wouldn't blame the Prince of Blood if he did.

"Alright. Time for a distraction! Why don't we go around and tell jokes?" Coatl suggested enthusiastically.

This only caused Metztli to palm herself across the face while Necalli shook his head, giving his cousin a look that said, *Really, man? Not the time*, without saying a word.

"I'd love to hear a joke," Acalan replied.

He didn't want to, not really. Coatl's jokes had a tendency of not actually being funny. But they were worth listening to just to see the look of satisfaction on Coatl's face. Listening to stupid jokes was better than talking strategy anyway, at least, that's what Acalan believed.

METZTLI

They had far more important things to do instead of sitting around listening to Coatl's attempts at being funny. It was not, in any way shape or form, Metztli's desire to kill anyone else but in a tournament like this their choices were clear. You either killed or allowed yourself to be killed, and Metztli had spent her entire life preparing to bring Acalan home, even if that was the last thing she ever did.

Her thoughts were distracted by her brother's laugh. She'd known him long enough to tell that it was only half genuine. She couldn't deny that they all needed a distraction, but was Coatl's comedy really the most ideal form of it? No. If they wouldn't listen to her pleas and seek the heirs out, then the least they could do was find a way to distract Metztli in which she was actually entertained and not just pretending to be. Or find her something to eat.

Metztli had graciously taken the orange Necalli had offered her that morning. That was the only thing that she had eaten and the growls coming from her stomach were beginning to grow louder and louder. She needed to eat. Or more so, they all needed to eat. Especially with the possibility of a fight coming soon. The last straw was when Xuki whined. Their dog was hungry too and being that Metztli and Acalan had chosen to take on the responsibility of caring for him. It only felt right that they at least kept him well fed.

"Acalan…Let's go hunt," Metztli said, interrupting one of Coatl's very pointless jokes. "Necalli and Coatl did it last time, it only seems fair that we do our part as well."

She stood and pulled her spear out of the ground. With any luck they'd run into a few birds. Honestly anything with a little bit of meat on its bones would do all of them well.

"Oh..uh yeah, sure," Acalan responded hesitantly as he stood, too.

"Acalan can stay if he wants. My legs are starting to go numb from all this sitting…I'm pretty good at hunting myself," Necalli suggested.

He didn't wait for Metztli to respond or say it was okay. He just stood, grasped his Macuahuitl, and assumed it was fine. It wasn't fine though, the alliance was stronger now than it had been before, but that didn't mean Metztli felt comfortable leaving Acalan, even if it was with Coatl.

"I'd rather go with my brother," Metztli responded plainly.

She didn't want to offend anyone, even if it was in her nature to do so. The only benefit to going with Necalli would be the opportunity to pick his brain a little more about the conversation that they'd been having the day before when Acalan had interrupted them.

"Have we not proven to be trustworthy yet?" Necalli questioned with a grin far too handsome for his own good.

Metztli sighed in response. They had saved Acalan and Metztli from being eaten by a jaguar, and if Necalli really wanted to harm her, he would have done so while she was sleeping early in the morning. But he hadn't and Coatl had proven to be pretty harmless too. As long as they stayed close then maybe she could leave Acalan with Coatl – at least for a little while.

"Fine," Metztli agreed. "We won't be gone for long. If either of you need anything just scream, or send Xuki."

She didn't move until Acalan nodded in agreement. He seemed happy to stay behind. Admittedly, Acalan had always been this way. He'd always much preferred staying in the comfort of the palace they called home instead of venturing out into the forest. Even killing animals seemed to stain his being.

Metztli had always assumed that he would grow out of this. That someday he'd happily follow along and embrace who he was and everything that was expected of him as the heir to their empire, but Acalan never had. He was ready to rule an empire, of that Metztli was sure, but when it came to making difficult decisions, Metztli was unsure how her brother would handle them. If everything went their way then he'd still have her to help him. That's all that Metztli could hope for.

"What do you normally hunt back home?" Metztli questioned when she was sure that they were far enough that neither Coatl nor Acalan could hear them.

She was taking a risk in leaving her brother alone with Coatl even if he was an ally, so it only made sense that she try to gather enough information to piece together whatever it was that everyone was keeping from her.

"In Texcoco? Nothing," Necalli responded with a bit of sarcastic laughter that confused Metztli. He had said he was a fairly good hunter so surely the answer couldn't truly be nothing.

Necalli spoke again before Metztli could.

"We used to hunt in Texcoco when I was a little boy, but things have changed since then. There's hardly any wildlife left, so we go to nearby cities where we can hunt. It's difficult. I'll say that," he explained.

Metztli knew that the House of Blood lived under unfortunate circumstances, but she had no idea it was that bad. It felt unfair that they were forced to commit so many atrocious sacrifices and in return didn't see anything come from it. Eztli, their goddess, was truly cruel.

"How can you worship a goddess that requires so much from you yet gives so little?" Metztli questioned.

"I've never bent my knee for anyone Princess, not even Eztli," Necalli said. "We just do what we must to survive…Besides, I reckon the House of Flor has it worse than us."

It was strange for Metztli to hear anyone speak of the gods in a poor manner and even stranger to know that Necalli shared the opinions that she'd held for so long. Nemiliztli had at least always provided for them and allowed them to leave comfortably, but Eztli did none of that.

"The House of Flor?" Metztli questioned.

The thought that the House of Flor had it worse than any other house was simply absurd. They were all filthy rich, even the common folk were bathed in rare gems and riches while people were starving in other cities.

Necalli stopped walking besides her, prompting Metztli to turn and look at him. He was sporting another glare that made her feel like she really didn't know anything about the way life was outside of Tu'nethe. Truly, she did not. She only knew what she'd been taught.

"The gods take beautiful men and women in return for prosperity in their house. Did you not know that?" Necalli asked.

Metztli noted the way he frowned as he questioned her. As far as she was aware, the House of Flor remained as prosperous as they did due to their trading with other cities. Chalco was one of the only places in Mexica where you could find rare gems and fabrics, even wine and other artisan crafts. So no, Metztli had no idea that they'd been trading lives for prosperity all along.

"Isn't that similar to what your house does as well?" Metztli argued as she started walking again.

She hadn't meant her words to be rude or condescending. The princess was simply curious as to what Necalli thought made his house so different. They were both giving lives in return for something. At least the House of Flor was. The House of Blood seemed to be receiving nothing in return for their efforts.

"No, it's different. Like I mentioned before. Most if not all who we sacrifice are willing participants. They're choosing to die in the name of Eztli.

"In Chalco the gods simply arrive and take whoever looks good in the moment. It's worse because they take them alive and do whatever they want with them. Just think about how restless you would feel if a god took Acalan simply because they thought him to be handsome. These people are never seen again. They could be dead, but they could very well be kept as pets…that is much worse if you ask me."

Having it explained in that light certainly made it feel like the conditions outside her home were much worse than she had assumed. There were bonds that were meant to be kept sacred. Reasons for why she was expected to stay pure just as Acalan and any other heir was expected to be.

To be clear, Metztli had never agreed with the idea that anyone but herself had a say when it came to her body and who she chose to share it with. But that was the real cruelty in how the House of Flor lived, wasn't it? The thought of having no say in those sorts of matters made bile threaten to rise in Metztli's throat. In Tu'nethe, men and women who committed such heinous acts were killed, but what could one do when it was the very gods who committed sin?

"That's just…it's awful. Do you think Xochitl and Atlatonan intend on changing things if they win? Surely if they did, they could wish for change, for protection for their people, couldn't they?" Metztli asked.

The princess was only slightly shocked to find that Necalli shook his head no. Her eyebrow raised in confusion. Given the opportunity, why wouldn't the sisters fight for change? That made no sense, at least not in Metztli's mind.

"They would have to feel some sort of empathy for the god's victims in order to do so and they do not…You could change things though. You could change everything if you won," Necalli confessed while he took a few steps to get ahead of her.

"And how exactly would I do that?" Metztli questioned, pacing a little bit further to catch up with Necalli.

"I don't know. I just wish there was a way for me to live long enough to see it," Necalli declared. "There's greatness written about you in the history of Mexica. I would have given anything to be a part of it. And not for notoriety. I couldn't care less what the histories say of me. Just knowing that I had helped you would have been enough for me."

The princess immediately stopped in her tracks. The words he spoke seemed so out of character and yet genuine at the same time. Aside from that, the mention of histories brought something back to Metztli's memory.

The morning before the other five houses and their people arrived, Metztli had walked into Acalan's room, only to find him asleep at his desk or more specifically, he was asleep on a historical text that she didn't recognize. Not only that, but instead of training that morning as she had planned to, Acalan had insisted that he needed to speak with Atzi immediately. Everything was slowly starting to come together with Necalli's mention of her history already being written.

"Will you tell me what everyone is hiding from me? That would help. You might not be written about in the histories, but I would always know that it was you who told me everything. I would never forget it." She grasped Necalli's hand to stop him from walking away.

The princess batted her eyelashes softly, moving her gaze from his eyes down to Necalli's lips and back again. This could work. She wanted it to work more than she was willing to admit.

What happened next unfolded much faster than Metztli could truly comprehend. One moment she was looking at Necalli and the next he had her jaw cupped delicately under his fingers. She didn't move an inch, not when he took a step closer and certainly not when he leaned down to press his lips on hers.

They moved in a gentle battle for dominance. Metztli had promised herself it would never come to this no matter how much she wanted it to. It was reckless but she could very well die in the coming hours, so she made no move to separate from him when his hands moved down her body, pulling on her waist and moving her closer to him.

Necalli pulled away breathlessly, resting his forehead on hers gently. He was so much gentler than she imagined he would be.

"I can't tell you, I'm sorry," Necalli confessed in a quiet whisper. "I promised Acalan I wouldn't…I just, I needed to do that at least once before this ends."

Metztli's instincts told her to rage with fire. He'd taken the opportunity to kiss her, but he wouldn't give her anything in return. And yet, she found herself simply nodding before leaning up to kiss him one more time.

Just one more time.

ACALAN

The more that Coatl spoke, the funnier than Acalan realized the man was. Albeit it was a little unexpected from a man who had grown up the way that Coatl had. Acalan couldn't imagine a life where he was fatherless, much less an orphan. But from the way that Coatl described his childhood, it seemed that Yaotl, the emperor from the House of Blood, had truly done everything he could to give Coatl a happy life, even if he wasn't the man's son.

It was getting easier and easier for Acalan to understand why Citlalic was the way that she was, so bright and full of life. He found that both Coatl and Necalli were honorable in their own ways, too.

Acalan now knew the reason why Citlalic remained completely unmarked while Necalli and Coatl carried many markings of sacrifices on their bodies. Every sacrifice that Citlalic had been expected to make, Necalli and Coatl had taken turns doing for her, if only so that she could remain pure of heart.

"What do you like about my cousin?" Coatl questioned with a genuine smile on his lips. "I mean no disrespect. You seem like the perfect suitor for her. I only ask because she is like a sister to me. Had anyone else asked for her hand to dance I would have said no."

Acalan also smiled at the thought of Citlalic and all the reasons why he found himself pulled towards the Princess of Blood.

"My entire life I've felt like an outsider in my own home. I have a beautiful family of course, and I'm grateful to have parents and a sister who love me unconditionally, but I've never truly felt seen, not until I laid eyes on Citlalic for the first time." He felt his palms go sweaty and cheeks grow warm.

The prince didn't have many regrets in life besides having failed as an older brother, but he did regret not having spoken to Citlalic before leaving. He should have done so. He should have told her he loved her at least once before entering the Pyramid of Tributes.

"Well, if that's not the sweetest thing I've ever heard, I'm not sure what is," Coatl said. "I know she feels the same way about you, she always has, even before we really saw you."

The sentiment was so genuine that what he'd said almost didn't register in Acalan's mind.

She always has, even before we really saw you.

Suddenly everything made sense. Acalan didn't need to ask any more questions. The gods were always listening, and he wouldn't allow the woman who he very well considered to be his future wife to be endangered by his carelessness. Instead Acalan stood from where he'd been sitting and found his journal and a pencil that had been sitting at the very bottom of the bag he and Metztli had been sharing.

Citlalic – Visions or dreams? Acalan jotted down quickly.

Either of those answers would now make sense. It explained why Citlalic knew everything that she did, and it certainly explained why she had been so taken with Acalan from the very moment they'd met. This new knowledge filled Acalan with a sort of encouragement. When Citlalic had spoken of how the tournament would end, it was not just because of the prophecy, but because she had already seen how it would end in her mind. Whether that was through visions or dreams, it didn't matter.

He'd suspected it was a sort of gift that had allowed her to know these things, but he also knew what happened to people who were found to have these gifts. The gods viewed them as threats, and they had all been killed a long time ago. In fact, from all the literature that Acalan read, he knew that someone with a gift hadn't been discovered in a very long time. Whether that was because such special abilities had simply died out or because they knew better than to openly display their gifts, Acalan wasn't sure. But he would fight to make their world a safe harbor for Citlalic. That seemed like the least he could do for someone who he loved.

"What are you writing, dear brother?" Metztli's voice rang through the air, scaring Acalan and causing him to jump slightly at the sound of it.

He closed his journal and placed it behind him knowing his sister would hardly notice the gesture.

"Love letters, you know, the usual," Acalan responded confidently as he moved his gaze to meet her.

There was something different about his sister, but he couldn't place his finger on what it was exactly. Not until he moved his gaze to Necalli and noted the slight guilt that flooded his features. Well, that explained why it had taken them so long to return. Acalan wanted to smile but at the same time couldn't find the strength to. He'd made Necalli promise to stop all advances on Metztli. Not because he was intending to be overbearing and protective, but because he didn't want Metztli to mourn Necalli when the tournament was said and done.

"No luck with hunting," Metztli said. "We found some eggs in a nest but that's about it. Guess we're eating nuts and raw eggs for lunch."

If Acalan hadn't noticed the way that Necalli had avoided his gaze, he would have believed that nothing had happened. But now he knew without a doubt that something had.

"Well, father used to make us eat raw eggs all the time growing up," Acalan said. "Add a little bit of salt and we'll be just fine."

He wasn't exactly jumping at the idea of eating raw eggs again, but it was still better than having an empty stomach.

"I'm not worried about us, I'm worried about Xuki. I don't think dogs can eat raw eggs and he looks hungry," Metztli continued, turning her gaze to their dog.

Acalan turned to look at Xuki too, even curiously tilting his head as if to examine the dog's condition. He looked just fine but if Metztli thought the dog was hungry then he probably was, and like she'd said, Acalan hardly agreed that Xuki would enjoy raw eggs without them making him sick.

"He can have some of my dried meat," Coatl suggested as he looked through his own bag to find something for their dog. "We still have some and Xuki seems to enjoy it."

"Are you sure, Coatl? I wouldn't want you to waste your food for Xuki," Metztli responded sincerely.

Had this conversation been a few days ago, Metztli wouldn't be speaking so kindly to Coatl, nor would she be finding a meal for their dog. In fact, a few days ago Metztli had been insistent that the dog was only Acalan's responsibility. She could pretend to be cold, but Acalan knew his sister's heart was full of warmth and love, she just had to open herself to the possibility of receiving it. This was something that Acalan hoped she would do before he had to tell her the truth of who she was.

"It's okay, this little guy needs to eat too," Coatl said with a big smile on his face as he offered Xuki a small piece of dried meat.

Xuki took it happily and wagged his tail. The dog was currently eating better than they were but that only seemed fair considering he'd accidentally found himself in a tournament to the death.

In the meantime, Acalan found his small sack of salt. It had been quite useful over the last couple days. Oddly enough, the prince was sure that they would both make it back, just as they had always dreamed of doing. Citlalic had seen it happen already, and if she had, then it had to come true.

Each of them had a few raw eggs sprinkled with salt and a handful of nuts for lunch. It wasn't the perfect meal, but it kept their stomachs full. Well, only relatively full because Metztli had gagged twice as she found the strength to actually swallow the raw eggs, and even once she'd gotten them down, Acalan could see that she was fighting to keep them from coming right back up. He couldn't blame her.

After their lunch, the four of them decided to move once more for the evening before settling down and finding a place to rest. In the midst of their journey, they'd found a few bushes with berries on them – ones that Acalan recognized to be safe, so they nibbled on those for a little while as they collected more for later. The tartness of the tiny berries felt far better in their stomachs than the raw eggs did, and they had seemingly put everyone in a better mood – even Metztli who was currently walking ahead of Acalan and having a very deep conversation with Coatl about whether mole or pozole was the superior meal.

"I'm not sure if the berries or you put her in a better mood," Acalan whispered to Necalli who was walking alongside him.

Necalli had been relatively quiet since he and Metztli had returned to them. Acalan didn't need to hear an explanation to know why, but he did want to thank the Prince of Blood for doing whatever he had to make Metztli's aura brighter than it had been even before they even entered the Pyramid of Tributes.

"Oh, I don't think it was me. We both know how she feels about me," Necalli argued, obviously trying to deflect from the idea put forth by Acalan.

The way that Necalli responded made Acalan laugh, which was something that he didn't think he would find himself doing so often within the Pyramid of Tributes. It was even stranger to think that he would be returning home with fond memories of the heirs from the House of Blood. He would though, he would always remember Necalli and Coatl and everything that they'd done in honor of his sister. Everything that they'd done to pave the way for the prophecy to come true.

"I think you're right. We both know how she feels about you… if our circumstances were different. I would have happily given my blessing, just so you know," Acalan said as he playfully bumped into Necalli's shoulder.

It was a delight to see Necalli's eyes brighten at the thought.

"I'm honored. You should know you have my blessing too, with

Citlalic, I mean. She'll be happy with you as long as you feed her chocolate and let her sleep in until she feels like waking up…and you know if you wanted to name your first son after me or something, I wouldn't be there to argue," Necalli teased.

He might be teasing, but Acalan took quick inventory. Chocolate he could provide in abundance, and he, too, enjoyed sleeping in until it was inevitably too late. He was sure that realistically there was much more that went into a happy marriage but if those were the fundamentals then they would be just fine. Naming their first-born son after Necalli seemed like a given and the next after, Coatl. That was the least that Acalan could do to honor the sons from the House of Blood.

In their journey they had come upon a few places that would be comfortable enough to sleep, but all four of them had continued walking until they finally found themselves tired enough to settle down for the evening. Acalan was glad that they hadn't stopped before because where they were now, there was a small spring of natural water. They'd run out of water earlier in the day so all of them, including Xuki, drank to their heart's content before setting their things down and making themselves as comfortable as they could.

"I'll take the first watch tonight, just in case one of the other heirs decide to make a move," Metztli said as she stuck her spear into the ground and made herself comfortable against a tree.

Acalan couldn't find a reason to argue. They'd both slept plenty the night before and his sister was right, it was quite possible that the heirs were simply waiting for them to get comfortable to attack.

"I can take the first watch too," Coatl offered. "My stomach is starting to hurt a little bit from the raw eggs we had earlier, so I doubt I'll be able to sleep anyway."

It was strange, just a few moments ago he'd looked fine but now he definitely looked like he was on the verge of getting sick. Acalan hoped this sickness would pass before it became a problem.

Once that was decided, they all ate what they could. The berries they'd gathered from before were quickly gone and, while their stomachs weren't full, all four of them bore content smiles on their faces. These were the memories that Acalan would keep with him when the tournament was over. Not those of bloodshed and panic, but these tender moments that the four of them had shared. Someday he would tell his children about these nights, instead of revealing what they'd had to do to win. It was bittersweet, knowing how everything would have to turn out in order for him and Metztli to win, but seeing everyone relatively happy was better than sulking.

Much, much better.

METZTLI

The air was far chillier than it had been over the last few days. Metztli had even considered laying down next to her brother to conserve body heat and find the warmth of a blanket. But she knew if she laid down and accidentally closed her eyes, she would fall asleep, leaving Coatl alone on guard. He was only feeling increasingly worse so that certainly didn't seem like the most intelligent thing to do.

Metztli herself felt just fine aside from being cold. How she was doing emotionally was another story on its own. Earlier, the princess had allowed herself to kiss Necalli. Initially she'd just allowed him to kiss her, but after that, she'd kissed him and it hadn't felt the way she thought it would.

In her mind she thought that Necalli's lips would be calloused with all the tragedies he'd been forced to experience but they weren't. Instead, she found that they were soft and gentle. When she'd kissed him, it had been so slow, or at least it felt that way because she forgot about everything else as they moved together.

That had been a mistake. Metztli had only promised herself two things. That she would not, under any circumstances, return Necalli's advances, and that she would do everything it took to see her brother return home. The latter she could still do, but the first promise was broken, unable to be fixed or mended in any way. If they won this tournament, she would go home and she would always remember the way his lips had held her own. How could any man ever compare to Necalli now?

They wouldn't.

In a single kiss, she had signed herself up for a life full of misery and always wondering what could have been if they weren't heirs to the great houses of Mexica. Being an heir ruined everything. It was the reason why she found herself in this stupid tournament to begin with, and it was the reason that she would have to say goodbye to Necalli forever. Maybe in another life she wouldn't be forced to know that torment, but in this one, she did.

"You're shivering," Coatl whispered, concerned.

Metztli was in fact shivering, but she wasn't sure if it was because of the cold or because of the overwhelming emotions she was feeling.

"Every other night has been warm, but tonight the gods have chosen to make us cold," Metztli responded.

She could endure the loss of warmth she'd become familiar with, but she could not endure the conflicting emotions she was feeling. On top of already feeling cold, her heart made her feel even colder. This was exactly why Metztli had denied herself the pleasure of seeing Necalli in a different light. Perhaps she should have slapped him across the face when he'd kissed her instead of playing along.

"Do you want my blanket?" Coatl asked as he slipped his own blanket off his body and offered it to Metztli. "I'm feeling a bit warm, if anything. I really shouldn't have eaten as many raw eggs as I did."

The princess regretted that they hadn't been smart enough to pack two of everything in each bag. She thought she'd packed as best as she could, but Coatl had packed even better. It was like they knew that one of their bags would be taken from them. Maybe they did. They seemed to know a lot more than Metztli did anyway.

"Thank you…I'm sorry about the eggs. It was really all that Necalli and I could find. Hopefully we will have much better luck hunting tomorrow," Metztli said as she wrapped her body in the warm blanket.

It did nothing to aid in how she was feeling, but it was warm at least. She felt the slightest tinge of guilt for having not brought back more food, maybe if she hadn't spent so much time kissing Necalli, they would have caught something that wouldn't have made Coatl sick.

"It's okay. You did your best. I just hope this feeling wears off soon," Coatl replied, almost pleading with his body as he tightly gripped his stomach.

Metztli knew what it felt like to be sick to your stomach. It was perhaps one of the worst sicknesses just because it depleted one's body so quickly. Luckily, she did know an old remedy that might help.

Without saying a word, Metztli looked around, praying that Acalan hadn't put their little sack of salt back in their bag before deciding to use it as a pillow. She didn't want to wake her brother but she did want to offer Coatl some relief. She smiled when she spotted the sack of salt sitting by a rock.

The princess tiptoed as quietly as she could. Necalli was also sleeping quite peacefully. Whether it had anything to do with the fact that Metztli had kissed him earlier, she had no idea. She did, however, manage to obtain the salt without waking anyone.

"Here, eat some salt," Metztli said as she offered the sack to Coatl. "My mother says it helps with stomach illness."

He seemed hesitant at first to take it, but she shook it at him and he took it, lightly grazing his skin over her own.

Coatl was warm. Not in a comfortable way, but in a way that made Metztli's eyes widen with worry, so much so that she didn't ask permission before she held her palm to his temple. After doing so, there was absolutely no doubt in Metztli's mind that he had a fever. That explained why he'd been so eager to let her use his blanket.

"How are you really feeling?" Metztli questioned.

Her gaze told him to be honest with her. There was no point in lying now that she knew he was at least sporting a fever, perhaps much worse. She shouldn't be worried about Coatl. In fact, before Metztli had entered the Tournament of Heirs, she probably would have been happy to find one of the heirs sick. But she knew Coatl now. She knew the kind of man that he was and she'd grown to care for him. Necalli, too.

The latter was much more difficult to admit.

"I think I…I just need to throw up. That will do the trick…is it okay if I step away for a moment? I don't want to disturb Necalli or Acalan." Coatl stood, slightly stumbling over his own steps.

The sight before her didn't make Metztli feel any better about the situation at hand, but she nodded anyway and watched as he walked away.

Metztli was worried to the point that she almost became sick as well, especially when she heard the sounds coming from him. It was a miracle that Acalan and Necalli hadn't woken up on their own, and though she would have much rather let the both of them rest peacefully through the night, she still found herself kneeling beside Necalli and shaking him awake. At first, he simply lifted his blanket as if she would climb underneath it with him. Even in his sleep he was far more confident than Metztli had ever known a man to be.

"Wake up! I think Coatl is really sick," Metztli whispered harshly, which managed to startle Necalli enough that his eyes fully fluttered open.

"What?" Necalli questioned, still half consumed in his slumber.

Metztli took a deep breath before speaking again. She hated explaining herself twice but in this instance she would.

"Coatl is sick. I don't know what to do, he said he just needed to throw up and that he'd be back," Metztli clarified, this time making sure that Necalli heard every single one of her words.

For a moment, she moved her gaze from Necalli's confused glare to her brother. How Acalan remained snoring as he cuddled with Xuki was a mystery, but she wouldn't wake him until it was necessary.

"I'm sure he's fine. He has a sensitive stomach. I promise that's all," Necalli tried to reason with her, but his words did nothing to dissuade the feeling that everything was about to go terribly wrong.

Footsteps approached, which prompted Metztli to whirl quickly and try to find the source of noise, but she found nothing. She was only realizing now that she was likely growing paranoid over how quickly the tournament could end from this point forward.

"See I told you he'd be—"

Necalli stopped, staring wide eyed behind Metztli. Within his eyes, the princess could see plenty of things, but most of all she saw fear.

Gut wrenching terror.

Before she could truly comprehend what was happening, or what had frightened Necalli to this extent, he'd pushed her out of the way, so quick that her head hit the dirt.

"ACALAN!" Metztli shouted in a fiery roar as she stared down at the sight before her.

Coatl had returned but he wasn't himself. The man who had left would never think of hurting any of them, but the creature that returned was lunging towards Necalli's throat. It was only then that Metztli realized that he was holding a blade in his hand which could only mean one thing.

This creature intended on killing them all.

One moment she was on the ground and the next she was sprinting towards her spear before sliding to Acalan who was clearly disoriented and confused.

He needed to run. Metztli wouldn't leave Necalli to fight this beast on his own, but Acalan needed to get as far away as he possibly could on his own.

"GO!" Metztli screamed at her brother.

There was too much happening at once. Necalli was being overpowered. Acalan was still trying to get a grasp on the situation at hand. Xuki was barking up a storm and biting at Coatl's legs and Metztli was ready to fight. That's what she'd trained her entire life to do. It was her duty as the second born heir of their house.

What Acalan did next however, was unexpected. Every other time they'd been confronted with violence her brother had frozen, but this time he'd stood as quickly as he possibly could, only allowing himself one quick breath before he aimed his bow at Coatl's heart.

Time seemed to slow as the arrow soared through the air. Metztli didn't allow herself the opportunity to breathe until she watched the arrow dig itself into Coatl's chest, landing in a place that should have dropped Coatl down onto his knees.

But the man remained standing.

He turned slowly, gawking at them with blown pupils that could be seen even in the darkness. He let Necalli go, using the hand that had been grasping his cousin to rip the arrow out his chest in one clean tug. Metztli's breath quickened at the sight. Shivers spread down her body. They were not fighting a man. They were fighting a god made beast.

"STAY BEHIND ME!" Metztli shouted at her brother.

The only way she could truly protect him now was by keeping

him close and finding a way to kill Coatl. That wasn't something that Metztli wanted to do, but she kept reminding herself that he wasn't himself anymore. And that when they killed him, it would be out of mercy and nothing else.

"The head! Metztli, aim for his head!" Necalli shouted as he lay on the ground, still catching his breath from nearly being choked to death by his own kin.

Metztli didn't have a better strategy, so she listened carefully as Coatl approached them, swinging his blade in an uncoordinated manner. She was graceful in the way she was able to dodge every one of Coatl's attempts, even more so when she slid underneath his raised arms and kicked him in the center of his back with all of her force. He'd be easier to control on the ground.

That did nothing though. He was far too large, like an old tree that refused to fall. Instead, he turned and lunged towards her again.

"ACALAN STAY BACK!" Metztli commanded.

From the corner of her vision, she could see her brother itching to fight, trying to find the perfect moment to attack. As bad as it sounded, Acalan would be of no use at this moment, not when it came to hand-to-hand combat. Coatl was moving far too frantically for Acalan to properly aim an arrow towards his head, but they had to find a way. This couldn't be the reason none of them returned home.

Metztli continued attacking him with her spear, though she was doing much less of that than she would like. All of her energy was being spent dodging his attacks. And now she couldn't find the right angle to aim for his head as Necalli had instructed. This was unfortunate for someone who had as little patience as Metztli did. Perhaps that's what drove her to slide past him again, gripping her spear with both hands as she lunged forward, raising it above her head and aiming for Coatl's head.

One mistake is all it took to die in the Tournament of Heirs.

One moment of impatience is what it took for Coatl to grasp the spear in his own hands before it even hit his skin. He wrenched it away from Metztli with a strength that caused her to roll forward straight in a tree. All she could do was watch as he dropped his knife, grasped both hands on her spear and broke it in two.

Before Metztli could scream for help, the beast's hands had already found purchase on her throat, suffocating her while he lifted her off the ground. Her body jerked uselessly as she tried to fight him off but there was no use.

This was it.

She was going to die.

ACALAN

calan watched as Coatl pinned his sister against the tree. By now, he'd already come to terms with what had to be done.

"ACALAN NO!" the Prince of Blood shouted as he tried to regain control of his body.

But Necalli's command did nothing to stop Acalan from threading another arrow through his bow and aiming it towards Coatl.

His sister was the prophesied heir. Her survival was more important than anyone else's, and to let her die was to let the prophecy die too. Mexica needed this prophecy to come true more than Acalan needed to stay alive.

Atzi had been clear in her words. It was only a shame that it had taken Acalan so long to see the truth in them. The prophesied heir was many things. A daughter from one of the great houses of Mexica, first and foremost. Someone who the will of the god's did not work on. It never had with Metztli. And lastly, someone who would have to suffer great loss before coming into power.

Acalan's mistake had always been in assuming that simply surviving through the Tournament of Heirs was enough great loss, or that losing Necalli would equate to the same. It wouldn't. He knew that now as he lifted his bow and carefully aimed it for Coatl's head.

"I have to," Acalan responded to Necalli before letting his arrow fly. It landed at the base of Coatl's skull.

The hit caused Coatl to drop his sister almost immediately, leaving her gasping for air and gripping at her throat as she fell to the ground. She was pale enough that Acalan knew it would have only taken a few more moments for death to come swiftly. That was something that Acalan couldn't allow to happen.

The prince stood his ground, bow in his hand as Coatl turned, stumbling slightly as he made his way to him. Acalan didn't move an inch. Whatever Citlalic had seen in her dreams or visions didn't account for this, of that, he was sure.

He suddenly understood why his sister favored fate over destiny. A subtle smile could change the trajectory of everything. Perhaps it had been Acalan's fault that they were in this situation now because he'd been the one to accept the heirs from the House of Blood with such open arms. Or maybe it would have ended this way even if he hadn't.

Necalli pushed forward, still unsteady as he jammed a blade into Coatl's side. It did nothing but anger the beast and Coatl pushed Necalli away, causing his body to fall to the ground. Acalan took a deep breath then and dropped his bow, preparing himself for what was to come.

Coatl's blade slid through Acalan's ribcage. The prince gasped at the pain. Memories of their childhood and the loving home he would never see again flashed through his mind. Vivid images of his mother and father, of Atzi and Citlalic and everyone else who he loved.

That was the only thing that comforted him as his body gave in and collapsed onto the ground, blood pooling over the fabric and spilling onto the ground beneath him.

Acalan was only vaguely aware of the pain that coursed through his body as he heard an earth-shattering cry from Metztli. She crawled to him.

What could possibly be a greater loss than that of one's best friend?

Acalan's destiny had already been decided the moment he shot an arrow through Coatl's neck, but he turned away to find the man, just to ensure that his sister would be safe. It seemed that even an arrow through the neck wasn't enough because Necalli continued wrestling with the beast. He was winning now thanks to Acalan's efforts, and that would have to be enough.

"NO! NO! NO!" Metztli cried, tears streaming down her face when she finally reached her brother's side. "I can fix this. I have to fix this!"

The knife remained within Acalan. That was probably the only thing keeping him alive and away from death's doorstep for now.

"Shhhh. It's okay," Acalan whispered in an attempt to calm his sister, though he knew that nothing would really be able to do that.

He screamed in pain as she applied pressure near the wound, soaking her hands in his blood. There was no fixing this, time was running out and Acalan knew what he had to do next.

"Metztli...I need you t-to listen," Acalan started, fighting through the pain.

There was only so much blood a person could lose before falling unconscious, and he'd already lost more than enough. It was a miracle that the blade had somehow missed his lungs.

"You don't get to die on me! Shut up and let me save you!" Metztli screamed, full of despair.

But nothing could be done now. Acalan was going to die and somehow, he was at peace with that. The only thing he could think to do was use the remnants of his strength to brush away the strands of hair that were sticking to her face.

"Metztli, there's a prophecy," Acalan muttered. "It speaks of you. I need you to listen."

Atzi had told him that it would be clear to him when the moment came to tell her. Nothing could possibly be clearer than this.

"I don't care about a fucking prophecy. YOU CAN'T DIE," Metztli replied, her voice cracked beneath the weight of her emotions. It was heartbreaking to watch but Acalan knew it had to be done.

"You're the key to this tournament ending for good...you're the only one who can stop the gods and their reign," Acalan said. He was suddenly cold, his lips felt parched and his body weak. "It's you Metztli. It's always been you."

Death was coming for him, and he needed his sister to understand who she was before he was gone for good.

"Trust Necalli, Citlalic, and Atzi. They know. They'll help you. The tournament rules say two blood bound heirs can win. Necalli knows how that can be done. You win this. You win this with him, okay?" Acalan commanded gently, hoping that Metztli would stay true to his words. "You win, and you tell mother and father that I loved them very much. You tell Citlalic that I'm sorry I couldn't keep my promise."

"No…no Acalan, please don't die. I need you. You're my brother, I need you…I won't ask anything else of you, I'll be a good sister, just please don't die." Metztli wept.

If Acalan could survive, he would. But there was no way for that to happen now, not as he bled out on the forest floor with a knife stuck between his ribs.

"Remember what Atzi said," Acalan managed to mutter. "I'll never really be gone. I'll always be with you. I love you, don't forget that okay? No one believes in you more than I do."

"Then stay alive, please, just tell me how to fix this," Metztli pleaded.

But Acalan was too far gone for any remedies. A stabbing required far more intervention than just rubbing salt in the wound. Besides, everything before him was blurry now and his body had gone numb. His time had run out.

"This is the only way," Acalan whispered before taking his final breath.

METZTLI

Acalan was dead.

From the moment that Metztli had been strong enough to hold a blade in her palm, the princess had known she only had one responsibility in life. And that was keeping her brother alive long enough to see him sit their father's throne. But now he laid lifeless on the ground, in a puddle of his own blood while she wept and screamed for him to say something, to breathe and come back to her.

The trumpets rang, signaling that Acalan was truly gone. She had failed.

It didn't feel real. None of this felt real. The princess kept trying to convince herself that this was all a part of a bad dream that she could wake herself from if she tried hard enough. That if she screamed loud enough or continued to shake her brother's body, he would wake and tell her to stop.

She didn't care about whatever prophecy her brother believed in. Nor did it matter that there were others who believed in it as well. She would have happily seen the world burn around her if it meant saving Acalan, and she would never forgive herself for having lost him. If she had only been smarter, quicker, more lethal, Acalan would still be alive, or maybe she would be dead in his place.

That felt like a better alternative than this.

Metztli couldn't stop the tears that poured out of her or the screams that escaped her lips. Her body collapsed, falling onto her brother's chest as she held him close. His blood seeped into her clothing and her skin, but she didn't care. She just wanted to hear his heartbeat, instead of sitting in this unbearable silence. She heard nothing though, just her own ragged breathing and the sound of her sobs.

Everything had gone terribly wrong.

"Metztli…we have to go," Necalli's voice broke through. "We made too much noise."

For a moment, she'd forgotten that he even existed or that Coatl had been possessed. She could only imagine that Necalli had killed him considering the silence that surrounded them but it was difficult to focus on anything except her brother's dead body.

She wondered if it was better if she died, too. At least that way she wouldn't have to face her family. The thought of having to look her parents in the eye and tell them she'd failed made Metztli's sobs grow louder.

"Metztli…please, let me help you," Necalli whispered as he placed a gentle hand on her shoulder.

The suggestion made her laugh through her grief. Help? How exactly was Necalli to help? It was his cousin who had been possessed and had killed Acalan. It was because of Necalli's stupid fucking charm that they'd agreed to an alliance in the first place. There was nothing that Necalli could possibly do to help.

In a spurt of rage, Metztli pulled the blade out from Acalan's chest, whirling around and pressing it into Necalli's throat just hard enough that she drew a drop of blood. Necalli let her as he put his hands up in surrender like he was guilty of something. Maybe he was.

"How the *fuck* are you supposed to help me, Necalli Cruz? My brother is dead. *DEAD* because of your cousin. I should slit your throat and rid myself of you," Metztli hissed.

She considered it for a long moment. It would be so easy to slide her knife against his skin and be done with it.

Trust Necalli.

Acalan was dead but his words lingered in the air, haunting her. She knew there were only two options at hand. She could believe her brother and let Necalli live, or she could kill Necalli and rid herself of any of the responsibility that Acalan had given her. It was impossible for Metztli to think logically at this moment. She was too overwhelmed with grief.

"Is this what you wanted all along? To kill my brother?" Metztli questioned. Her voice cracked at the mention of a betrayal that large but she needed to know.

She needed Necalli to say anything that would make it easier to kill him without feeling any regret for doing so.

"This was never supposed to happen," Necalli responded in a fearful whisper. "I was ready to die for the both of you. I killed Coatl for you."

Metztli wanted to believe him. She had seen the fear displayed on his features when he'd seen his cousin. She'd been too distracted with her brother's death to watch when Necalli killed Coatl or to hear the first trumpet sing. But one glance to the side and she knew that it was true.

"Tell me it's all a lie," Metztli said.

Her thoughts weren't really making sense. She just needed answers, anything to justify killing the Prince of Blood.

"It's not a lie, the prophecy is real," Necalli promised. "My sister has dreams that come true. She dreamed that our mother would die during birth, and she did. She dreamed she would fall in love with Acalan and that happened too. She's had dreams of this prophecy and of you defeating the gods. It's all true, I promise."

His words did nothing to calm Metztli. If anything, they sent her into more of a panic.

"So, she knew then?" Metztli questioned as she dug her blade deeper into Necalli's skin. "That Acalan would die. She knew and she did nothing to stop it!"

If what she believed was true, then she would now have a perfectly good excuse to kill Citlalic the moment the opportunity arose.

A life for a life, an heir for an heir.

"No! He was supposed to survive. She had dreams of the two of you winning the tournament...I don't know what went wrong. My sister's dreams have never been incorrect," Necalli said, pleading with Metztli to believe him. But as much as she wanted too, it all felt wrong.

Metztli flinched slightly when Necalli's hands moved to the necklace he was wearing. It hadn't seemed special before, but now he opened it to reveal a tablet of some sorts.

"Look. It's nightshade. Coatl and I were ready to die when the four of us remained. It was never meant to be you and I standing here. I'm sorry that it is but let me help you Metztli, please," Necalli begged.

Metztli moved her gaze to Coatl's body. Necalli wasn't lying. She could see the same necklace wrapped around his throat too.

"Apologies aren't going to bring back my brother," Metztli said as she loosened her grip and let Necalli go.

Even if she wanted to kill him, she knew she wouldn't have the mental strength to do so. Acalan had been clear in his last words.

Trust Necalli.

Metztli didn't know how she was going to do it, but she had to honor the last thing her brother asked of her.

The princess dropped the blade in her hand before returning to her brother's side. He looked peaceful despite the way he'd died. She wept as she shut his eyes and laid him to rest. Every inch of her being hated herself as she did so. Acalan was many things. He was the purest of hearts and the most gentle of souls. He should be alive in her place. The prophecy should have spoken of him and not her. He should be the one who got to return home.

"Metztli...we really have to go before the other heirs decide to come find us," Necalli said.

She knew that four other heirs still remained, and they were now outnumbered, but leaving her brother there to rot...That was something that she couldn't fathom bringing herself to do.

"Do you think they clean the bodies before delivering them to our families?" Metztli asked between her tears.

Looking over her shoulder, she fell apart again. Her mother might very well die of heartbreak if she saw Acalan in this state. Metztli was staying alive purely out of spite for the gods and because her brother had ordered her to.

"If they don't, I'll kill the gods myself to make them pay for it," Necalli responded as he knelt beside Metztli.

It was only then that Metztli realized Xuki was nowhere to be found.

"Xuki!" she shouted in a panic.

She'd already lost her brother and Coatl. Losing their dog would be a punishment far too great for her to handle. She waited patiently until she finally saw Xuki come out from the forest, limping and whimpering. They'd all fought valiantly but it hadn't been enough.

"I can't leave him," Metztli whispered as she held Xuki in her arms. The dog was trying to lick the tears off her face but there were too many to wash away.

"I can't protect you if all four of the remaining heirs come for us. I know this is…difficult, but I'm begging you to let me help you win the tournament," Necalli pleaded.

Metztli took a deep breath before coming to the realization that she had no choice. All she could do was lean down to press one last kiss onto her brother's cheek before she stood with Xuki. Necalli stood too, collecting the remnants of their things including Metztli's spear that had been split in two.

"Leave it," Metztli said. The damned thing had failed her in a moment of need.

"You're going to need it," Necalli started to argue with her, but Metztli knew she was filled with enough rage that she could kill someone with bare hands if she needed to.

"I said leave it," Metztli ordered once more before closing her eyes tightly, still half hoping that this was all just a bad dream.

Necalli listened to her, dropping the broken spear. They had already taken a few steps when Metztli stopped and placed Xuki on the ground. She ran back to Acalan's body, kneeling next to him one last time.

She wept for a moment before her gaze found his bow and arrows still in one piece.

This was it, there was no more time to mourn. She needed to win this tournament if only to look the gods' in their faces and blame them for her brother's death.

Metztli stood and swung the arrows across her body, holding the bow close. She whispered one last goodbye and turned.

All she could do now was win in her brother's honor.

DAY FIVE OF

The Tournament of Heirs

Metztli

Silence loomed over Metztli and Necalli. The prince had guided her and Xuki to the waterfall where they'd all bathed a few days ago. She was grateful for the opportunity to wash herself. The sun had risen and brought light to the blood that remained on her body. It was Acalan's blood – not Necalli's, Coatl's or her own – but her brother's, the one person who she was responsible for, the only life she ever truly cared about, now gone.

The princess wept silently for as long as she could, even when Necalli dragged her into the water and helped cleanse any evidence of death off her body. Sure, she was clean now, her brother's blood had been swiftly taken away by the natural movement of the water, but her soul remained marked by his death and this prophecy that she knew nothing of and could not bring herself to care about.

Metztli could only assume that the prophecy was wrong. She'd always had a distaste for the gods, that was certain, but that didn't mean that she was somehow going to rid her people of them for good. She couldn't help but think that Acalan would have been better suited for that sort of thing. He would have found a peaceful resolution and right now all that Metztli could think about was shooting arrows straight into the god's hearts. As if that would do her any good. The gods were immortal. Killing them was impossible regardless of what a prophecy said.

She did not argue or resist when Necalli held her close to him. Metztli wouldn't dare look, but from the way he embraced her and the slight sniffles that escaped him, she could only assume that he was crying, too. That made sense. She couldn't imagine that killing one's cousin was an easy feat, even if Coatl had been possessed and ready to kill them all.

To say that they were in a terrible position was an understatement. With Acalan and Coatl dead that left Necalli and herself outnumbered. It would take a miracle for either of them to win now.

The tournament rules say two blood bound heirs can win.

Necalli knows how that can be done.

Acalan's voice echoed so vividly in her mind that Metztli was almost convinced that he was close by, still alive and breathing instead of laying in the middle of the Pyramid of Tributes, lifeless and cold. She hated how little she knew about what her brother had spoken of. If anyone would have just told her about the prophecy before then maybe she could have been better prepared or would have been able to find proof and evidence that it wasn't about her.

It couldn't be, and even if it was, she couldn't imagine that she could do anything about the gods now. Not with her brother dead and Necalli as her companion. There were still holes in his stories, half-truths that did not make sense. Really, she had only kept him alive because her brother had told her to trust him.

"Can I ask you something?" Metztli whispered, finally opening her eyes as she realized that sitting and sulking would do no one good.

If she survived the tournament, then at least she could go home and mourn in the comfort of her home. She could walk through Acalan's room and simply take in his scent while it remained vivid.

That is, if her parents didn't banish her for having failed in the one duty she'd been given. If they couldn't find the strength to forgive her, she would understand. She was unsure if she would ever forgive herself for letting her brother sacrifice himself for her. It should have been the other way around. Metztli had always prepared for her death to come before his.

"Anything, always," Necalli responded, taking the opportunity to loosen his grasp on her.

She didn't realize how tightly he had been holding on to her. It felt comfortable knowing he was weighing her down, as if she would somehow drift away if he let her go. Maybe she would, but Metztli couldn't find it in herself to care at all.

"How much do you know about the prophecy? Is it…something well known in Texcoco?" she asked.

She'd realized earlier that there was so much she did not know about the other houses of Mexica. Perhaps this prophecy was just something that had been kept from her, too.

Necalli shook his head vigorously. That was enough for Metztli to know that the answer was no. In hindsight that made sense. If the prophecy was true, the gods would have likely done anything to stop the news of it spreading. They'd always made themselves look invincible, and maybe they were. But now there were whispers that called everything into question.

Whispers that Metztli could make a reality if she just believed in herself as much as her brother believed in her.

"Coatl knew more of it than I did," Necalli responded, turning his gaze down to his hands as he spoke of his cousin. "I guess I always figured there was no use in learning all the details of it. Not when I believed I would never return home after entering the Pyramid of Tributes."

Metztli didn't need to see his eyes to know he felt shame over what he'd done. There were many unforgivable sins, and killing your own blood was amongst the highest of them.

"I'm sorry," she said. "It must have been difficult living that way. Always assuming that you would die for someone you didn't even know."

Her sentiment was genuine. Dying for her brother had been easy for her to accept even at a young age. She loved Acalan. She would have done anything for him, even die in a tournament that was just entertainment for the gods. To die for a complete stranger, though? Just because your sister claimed there was a prophecy about a princess from a different, more fortunate house.

That couldn't be easy.

"It was more than that for me and Coatl," Necalli started. "We just thought that if you could put an end to the gods' reign that our people might have better lives. My sister wouldn't have to hide who she is and the gift that has been bestowed upon her. I was ready to die for my people. And then I met you, and I realized you were worth dying for too. You and Acalan both."

It was an honorable explanation, one she didn't expect from the heir to the House of Blood. But then again, Necalli had always been full of surprises.

"I don't think I am who you all believe me to be," Metztli confessed what she felt was true. "I'm the second born heir to a modest house. I know of nothing other than fighting and I've proven to fail in that aspect as well. You all must be wrong. The prophecy cannot speak of me."

She might be the sole heir to her house now, but before she'd been set to inherit nothing. She had liked it that way, knowing that she only had one responsibility was much better than this.

"Your priestess seems to feel differently, and so do I," Necalli replied, this time holding his head up high and looking straight into her eyes. "You truly cannot think so low of yourself. That's not the Metztli I know."

Acalan had mentioned Atzi knowing, but having it confirmed filled Metztli with rage. If it was Atzi who filled Acalan's mind with the idea of a prophecy, then she would pay for it. Metztli would make sure of it.

"You don't know me," Metztli argued. "And you shouldn't trust anything Atzi says. She's cruel, always has been."

She had felt differently about the priestess when she'd entered the Pyramid of Tributes, but now that she knew the truth, Metztli couldn't help but despise the old woman even more than she ever had. At least now she knew why it always seemed like the priestess had spoken in half-truths. That made her a liar in Metztli's mind.

"She said you would say that," he countered. "Both parts – about her being cruel and you doubting who you are."

His words should have angered her more, but they did not. Metztli was already too full of rage to add more to it.

"Even if I am who you think I am, I don't see how I can make a difference. Only one of us can leave here, and then what? I kill the gods on my own?" Metztli asked.

Necalli had said he didn't know much of the prophecy, but he surely knew much more than she did. While the prince might not know everything, he had to know something that could help her figure out the mess before her.

"That's not true," he said, his tone was stern, like he knew that what he was speaking of was certain.

Metztli's eyebrow raised in confusion and anger. Why did everyone know more than she did? If they believed she couldn't be trusted with this information, then how could she possibly be capable of being the prophesied heir?

"Two blood bound tributes can win," Necalli tried to clarify.

But that still didn't make any sense. She was blood bound to her brother, just as every other heir and their companions were blood bound. And now Acalan was dead, and Coatl was dead too.

She must have been missing something.

"Acalan is dead. That means only one of us can win," Metztli insisted. Necalli shook his head no in response.

"You're right, blood bonds are found in families, but they can also be formed," Necalli explained. "Wouldn't I know about this? Considering which house I belong to?"

While Metztli wanted to understand, she also couldn't bring herself to. If blood bonds could simply be formed, why hadn't anyone ever used them to bring two heirs from different houses home to victory?

"It's never been done before," Metztli argued, hoping that she could talk some sense into Necalli.

Even if it was something worth considering, they would have no way of knowing if it could actually work.

"Oh, come on. I know you're not dull. It's never been done before because the houses don't want to share a victory like this. The winning heirs only get one wish, not two. It's easier to kill one another than decide who gets to rule over Mexica and who gets to ask the gods for something," Necalli reasoned.

Metztli hated that he was making so much sense. If he was

speaking nonsense, it would have been much easier to ignore him.

"How is it done then? If we wanted to be…bound together," Metztli inquired.

Knowing what she did about the House of Blood, she couldn't imagine that any of the rituals would be the sort that she wanted to be involved in, but it was worth knowing. If they could both survive this tournament and return home, then at least Metztli wouldn't be entirely alone.

Necalli sighed as he brushed a hand through his damp hair. He looked at Metztli for a moment before turning to look back at the water. That was enough for Metztli to know she wouldn't like the method needed to bind herself to him.

"There's an easy way, and a hard way," he said, prompting Metztli to roll her eyes.

"Well, obviously I favor the easy way," Metztli replied sternly.

There was no use in wasting time. Now that only six of them remained, they'd be lucky if they made it to nightfall without being massacred by the four remaining heirs.

Necalli shook his head, refraining from telling her everything. That was an unwise thing to do considering how she was currently feeling. She would have strangled him if she thought any good would come from it, but if she wanted to win the Tournament of Heirs, then she needed an ally, someone to depend on until this was all over.

"I don't think you will," Necalli responded in a soft whisper. That was enough for Metztli's anger to begin spilling out of her. If she was this prophesied heir, surely Necalli didn't have to be so hesitant to tell her things, regardless of how harsh they were.

"SPIT. IT. OUT," Metztli half shouted as she restrained herself from physically attacking Necalli again.

The princess only lowered her voice when Xuki whined. The dog hadn't wagged his tail or much less moved since they'd settled down by the river. They were all grieving in more ways than one.

"Fine, but you cannot attack me. This is the easy way. It's not necessarily a desire of mine, at least not right now," Necalli explained.

His words did very little to ease Metztli's mind.

"We would have to be…intimate…" Necalli explained. "Or else we could sacrifice one of the remaining heirs and perform a ritual. Those are the only two ways I know of this working."

The Prince of Blood made quick work of moving away from Metztli, obviously concerned with the idea that she might really attack him. She didn't though. She simply didn't have the energy to do so.

"It can't be that simple. Plenty of people are intimate – that can't just make them blood bound to one another," she said. Truly just trying to make sense of everything.

"Well no, you're right…it's just something that occurs when two people who have never…you know…Why do you think they expect us as heirs to stay pure before marriage? Otherwise, a blood bond can't be sealed," Necalli explained. While his reasoning did make sense to an extent, Metztli had always assumed that those standards had only applied to female heirs, not male.

"And you expect me to believe that you're pure?" Metztli questioned with a raised eyebrow.

Out of everything that Necalli had said, that was the one specific detail that Metztli had a hard time believing. If the princess wasn't in the middle of grieving her brother she might have even laughed at the slightly offended expression on Necalli's face, but what else was she to believe after the way he'd spoken to her before? Or the way he had kissed in the forest just a day ago?

"I am the purest of hearts, truly," Necalli argued, pulling his palm across his chest.

The prince looked absolutely gobsmacked at the idea that Metztli would assume anything else. Actually, she assumed that he was still lying to her about it even now.

"The only thing pure about you is that you are purely intolerable," she retorted.

"Was I purely intolerable when you kissed me yesterday?" Necalli asked, taunting Metztli in return.

This was what they did best, pester one another until someone yielded.

"No. But you're slightly less intolerable when you're not

speaking," Metztli replied.

The smallest of smiles arched over her lips. They could tease all they wanted, but that didn't mean that she truly believed he was pure. She believed quite the opposite, actually. It was difficult to imagine that Necalli of all men had gone his entire life without ever being with at least one woman.

"If you thought you were going to die in the Tournament of Heirs, why not indulge?" Metztli questioned.

"Honestly?" Necalli asked, prompting Metztli to roll her eyes again. "I will not lie to you. I did indulge quite a bit. Just never that far…every time the opportunity arose – and it did often – I couldn't bring myself to go through with it. It felt wrong, so I never did.

"I just thought if I was going to tie my soul to someone else's, they should be important to me, and all of the women and men I was with never struck me as important. I knew they just wanted to be with me because of what I had to offer and not because of who I was," Necalli explained.

Metztli still had a difficult time fully believing him. He'd offered to sleep with her plenty of times before, even when he had barely known her. It was just hard to understand why she was so special.

"And you would be okay being blood bound to me?" she questioned. "From the way you speak of it, it sounds like it would be for the rest of our lives. Would you really want to be bound to me forever?"

She needed to know if this was simply something he was willing to do to survive or if he had other reasons for wanting to be tied to her.

"This isn't a question of if I would be okay with it," Necalli started, turning his head away but looking at her from the corner of his eye. "This is a matter of if you would want to be bound to me forever. In every life, I would find you. It's infinite as you said. So, if I'm really intolerable…"

Hearing his words, Metztli finally understood.

In every life I would find you

"Is that why you were so eager to bed me before? So, you could find me in another life?" Metztli questioned, her tone was softer than before and far more vulnerable than she would have cared for it to be.

"Yes," Necalli responded simply but confidently.

Metztli was unaware if it was the overwhelming emotions that flowed through her body or something else, but she found herself inching closer to him. With ease, Necalli wrapped an arm around her, adjusting so she could rest her head on his chest.

In another life, she would have wanted to do things differently. She would have wanted to make this decision simply because she wanted to and not because their lives depended on it. But in this life, it was this way, and she had no choice but to make the best out of it.

"I think it would be rather difficult to capture one of the remaining heirs and keep them alive long enough to perform a ritual," Metztli whispered.

She wanted to turn to look at Necalli, but she didn't. She was too scared to see what his reaction to this would be.

"It would be very difficult. Impossible even," Necalli replied.

A small smile appeared on Metztli's face. Perhaps her brother had been right and she did need Necalli to do this. If she was the prophesied heir as everyone believed her to be, then she would need someone who believed in her more than she believed in herself. It felt wrong to let Necalli in, but she didn't see another choice. Metztli had always been selfless by nature, and if this was the one selfish act she ever committed. Then so be it.

"I guess that only leaves us one option then," she said calmly, this time allowing herself to look up at Necalli instead of avoiding his gaze.

Acalan was gone. There was no opportunity to bring her brother back from the dead, but if she could save Necalli from death, then maybe, just maybe she could start forgiving herself for having failed her brother.

A life for a life, an heir for an heir.

"Yes, I suppose you are right," Necalli responded, looking down at her.

He looked far too handsome in this light, the curve of his jaw illuminated by the sun above them.

"Promise me that you're not lying about this or the prophecy," Metztli demanded as she stared at him with wide eyes.

She'd always been good at reading others. Her father might have been bestowed a gift from the gods, but she didn't need one to tell if Necalli was lying to her or not.

"I would never lie to you, Metztli Amos," Necalli stated. She believed him, even if she knew better than to place any trust in the Prince of Blood.

In one swift movement, Metztli swung her body onto his, straddling his waist and enfolding her lips with his. When they'd kissed the day before it had been gentle and slow but today it was different. She drained every bit of emotion that clung to her body and soul into him. Necalli accepted it with ease, gripping onto her hips tightly as he kissed her back.

Their clothes were still damp from bathing in the water, but that didn't stop Metztli from pulling at the hem of her shirt and trying to wrest the sticky fabric from her skin. She only pulled away when Necalli did first, breathless as his expression filled with worry.

"Wait," Necalli stammered as he kept his grip on her waist tight.

"Not like this, just…give me a moment, okay? Stay right here, and I'll be right back."

He shifted her body off his, grabbed his bag, and retreated into the forest before Metztli could argue. She knew what he was doing of course, there was this notion that moments like this should be special and perhaps they should be. But considering what they'd been through in the last day, none of that seemed to matter, at least not to her.

"Can you stand guard?" Metztli said to Xuki, who was still lying on the ground.

She felt awful that she couldn't mend the dog's leg, but if they all survived this, she would have the best shaman take care of him. This stray would never know anything but royal treatment, it was what he deserved for having fought alongside them so loyally.

"If you do, I'll make sure there's a big turkey leg waiting for you when we go home, and a big fluffy bed too. You're a prince now Xuki. The only one the House of Life has left," Metztli mused.

Necalli had been a nice distraction, but grief was still present in Metztli's mind. She imagined it would linger for a long time, perhaps forever, so it was something worth getting used to.

Xuki barked in return, obviously amused with the talk of food and a warm bed. If Metztli's parents decided to disown her that would be quite fine. They would have to take in Xuki though, that was not negotiable.

"Why is he barking?" Necalli asked as he emerged from the brush.

"We made a deal," Metztli said.

Necalli looked confused at the notion, but it was the truth.

"Alright then…well, if you want to follow me, I guess…or not," he said. "Really if you wanted to sacrifice someone instead of this, I would not argue with you."

The way his voice jumped from quick phrases to slow words nearly made Metztli laugh, but instead she stood from where she'd been sitting and gathered her belongings.

"Why are you so nervous?" Metztli teased as took Necalli's hand.

"Do you want me to write you a list?" Necalli responded playfully as he led the way.

If anything, she should have been the one nervous to go through with this. She'd kissed other men before but anything else she'd experimented with had been by herself, in the privacy of her room. Here, she was out in the open with a man who knew far more about what they were going to do than she did.

They didn't walk far, just barely deep enough in the forest that they were no longer in the open.

"I thought it might be more comfortable like this," Necalli said as they came upon a glade, hidden from view by trees.

He'd laid out a blanket and used the other to make a sort of makeshift pillow. It wasn't a lot, and perhaps it shouldn't have mattered to Metztli, but it did.

Metztli loved being Acalan's sister, often it was the one thing she took the most pride in, but she would have been lying if she didn't confess how easily she'd been overshadowed by her brother. Understandably so, of course. Acalan had been perfect. But now the fact that Necalli had even taken her comfort into consideration made her feel special and that wasn't something she was used to feeling.

"It's perfect," Metztli responded and it truly was.

"Great…so, we should…Or I mean we could-" Necalli started.

Honestly, Metztli found it a bit entertaining to watch Necalli stumble over his own words. He'd been so poised before, always knowing how to work his charm, but now he was different. She found pleasure in knowing it was because of her and no one else.

"Remember what I said…about not talking?" Metztli interrupted with a playful smile.

She would never truly forget about the events that had occurred within the Pyramid of Tributes, but she could try. Just for this moment she wanted to try and forget that any of it had ever occurred.

"You think that's funny?" Necalli replied, grinning.

Metztli took the opportunity to set her things down. This was happening, she had never imagined that it would happen like this, but perhaps it was better that she'd never had any expectations for this specific moment at all.

"I've always thought of myself as a bit of a comedian," Metztli said as she wrapped her arms around his neck.

Necalli hummed in response, placing one hand on her waist while the other gently cupped her jaw and pulled her in. He was slow and gentle with his movements at first until they fell into a comfortable rhythm. Metztli appreciated it, she truly did, but all she could think about was the fact that they needed to do this quickly or risk being caught in a less than favorable position.

Metztli pulled on the hem of Necalli's shirt a few times before taking the initiative and tugging it up and off his body. His skin was cold from the water but she could fix that. She was more sure of that than anything else.

She expected for Necalli to do the same with her clothing, but he did not. Instead, he allowed his mouth to roam down her neck, pressing warm kisses into her skin. He didn't seem brave enough to unclothe her. Once again, Metztli found it a bit strange how gentle Necalli could be. For a moment she wondered if he had lied before when he'd said he had indulged in other's.

At the first opportunity Metztli slipped out of her shirt, grateful to be out of the damp clothing. Necalli practically growled at the sight of her nearly bare, but there were still a few layers they would have to get through to be able to fully bond. The quicker the better, that's what Metztli thought as she slipped out of her skirt too, revealing the few blades she had strapped to her body.

"Wait…Let me look at you," Necalli paused, taking a step back to really take in the sight before him.

Everything else Metztli had been comfortable with, but this almost felt too intimate, so much so that she stepped forward, closing the gap between them before kissing him again. In another life he could have looked for as long as he wanted to, but in this one there was a time limit for everything.

"You're far more eager than I expected you to be," Necalli teased as he pulled away. But he did nothing to stop Metztli from undoing the buttons of his skirt, and she didn't correct his assumption.

Had they been in any other situation she would have wanted to take her time exploring him, but they couldn't, not when anyone could fall upon them.

"We don't have time for slow. Not today," Metztli replied.

For a moment there, she'd assumed her comment would be discouraging, but instead she found that Necalli's face lit up at her words.

"Does that mean there's going to be another time?" His hands found purchase on her waist, pulling her in close.

They had a long way to go but that movement had been far more encouraging than any other that he'd made.

"Maybe, if this is good."

Saying that instead of saying she was unsure of what would happen if they left the Pyramid of Tributes together, felt better. It seemed to be exactly what Necalli needed to hear as well because only a second later and his lips were on hers again. This time everything went quicker. His grasp on her was tighter and before Metztli could think properly, he was guiding her towards the blanket. She'd never been with a man, but she knew how this worked, or at least knew the process well enough that she didn't argue when he laid her down and hovered over her, kissing down her neck and over the swell of her breasts.

"Does that feel good?" Necalli questioned with a slight sheen of worry written on his face. Metztli nodded softly.

It did feel good, much better than she had expected.

"I'm trying to be quiet," Metztli responded in a near whisper.

Her words made Necalli laugh slightly as understanding washed over him.

"That might be difficult," Necalli replied as he traced his fingertips down her chest and belly, leaving a trail of goosebumps on her skin…

"I think I can manage," Metztli argued in return as she let her own fingertips trace the muscles that chorded his arms.

"Are you sure you want to do this?" Necalli asked, halting everything so that he could really look at her.

From the expression on his face, she knew he was being sincere. Even though she was loath to admit it to herself, she had thought about bedding him. Deep down, she couldn't deny the pull she felt from the very moment she'd laid eyes on Necalli.

"Yes," was all that she could say in response.

That confirmation seemed to be enough for Necalli because from that point forward everything that he did was masterful. From the way he kissed her to the way he managed to slip her undergarments off her legs without ever having to separate from her. It was only when one of his hands trailed lower down her body than she'd expected that she pulled away.

"What are you doing?" Metztli questioned with a raised brow.

She was inexperienced, but she knew that he was currently using the wrong body part needed for this activity.

"You've never touched yourself before?" Necalli questioned in return.

Suddenly Metztli's cheeks grew warm. Of course she had, but she wasn't sure how the answer to that question would be relevant now.

"It'll hurt less if I um…prepare you for it, or so I've heard…just try to relax okay? If you want me to stop, just let me know and I will."

She was grateful that he hadn't given her the opportunity to respond before because having to explain to him what she had done and what she hadn't, wasn't necessarily a conversation she wanted to have. She nodded softly as his hand parted her legs.

A slight gasp left Metztli as she felt his fingertips graze her heat. She suddenly understood why he had said it would be difficult to be quiet as he used her own slick to rub small and slow circles into her. It felt even better than when she touched herself. How or why, she did not know, nor did she care when Necalli's fingertips stumbled up the bundle of nerves between her legs, prompting an eager moan to slip from her lips.

Necalli soaked in every one of her sounds. His mouth fell slightly open, breathing in her moans and whimpers and using them as motivation to keep his subtle movements going.

Metztli's hand found purchase in his hair, pulling slightly every time he coaxed another moan from her. It wasn't until she felt a finger slide through her folds and into her heat that she pulled hard enough that Necalli moaned too.

"Perfect aim, every time," Necalli teased with an arrogant smirk.

Metztli would have been happy to smack it right off him if she wasn't enjoying herself so much. But she could barely think clearly and only managed to mutter broken words in return.

She wasn't sure if there was a word that could truly describe how she was feeling. All that she knew was that pleasure was radiating through her body, making her feel warm and fuzzy with delight. So much so that Metztli found herself squeezing her eyes shut in response.

"You don't get to do that. Look at me," Necalli asserted softly as he leaned down to whisper straight into her ear.

The tiny hairs on Metztli's neck raised at the sound of his voice. She hated being told what to do. She always had, but that didn't stop her body from naturally responding. Her eyes opened, searching for him again. Metztli had always found Necalli to be handsome, but in that moment he looked more beautiful than anything else…

"Good, you're doing so good," Necalli responded before easing a second finger through her.

This time there was nothing that Metztli could do to stop the louder moan that escaped her.

"Shh, I know it feels good but you have to stay quiet, remember?" Necalli warned.

He was teasing her. Metztli was more than aware of that. Somehow, she did not mind it. If anything she found his words endearing. His praise was hitting her in the most perfect of places, and his fingers were doing more than enough to satisfy her too.

"Do you want me to be silent then?" Metztli asked breathlessly.

Only a few seconds later she felt his thumb begin to caress her bundle of nerves again. Metztli was well aware that she needed to be quiet, but his sudden touch made her moan even louder than before.

"If I had it my way, I would have you screaming," Necalli practically growled.

The possessive nature of his tone caused Metztli to melt beneath his grasp. There was a familiar pressure beginning to build her stomach, somehow it was more intense than when she brought herself to this state. All the princess could think about was finding her release.

"You can let go, I've got you," Necalli reassured her. His pace remained the same but there was more pressure now.

He was magnificent at this and certainly as skilled as he had led Metztli to believe. The princess did not respond with words, instead she raised her hips slightly, meeting Necalli's movements halfway and purring when she felt him even deeper within her.

Necalli continued praising her, reminding her how beautiful he thought her to be, how perfect he found every sound that left her. Each word pushed Metztli closer to the edge until she found herself squeezing his arm and screaming his name. Her legs were shaky, but Necalli didn't stop, he waited until the pleasure had truly washed over her before moving his hand and resting it on the lower half of her stomach.

"Did I disappoint?" Necalli questioned, a slight smirk painted over his lips.

"I finish quicker on my own," Metztli replied, a soft smile on her lips.

Necalli was far better than she could imagine any man to be, but they weren't bound by blood yet, and they'd already taken more time than Metztli would have liked.

"What's next?" Metztli questioned.

Albeit she was just somewhat unaware of the order of these things. Necalli had said that he needed to prepare her, but was she prepared now that she'd climaxed? She hoped so because she found her body buzzing for more.

"Well…We could continue, or we could stop. I could die happily knowing I've brought you pleasure once. You don't need to do this just to save me," Necalli said. His tone was calmer now as he traced shapes into Metztli's stomach.

The sentiment was kind, generous even, but Metztli knew what she needed to do. If she had any opportunity of saving another soul from being lost too soon, she had to see it through. Prophecy aside, if she let Necalli die for her, she wasn't sure how much of her heart would remain.

"Don't think about it that way," she said. "I want to continue… Besides, this might be your one opportunity, don't talk yourself out of it now."

If they were going to do this then she needed Necalli to relax.

"Well, it would be awfully ungentlemanly of me to deny a princess's request," Necalli said, smiling before leaning down to press a kiss into Metztli's lips.

"Ready to be blood bound then?" she asked.

This was it. Once they did this, they could both leave the Pyramid of Tributes together, but she now knew that would only be the start of what had been written in their destinies.

METZTLI

I t was all said and done far quicker than Metztli had imagined. She'd thought that perhaps she would feel different. Not because she was no longer pure but because of the blood bond that now tied her to Necalli forever. But aside from the slightest ache that remained, the princess felt quite the same.

The Prince of Blood on the other hand was currently snoring on her chest, obviously well spent from their activities. Despite being half nude in the middle of the forest, Metztli couldn't find it in her to wake him or tell him to move. Neither of them had slept the night before, not for a single moment. So she stayed put, running her hands through his hair while he slept peacefully.

Necalli had insisted that being intimate was all they had to do for this to work and Metztli supposed that in some way it made sense, but there was still a deep-rooted fear within her that even if the both of them remained, she would somehow lose Necalli, too.

It was strange, how drastically her life had changed from one day to the next. Her brother was gone, and all that he had left in his passing was mentions of a prophecy that Metztli didn't quite understand and a wish to keep Necalli alive.

The princess was far from trusting Necalli though. They'd gotten closer than they were before, and she realized now that he wasn't as malicious as she had originally thought him to be, but she knew better than to fully give her trust to anyone. The last time she'd done so, her brother had been killed right in front of her while she knelt, gasping for air.

Metztli continued reminding herself that they just had to get through the tournament. If they did that then she could confront everyone who had ever known about the prophecy and kept it from her. Citlalic would be difficult to confront, considering that Metztli knew she had secrets to keep, but she would find a way to do it in a manner that her brother would have been proud of. That was the least that Metztli could do now that her brother had crossed into another life.

On the other hand, Metztli had a long list of things she intended to do to the old priestess. Not as punishment for being cruel to Metztli her entire life, but for filling Acalan's mind with the idea of the prophecy in the first place. Had he not known about it, perhaps he wouldn't have sacrificed himself for her and he would still be breathing.

Her brother had been clear in telling Metztli to trust the old woman, but that possibility seemed highly unlikely considering how Metztli was feeling about the priestess. If anything, Atzi would be lucky to leave Metztli's questioning in one piece.

"What am I gonna do with you?" Metztli whispered to herself as she looked down at Necalli.

She'd done what was needed for the both of them to survive, and she would be lying if she said she hadn't enjoyed herself while doing it, but she was worried that when Necalli finally woke from his slumber, he would assume there was now something between them.

Maybe there was, aside from the blood bond between both of their souls, perhaps there was a reason that she was letting him sleep comfortably on her chest while she stayed wide awake, questioning the events that had occurred while she'd been inside the Pyramid of Tributes.

Those thoughts didn't leave Metztli's mind and if anything, that was a good sign. For the first time since her brother had passed, she was finally able to think more clearly. That is, until she heard the pattering of small paws nearing. Metztli recognized them to be

Xuki's but she watched cautiously anyway.

A deep breath left her lips when she saw her limping prince of a dog.

"What is it sweet boy?" Metztli questioned as she shimmied out of Necalli's grasp.

She noted how Necalli nearly shook awake. That wasn't her intention but if it was between him and Xuki she would always pick the dog.

Xuki whined in response as he sat on his hind legs, still avoiding putting pressure on his left.

Metztli could only assume that Xuki had either gotten lonely or was in pain.

Metztli took the opportunity to dress herself. She was happy to find that her clothing was now dry, so she strapped all her blades back onto her body before slipping back into her clothing. After finding a comfortable spot against a tree, Metztli beckoned for Xuki to come and sit in her lap, which he did.

"Do you miss him?" Metztli whispered as her eyes began to fill with tears.

She imagined that this feeling would never really go away. Even if she survived the Tournament of Heirs and even if she somehow lived long enough to fulfill this prophecy that she knew so little about. Metztli knew that her heart would always ache for her brother.

For what remained of her life, she would never truly be complete. Acalan was not only her brother. He was her best friend, and no one would ever be able to replace him.

"We can sleep in his room when we get back home...I bet you'll be able to recognize his scent," Metztli said as tears began streaming down her face. "But we can't touch any of his books, understood? Those must remain exactly how he left them."

Xuki licked her face clean of the tears and that was comforting. Perhaps someday she would come to fully trust Necalli, but until then all she had was Xuki.

It wasn't until pup's whines turned into barks that Metztli became concerned. He never barked, not unless they were in danger.

Metztli moved as quickly as she could, wiping the tears off her face before moving to shake Necalli awake.

"What is it?" Necalli asked as he stood frantically and began to dress himself.

"We have to go," Metztli said as she quickly folded their belongings before stuffing them back into their bags.

She had just swung Acalan's arrows across her body when a scream tore through the air. It was a woman, no doubt. That wasn't necessarily helpful information considering that aside from Metztli, three other women remained. But if a woman was screaming that meant that the alliance formed between the House of Wind and the House of Flor was now broken. With any luck they'd kill each other and leave Necalli and Metztli to finish the job for good.

"Give me your bag!" Necalli half shouted at Metztli.

She didn't argue. Running with a bow on her body was already strange and unfamiliar to her, and she had to carry Xuki in her arms out of fear that he wouldn't be able to keep up with an injured leg.

As they ran through the forest, they heard another earth-shattering scream. Metztli didn't stop running, nor did Necalli. They wouldn't know for sure. Not until the trumpets sang and the marks on their arms disappeared, but two women could only mean one thing. Either each house had lost an heir, or the House of Flor was no longer in play.

They didn't stop until they reached what Metztli could only assume was the opposite side of the pyramid. She knew that much because they'd hit a stone wall that looked eerily familiar to the one her brother had broken her out off.

There was nowhere else to go for now, so the princess set Xuki down before hunching over in an attempt to catch her breath. The feeling was too familiar to how she'd felt when Coatl nearly choked the life out of her, but she had no time to panic or mourn, not when danger could still be near.

"Do you think the House of Flor is gone?" Meztli questioned, still winded as she searched for her flask of water.

Considering the screams, the trumpets should have sang already. But they had not.

"I don't know…The first scream didn't sound like Atlatonan or

Xochitl," Necalli responded.

From the expression on his face, Metztli inferred that he was certain about what he was saying, but if his words were true then that had to mean they would just kill each other off, right? Or at the least just leave them with one heir left to defeat.

Before Metztli could respond, the song of death filled the Pyramid of Tributes once again. Metztli pulled her arm in front of her, anxiously waiting to see which mark would disappear.

"I was right," Necalli confirmed. "The sister from the House of Wind." Necalli confirmed.

Metztli nodded in response. The screams had been heard so closely together and in her mind that meant that a second song would ring out soon enough. Both screams had sounded like they were women, so that could only mean that one of the sisters from the House of Flor was dead or dying. There was relief in that notion, but Metztli wouldn't allow herself to really feel it until it was confirmed.

Both Metztli and Necalli stood silently, waiting to hear something, to find out anything about their standing in the Tournament of Heirs. Luckily Metztli had been right, and it wasn't much later that a second song filled the Pyramid of Tributes, and with it a mark from the House of Flor disappeared.

"Does this...Does this mean their alliance is broken?" Metztli questioned.

She was ready to end this and face the reality of returning home. Avoiding doing so would only hurt her more in the end. It was better to face her parents and confront the consequences than to spend another day in the Tournament of Heirs.

"I-I could only assume so," Necalli responded, not sounding very confident.

"What do we do? If only two heirs remain...those are good odds for us Necalli," Metztli said as a sudden burst of adrenaline zoomed through her body.

"We should wait, just a little while. You haven't slept at all, and all you carry is your brother's bow and arrows. I don't want to risk it until we're ready," Necalli responded as he shook his head.

That wasn't necessarily the reaction Metztli had hoped for. She felt ready to end this now, so why wait for her feelings to change?

"I'm just as proficient with a blade, and I feel fine. We've been preparing for this our entire lives, Necalli, why wait?" Metztli asked, taking a step forward and holding her chest high.

It was in her nature to look for an argument and she thought that Necalli would slip right into her trap, but he didn't. Instead, he merely nodded no before cupping her jaw with his delicate hands.

"I know you want to end this. Trust me, there is nothing more that I want than to get you home, but I just…I have a bad feeling about this. We know nothing of the weapon that Cuauhtémoc carries, and the remaining sister from the House of Flor will be filled with rage," he continued. "Please, just give me a few hours to think this through. Rest, practice shooting your brother's bow, do anything. But please, just give us a few hours." His tone was serious and yet gentle all at once.

Metztli had learned a lot about following her instincts over the last few days. And while she felt ready, if Necalli did not, then a million things could go wrong. The night before was all the proof that Metztli needed of that.

"Fine…but just a couple hours, that's it," Metztli responded as she sat herself against the wall.

The next time she slept, she wanted it to be in the comfort of Acalan's room or her own, not on the ground. Four nights of that had been enough and she would do whatever it took for this to end before having to spend another day within the Pyramid.

"That's all I'm asking for," Necalli replied as he sat himself down next to her.

A silence fell over them that was strange and unprecedented. They hadn't had the opportunity to speak before having to flee. They'd done the deed and then Necalli had fallen asleep. She wasn't complaining of course, it was just that she was awfully aware of how close he was sitting to her. And now that she knew him intimately, she wasn't sure that they would ever be able to go back to the way things had been before.

"Will you return to Texcoco if we win?" Metztli asked after a few moments. Her tone was far more vulnerable than she had intended it to be, but the question was fair. She needed to know.

"No, my place is by your side now, until you send me away," Necalli said as he slipped his arm around her shoulders.

It was far too natural the way that Metztli curled into him. She didn't like it. If anything, she despised this. What her heart wanted and what she needed were two different things.

"You have responsibilities," Metztli reminded him. "You're the oldest heir to your house."

"My sister has been preparing to take care of our house since she first had visions of you. My responsibility lies with you and no one else. I will remain in Tu'nethe for as long as you want me there…but don't think about my responsibilities, think of something else. Have you considered what you'll ask the gods for?" Necalli questioned.

She hadn't thought that far ahead. Metztli had always assumed that her brother would take the wish and ask for something worthy of a prince. But now that Acalan was gone, the wish would be left with her to do with it as she pleased. Up until now she'd only fantasized about confronting the gods for being so cruel. But if she won, they would owe her something.

Metztli was quiet for a moment as she considered what she would ask for. There were so many things she could use the wish upon. Her brother would have asked for peace and prosperity for their people, but she knew that her father was capable of maintaining that on his own. If the prophecy claimed that she was the key to peace, then perhaps this was the way that she could end the Tournament of Heirs for good. Taking down the gods would be a challenge on its own but if she managed to end the tournament, that would be a good start. There was no doubt about that.

"I'll end the Tournament of Heirs," Metztli responded.

She looked up at Necalli, expecting to be met with a look of satisfaction. Instead, she was met with something else entirely.

"That won't work, Metztli," he said. "It's written into the rules. That's the one thing you cannot ask for."

Metztli sighed. She'd thought her idea was quite clever but of course, it was not. Acalan had probably known it wasn't that simple, but she wasn't her brother, nor had she ever looked deeply enough into the rules of the tournament, at least not in the way Acalan had.

"Help me come up with something else then," Metztli suggested. Necalli wasn't her brother. She didn't believe him to be nearly as wise as Acalan, but perhaps he could help in some way.

Necalli thought for a moment.

"Fine…but only because you asked so nicely," he finally said, prompting Metztli to roll her eyes as she inched closer to him and began thinking up wishes.

"I think it's time to go," Metztli said, her tone gentle and soft.

If they were going to do this, then they needed to be on the same page, perfectly in sync. That's what it would take to win the Tournament of Heirs together.

"I can't convince you to sleep through the night?" Necalli questioned.

That was perhaps the smarter option, but Metztli just wanted this to be over. Aside from wanting her brother back, there was nothing else that she wanted more than to be done with the Tournament of Heirs. Forever.

"If we sleep, they'll sleep," Metztli explained. "It's better if we hunt them now when they're likely still tired from fighting earlier."

Necalli sat with her words for a while before standing and grasping his Macuahuitl, surrendering to Metztli's desire.

"Time to hunt," he said as he placed both of their bags on his back.

"Hunting is what I do best," she responded as she scooped Xuki in her arms.

Slowly they walked back into the forest, there was no going back now.

The Tournament of Heirs would end before nightfall and Metztli Amos would be damned if she did not survive. If only for the opportunity to honor Acalan's life, to end this vicious tournament, and ensure that no other heirs would ever have to know the pain she'd felt when she'd watched life leave her brother's body.

That would be enough.

METZTLI

The remaining heirs had hidden their tracks well. Metztli knew this to be true because she and Necalli had been looking for a while now and there seemed to be little to no signs of life anywhere.

They'd first gone to the river where Metztli and Acalan had first spotted the heirs from the House of Wind and Flor. The princess had hoped that perhaps they'd be in need of water or respite after whatever had occurred between them. But alas, upon arrival it appeared that no one had been there for days. They had no better luck when they returned to the waterfall or ventured to the grassy plain that resided in the center of the pyramid.

It was frustrating to say the least. If there had been a fight, then they should have already come upon dried blood or evidence of struggle but it almost felt like the pyramid had been abandoned. Metztli wasn't known for her patience, but she tried to remain calm as they continued searching. After all, the idea that this could all be finished was more than enough motivation to continue in their search efforts.

"If it gets dark, we'll have to wait for tomorrow," Necalli said as they hunted in vain for any sign of the two remaining heirs.

"We don't have that kind of time," Metztli replied.

"They could be anywhere, Metztli. Literally anywhere," Necalli said, and while his words were true, that didn't mean that Metztli accepted them.

The princess remained silent. That seemed like a better idea than growing the tension between them.

"Maybe Xuki can track them!" Necalli suggested. "He's a smart dog."

From the tone of his voice, Metztli could tell that the prince was growing increasingly frustrated as well.

"He doesn't know what they smell like, Necalli, and even if he did, his leg is hurt. I don't want it to get any worse," Metztli responded with a deep sigh.

"What if I wrap his leg with something? He might still be able to track the smell of fresh blood…I know this is difficult but otherwise we might be looking for them for days."

Metztli stopped in her footsteps, placing Xuki on the ground before running both of her hands through her hair. She wanted to scream from the top of her lungs, if only for the opportunity to let out all of the feelings she'd bottled up in the last day.

Two arms wrapped around her tightly.

Necalli was flawed, but he did have a strange way of comforting Metztli whenever she was in need of it.

"The quicker we figure this out, the quicker the tournament ends. I know that's what you want, I'm just trying to help. That's all I want to do," Necalli spoke softly in her hair.

The worst part was that Metztli believed him. Every single one of his words sounded genuine to her ears and he was right. She'd been adamant about ending the tournament as quickly as they could. Even if Xuki was injured, he might be their only hope at finding the remaining heirs before nightfall.

"Fine, but he complains even once I'm carrying him again," Metztli said as she pulled away.

Metztli watched carefully as Necalli dug through his bag, after a few minutes he finally found the old rag he was looking for. He took a seat on the floor before calling to Xuki. The dog, as smart as he was, had a difficult time saying no to the potential of being a pet, so he stumbled over to Necalli and wagged his tail as the Prince of

Blood wrapped his leg.

Metztli held her breath until it was all said and done, watching closely and waiting for Xuki to move. When he finally did, the dog walked happily and wagged his tail until he was in front of Metztli again, sitting and waiting for orders.

Strays were quite intelligent by nature, having to fend for themselves was never an easy ordeal but Xuki…sometimes it felt like the dog really listened and understood the conversations that were being had around him.

"Feels better?" Metztli asked him.

He certainly looked better now that he had a little more stability on his hind legs. Xuki just panted in front of her with a toothy smile. Considering that the dog couldn't actually speak, Metztli figured that was as close to a yes as she was going to get.

"Can you find the other heirs, good boy? Don't get too close, we'll take it from there, okay?"

Xuki quickly got off his hindlegs and started walking, sniffing around, pausing here and there while his ears perked up, searching for any evidence of life. Necalli had been right, Xuki would be much quicker at finding the heirs than they could have been on their own.

"I don't want to say I told you so but…" Necalli teased before pacing ahead a few steps so that Metztli couldn't outright attack him for his taunting.

Metztli was quick though, and before Necalli could move to make more space, she had him pinned between herself and a tree.

"Say it," Metztli whispered in a sultry tone she hadn't even been aware that she could produce.

The princess could feel Necalli's breath on her lips and the way his gaze burned in her skin. The feeling was intoxicating and replaced any other emotion that remained in her body.

"What do I get in return, if I do?" Necalli questioned softly.

It would have been so easy to reach up slightly and kiss him. Quite frankly that's exactly what Metztli wanted to do. Every time she'd kissed Necalli, she'd felt alive. It was almost as if she'd never been truly living until he kissed her in the forest just a day ago.

"I let you live," Metztli responded as she fought back every urge to bring her desires to fruition.

"I want something else," Necalli retorted.

He didn't need to say what he wanted for Metztli to know he wanted to feel her lips on his.

The princess smiled as she pulled away and reminded herself that they had a task at hand that was far more important than kissing her ally.

"Stop distracting me," she said before moving to follow behind Xuki again.

Necalli scoffed before catching up to her and bumping into her shoulder playfully. If they won the Tournament of Heirs, they would have plenty of time to fool around. Or maybe they wouldn't. Metztli remained unsure what role she wanted Necalli to play in her life.

They trailed behind Xuki for a long while until their feet began to hurt. Metztli began to question whether they'd been walking in circles and weren't actually any closer to the remaining heirs. A deep sigh of relief escaped her when Xuki finally sat down and gestured his head to one direction. That had to mean something.

"I don't hear anything, do you?" Necalli questioned in a soft whisper.

Truthfully, Metztli's hearing was keen, and she didn't hear anything at all, but if Xuki had stopped then he must have sensed something. Metztli stayed quiet.

Necalli raised his palm, signaling for Metztli to wait while he investigated a little more. While the gesture was kind, it only prompted Metztli to roll her eyes and follow right behind him. If they were going to be a team for the remainder of the tournament then they needed to act like one.

Suddenly, Necalli gave a sharp gasp before whirling around as if to block her from the sight he had come upon. But Metztli couldn't help herself. Even after seeing the terror in Necalli's eyes, she still found herself inching ahead.

But the moment she saw it, she was filled with regret.

"No…no, that…that can't be," Metztli shrieked as she took a few steps backward and turned.

One look at the mutilated bodies was more than enough for her.

The princess shook her head as she tried to make sense of everything but that was nearly impossible considering what she'd just seen.

The bodies of Atlatonan of the House of Flor and the sister from the House of Wind, were laid out beside one another. Their chests had been ripped wide open, leaving a cavity where their hearts should be but weren't. There was blood everywhere, seeping from their chests into the ground underneath them. It left an odd stench in the air that reeked of metal and betrayal. As Metztli studied the bodies there seemed to be no evidence of struggle, but that couldn't possibly be true.

Necalli remained silent. He had turned pale and wouldn't look at her, not when she approached him and certainly not when she placed her palm on his cheek.

Metztli was confused. Surely Necalli had seen plenty of sights just like it considering the rituals he'd been a part of.

Oh, Metztli thought to herself as the realization clicked in her mind.

They hadn't come upon bodies mutilated during the breaking of an alliance.

They had just come upon bodies used in a ritual.

A blood bond sealed in death and sacrifice.

"It can't be. Necalli, how would they know?" Metztli questioned softly.

Even if the sight was now clear, there were still questions to be answered. Necalli and Metztli had only completed their own ritual because it was that or imminent death for one of them, but Xochitl and Cuauhtémoc could have still won with their companions.

Really, Metztli couldn't think of a single logical reason why they would have killed their own blood to be bound together forever.

"Xochitl would know...It came up in conversation before. I didn't think anything of it. We were children back then," Necalli responded as he shook his head and squeezed his temples with one of his hands.

His eyes remained shut as he spoke, and while his words had confirmed what Metztli believed to be true, it still seemed completely beyond reason that Xochitl would kill her own sister. Metztli would have given anything to save her brother, even her own life.

"But why would Xochitl kill her own sister?" Metztli questioned as she tried to keep her tone as even as she could.

Even if her mind was racing, even if she was full of terror, it was better if they both remained calm and just tried to figure this out.

"I-I can't think of anything. In truth I haven't been amicable with Xochitl in years. It's a long story but it doesn't matter, I just…I can't explain this." His eyes opened but continued to avoid her gaze.

His answer did little to satisfy Metztli. Xochitl had spoken about Necalli like they'd been friends and Necalli had done the same before, so the Prince of Blood had to know something that could explain why she'd sacrificed her own sister.

"Does she know? About the prophecy?" Metztli questioned with a tone slightly more forceful than she had used before.

The princess took a step forward, limiting the space between them so that Necalli would have to look her in the eye. They were blood bound now. The option for withholding information had ended the moment she'd allowed him to know her intimately.

She watched as Necalli paused for a moment and closed his eyes again. It looked like he was sorting through old memories.

"It's possible…Xochitl and I spent a lot of time together before our friendship faded. I wasn't always in the right state of mind, so I don't know. I would have never said a word about it if I knew it would end like this," Necalli confessed. He sounded sincere.

He turned and looked at Metztli.

That had been a mistake.

Metztli had many skills, one of her most useful was her ability to read people. She quickly thought back to when Xochitl had stopped her the night of the Celebration of Tributes to deliver a warning about Necalli's charms. It was only until that very moment that Metztli realized that amicable was perhaps not the word that Xochitl would have used to describe her past friendship with Necalli.

"Did she love you?" Metztli questioned as she took a step backwards.

It wasn't really a betrayal, but it felt like it. Jealousy surged through her body even if she didn't understand where it was coming from.

"What?" Necalli questioned, taking a step closer to Metztli. That wouldn't help, not now.

"She warned me about you, but it had nothing to do with the Tournament of Heirs, did it?" Metztli responded.

"Metztli, we were…we were teenagers, I-I didn't know what I was doing, I just…" Necalli started.

It was confusing how sincere his tone was. It only aggravated Metztli more as she sensed it.

"She wanted to be bound to me and I-I knew it wasn't the right thing to do. I didn't think It mattered," Necalli continued.

In the grand scheme of things, it really didn't. The ritual had already been done. There was nothing that either of them could do to go back in time and stop it. Her reaction was fueled by pure spite and jealousy at the idea that Xochitl had held him first. It made her blood boil even if Necalli had rejected Xochitl's affection in the end.

"Next time someone might have a personal vendetta against you, you could consider telling me. That's the sort of information that I need to know," Metztli hissed in response.

That was all the princess could manage to say without outwardly displaying her jealousy.

"I'm sorry, I really didn't think it mattered anymore. I wasn't keeping this from you on purpose," Necalli said, almost pleading with her to believe him.

Metztli could only nod in response. She wasn't sure what to say or how to say it. What had been done was already done. If anything, this could be dealt with after the Tournament of Heirs was over. Until then, they had to find a way to win.

"Let's just go…It'll be dark soon anyway."

"Metztli, I'm really sorry. You have to believe me," Necalli stammered as he ignored her request to leave.

She couldn't help but wonder if it was their bond that was pulling her towards him.

"Unless you want to sleep next to dead bodies, I suggest we go now," Metztli argued.

She wanted to forgive him, just not now. She would rather sit with the feeling than completely succumb to the bond they now shared. Finally surrendering, Necalli sighed as he nodded and started moving. Metztli whistled for Xuki to follow her before moving and only stopped when she realized he was not.

"Come on boy, you did your job. Now, let's find a place to rest for the evening," Metztli cooed at the dog, beckoning for him to join them.

Xuki stayed seated.

"Do you want me to carry you?" Metztli questioned with a pout.

Before anything else could be said, an arrow shot right between Metztli and Necalli, only missing the princess by a few inches at most. Her heart raced as she realized why Xuki hadn't wanted to move. Her orders had been clear, he was to find the remaining heirs, and he had.

Amid chaos and confessions, Metztli and Necalli had fallen into a trap.

"RUN!" Necalli shouted, pushing Metztli ahead of him.

They'd gone looking for a final confrontation, but they'd intended it on being on their terms.

The arrows didn't stop coming. They flew past Metztli and Necalli, never hitting or grazing them, just taunting them with a promise of death. When Metztli realized this, the princess took the first opportunity to find shelter behind a tree.

"Go Xuki, I'll find you when this is over," Metztli ordered as she crouched, beckoning for the pup to leave them.

The dog whined and barked, obviously rejecting the notion of leaving them to end this on their own. Metztli should have made her brother run the moment that she realized Coatl had been possessed, but she hadn't. Perhaps he would have still lost his life regardless, but she would never know and she didn't want to have the same regret with Xuki.

"GO NOW!" Metztli shouted and only then did Xuki run away, looking behind himself with every few steps.

That was fine. Xuki could be as angry as he wanted with her. She would make it up later when they all left the Pyramid of Tributes alive.

"What are you doing?" Necalli questioned as he gripped his

weapon, ready to attack at any given moment.

"This ends now," Metztli responded as she slipped her brother's bow and arrows off her body and placed a blade in each of her hands.

This was it. They had to fight regardless of how unprepared they might be.

"Are you sure about this?" Necalli questioned, fear written all over his face.

The honest answer was no, but she knew better than to respond with it.

"It's time to go home," Metztli said simply.

Whether they survived or not, they would return home after this. Strangely enough, Metztli found comfort in that.

Necalli nodded before taking a peek over the side of the tree. Another arrow flew past his head, followed by at least a dozen more.

"That has to be the weapon…the aim is off just slightly and it's far too quick for it to be a bow," Metztli said as she tried to come up with a plan.

Being that the remaining heirs hadn't reached Necalli and Metztli yet, she could only assume that they were still somewhat far away. With the force that the arrows were coming with, she knew that this weapon could do serious damage if they were met face to face with it.

"I'm faster than you are. If I run, then I can distract Cuauhtémoc while you take care of Xochitl," Necalli suggested.

Metztli's immediate reaction was to disagree. Separating was dangerous and they had no guarantee that if they did, the other heirs would separate as well.

"No, absolutely not. I-I can't protect you if you leave," Metztli confessed, her voice breaking slightly.

There was no reason to smile but Necalli did anyway before he dug his hand into the back of her hair and pulled in her for a kiss.

"This is the only way I can protect you," Necalli said as he pulled away.

Metztli watched as he took a few steps backwards, muttering something before he darted away screaming, calling all the attention to himself. He was brave, so much braver than Metztli had ever given him credit for. She only hoped they both lived long enough for her to tell him.

The princess allowed herself a few breaths before venturing out into the open herself. Whether she was met with Xochitl or death, she was ready for this to end.

"DON'T BE A COWARD XOCHITL," Metztli screamed from the top of her lungs as she adjusted her grip on the blades. "LET'S END THIS ONCE AND FOR ALL!"

The silence was suffocating. Xochitl was treating her like prey but that's not what Metztli was. She was a predator through and through, and she was hungry for blood.

"Are you surrendering Metztli Amos?" Xochitl questioned as she sauntered out of the forest and came into view.

The way that the woman spoke with such cold fury brought chills to Metztli's skin, but she smiled anyway.

"Would I be holding two blades in my hands if I was ready to surrender?" Metztli questioned as she adjusted her stance.

"I was hoping you'd be a little more distraught considering the death of your beloved brother…It was a shame really. I was hoping to taste his blood fresh, but it was all dry by the time we found him," Xochitl spoke with a tone full of hatred and poison.

They were circling each other now and it was taking every bit of restraint in Metztli's body not to lunge forward at the mention of Acalan. She only hesitated as she sensed that it was all bluff. Xochitl was just trying to get into her head before the fight began.

"Did you taste your sister's blood too? Are you so feral with bloodlust that you simply couldn't resist?" Metztli questioned.

Xochitl spat, and satisfaction coursed through Metztli as she realized she had gotten a rise out of the other woman. Heightened emotions made people stupid and uncoordinated. And that would only make Xochitl easier to defeat.

Xochitl lunged at Metztli, slashing a blade across the air in front of her while she gritted her teeth and displayed them fully. It was going to take a lot more than that for Metztli back down. The only thing that really scared her in the moment was the fact that she couldn't see or hear Necalli.

"Oh, don't tell me that the mention of your sister is a sensitive subject," Metztli taunted as she flipped the blade in her dominant hand.

It was a simple gesture that she was calm and collected, ready to strike and devour the moment she was given the opportunity to.

"Don't speak of her!" Xochitl shouted, lunging forward again.

Metztli slid out of her grasp with ease. If Xochitl wanted the opportunity to stay alive, she was going to have to start working a lot harder for it.

"Why not? Don't you want to remember the way you carved into her chest and used her for your own selfish gain?" Metztli continued, mocking the princess for what she'd done.

She deserved it. One does not get to commit such a cruel act without being punished for it.

"You're just like him," Xochitl growled. "You pretend to know everything when you know nothing at all. I did what had to be done. She knew this is what I had to do. I wouldn't expect you to understand."

The pair circled one another for just a few moments. Ultimately the princess found that she was wrong, there was nothing that Xochitl could say that would justify what she had done, even if her sister had somehow been a willing victim.

"I would have never brought harm to my own blood. You know nothing of loyalty, and you reek of betrayal." Metztli raised her blade and rushed forward.

The sound of the metal clashing filled the air. She'd gotten much closer to Xochitl than she had before. The woman knocked her head backwards as if she was going to headbutt Metztli, but before she could, Metztli turned quickly, dragging her blade downward and cutting a thin line along Xochitl's arm.

"Better than reeking of failure. Don't worry. I'll make sure no one remembers you when I leave the Pyramid of Tributes. My destiny is bigger than yours, I just wish I could keep you alive as my pet long enough for you to see it," Xochitl snarled as she swung wildly.

Instead of dodging this time, Metztli used Xochitl's frantic movements to her advantage. She took a small step forward and to the side, lifting her knee until it met Xochitl's stomach before pushing the woman down by her shoulders. She moved to swing her blade at the princess, while she was on the ground, but Xochitl rolled over just before she could. Metztli stumbled but regained control quickly.

"Nice try, but I won't die that easily," Xochitl hissed as she righted herself.

"Why not? If you care about destiny so much then you should know yours ends right here, right now," Metztli spat as she lunged forward again, this time slashing her blade low and towards Xochitl's legs.

The other princess managed to move out of the way fast enough, but she made a mistake in moving forward too quickly. It gave Metztli just enough time to lift her leg and kick her straight in the chest, sending her flying onto her back.

"You think you're so righteous, don't you?" Xochitl barked as she rolled over once again and lifted her body off the ground, steadying herself.

"The beloved House of Life, so peaceful and prosperous... You know NOTHING!" Xochitl screamed as she moved forward, hungry for blood and for Metztli's life.

Now that she knew the truth behind the House of Flor, Metztli pitied Xochitl as she dodged and blocked every one of her intrusions. She aimed low when Xochitl aimed high, fighting for any opportunity to end this quickly. Their blades clashed together once more. Each woman applied all their strength to stop the blades in front of them from moving any further.

"I know you're a coward," Metztli said. "I know you allow your women and men to be taken while you sit and accept gifts and praises from the gods. You're nothing but a pawn in this story, Xochitl. You won't be missed."

This wasn't a physical attack, but it worked just as well, angering the princess even more and causing her to take a step backward before she began to circle Metztli again like a vulture.

"Do you think you're any better than me? I did what I had to do to survive. The gods will face their own retribution...but you...you let your brother die for you, and Necalli will die too. Cuauhtémoc will make sure of it…and for what? A prophecy that you're not strong enough to fulfill? Save yourself the burden and let me take care of this," Xochitl spoke as blood continued dripping down her arm.

If only it were that simple.

Metztli hadn't asked to be a part of the prophecy. Quite frankly she was still having a hard time believing that she was the prophesied heir at all, but Acalan believed she was. She would have gladly handed over the responsibility to anyone, even Xochitl, if it meant being able to keep her brother. But he was gone, and Metztli would rather die trying to honor her wishes than to hide from them.

"Is that what this is about?" Metztli scoffed. "You're jealous that the prophecy doesn't speak of you?"

The expression on Xochitl's face was a clear yes. Metztli had no attachment to the prophecy aside from the desire to fulfill her brother's wishes, but it did fill her satisfaction knowing that she had something that Xochitl wanted. Or perhaps two things if Necalli was included.

"How do you know it doesn't speak of me?" Xochitl snarled. "I'm a female heir just like you. I've suffered great loss and I know I have what it takes to see it through. You don't. You never have, and you never will Metztli Amos. The sooner you realize that, the quicker I can kill you and be done with it."

Maybe Metztli didn't have what it took to fulfill the prophecy. Perhaps Xochitl was right, and they had it all wrong. It didn't matter though, Acalan had believed in her and that's all she needed to know to keep going.

"Kill me then, prove that you're better than me. If you want the prophecy so bad, then take it," Metztli taunted as dropped one of her blades onto the ground between them.

Xochitl leaped forward, both blades still steady in her own hands. It finally felt like she was actually trying to fight instead of crossing blades with Metztli and delaying what needed to be done. This was a dance that Metztli was comfortable with, one that she knew well. Both women moved in sync counteracting each other's blows until Metztli allowed for Xochitl to take her to the ground with a kick swift to her legs. Xochitl threw one of her blades to the side as she straddled Metztli's body and charged the blade at her neck, only for Metztli to wrap her hands around the blade, allowing it to pierce through her skin.

She did not feel fear.

She had Xochitl exactly where she wanted her.

"I pity you. No one has ever taken you seriously a day in your life, have they? Not the gods, not Necalli and not I," Metztli spat as she pushed against Xochitl's blade.

The woman laughed from above her, so loudly that Metztli almost didn't fully process the scream that scattered through the wind.

It was Necalli. She'd heard him scream before. She didn't need to see him to know it was him. It was time to finish this and to bring the Tournament of Heirs to an end.

"Hear that? Necalli's facing what he deserves, and you are as well. I'll do you the courtesy of allowing you a few last words. I'll even pass them on to your grieving parents," Xochitl hissed with a demonic smile on her face.

Her teeth were fully visible and ready to sink into Metztli's throat at the first chance, but Metztli did have something to say. Just one word that would end this as quickly as it had started.

"XUKI!" Metztli shouted from the top of her lungs.

Xochitl's brow furrowed in confusion as she let up on the blade just enough for Metztli to shift her grip to the handle. It couldn't have been more than a breath later that Xuki flew from behind Metztli, teeth bared as he pounced on Xochitl and dug straight into her neck.

Xochitl went flying back as she swung her arms frantically trying desperately to fight off the tiny beast. Except it really wasn't a beast but a stray pup that was completely and utterly loyal to Metztli. She had sent him away, but she knew he wouldn't go very far. His attack gave Metztli just enough time to flip on to her stomach and reach for her brother's bow and arrows.

In one swift movement she was hovering above the other princess who held onto her neck and tried to speak, only to discover she was choking on her own blood.

"You're not the prophesized heir," Metztli growled before whistling for Xuki to retreat. He did, his mouth and paws covered in blood. Xuki walked to Metztli's side and stood next to her, ready to pounce again if he needed to.

"I am," Metztli spoke confidently before letting the arrow fly straight into Xochtil's skull.

The trumpets sang only a second later. Metztli stood above her body for a moment as she watched Xochitl's mark disappear on her arm.

Only three remained.

Metztli sprinted after Xuki, eager to find Necalli before it was too late. The screams continued as she flew past the greenery. There was no use in being silent now. What mattered was finding Necalli and helping him, even if her hands burned from where Xochitl's blade had sliced through her. They were wounds that would need tending to but not now, not when she was rushing through the forest in search of her companion.

Another scream filled the air, this time louder and far more fearful than the ones earlier. Metztli only ran faster, not willing to stop to check her arm as the song of death filled the air. She was running faster than Xuki now.

She only paused when she reached a seemingly empty field. She didn't recognize it at all. Metztli was sure that they had walked through the entirety of the Pyramid of Tributes and not once had they stumbled upon this open field. The gods in their cruelty must have altered the landscape to make the fight between Necalli and Cuauhtémoc more entertaining.

"Necalli!" Metztli shouted as she looked around her.

The grass was tall enough that she couldn't see more than a couple feet ahead of her.

Luckily, the princess heard a familiar moan, albeit this one was full of pain. But it was enough that she was able to stumble through the grass and follow the noise, only to find Necalli on his back, a bright smile on his lips as he caught sight of her.

"You scared me!" Metztli screamed as she knelt beside him.

Xuki eventually joined. Their pup licked the dirt and sweat off of Necalli's face.

He looked like he was in pain but there was no blood on his body.

"Are you hurt?" Metztli questioned.

She wanted to reach out to touch him, but her hands were soaked in blood – mostly her own but she had no doubt that Xochitl's was mixed in there too.

"I think he cracked my rib," Necalli whispered.

A cracked rib they could deal with now that they had both survived.

"I heard the trumpets…where is he?" Metztli questioned.

Cuauhtémoc was dead but fear still lived within her.

"He stumbled away after I managed to slip the nightshade into his mouth. It wasn't much of a fight after he ran out of arrows, but he used the damn thing to hit me in the ribs."

Metztli shook her head softly as she imagined how it had all occurred. The slightest smile appeared on her lips when she realized they'd won. Now, they just had to wait for the gates of the pyramid to open.

"What happened to your hands?" Necalli questioned as he tried to lift his body off the ground.

Metztli stopped him by pressing a gentle hand against his chest.

"Long story. I'll explain later…We won, Necalli," she said softly.

It hadn't been in the way she imagined or had hoped it would happen, but they had won. She would have done anything to share this moment with Acalan instead, and she would have done anything for the prophecy to be a lie. Maybe it was, but she saw now that if there was a possibility of it being true, she had to see it through, for Acalan, and for every other life she'd taken within the Pyramid of Tributes.

"You know what has to happen next, don't you?" Necalli questioned with worried eyes.

Metztli responded with a firm nod. Their plan was insane. It would be a miracle if they both walked away with their lives, but it had to be done.

The trumpets sang once more. This time the song was one of

celebration, but it did nothing to lighten Metztli's spirits. Winning the Tournament of Heirs was just the beginning. She knew that as she helped Necalli stand, wrapping his arm around her shoulder so she could help him walk.

This was only the start of something much bigger than she had ever imagined herself being a part of.

METZTLI

s they reached the gates of the pyramid, they were met with the same acolyte who had inducted Metztli and Acalan into the Tournament of Heirs. He bowed slightly at the sight of them and said nothing as his gaze caught Xuki. Instead, the man just turned and walked ahead of them, leading them to the gods and what Metztli assumed would be a colosseum full of people waiting to find out who had won the Tournament of Heirs – her family included.

Metztli wasn't ready to face them. It was agonizing to try and imagine their grief when they realized Acalan was gone. Trying to imagine what they would think when they saw her with Necalli was equally difficult.

The House of Blood was as good as a sworn enemy to the House of Life, but Necalli had saved Metztli on more than one occasion. Acalan had trusted him, and they'd been allies for days without Metztli's parents ever knowing it. As she walked through a dimly lit hallway, holding up Necalli and helping him walk, still wearing her brother's bow, she only hoped that her parents would allow her the opportunity to explain herself before they judged her.

But what she would say was a mystery in every regard. She still didn't understand the prophecy to its full extent. All that she knew was that it said she would bring an end to the gods' reign and that her brother had believed in it enough that he had given his life for hers.

The ultimate sacrifice, sealed in love, blood, and loyalty.

Metztli would not let that sacrifice be in vain.

As they approached the entrance to the colosseum, the roar of the crowd grew louder. Metztli's heart dropped to her stomach. She wanted to confront the gods, but she did not want to face her parents.

How could she look her mother in the eyes and not see Acalan? How could she face their father who had only given Metztli one responsibility? How could she look at them and explain that it was destiny that had led her there and left Acalan behind? She wasn't sure if they would ever believe her, even if Atzi backed up the claims of the prophecy.

The acolyte raised his hand silently, ordering them to stay put when they finally reached the opening. He said nothing as he walked away and into the colosseum. Waiting would only make Metztli feel worse, she knew that because her breath hitched in her throat, making it feel like she was going to suffocate on her own thoughts.

"Breath, Metztli," Necalli reminded her as he rubbed circles into her back.

Metztli squeezed her eyes shut as she took a deep breath. That was the thing about bravery, it was needed in the moments when it was most difficult to produce.

"Whatever happens, I'll be right here, just…remember the plan and we'll get through this together," Necalli said.

It did little to calm Metztli's nerves, but the sentiment had been kind anyway. As long as she followed the script, then this would go her way.

It had to.

It was only a few moments later that they heard them, despite not being able to see them yet. The gods were beginning their speech before the winning heirs would be presented. She had no way of knowing which god was speaking but it irked the princess to hear them speak of the Tournament of Heirs like it was some form of entertainment and not something that had changed her life forever.

Regardless, Metztli paid close attention to every one of their words, all lies. Their imperious voices filled Metztli with rage. It was because of them that Acalan was dead. They had taken her brother away from her and Metztli was ready to seek retribution.

She thought of nothing else when the acolyte returned, beckoning for them to follow. The crowd cheered before going silent again at one of the god's commands. It was time for the heirs to be presented and she could only imagine that they were all anxious to know who they were.

In some ways, the people of Mexica were just as bad as the gods for allowing themselves to see this as entertainment when all twelve families would mourn losses that were indescribable. Metztli reminded herself that this was only because of what they'd been taught to believe. If she could change things, then she had to. Acalan would have wanted for her to do so.

"You go first," Metztli whispered to Necalli as she slipped his arm away from her shoulder.

She would be right behind him if he needed her. Really, she was just avoiding the inevitable. Necalli nodded softly as he gripped his side, limping behind the acolyte who had been sent for them. Metztli realized that she had only gained herself a few seconds but nothing more as she followed behind him.

Necalli walked into the brightly lit colosseum first. Cheers filled the arena, but they were drowned out by the gasps and mournful cries of every empress and emperor present. Metztli swore she could recognize her own mother's cry through them all which prompted her to stop, afraid to be shown to all of Mexica and ashamed that she was not standing with Acalan to her side. It was only when Necalli paused, looking over his shoulder at her, that she moved, taking a single step into the light.

The crowd went feral at the realization of what had been done and who had won. A mixture of disapproving shouts and cheers were made but all that Metztli could hear were the cries of two women in particular.

She looked through the crowd and found Citlalic first. The princess should have been happy to see her brother, but instead she cried in despair and sank into her seat.

When Metztli found her own family, she only saw the way her father was holding up her mother. Xara's face was full of sorrow and disbelief, as was his.

The only thing that Metztli could do was mouth, *"I'm sorry,"* as she followed behind Necalli, eventually standing to his side when they were finally in front of the gods who sat at their altar.

They were glorious, Metztli couldn't deny that as she stared up at them. They were all stunning and dressed in the most beautiful of clothing while Metztli and Necalli stood in front of them, drenched in dirt and blood. That was enough of a reminder of what they'd lived through for Metztli to fill with rage again.

"I must confess, I'm impressed you two were the first pair to figure out a new way of winning," a god with long hair spoke. His voice echoed through the coliseum even though he spoke directly to Necalli and Metztli.

She didn't need him to introduce himself for Metztli to know he was Nemiliztli, the God of Life, in his full glory. He was covered in turquoise and gold, representing life even though Metztli knew he enjoyed taking it more than he enjoyed giving it.

"Isn't that marvelous?" Nemiliztli addressed the crowd. "The Tournament of Heirs will never be the same thanks to these two champions"

He was right. The Tournament of Heirs would never be the same. Metztli was determined to make sure that was true. The crowd in all their stupidity cheered. The princess had to remind herself that they had no choice, not when the gods were before them.

"Why don't you tell us your names, which houses you represent, and why on earth there is a dog with you," a goddess questioned in turn.

From her red and silver garb Metztli could only assume she was Eztli. It angered Metztli to believe they hadn't even taken the time to know these simple facts before presenting them as champions.

Metztli wanted to growl at the goddess as their gazes met, but she was too stunned to do so. Every other god and goddess wore a face of amusement, but Eztli did not, If anything her eyes were full of anguish. That was not something Metztli had thought the Goddess of Blood was capable of feeling.

"Necalli Cruz, heir to the House of Blood," Necalli responded first.

Metztli was grateful for it because he gave her just enough time to inch closer to Xuki. He was hers. They would not take the dog from her, and anyone who tried would lose their lives.

"Of course, you bring honor to me and your family, Necalli Cruz…and you are?" Eztli turned to look at Metztli once more.

It was even more difficult to speak than Metztli assumed it would be. Even more so when she looked up at the crowds and realized just how many people were watching. There was no room for failure here, none at all.

"Metztli Amos, second born heir to the House of Life," the princess announced after taking a deep breath, reminding herself to keep to the script.

That was the only way she would get what she wanted from the gods.

"And the dog is yours, I'm assuming?" Eztli continued.

Metztli had to stop herself from rolling her eyes. The Tournament of Heirs was meant to be a form of entertainment for the gods, but it didn't seem that any of them had actually watched. They probably waited until right before blood was about to be shed to care at all.

"Yes. My…my brother Acalan believed him to be a stray, but he fought valiantly. He's mine now," Metztli explained as she looked down at the pup.

Stray or not he was a prince now. Metztli was ready to make that clear if anyone misunderstood her words.

She watched as some of the gods raised their brows and scoffed at her, but their opinions didn't matter. They never had before, so there was no reason she should start caring about what they thought now.

"I'm afraid this does happen from time to time…the dog is yours if you want it," Nemiliztli declared as if his words were a kindness. "No one will miss a stray otherwise"

"I'm assuming you two know how this will proceed. You've chosen an interesting route and while I applaud you for making the tournament exciting, the awards remain the same. Only one house may rule and only one wish can be granted. Have you two decided who will take each?" Nemiliztli questioned them with a tone full of false compassion.

Did he truly expect them to be grateful after what they'd lived through? It wasn't fair that the God of Life be seen as so righteous and fair when it was he who found the Tournament of Heirs most entertaining. Metztli had never had a personal vendetta against anyone, but she did now.

She wanted the God of Life dead.

"Both are hers to take," Necalli stated confidently, prompting gasps throughout the crowd and a look of confusion on Nemiliztli's face.

Metztli scoffed before she could stop herself. Was it really that difficult to believe that Necalli was willing to give Metztli everything? By the time that Metztli wiped the expression off her face, Nemiliztli was already angry. Metztli found satisfaction in that, especially knowing what was to come.

"That doesn't seem fair," Nemiliztli said as he sat back into his chair.

It was obvious that the god was expecting them to either share the winnings or perhaps even fight for them, but that would not happen. Not today.

"That is what we have decided," Necalli argued in return.

He straightened to his full height despite the pain that Metztli knew he was feeling. She took pride in knowing that Necalli and Acalan believed in her so much, but she couldn't disappoint them, nor did she intend to.

"And what do you wish for, Metztli Amos?" Eztli questioned as she looked right into Metztli's eyes.

In a moment of panic Metztli's gaze moved away from the goddess to Necalli who nodded softly, confirming what needed to be done. That wasn't enough though. Metztli found herself looking for her parents, but it didn't help to find them, considering the state that they were in. It wasn't until Metztli found Atzi in the crowd that anything changed.

The priestess wore a face with no expression. But when she found Metztli's eyes she nodded yes.

"I wish for the Tournament of Heirs to end. Forever," Metztli announced, taking a step forward to show she was serious.

The crowd behind her stayed silent for the first time since they'd been presented. Most of the gods laughed at the notion but she knew they would. This was all a part of the plan.

"Oh, my child…I'm afraid that cannot be done. You must-" Nemiliztli started.

Metztli didn't give the god an opportunity to finish his sentence before she was interrupting him.

"Why not? Has enough blood not been shed? Why should we pay for the mistakes of our ancestors?" Metztli questioned furiously.

That seemed to quiet the gods and she couldn't blame them. It was likely that they'd never been confronted with these questions before.

"*That is not for you to decide,*" Nemiliztli snapped as he stood from his seat in complete disarray.

The sight brought Metztli more delight than she assumed it would.

"It should be," the princess argued before turning to face the crowd.

"I just survived a tournament to the death. Five days of misery, I watched as my brother died in my arms. I killed to survive. I shed blood, and for what? For the gods to continue telling us what to do? They claim I have a wish, but they will not fulfill what I desire. Do you all not see how cruel the gods really are?"

Most of the faces in the crowd looked afraid but there were others who looked intrigued. Good. There was power in numbers and Metztli was going to need power if she was to accomplish this.

"THAT IS ENOUGH!" Nemiliztli screamed as he walked down the steps of the altar.

Metztli turned to face him. He believed her to be a naïve child, but she was not naïve. Her destiny had been written in the stars and the sooner that Nemiliztli understood that the better.

"I will give you one more opportunity to make a reasonable request or you leave here with nothing," Nemiliztli whispered as he found himself face to face with the princess.

He might have expected her to crumble under the pressure of his glare, but she did not.

Her father had once told her to never let a man disrespect her and Metztli intended to stay true to that, even if the man was an ancient god who believed he ruled over her.

"Fine. Just let me address my people," Metztli responded, giving the impression that she had surrendered and there would be no further arguments from her. Nemiliztli took a few steps back and crossed his arms in front of his chest as Metztli turned to address the crowd once more.

"The people of Tu'nethe knew my brother to be the brightest of souls," Metztli started, quickly finding her parents in the crowd. "Anyone who knew him would agree that he was far wiser than his age should permit. I wish that it was he who stood before you today."

This message was much more for Xara and Tenoch than it was for anyone else.

"Acalan hated violence. There was nothing that he cherished more than life itself…My brother bled out in my arms after saving me from an attack. He will always be remembered, and his death will be mourned for centuries to come…In his final moments, my brother revealed something to me, something that affects everyone here today. And I think it's only fair that you all know it too." Tears welled in her eyes.

She didn't move to wipe them as she turned back around to face Nemiliztli again.

"My entire life I've despised the gods. I cringed at the idea of you all. I always thought that there was something wrong with me for feeling the way I did, but now I know that there is nothing wrong with me at all. When I was in the Pyramid of Tributes, what motivated me was the thought of seeking retribution. Not from the other heirs but from you," Metztli stated, looking straight through Nemiliztli's soulless eyes.

He was angry and he should be. Metztli Amos was about to undo any sense of peace the god had ever felt in his life.

"My name is Metztli Amos, I'm the second born heir of the House of Life. Daughter of Tenoch and Xara Amos. Sister of Acalan Amos…"

As she spoke, she felt empowered by every single one of her words. She forgot that a crowd was surrounding her. Instead, her attention remained fixed on the god before her.

She would not yield.

"I stand before you as the prophesied heir, and I only ask for one thing. I wish for the opportunity to meet you on the battlefield, so that I may kill you myself. And when I do, the god's reign on mortal life, will end forever," Metztli announced.

Screams and shouts of panic were heard around her, she recognized the sound of her father's voice pleading to let him speak with his daughter and to disregard her desires. But his pleas went unanswered.

"Declare your wish properly," Nemiliztli hissed as he took a few steps forward to meet Metztli face to face.

The princess smiled. She'd never felt more sure about anything that she'd ever done in her life. She was confident that Acalan would have been proud to see her in this moment, face to face with Nemiliztli himself and without a single shred of fear left.

She knew what she had to do next.

"My name is Metztli Amos, and my one wish is for war."

Acknowledgements

First and foremost I would like to express the extraordinary debt I owe to my family members and friends who have shown me nothing but absolute love and devotion throughout this entire process. The Tournament of Heirs would be nothing but a wishful thought if it wasn't for the continued motivation you all gave me over the last year.

Dad, I thank you for allowing me to pursue my dreams and for pushing me to be the best version of myself that I can possibly be. You had to sacrifice your own dreams in order to give me a better life and for that I am infinitely grateful. I know I cannot change the past or give you the childhood you deserved but know that this story is for both of us. *Por eso le eche ganas.*

Mom, thank you for putting up with all my ideas and letting me brainstorm with you over lunch and a Dr.Pepper. Often I found myself in search of a listening ear and you were always more than willing to let me ramble. Your dedication to making this debut memorable did not go unnoticed. This story wouldn't have been possible without you.

Noah, you are only seven but you are the absolute light of my life. When you came into our lives, I had no idea that I could grow to love someone as much as I love you. I want to thank you for being the best little brother a girl could ever ask for and for sharing your brilliant imagination with me everyday. Stay bright and never stop being yourself.

Amanda, before knowing you I did not know the meaning of womanhood and I certainly did not know how special a friendship could be to me. You are an inspiration in my life and you have taught me more lessons than I could ever count. Thank you for showing me the beauty of female friendship and for allowing me to be a part of your life. Here's to bonding over books and growing old together.

Rachel, it seems like yesterday that I reached out for the first time. Without you the Tournament of Heirs would not be what it is today. I thank you for guiding me through the writing process and for always being the helping hand that I needed. I could not have asked for a better editor and in the process you've become my friend. I hope to edit many more novels with you and hey, maybe I will write a spicy contemporary romance someday!

Finally to all my readers, It is an understatement to say that I've been overwhelmed with all the love and positivity you all have shown me since I announced my debut novel. It is because of you all that I strived to make The Tournament of Heirs as brilliant as I could possibly make it. Following my dreams was the most difficult thing I have ever done, but you all made it so much easier. Know that I have a deep admiration for every one of you, and I consider myself lucky to have you all as my readers.

About the Author

Amilea Perez currently resides in Utah where she is a full time student. When she is not studying or in the chemistry lab. She enjoys spending time with her family, binging TV shows, watching movies and most of all working on *The Mexica Chronicles* Series.

Growing up, Amilea craved seeing her heritage and roots represented within media and in a higher education setting. With the guidance of her parents she came to realize that change cannot occur without effort. Knowing this Amilea pursued a bachelor's degree in Biological Chemistry and was honored with the title of Utah's Young Humanitarian in 2023, due to her efforts in providing adequate medical access to underserved communities.

While Amilea takes great pride in her academic and humanitarian achievements, she still hoped to someday see more representation of her culture in the media. Amilea began writing fan-fiction in 2020 in order to fill her desire for artistic expression and it wasn't long before she found her heart set on writing her debut novel, *The Tournament of Heirs*. Amilea Perez hopes to continue writing diverse stories for a long time and to inspire other Latin/x writers to do the same.

Follow Amilea Perez on social media to stay up to date with her projects!

Website: Amileaauthor.com

Instagram: Amilea.writes

TikTok: Amilea.writes